VENERO ARMANNO

TRAVEL UNDER ANY STAR

un

CONTENTS

TRAVEL UNDER ANY STAR

For many Ks

Once again I was on that beach with its crystalline waters, and Stina walked across the hot sand in her bare feet, in the beauty of young naked skin so open to the sun. I saw her image even though it was close to forty years later; in my own mind, of course, a single day hasn't passed.

It happens this way sometimes and is worse when I drink, and today I suffered a hangover of epic proportions, result of the irresistible charms of a five-star hotel called the Tropic Towers, the sort of place I'm completely unused to. Bed, view, gourmet food and extensive mini-bar all on a film production's account; what could be better?

William Flood had got me here; how strange that he should remember someone as unimportant as me after all these years. Then again, it's a reunion of sorts. There's me, him, and the young man's dreams we'd shared. The auteur's remaking his own cult hit of the late 70s, Black Beach Killer. The title's been updated to the more new-millennium sounding Black Soul Killer; it might be the only point of originality in his entire production, but who am I to judge?

The important thing is that the original was meant to be Christina Vågberg's film, even in her second-string role as the plucky heroine's sexy best friend. Back four decades William Flood's blood-soaked script would have given her screen and scream time galore, an entrée to the world of movie acting and first opportunities for a nascent talent, but things had gone wrong. My fault, as it turned out. A young star-that-never-was died. A year later I sat in a movie theatre and watched the movie William Flood had ended up making: our auteur hadn't had more than twenty seconds of her performance to use—just one long sexy walk up glittering beach sands—and all of it without the unforgettable music of her Swedish accent.

Stina smiled, she shone naked and silent, she lived there in the eternity of celluloid, and now she was being remade.

He shades his eyes and moves aside from his latest acquisition, a late-model Arri Alexa digital motion picture camera. Embedded in the parchment of his face is an enigmatic smile. Despite the fact that the camera's set up in a sort of tent, the sun has managed to cook the skin on his brown skull. Still, I can't help thinking how fit this man seems. Fifteen years older than me, William Flood's like a wiry, aging middle-distance runner leaning in for a view of the next unforgiving leg of the course ahead.

Around us, those few crew who don't have anything to do shelter under more makeshift awnings and rectangular, desert-style tents. They're poised to see what unfolds, what their director's eye will seek to capture. I have no idea what's coming, only what William Flood's told me: It's a beach scene today and it's going to be hot, better wear loose clothes.

'We've got local girls populating the strip down there, see? And those half-dozen strapping lads? Boys from the local meatworks. They can't believe their luck. Paid to spend a day naked with a multitude of naked young women. I can only imagine tonight's shenanigans. I feel like Father Christmas.'

The director's genuinely happy, and why shouldn't he be? His career entered that middle sphere between mediocrity and oblivion after his first three or four films. He's almost as forgotten today as most men are their entire lives. To have a second chance is a miracle he'll no doubt give his all.

'God's greatest gift, youth,' Flood shakes his head, still squinting at the endless beach in his control. 'No matter how much you do or don't do, there's always a moment when you just want to go back …'

The director indicates the Alexa's viewfinder.

'Go on, take a look. It'll give you an idea of the framing on the big screen. This thing's going to be ten times bigger than the original.'

When I focus into the lens the too-bright beach world keeps blurring. My eyes water and there's that persistent post-alcoholic ache at both temples. What I really need is a new prescription for my glasses, a mug of coffee and some painkillers. Despite this, what I do make out is certainly impressive.

'Okay,' he says to those around him. 'Set … get them to call action.'

Someone with a megaphone receives the message via his ear-piece. From out and up on the highest dune he calls it with a screechy metallic timbre. In an instant the beach scene moves into a new sort of life. I try to straighten from the Alexa's viewfinder but the director's hand goes onto my shoulder, gently keeping me there.

'Don't look away just yet.'

'But it's that scene, right?'

'And beat for beat. You watch.'

The day's sea-breeze sweeps across the crests of the breakers. Young people's hair streams and blows. I taste the salted wind; can feel the way clear, breaking waves ooze forward with a physical motion like mercury. Young women stretch themselves on colourful towels wearing only their bikini bottoms; others jump in a game of volleyball; even more seem to be playing games with the wavelets. There are wet golden breasts and nipples firmed into flesh-toned bullets by the coldness of the sea. The crew feasts their eyes and so do I. None of us is immune, uninterested. The boys from the meat works gape like hungry dogs. Of course I know what this is, it's the short prelude to the scene Stina was so worried about. She'd been terrified of what she needed to do and of what William Flood had planned for her. In the character of the irresistibly sensual 'Stacey-Lee, student-exchange from Stockholm', she was to walk out of that ocean, come up from the waterline past everyone else, maintaining an insouciant saunter, a slight swing to her hips, and pass the camera—all the while perfectly naked. Then the much younger William Flood's lens would follow her up a long sandhill to where she would collect her towel and things. There, before she even has time to dress properly, an ugly hand would reach out and drag her screaming and fighting into the quiet of trees and brush and secluded sand dunes. The worst to be enacted upon her, brutally and in close-up.

Well, that's what the whole thing had been, a thriller-slasher-teen-based piece of garbage, one late-seventies precursor to the Halloweens and Friday the 13ths and Elm Streets of the eighties.

Now the day shimmers beneath this blistering sun, a hot southern hemisphere Christmas around the corner. I feel a sourness in my belly like a collection of years swallowed down hard and kept there. All around the sun-dazzled, roped-off stretch of beach, and even further back where more beachgoers and observers have camped themselves, extra tents, umbrellas and wider canopies have been set up. Everyone will need cool shelter as soon as these open-air scenes are done. For the moment, grips, make-up artists and stunt people swelter and bake.

Just like '78.

And, with a strong clenching of my heart, there she is in the magic frame of the electronic viewfinder. It takes a moment for my mind to catch up with the reality in my eyes. Okay, it's not Stina but some modernised version of her. Here's a willing young actress who'll appear naked in front of—let's face it, given the proliferation of illicit medias available these days—what will turn out to be just about the entire world.

'It's really beat for beat?' I ask William Flood, hoping it's not, but he's busy now, too busy concentrating and muttering quietly to his DOP and assistant. Almost-septuagenarian hands and fingers move nervous as birds over the ochre hues of his thinly muscled, sun-brown legs.

He doesn't need to reply, anyway. I can see it's just as it had been.

The actress saunters toward us along the sands, hair flowing away from her face, that sexy little swing to her hips captured just right—it'll be one perfect take. Her breasts are much bigger and rounder than Stina's; she's definitely not as pale-skinned. She has no pubic hair at all. A modern touch. Then she comes closer and closer and everyone around this camera knows for certain that there are living angels in this world.

The Alexa eats her up. We eat her up.

She passes with a sly sort of curl to the corner of her mouth; she almost has that right. There was nothing ever sly to Stina, but the curl at the corner of her mouth, that was a trait never to forget.

Then it's over, this part's done. A second crew follows her up the steep sandy hill using a Steadicam. Technicians scurry toward the next set-up. The scene will be a big one, with this sea-goddess about to be sacrificed like a goat at some bloody pagan ritual. That was the part Stina had been so afraid of; for all the plastic weaponry and make-believe blood, William Flood's choreography had been physical and intense. Even in slow-step rehearsals her body had come away bruised, her eyes had rimmed with tears. I can't help wondering how this present incarnation has taken to it all.

Though I'll never see it.

William Flood's hand has gone to my shoulder again, this time because my face has started to crumble.

In that viewfinder, Stina. In my heart, Stina.

'Man,' he says, 'I knew I'd need someone to share that with. Thanks for coming.'

There's a new look in his face. Making this movie might be a dream come true, but it hurts him too.

Off in the sunny distance they're already calling for William Flood's counsel.

'It takes you back,' he speaks, wistful as a fading cloud.

Takes you back?

It goes a lot further than you know, old man, because Stina was mine before you even knew she existed.

Part One

I.

'Every child move quickly and quietly to a desk. Boys in the front rows, girls together starting at the centre of the room. No boy and girl at the same desk. You, the small one there. Eco ... whatever your name is. Look after that new boy.'

John Ecolangeli is whatever my name is, but I heard myself become 'Eco', all because an Australian nun couldn't be bothered pronouncing my full surname and for evermore spoke it as in 'Echo'. That's also how I ended up next to a kid who had a face like thunder—dark, mean and confused by what was going on around him. He didn't move a muscle as all the other children scampered to their new desks of the 5th grade.

This one standing beside me had to be brain-dead. Mystifying in his muteness. I dragged the behemoth by the arm and got him settled in.

The boy smelled of sweat and garlic and something peppery. His hair was dirty. I could see specks of grunge in the close-cut roots; I had to face the other way. When I did a girl with blonde plaits, light blue eyes and skin so pale she was like some figure from an antique Nordic painting whispered 'Eco' at me. She gave a small nod, as if she understood something I didn't.

A curl was in the left corner of her mouth and despite the grey of a stormy January outside, a light moved through the room.

2.

The nuns really ought to have known my proper name. After all, this was a school I'd been enrolled in from the very start, but they hadn't liked me since the incident with the zebra crossing and the black bus.

I was in the first grade then, innocent and gullible as a kitten. Some older kids had been speaking in the playground about the way road traffic always has to stop for pedestrians at zebra crossings. There was some kind of incontrovertible principle to the thing. I interpreted this as a magical force field in operation—or perhaps a purely scientific one. Something like the force field my hero Professor John Robinson used to protect the inhabitants of the Jupiter II from aliens and terrifying intruders on Lost in Space.

By the next morning I'd formulated a test. Well, maybe it wasn't so much a test as a way to watch the force field at work. Once I'd walked on my own through the leafy and winding streets of New Farm, as I did every school day, I waited at the long, wide, white-striped crossing in front of the school gates. It didn't take long. The first vehicle coming just happened to be the old rickety black bus that each morning delivered the nuns from wherever it was that they all lived together. Five years of age, I waited until the very last moment, then as a small group of other children sensibly waited behind, I took quick small strides out onto the stripes.

Not by any shape or means should I have made the age of six.

The bus was old but its brakes were good. I remember the black monstrosity slewing sideways in a screaming arc of smoking and skidding rubber; in my mind I was amazed and delighted and terrified by the strength of the zebra crossing's invisible power. I tried to skip off, and would have enjoyed a state of blissful wonder the entire day through, if—within minutes—amidst the screaming of so many horror-struck nuns, and many bone-rattling shakes of my body, I hadn't been dragged up to the office of the headmistress. There, Sister Mary Finney waited in her usual funk of dark disapproval for any and all miscreants. With a face made of petrified wood she meatily delivered six cuts of the strap—three per tiny hand—and sent me out, sobbing, with a bucket, broom, rake and rags to clean the school for the entirety of the day.

She hadn't asked me what I'd thought I was doing; none of the nuns tried to console me; of course, my parents weren't called and I wouldn't tell them about this myself. It was simply a black day to be overcome.

So with hands that felt as if they'd been stomped by an elephant, I cleaned grubby railings and pee-stained toilet floors. I collected rubbish around the grounds and emptied food scraps from the tuck shop's overflowing steel bins. I mopped the veranda outside Finney's office then had to go in and sweep her rugs. All of this should have been enough to get those God-loving women in their black robes and heavy rosaries to remember my name, but no, it wasn't to be.

Four years on, and I was still 'you there' or 'the small one at the front' but mostly, and now and forever, 'Eco'.

3.

I didn't need to feel especially persecuted. With every passing year the nuns seemed to like new kids even less, especially those late arrivals from overseas countries who were too old for the first grade and had to be shunted into other grades.

We always had a big influx of migrant children to the Mary Immaculate Catholic Primary School in New Farm, our city's 'Little Sicily'. Kids just like me; kids just like my new desk-neighbour.

Once we'd all settled into our places and the nuns were satisfied with the configurations—no boy was too close to any girl—the first to have to stand up straight and announce himself was a Chinese boy named Qui Shu. Amongst the kids his name became 'Queen

Shoe'. I was sent to the globe at the front of the classroom in order to find his country and continent. Nerves and trembling meant I pointed at somewhere close to Bombay. The nuns tut-tutted. I returned to my desk carrying the weight of their disenchantment.

'They're not out to impress,' Sister Mary Barnaby told the very young Sister Mary Felicity as the aged and half-deaf Sister Mary Ursula nodded agreement. These three set the tone: this class consisted of a bunch of complete dummies, and would be so treated.

Queen Shoe announced to the nuns who constituted our welcoming committee that he was something called a 'Buddhist'. He was sat down and forgotten.

The rest of the new arrivals were mostly European. I didn't take much notice of the three French children—two girls and a boy—or the Chilean and the Argentinean sitting together who seemed to hate one another already. I was more curious about the new Italian boys and girls. Some were from the north of Italy and were fair-haired, light-skinned, and, in a couple of cases, blue- or green-eyed. To me they hardly seemed Italian at all. Others were from the mezzogiorno, the centre of the country said to be rife with criminals and corruption (my father's two favourite words, always uttered in contemptuous Sicilian). Then there were the ones full of Moorish and African blood, from poor islands such as Lupari, Salina, Vulcano, and of course my great sad island of Sicily.

'Triste ma bella,' that's what my father always told me. 'Sad but beautiful,' a wistful sigh in his voice.

We'd left before I was three. The truth was, I barely remembered the place.

The nuns moved amongst the desks. Sisters Barnaby and Ursula—the first middle-aged, the second one ancient as an old tree—had faces like comic-book caricatures of witches, their noses hooked and their mouths twisted into perpetual grimaces. At least Sister Mary Felicity, who was no more than a teenager, had a pleasant mouth and warm, expressive eyes. We loved her immediately. To her we children seemed not to be just individual lumps of dog-turd that would inevitably end up soiling her polished black shoe. Her face was kindly, even sweet. None of us understood it at the time but Felicity was a novitiate, not yet eighteen years of age, wearing the white veil that differentiated her from the nuns who'd already made their lifelong vows.

Sisters Barnaby and Ursula stopped at my desk. They weren't interested in me but in this swarthy, fetid, sweaty lump of meat at my side. He looked like sin and stupidity on two legs. Mean too. We hadn't exchanged a word, yet somehow I was already scared of him.

'And what is your name?' Sister Ursula asked in a loud voice, account of her own deafness.

The boy's head remained down and he didn't give any indication of hearing the question. Sister Barnaby contemplated his filthy shock of hair and repeated Sister Ursula's question, but with a sharper edge.

When he didn't move Ursula screamed it herself, just in case he was as deaf as she:

'WHAT IS YOUR NAME?'

He was absorbed by the wood-grain of our desk. I would have answered for him, nervous sweat gathering on my upper lip and in my armpits.

'Stand up boy!'

He didn't.

Sister Ursula grabbed his ear and pulled the dead weight of him up to the tips of his toes. It was as if she wanted to wrench that ear off his head. As he stood I smelled more stale sweat, the most awful body odour. He might have swum in a sewer. All three sisters backed away. The abandoned ear had turned a flaming red.

'Glory! When did you last take a bath?'

Now the boy chose to look at them. His gaze was heavy-lidded, somehow pitiless, yet also filled with hurt. It wasn't clear to me if he understood what was being said, but I thought, Give this kid a knife and he'll cut your hearts out.

'Be a gentleman—answer us!'

I knew that the next step would be a visit to Finney for six cuts of her thick leather, then he'd be sent for a good talking-to from the parish priest of the church adjoining our school. Father Cagliari would give this boy what-for; he'd probably be made to clean the church floors for a good month of Sundays.

The lug didn't twitch. The class held its collective breath, each child afraid to move, all of us fearful of the consequences should the blazing eyes of the nuns turn our way. A bad, new smell twitched my nose. Nerves had made some child nearby let out an anxious fart. In a second I'd probably get the blame, and Sister Ursula was on the verge of making some new eruption of indignation, when a quiet but accented voice spoke up.

'Is it not possible that the obvious is the truth?'

Ursula had to bend her head to hear. 'What was that?'

It was the new girl in plaits, the one with the ivory skin. She was on her feet and I noticed she was a little taller than the other girls, and slightly pudgier, but with a serious and intelligent face. She'd spoken politely, yet the way her shoulders were slightly hunched, and the way her hands were rounded almost into fists, revealed what she was really thinking.

'Sit down, child,' Barnaby said.

'Is it not possible that this human cannot until now speak your language?'

She had her own problems with the language, that much was true too.

'I've told you to sit down.'

Though Sister Barnaby simply wanted to make her pipe down, Sister Ursula was confused. She couldn't quite make out the words being spoken, so she rounded on the girl, her imposing height towering over the kid like a black angel of death.

'And if this truth is so,' the girl spoke up into that ancient, wooden face, 'why scream at him? What good does it do?'

It must have been the build-up of tension. The need for

release. The way this new girl said it: Why scream at him? The class started to laugh. Sisters Barnaby and Ursula looked around, bewildered and enraged. Then with a hard glance at one another they knew what needed to be done.

This was the sort of thing you nipped in the bud.

Straight away. First day.

Very tense, and with exaggerated calm, they walked to the front of the room. At first the laughter increased, but the way Barnaby and Ursula stood there as holy statues silenced everyone. Small Sister Felicity waited forgotten to one side, her eyes cast down. Her hands clutched a rosary.

'Children, rise from your desks and form two lines. One line in front of me, one line in front of Sister Ursula. Sister Felicity will ensure that you shepherd yourselves properly. Keep the lines straight. No speaking.'

The two old nuns waited at the front, facing the classroom. From under their left sleeves they slid out their leather straps, black as coal, heavy as lead.

'The dumb boy, first in line with Sister Ursula. You, the smart girl, first in line in front of me.'

My neighbour had to be led to the correct spot, a bull being set into its place for execution. He still didn't seem to understand what was going on, even if the resentment in his eyes glowered more strongly than ever.

And so I and the rest of the class formed two queues behind these two complete strangers. Most of us knew what was coming; it was far from the first time a school-room had experienced what we'd named 'the mass slaughter'. There always came times when the nuns simply decided an entire class needed to be punished for something that a single child had done.

I was second behind the 'dumb boy'. Now he understood the strap and what it meant. He stared with undiluted hatred into Sister Ursula's eyes. She made him hold out his hand. We all let out a gasp at the force and speed with which she brought that thing down—at the echoing crack. The boy's entire body stiffened but he made no sound. Some of the children were already crying in anticipation of their turn. I wasn't crying. Instead I felt as if my bladder was full and I had to urinate or die.

With a pained expression young Sister Felicity gently turned the boy around by his shoulders and guided him back to his desk. It was as if she herself had experienced the blow.

I was next. I put out my hand. I didn't stare at my oppressor but looked to my right at the 'smart girl'; she was about to receive her cut. Sister Barnaby might have been middle-aged but she had the bulky appearance of an East European wrestler. She actually contemplated the girl's hand a moment, as if deciding how best to beat it. That hand was white and delicate as a piece of my mother's most prized china.

No—I pictured snow, the light snowfall of whatever country she came from.

A wave of something passed over me, not for the stroke of the strap I was about to receive, but for the delicacy of that girl's hand. How could anyone dream of hurting it? I'd push between the nun and the girl, stop this monster's act, run away with her into the streets of New Farm.

Yet the girl gazed at Barnaby with a smile that seemed oddly victorious.

The nun was inflamed, colour in her cheeks. She raised the strap right above her head and brought it down with the full strength of her beefy arm and shoulder.

At the last moment the girl pulled her hand back. Sister Barnaby's strap kept going and with a muffled thwock against the thick material of her robe, it struck her own right thigh.

Hell opened a side gate.

4.

That was our morning, first lesson of the first day. We were kept in at little lunch as extra punishment, for the transgressions of others. The girl whose name I still didn't know had been taken out of class and hadn't returned. The rest of us remained locked inside with one burning hand each. We were stone-silent until an assistant headmistress strode across the school grounds swinging a bell for what we called 'big lunch'. Finney must have been very occupied with the blonde girl as the ringing of the lunch bell was a task she usually reserved for herself. We escaped that stifling room to the mercy of sunshine and salami sandwiches—or whatever our respective mothers had prepared for us.

It wouldn't have surprised me if Headmistress Finney had sent the 'smart girl' home for the rest of the day, or even for the entire week. A blue mood had settled into me and I didn't want to sit with the other kids and make up stories and games. I especially didn't want to have to hang around with the lump, whose reeking presence and mute lack of understanding felt like being slowly sucked down into quicksand. He'd vanished somewhere, anyway. So I finished my sandwiches under a huge mango tree while others skipped rope, climbed monkey bars, threw a ball or created opposing sides in an imaginary battle derived from watching too many episodes of Combat!.

Wait.

There was something off in the distance. Someone. Past the sports oval, out across those greener fields spreading far away from the school into that no-man's land where you were never allowed to go.

5.

Yes, absolutely off-limits this part of Mary Immaculate, and everyone knew it. The new girl had ignored that and had found her way down. Now she was on her white knees, busy doing something in the long grass—or to the long grass. We were a long way from the main buildings, of course, off the school's official grounds. It was as if she'd made camp in some beautifully isolated new country. Jacaranda trees stood still and unmoving in the quiet hot day, no purple flowerings just yet.

'What are you doing?'

She was so absorbed in her task that she hadn't noticed me. As she looked up I saw the unmistakable streaks of dried tears on her cheeks. Her hair was slightly awry, as if someone had pulled on her plaits. Still, whatever had transpired in Finney's office, she smiled with that funny curling at the corner of her mouth. She was doing her best to not allow even the slightest upset or distress show.

'E-co,' she said, making it sound comic and dramatic at the same time. Then I watched her massage her palms and knew she was trying to rub the hurt of the strap out.

'Was it bad?' I asked. She shrugged no reply. 'How many did you get?'

'Six,' she said. 'Plus the caning.'

'Wow.'

'Is this normal?'

'Maybe. I don't know. It's a lot.'

In fact, the two punishments together were unheard of. This must have signified something incredibly serious. Had she given Finney more lip, made the situation worse? She must have. I didn't need to ask where Sister Finney would have applied the strokes of the cane. I'd had to bend over the back of a wooden chair for them enough times. The cane's strokes were often worse than the strap—a sharp, whipping instrument as opposed to a blunt one—and for days it would sting to sit down. I imagined the marks, the welts across her buttocks.

'What made her so mad?'

'They are all stupid.'

She moved a shoulder, a smaller shrug than before, and there was just a hint of a snuffle.

'My parents ... they have never asked me to, ah, sit with my ass across two chairs.'

I didn't think I'd ever heard a girl say such a word. My friends and me, we lorded it up with plenty of language collected from books, the street, older friends and even the men in our families—but for a girl to say 'ass', which wasn't even a word used in this country ...

'"Two chairs"? What's that mean?'

'My mother and my father, they tell me to always be the one thing I am and to stick with it as, ah, strongly as I can. They say, ah, if I believe something is right then I must never relent for what is wrong. You cannot sit your ass between two seats. Correct?'

I simply stared at her. That made just about the most perfect sense I'd ever heard. My parents had me buckling to authority—to all authority—at every turn. Just so that I could be seen to be doing the right thing, so that I was a good boy. It came from their fear of doing wrong in this country they barely understood.

But the new girl, she had that accent and slightly strange way of speaking; it took me a while to realise that her 'ah' wasn't a verbal tic, but a moment when she needed to translate from her own language to English. What was her language?

'But, what you said, it only got you into worse trouble.'

'My father says, ah, "This is the one and only life". I was in trouble already. How can it matter to make more?'

I looked over these green, long-grassed paddocks, contemplating her words. The sounds of children playing and screaming drifted from the school.

'Do you know it's not allowed—'

'—to be all the way out here? Ja, of course I know.'

'So what are you doing?' I asked again.

'Will you like to help with me?'

'Okay,' I said, though I didn't have a clue with what.

'Come on, E-co.'

She spoke my name in that lilting way again. It wasn't mocking or teasing, she simply appeared to like the sound of it. And her accent was of a type I hadn't heard before. I kneeled beside her.

'All right, this is how,' she said. 'We are creating, ah, we are tying knots. Like this. And this.' She demonstrated it for me, and that's just what she made, clumps of long grass knotted together. 'It is a trick we used to compose at my old school.'

'"Make",' I told her, 'not "compose". "A trick we used to make".'

'Ah, ja? Good, you must tell me my blundering.'

I thought I'd let her have that one.

'So, where was your old school?'

'In Stockholm.'

Maybe I'd heard of the place, maybe not. 'That's your home?'

'Ja,' she said, now making that sound funny too.

'Where is it?'

'Stockholm? This is Sweden.'

'So you speak ...?'

'Swee-dish,' she giggled, and to my total incomprehension she rattled something off that sounded musical and strange. 'Du har att förbättra din inlärning av världen.'

She liked what must have been the comically blank look in my face.

'I told you that you must improve your learning of the world.'

'Okay.'

Meanwhile I got into that very odd task with her. We slid around on our knees in the grass doing the stupidest thing, tying knots, and for the first time that day I felt happy. It was as if the black heavy robes of the nuns, their scowling faces, and all of Catholicism's dead weight, had been lifted from my heart.

'You know I am very older than you already?'

'But we're in the same grade.'

'What age do you hold?'

I told her, and she gave a small but triumphant smile. 'The month of your birthday?' So I told her that too. 'I am over one year your elder.'

'Then why did they put you in grade five?'

'Mistakes are made. My father will have this corrected.'

I contemplated her statement. 'What if they won't let him?'

'Hah!' she made an expression of disgust. 'These people have already proved they are, ah, not competent. They could not shovel the shit from behind a horse. Now, the trick will be how to make the nuns come and get their, ah—'

'What?'

The words stumped her at first, but then she had it.

'To come collect their true desserts,' she said.

I didn't have a clue what she was talking about. Desserts such as ice cream and apple pie? Before I could ask what she meant, a new idea struck her.

'Hey—I know! Find your great friend Livio.'

'Who's Livio?'

'Maybe this human is behind this tree?' she spoke with teasing indifference. 'Yes, I think it is so. Go look. He was here in the grass shouting like he is mad. This is how I came to be here. Then I caught my idea.'

All right, now I had it. The thing made a sort of sense. The new boy who'd been made to sit next to me, his name was Livio. He'd escaped all the way down here to shout and kick at the air, and she'd come down to find him. Then some weird idea to do with long grass had struck her.

When I circled the trunk of the largest eucalyptus in this vast, silent field, there he was, cloaked in shade as if he never wanted to be seen or found again. The mean-faced boy with the odour problem.

'Your name's Livio?'

He snuffled and rubbed his eyes. I wouldn't have expected a dumbo like him to even be capable of tears. It was like seeing a bear cry.

'Livio?' I repeated.

The boy wiped his face and nodded. 'Si, mi chiamo Livio.'

Exactly as the girl had suggested in class, and just as simple: he didn't speak English. I indicated that he should follow me. Slowly he found his feet. His knees were filthy, his socks were down, and while the girl's tears had dried on her face, his remained wet and hot. We returned to the girl's industrious mystery.

'His name is Livio,' I told her.

'So?' she smiled. 'He is called Livio Vida.'

I said to her, 'So you speak Italian?'

'Swedish and English only.'

'Then how do you make him understand?'

'Have you never seen the Tarzan cinemas? "Me Jane." Easy.'

'Your name's Jane?'

'Christina, young silly. But I like "Stina."'

'Stina?'

'Yes. And you?'

'Giovanni. Uhm, but that's only at home. Everywhere else I'm Johnny.'

'Johnny.' She stopped, then shook her head. 'E-co.'

And that was it. She never called me anything else again.

'Please will you make to ask Livio to help? We will do a lot before the bell rings, ah, if three work as one.'

'And then?'

'And then.'

Her smile had an edge, this time no sweet curling at the corner of her mouth. There was a sort of darkness to her expression that surprised me, as if a pure light could turn itself black when required.

'And then I will tell you my plan and we will see if you will like to be brave.'

She sat back on her haunches, rubbed her sore palms together some more, and gave me a softly accented rundown of this thing she called 'desserts'. It had nothing to do with food or sweets. Even as a curl of fear grew in my belly, I started to chuckle softly. That pleased her. I had to explain to Livio what we were going to do. If he wanted to join. He understood my rough peasant Sicilian. He did want to join, and gruffly spoke a few words back to me in the exact-same dialect; turns out he was from roughly the same region as my family.

And that was our start; a beast, an angel and me.

6.

At little lunch the next day, the three of us moved to a secluded corner of the playground and Stina showed us how to run the fight. She was like a movie director or something, and she was taller than either of us, and perfectly serious too. As she demonstrated what we should do I translated for Livio, who today had halitosis though his body didn't smell at all bad. He must have immersed himself into one hell of a soapy bath.

Stina repeated again and again, 'No real striking of the body, it is just for play.'

At this age, and small and a little tubby, I wasn't going to be hurting anyone. Livio though could probably have cracked me in half.

She composed a special note and said she would deliver it herself, so, in class, just minutes before Finney would come striding through the playground ringing her heavy bell for big lunch, Stina asked Sister Felicity if she could visit the bathroom.

'Go on, quickly now.'

Stina didn't return before we were let out. Livio and I waited near the busy tuck-shop, then she was walking briskly towards us, a happy look in her face. By now Finney would be back at her office, picking up the neat but childishly-printed note slid under her door.

Boys have planned a wonderful war in the oval at lunch.

'"Terrible",' I'd told her. 'Not "wonderful".'

'Ah? Time is too past now.'

Avoiding the nuns on playground duty, we were silent conspirators going fast and unobserved down to the sports oval. Then we went further along to the jacaranda and mango trees in the fields. We didn't know it, but all this overgrown land had once been farmland set up by German settlers. Now it was our stage. Stina pulled on a woollen beanie and tucked her giveaway white-blonde hair beneath it. The plan was that none of us should be recognised; Stina would peer from around the trunk of a tree, where she would be hiding.

From the distance we intended working at, Livio and I would simply look like two boys of indiscriminate age, indistinguishable from all the others at this school.

We positioned ourselves so that the extensive traps of knotted grass were between us and the oval. From that moment everything happened so fast it was like living inside a John Wayne western at the local Astor film theatre where families like mine went every weekend.

We saw them coming in the distance, not one, not two, but six nuns. They didn't seem to be in much of a hurry, not yet anyway, and glided gracefully in their robes. Finney must have told them to go patrol the oval and take a look at the field, make sure no fighting was going on.

Livio and I nodded at each other and started to go at it. We threw ourselves into the fight and we thought it was as wild and well-choreographed as any bout on Sunday's weekly World Championship Wrestling show.

From her spot behind the nearest tree Stina peeked out, starting to laugh and clapping her hands.

When Livio bellowed low I squealed high; when he let out a high-pitched scream I tried to make sounds deep and resonant as a bull's. We alternated like that and Stina fell onto her backside, holding her sides at the ridiculous noises we made, laughing so hard she could probably have wet herself.

We glimpsed her white thighs, her white underwear under the modest school skirt, and redoubled our efforts. For his part, Livio acted violent but was gentle as a lamb; he didn't hurt me in the slightest. Really, he was like a bad-breathed giant handling eggs. He picked me up, threw me down; I got over him and pretended to smash his face. At one stage he aeroplaned me on his shoulders and I squalled like a wildcat.

At all of this the nuns were running across the oval. They came into these green meadows. Livio and I went harder. We rolled and wrestled, got to our feet and exchanged superhuman blows. We sneaked glances towards the coming nuns. Dio mio but Finney herself was at the head of this platoon, which made my blood turn to spit, and she was moving as fast as her fat legs could carry her. She wasn't just shouting but waving her fists, and Sisters Ursula and Barnaby flanked her.

The first to get a foot yanked in the grass-knots and half-somersault was Barnaby, robes flying, then no less than our loving headmistress with such dark affection for her leather strap and whipping cane landed spread-eagled. One more nun fell flat and hard on her face before the others stopped, frozen, eyes darting as if for land mines.

Stunned by such incredible success, Livio and I halted our bellowing and fighting. We stared in wide-eyed surprise—then turned tail and bolted for our lives.

Stina kept up with us.

We ran far down into the field, further than we'd ever gone before. We discovered it abutted a road that led off to some ramshackle homes in the poorest part of our suburb. From there we doubled back out of sight, cowering behind trees and a line of rust-bucket cars. We took the most circuitous route possible then dashed panting all the way back up to the schoolyard, coming in the front way. Then we rejoined all the playing throngs. Our faces were hot and damp, uniforms soaked with sweat.

The bell went off. Time for classes to resume.

Stina had slipped off her beanie and now tried to hide it behind a steel rubbish bin—and lo and behold but that sweet young Sister Felicity was on playground duty, and she knew nothing of what had just happened, and she gave it back to her, asking, 'Christina dear, why would you throw away a good beanie?' We knew it then, we were sunk, well and truly, and that made us hold onto one another and laugh like clowns.

Sister Felicity looked on.

What else could she do but gaze at us with eyes that melted at the complicity of children?

7.

'What do you mean?' Finney asks with a quick glance away from my father.

Her number one henchwoman, Sister Barnaby, shrugs slightly. She also doesn't know what this swarthy Mediterranean is on about. The half-deaf Sister Ursula isn't present. We've been told she remains in a hospital bed. Finney can't make eye-contact with Sister Mary Felicity, who is present, because the teenager's eyes remain downcast, staring at the bare brittle boards of the headmistress's office floor.

'What is this "good way" you mention, sir?'

Finney enquires this of my father with mock-interest only. We're all standing in that box-like little office of hers enduring the heavy atmosphere of her administrative and moral outrage.

Liv and I have fresh streaks of tears down our cheeks. Stina looks calm and cool; she doesn't have any tears at all.

In the day and night before this meeting, in our respective homes, my parents and Livio's parents have raised themselves into terrifying figures of vengeance. We've been yelled at and screamed at in Sicilian. Our parents have boxed our ears, then they've wept at us, hurled bitter accusations, locked us in our rooms and subjected us to endless sermons through closed bedroom doors. We know now how evil we are, and just how much things will change.

Yet here in Sister Mary Finney's office these archangels of Sicilian doom are awkward and lost. They've appealed to the head nun and used their hands to create explanations and promises in the air. Their voices rose and fell as they begged for their sons to not be expelled. My father has promised that both he and Livio's father will turn their sons' hides black and blue. The families will pay Sister Ursula's hospital bill and bring her good home-cooked food every day. Every single day. And it goes without saying that any building construction or reconstruction work that the school needs will happen whenever it's needed, free of charge. He's used every bit of broken English he knows to vow that the soft life he and Carlo Vida have mistakenly let their boys live is over—'Is ovah, Sistah, ovah, dis is my big promise'—and from now on they will learn about hardship and real life, about humility and respect, 'Da good way, okay? Da good way Sistah.'

Contrasting these histrionics are Stina and her parents. The small Vågberg family stand a little to the side. They are silent and unmoved. This doesn't negate the concern in the faces of Mr and Mrs Vågberg, but they certainly aren't begging—and I can tell there's been no screaming and shouting in that little expatriate Swedish household.

Instead, at the very moment of their arrival today, Stina's parents made it clear to the nuns that their child's enrolment at Mary Immaculate was an aberration, an unfortunate mistake. Mr and Mrs Vågberg sent Stina to this place because they'd been told it was the natural repository for New Farm's new arrivals. The truth they wanted understood was that they had no truck with religion, wanted Stina exposed to as little secular babble as possible, and had meant to take their child out of the school as soon as was practicable—plus get her into the higher grade she should have been in right from the start.

More than that, they certainly weren't going to punish her for what happened in the fields.

'What about an innocent nun's serious injury? Should that go with impunity? This is an elderly person, and it's only good luck there weren't more who were hurt.'

Sister Finney had then held up her scraped palms to reveal her own injuries.

That old bat Ursula had broken a hip. If she'd been a horse or a cow someone would have delivered a bullet to her brain. We were told that at her age something like this was a very serious medical matter. Yes, it was, and that had refreshed my and Livio's onslaught of tears. We hadn't meant to hurt anyone. I was almost certain Stina hadn't meant to either. Finney's speech had chastened the Vågbergs, yet somehow I had the feeling that in their home they'd secretly laughed about the traps in the grass, about the tumbling nuns.

'My wife and I are very sorry for the sister's injury, and we will visit her tonight. However, we are here to discuss the reason why Christina did this thing. Our daughter has her side of the story. What is yours, Headmistress Finney?'

She ignored the question and turned her pale eyes on my father.

'Please explain what you mean, sir. What is this "good way" you mention?'

'Okay, da good way,' my father repeated, trying to get his idea across while patently ignoring Nils Vågberg's presence. He drawled his words in his deep voice. 'What I mean is we come dis cuntery for better life. Is so dat for da children we want dem live better than what we got when we was little, you know? Not food enough, no money, no sorta hope for what comes in da future. So we gotta give dem da better way and we gotta teach dem dat better way also.'

Finney was hurrying him on: 'And this means what in relation to these boys?'

'Relation?' He knocked his hard, tanned chest with his knuckles, his short-sleeved shirt unbuttoned to his sternum. 'Relation is I am fudder. Fudder.'

My ma took his arm and leaned in close, whispering in his ear. My father looked confused a moment, then his face cleared.

'I sorry. I no unnastan. What I mean is we get tough in da home. Tough. My son Giovanni he come with me. I bricklayer, you know? Da boy he gonna learn to work and sweat and den when he come to school he unnastan value of educazione and be good to his teachers, you no worry no more.'

'That's hardly enough to—'

'And den one day my son he gonna be teacher too. Is job got good respect and position, so I make sure of dat.'

Sister Mary Finney abandoned any pretence at listening and

was already signing papers that looked official and frightening. My father cleared his throat, something he did when he lacked confidence.

'Listen you no sign nuttin, you stop now Sistah, okay? In dis cuntery is gonna be same for fudder and mudder of Livio dere too. Livio fudder Carlo he work hard like me. I know he gonna lake Livio with him every Saturday from now on, be labourer in da sun, make him work and sweat. Is gonna happen all da holidays too, is true Carlo?'

Carlo Vida—who to all practical purposes had no English at all, a fact that held him back from becoming more than a simple day-labourer—managed to pick up his cue and nod with the Grim Reaper's dark emphasis. For all he knew his countryman could have been telling these teachers that the families meant to lake their sons to some secret place where they would be hit on the head with shovels and buried.

'So you let da boys stay where dey are in dis good school, right? You can be sure in dis cuntery no more Mr Nice Guy.'

Papà concluded his appeal, pleased with himself for being able to end on this note of colloquial English. The nuns would now know they weren't dealing with some illiterate migrant. For emphasis he turned a heavy-lidded gaze toward me, then to Livio.

The Sicilian Death Stare.

Both of us quailed.

I knew too that my father was forcing himself to not look anywhere in the direction of the real source of the trouble, Da bloody girl. He'd worked it out in his mind, of course: we were good boys who could be naughty, sure, like all kids, but this Christina Whatshername, she was pure female trouble. And her parents—Gesù Cristo! how they made him want to pull out his own teeth: white-skinned, Godless, immoral and probably Communist too.

'Sir,' Finney spoke, looking up from her completed forms. 'The word is "country". I wonder if you can say that?' With another glance at Barnaby, a glance this time meant to convey a certain airy wickedness, she added, 'The way you speak the word is not pleasing to my ears. Could you repeat this please: "Coun-try".'

My father looked to Ma for an explanation. Carlo and Agata Vida stared at the nun expecting not to understand anyway. My mother gave a minute shrug; now she had no idea what this woman was trying to tell them.

'"Country",' Finney encouraged him.

'Cuntery!'

Stina's father had thin sandy hair but his daughter's light blue eyes and calm exterior. He spoke up again.

'By God this is a shameful display. I have learned everything I need to know. You mean to—' he searched for a word—'you mean to elevate yourselves above others. One day there will be laws against frightful institutions such as this.'

Nils Vågberg spoke with meticulous care. His English was perfect, but it was as if he knew it could lack a flow; like his daughter, he had to translate from his thoughts. So everything he said came out with an impression of slow, judicious contemplation.

'What?' my father growled, misunderstanding, thinking the word 'shameful' had been directed at him. Ma took his arm very hard, by a fat bicep.

Mr Vågberg kept his gaze focussed on the headmistress's face.

'We will take our daughter away from this place, but for these good people here, you have already made up your mind about what you are going to do. Correct?'

'Of course. This is a discussion only.'

'And the purpose?'

'These children have been invited to leave the school. I've granted an opportunity for their families to learn why. At this juncture I am not calling the police. However, this can change.'

'Really? And why is it that you have not mentioned that you beat these children, and that is why my daughter took action?'

In her hard wooden seat Sister Finney straightened her back.

Mr Vågberg said, 'May we hear your side please? Perhaps the authorities would like to hear your reasoning for physical and emotional abuse? Tell me why exactly do you beat small children, Headmistress Finney?'

It was enough.

Finney stood from her desk. The heavy hem of her black robes swept the bare floor as she walked out of her own office, imperious as an ocean liner. That left Sisters Barnaby and Felicity. Felicity now looked up. Her eyes implored Mr Vågberg to not see her as someone who would ever harm a child. Their gaze met. He breathed in deeply through his nose. His thin lips were pursed tight. Nils Vågberg then closed his eyes a moment.

It was as if he wanted to construct one perfect sentence. It came out as two. A voice like ice was directed at Finney's great stern.

'You so-called God-fearing brute.' He turned to the others. Felicity flinched before him. 'Shame falls upon each one of you.'

I would never forget the expression in young Felicity's face, blanched of colour. It was as if this was the first moment she saw herself as others did, and not the way she hoped her God might.

My father was beside himself. This man had spoken like this to sacred nuns. My mother had to keep anchoring him. In my pa's mind this Vågberg fool had not only ruined everyone's chances, but he'd also abused Gesù Cristo's own brides. He literally shook with rage.

Then Stina's mother managed to make matters worse. She had the same good but slightly hesitant English as her husband, but her accent was a hundred times thicker. Her slim arm went around her daughter's shoulders, holding her close. Tears glistened in her green eyes. I thought her very beautiful and elegant.

'Vat our Christina did, ve are so proud ov. Ve are proud ov all these children. To stand up to you.' She looked at Liv and me in a way that made me wish she was my mother. 'Now you beeches go vock yourselves.'

There was silence. Finney was gone. My father turned to my mother, not understanding the peculiar words.

Then he got it.

Part Two

I.

Well, the beeches and that vock of Mrs Vågberg's rang in my father's ears, and he took it and everything else out on me. His punishment was as promised: labouring on stinking building sites each weekend, every holiday, any time his deep, gruff voice called out my name.

Other kids stayed home watching TV, or they played with their friends whenever they wanted, but I was forced to grow up faster, learning to haul bricks, mix concrete and dig foundations until my hands were blistered and bloody. My face, arms and shoulders turned dark brown, skin peeling, all in the days before people like my father believed in equating the sun with skin cancer. Not much more than a quarter century later he'd die from a melanoma on the back of an arm. A brief three months between diagnosis and his last breath, no great surprise when he was used to slaving outdoors half-naked, muttering to himself about the nuns and the school and those *miserabile* Vågbergs.

Brick by brick and block by block I helped him construct retaining walls and fences, fill in concrete foundations for new homes, pave driveways, and everything and anything that people wanted. And it always seemed to be summer; my face and shirt and shorts and socks never stopped being soaked with sweat; nausea squirmed through me from exertion and exhaustion; and the flies, the flies, the fucking flies, drinking perspiration from my eyes, from inside my ears, from above my lips, finding each and every crease and crevice of my body to crawl into and make their home, driving me mad.

This was adult life my father was showing me? This was the great wonder of the working world?

Of course I was forbidden, absolutely banned, from ever seeing Christina, and so I didn't. She lived far enough away, somewhere by the park and river, I thought, that I wasn't very likely to bump into her. Every day I wished I would. She'd been moved to the local state school, and must now have been placed one or even two grades above me.

The funny thing was that Livio Vida also turned out to be a year older than me, but there was no way—no way—anyone would have contemplated putting him into a higher grade. He barely passed subjects where he was, and more often than not his name and a grade of E or F went hand in hand.

Despite our differences, at our new Christian Brothers all-boys' school Liv and I were always together, and in those rooms and in those playgrounds I never heard a single piece of news about Christina Vågberg. I never saw her at the shops, didn't come across her playing on the swings or sitting in the grass by the riverside. She might as well have never existed, which was exactly how my parents wanted things to be—and if Livio's family hadn't purchased a small timber worker's cottage in the street adjoining ours they would probably have tried to ban me from being friends with him as well.

In those days there was plenty of building and bricklaying work for my father, but, strong as he was, he knew he wasn't going to be able to take it for another fifteen or twenty years. He wanted to climb that great unseen ladder to success and real money. In his mind this meant buying old neglected houses and tearing them down in order to build big new blocks of multi-storey flats. A property developer, that's how he imagined himself. A big-time landowner. Only problem was that he needed a lot of capital to get his project started plus a whole lot more to keep it going.

A bank manager with deep pockets needed to believe in him. None did, especially not after they met this naturally surly, deeply sunburned Sicilian who fumbled the simplest sentences while sitting in their offices with an expression of hungry disdain. He'd face each manager squarely, and in his brown features there'd be a look of entitlement married to contempt. Even I could see the way he turned otherwise friendly people off. My father simply was not good with authority; he didn't like anyone having power over him. Problem was, in this country, in his position, just about everyone did.

Every few months he would sit me in a kitchen chair and tell me what his revised plans were. I would have to write these down in English, but not only that, I had to memorize them so that in new meetings with the same old bank manager after bank manager I had to be my father's mouthpiece.

'Very interesting. Thank you very much, young man. Now, could you please explain again to your father that the bank isn't in the position to support a loan of that magnitude? Not without significant securities.'

Speaking Sicilian, my father would turn to me: 'Tell this thick-head about our house. That's the security.'

Which I'd explain, to something like, 'I do believe I've already made it clear that your family home is still under a significant mortgage.'

I'd translate, my father glowering, trying not to show his true feelings and failing. He'd bite down hard on his silence, grinding his white teeth.

For weeks afterwards he would be sullen around the home, quick to snap, and at work would attack his tasks with a ferocity that bordered on the maniacal. If I was with him I'd have to do my best to keep up while at the same time staying out of his way. He'd curse God, Jesus Christ, the Madonna and the prime minister of the day. He'd mutter about Mussolini being right—I never understood about what—then some nights he'd go out, in a pair of clean summer shorts, his shirt unbuttoned to his sternum, hair wet from washing and combed back fast and hard. Freshly shaved, grim-faced, he'd stalk to his car as if heading to an execution.

Instead it was to see his friends, he said, good, hardworking migrant men just like himself who had little English but immense faith in the promise of their new country. They played cards, drank, swore, made plans and argued out their schemes—always looking, I imagined, for the way in. Success. Money. They knew it was here. Here in the immeasurable opportunities this red-brown land offered. But how to actually get it?

In his absence my ma and I would breathe a sigh of relief, sitting together on the couch in front of a standing fan set on high. We'd watch the evening's television shows with singers and dancers or detectives and victims, me happy to be leaning into her despite the summer heat, her wearing a quiet expression that was, as ever, tinged with a sadness that never seemed to go away.

2.

Yet things always change and nothing and no one ever stays the same, and eventually the dust of being expelled from school had to settle.

As time passed, that black event became an echo of misery that mercifully faded. Papà's iron hand relented when he was more satisfied with my academic results at the Christian Brothers school—a place which to me was just another hellhole of Catholic pain, guilt and sexual frustration. To this day the very image of the most severe of the brothers—a dog-faced, untrusting and untrustworthy hound of a man named Brother Percival Baxter—walking through the school grounds tolling his bronze bell still brings nervous sweat to the back of my neck.

He was a male counterpart to Headmistress Finney, of course, and in a perfect world they would have found one another, married, and cancelled each other out. Baxter and the rest of his holy men were holy terrors through and through; their thoughts and dreams were utterly unknowable to the boys in their charge. We lived in gut-tightened fear of each and every one of them, and this was something the parents of all we mostly migrant boys liked. None more so than my pa.

'The strong hand makes the strongest children,' he'd tell me, plus other fascinating aphorisms he dreamed up on the spot.

Another thing that made my father happy was the way I pulled my weight when I worked with him. Despite any earlier indications to the contrary, I seemed to have inherited the trait of handling backbreaking work just the way any other self-respecting Sicilian donkey would: blindly and with dogged determination.

So his iron grip loosened by minute degrees, eventually allowing me to think in new directions. In my own directions.

By then I was spending all my pocket money on fantastic new records, and soon decided that what I wanted more than anything in this life was an electric guitar and amp. A cheap combo set was waiting for me on my fourteenth birthday. The guitar was kitsch-blue, ugly, an embarrassment. The amp wouldn't have served a ten year old's picnic-party turntable—thus was my reward for topping my English and History classes.

Despite the abject crappiness of the musical equipment, not to mention of whatever talent I had to offer, a little neighbourhood rock band let me join. The three other boys were several years older and let me in because I'd taught myself the chords and a fair few of the melody lines for a half-dozen Creedence tunes. They wouldn't need to work them out for themselves. None of these songs were difficult, but there you go.

I could be their second rhythm guitarist, not the rhythm guitarist, as long as I kept that amp turned down low. It didn't matter, we played nowhere, only the empty garage the singer's parents couldn't afford to occupy with a car.

Being in a band with a couple of older neighbourhood boys was acceptable to my parents because my grades, as if by some miracle, remained high. Going to that airless little garage four blocks away gave me moments of liberation. In the meantime my mother and father slowly came to the realization that when their son was happy he did better at school. Maybe they could ease up on how strict they were, on how heavily they placed their expectations on his shoulders.

He's a good, smart kid.

I hadn't heard that for a long time, not since before the meeting in Finney's office.

Soon our little quintet's bass player moved on and lo and behold I managed to get Livio into the group. Why not? Our so-called music was a violent discord anyway.

As a total beginner he was as okay on the bass as I was on the guitar, which is to say, not much. When he played his simple fumbling notes he'd stand almost completely still, as if the music could not hope to move him. His eyes would stare dead ahead like the twin muzzles of a tank, flat and black. It didn't move anyone else either—the band as a whole appeared acutely tone deaf. I was always the one to have to work out the new tunes. The ridiculous complexity of Stairway To Heaven drove me absolutely insane; we dropped it for yet another go-around of Smoke On the Water.

To make things worse, neither Liv nor I were allowed lessons. That was a bridge too far for both sets of parents. What if we actually learned to play well and abandoned dreams of university and professional careers to become drug-addicted long-hairs like those fools on television? So we had to make do on just about zero natural talent and no training whatsoever.

What was strange was that I completely rejected a more natural gift for the piano. I learned it mostly by ear, but with a touch of guidance from my mother. A few sticks of unwanted furniture had come with the house when my parents had purchased it, and that included someone's leftover old upright.

The thing needed tuning and was kept in one of the less visited rooms, full of dust and abandoned toys, empty boxes.

Some convent nun at my ma's school back in Sicily had taught her the rudiments of playing, and had even told her she was a natural, but music hadn't been something she'd had the time to engage with.

She must have had more than just a passing interest, though, because on rare occasions I would hear her softly playing, slightly warped yet otherwise lovely melodies melting through the walls. Once I wandered into that half-darkened room and jumped in fright; her shadowed silhouette was seated there, hands easing over the keyboard but no music being made. It was her form of practice, moving her work-hardened fingers over the keys yet not pressing down.

'I can hear the music in my mind,' she told me in Sicilian, 'that way it comes out perfect.'

'What are you playing?'

'First, the scales. Then a few hymns.' Now she did play something for me, and the creaking piano sounded seven-eighths good. 'The nuns taught me. I don't know what hymn this is.'

She slid a little to the side on the old wooden seat, meaning I should sit next to her. Despite all our rich Italian food my ma was always slim and slightly frail. Next to her I was becoming a teenage lump of lard. That afternoon she showed me how to play the melody, at least the easier bits, fingers moving here, palms raised there, and it wasn't until years later that I realized she and the old Sicilian nuns had mistaken Debussy's Claire de Lune for an old church hymn.

Even if I did have a knack, to me the piano was too reminiscent of my curiously withdrawn mother sitting in dusty shadows with her half-remembered tunes from so long ago. The white and black keys and the little stool reminded me too much of Liberace and cheesy variety shows. Even the supercool Elton John (he's the Rocket Man!, the Teenage Idol!, the Madman Across the Water!) couldn't persuade me to take up that instrument. The piano was my ma's sadness and my ma's sadness was the piano.

I wanted to live: electric guitars raised hell. Look at Town-shend, Page, Blackmore and Hendrix—imagine creating thunder from your fingertips to a wall of Marshall stacks.

Still, I couldn't deny an affection for our defeated keyboard, and the little melodies I sat there and made up sometimes mesmerized me for long stretches of lost time. The fact that I secretly wrote verses of things that looked suspiciously like attempts at poetry was yet another thing about myself I couldn't quite understand.

Then I had one rare and beautiful secret to keep to myself.

3.

A Saturday came that my father didn't need me on his latest work-site; it was hot, it was 1975, I was nearly sixteen.

This year Ken Russell had turned Tommy into a feature film. He already had this new one called Lisztomania. I went to the Regent Theatre in the city and sat with an ice cream cone, chocolates and a drink. It wasn't anything out of the ordinary; none of the other boys at school, including Livio, who remained far and away my best friend, thought too much of the movies on a Saturday afternoon. Especially when they could be at a beach, a public swimming pool, or out playing sport.

While I settled into the muted light and chilly air conditioning with row after row to myself, the cinema felt as quiet and enveloping as the Cathedral of St Stephen three blocks away. The way it ought to be. I'd never liked a packed house, chattering patrons of all ages, the sound of popcorn and crisps being munched too loudly. This particular movie had the virtue of unpopularity, no one wanted to know about it, and after the briefest of runs today was its last day screening.

I couldn't have been happier. Not to be working with bricks and mortar, not to be arse up with sweat in my eyes and flies crawling into my nostrils. Not to be with my old man.

The lights went down, the ads started, the trailers for coming attractions (That one about the shark looks good, Aloha, Bobby and Kose looks like shit.), then there was the slow, tantalizing ritual of the closing of the curtains and their slow re-opening to reveal the full glorious breadth of the cinema screen.

And a tall teenage girl who only looks a little like the Stina of a half-decade ago quietly slides into a seat up front, dead centre.

4.

It's hot. She's cool.

I'm nervous, dressed in old jeans that pinch at the waist and in the crotch. Cheap, worn Dunlop sneakers and a western shirt with snap-buttons that my expanding belly's always popping. The epitome of unhip, even by 1975's own very unhip standards. She's fresh and relaxed in a light cotton print summer dress with her hair away from her face in a ponytail, sandals on her feet. She wears no makeup—not that I really know anything about such things—and there's no polish on her short fingernails. I don't need any figuring to know she's close to seventeen. It's a world of difference; funny thing is, that sense of difference doesn't exist between Liv and me.

The way she is, I can't help thinking that if she does herself up just one bit more there won't be the nightclub or bar that won't let her in.

'Wow, look at you,' she says, those light blue eyes I remember so well opening wide. A surprised sort of happiness is in her face. 'Do people still call you "Eco"? I really hope so, it suits you so much.'

The accented lilt to her voice, it's so much more subtle than I recalled. She no longer hesitates over words. That curl, though, it still comes into the left corner of her mouth.

'Sometimes they do ... yeah, all the time. Uhm, do you still like "Stina"?'

'There are friends who call me call me Christina or Chrissie ... those never sound right to me. I do like Stina best. But look at you! Look how long your hair is!'

She steps back and gives me a full appraisal. I squirm. She's lovely and I'm a lump; bad haircut, overweight, spots. I've never felt so ugly as at this very moment. I'm sure I even have bad breath. Boiled artichokes with pecorino pepato cheese plus garlic for dinner the night before, what can you expect?

If she finds me repulsive she's kind enough not to let on.

'How are your parents?' she asks, and even though they'd made it clear how much they hated every Vågberg on this planet, wherever they roam, her voice doesn't hold a trace of ill will.

'The same. Exactly the same. What about yours?'

'Hmm, sometimes I don't know,' she shrugs, and the way she doesn't elaborate suggests some bigger story. 'So what are you doing at the movies, all by yourself?'

'Same as you?'

She keeps smiling. 'Going with someone spoils it?'

'Maybe.' I've never really thought of it before, but now it seems true. 'Uhm ... there were horror films,' I start to say, 'from the thirties ...'

'Where?'

'At the Lido here in town. In January. I saw all of them.'

'By yourself?'

I nod a slightly shamed yes.

'Pity ... I missed them.' She considers me. 'Didn't it make you sad to always be so alone?'

'I don't really know. It was kind of fun.' I try not to sound pathetic, a loser. There's no doubt in my mind that Stina's gone solo to Lisztomania simply to take a break from her rich and active social life.

'Which films did you see? Of these horrors, I mean.'

It makes me feel better to tell her about Karloff as Frankenstein, Chancy as The Wolf Man, Lugosi as Dracula, and my favourite, Claude Rains as The Invisible Man. Of course, she's seen all of these on television.

'Some of the comedy was just a bit too awful in The Invisible Man, but yes, I liked it a lot too. Why is it your favourite—did you imagine what it would be like sneaking into girls' rooms?'

I had and still did, and even just the thought of it could make me masturbate three times in a single night. I'm sure she notices me blush.

Stina lets me off the hook. 'Have you read the book?'

'A couple of times. I really liked that line, "Drawbacks I saw none."'

'Hmm,' she smiles. 'What?'

'It's when he first thinks about being invisible. What he can do and what he imagines he can sort of get away with.'

'Ah, you have a good memory, yes,' she says, genuinely impressed. 'I remember that part of the book. I understand that thinking. New ideas can seem so promising, and then, reality.'

It's so strange to be standing in that cool foyer having this conversation with her. She seems as natural as sunshine, mature beyond her years. Certainly more mature and aware of herself than I am.

Stina asks, 'Do you read a lot, or are you more of a sports person?'

'Not sports. I hate football. I hate soccer. I hate cricket.'

Stina laughs, 'Tennis? Handball?'

I laugh a little too. 'Fuck 'em all.'

'Yes,' she agrees. Then: 'Vock dem-oll.'

And that really makes me laugh, because I understand the reference to her mother's heavy accent.

'So, uhm, I do read a real lot.' Part of me still squirms, but a larger part's beginning to feel a whole lot better. She has this way to make a boy feel comfortable. 'When I go to bed, I've always got this stack of books in my room.'

Stina takes a sigh at that, as if she thinks this is the best idea ever. Her face—God, it's so alive. She doesn't seem to need or want the sort of mask most people wear every minute of every day. All this time has passed, and we're not little kids any more, and she's happy to be seeing me. Extraordinary.

'By the way,' Stina speaks, now with a touch of her own

shyness, 'they weren't all made in the thirties. The Wolf Man was 1941. George Waggner directed it. And a man named Siodmak wrote it.'

'Okay,' I say.

'Do you remember the curse?'

One short breath each, then: '"Even a man who is pure at heart, and says his prayers by night, may become a wolf when the wolf bane blooms and the autumn moon is bright."'

We stare at each other, completely surprised.

'Siodmak wrote the sequel to The Invisible Man. Isn't that strange? Hollywood must have been small and amazing then. Vincent Price was in that film.'

'How come you know?'

'I'm interested in movies.' Stina studies the ornate ceiling above us. 'I'd love to—' then she changes her mind from whatever she meant to say. 'Hey, isn't this place wonderful? My idea of heaven is a beautiful old art deco theatre, something built in the 1920s maybe, with statues and velvet coverings everywhere, and comfortable seats, and a screen you can see wherever you sit. Bring my body here, I will be the happiest corpse ever.'

'So will I.'

'I'm not in a hurry. Do you want to walk home?'

I nod.

'You live in the same place?'

'Yes.'

'Well,' she says, 'me too.'

5.

We left the Regent's foyer and started to follow Queen Street out of the city. Late afternoon and the bitumen felt as if it was steaming, like it had turned to gum underfoot.

In those days there wasn't the big mall yet, just cars and buses going up and down, and Rock 'n' Roll George cruising past as usual, on cue, ever-present in his 1952 cream-coloured

FX Holden. We watched him come along then slowly pass, first in profile, that craggy half-handsome, half-dark face, then him glancing our way and seeing Stina on the footpath, almost smiling, giving a small nod of appreciation, and who wouldn't at someone like her? Maybe he'd noted Stina many times on this strip, cruised up and down just to get another look at her. At all the girls like her.

No, there was no one else like Stina, not in this town.

I was too young and inexperienced to suggest we do something like stop somewhere air conditioned and have a coffee—a milk shake, more likely. How much money did I have in my pocket? Not enough for either, anyway.

At first it was still and humid, but now as if God decided we'd all suffered enough a late afternoon breeze began to rise. Cooling, making the city sigh. Shadows lengthened. Glorious. Shade and more shade. Such simple things, yet a walk in paradise.

So we watched the sun set into a last burn of red and gold on the horizon past the buildings. Stina said something about the colours and oil paintings, but I didn't know much about that.

John Turner? Who?

At my school there were no classes in art. Woodwork and every sport conceivable, sure enough; painting and visual creativity, you must be joking.

It'd take an hour to get home, a nice time of evening to walk. It'd be dark. I imagined something out of a movie, a powerful scene of me drawing Stina into a grove of trees inside New Farm Park and kissing her. Pulling her down into the grass. I had to shake the thought from my mind, though it resisted being dislodged. I didn't even know what to talk to her about, much less how to make adult-style moves.

For the only females I had anything to do with were family, old family friends, neighbourhood mothers and the occasional shop attendant. The girls I knew were in magazines with their beautiful breasts out and their asses upturned. The censorship laws of our state meant it was just about impossible to find anything more graphic than that. Even Portnoy's Complaint and The Little Red School Book could still cause heated arguments amongst those who thought they never should have come off the banned books list.

Despite the best intentions of the law I was a teenager who'd taken to the art of masturbation as if to a holy vocation. In the shower, in the toilet, last thing at night with a packet of tissues hidden beneath the bed covers.

Only after the deed was done could I calmly turn the pages of the library books stacked on my floor—and whatever I'd learned about the opposite sex came from my more hidden stash of books: Everything You Wanted to Know About Sex But Were Afraid to Ask; The Joy of Sex; Fear of Flying; even The Female Eunuch, which I hadn't much understood. I'd devoured these tomes several times over, but in just a few minutes of Stina's company I knew they hadn't taught me a thing.

How do you talk to a girl?

She wanted to know what I'd been doing and whether my school was any good. I stammered through stupid answers. She said she liked her school well enough, and the friends she had there, but she felt restless, always restless. Maybe life was somewhere else. Life couldn't be this small place, not Brisbane, 1975.

I didn't think to ask her what exactly she was restless for. Maybe she didn't even know; I certainly didn't.

By the time we'd discussed school subjects, the ones we did well in and the ones we wished had never been invented—physics and economics were her downfall, same for me if you added science—we'd made our way into Fortitude Valley. The place was, of course, quiet as death on a late, lazy Saturday.

Old Italian men sat at round tables on the footpath by pizza and pasta cafés, drinking espressos. A few Chinese restaurants steamed with the aromas of cooking duck and pork. The people who wandered around looked lost.

Despite the cool change I was sweating. Stina didn't appear to perspire at all. My talk faltered. I didn't know what to say or how to say it—but Stina wasn't about to let awkward silences spoil this walk, this unexpected meeting. So she brought up the film we'd just seen, which had been crazy and chaotic, and had mostly gone over my head.

'Did you like the parallel between how popular Liszt used to be and today's rock stars?'

I told her I did, though the truth was that I hadn't thought about that at all.

'And the part where the court ladies stroke his ego and make a chorus line for him? I know that was a dream sequence but Liszt's ten-foot erection—isn't that what it must be like to have so much fame and adulation?'

'Uh, yeah ...'

'It would have to make you feel very powerful. And enormous.'

She wasn't teasing me. All the same, my breath came hard and the blood seemed to sing in my head. Just to hear her say something like this—to mention an erection, to include intimations of sex in a simple conversation—well, it made that mindless and uncomfortable stiffening present itself straight away, an angry fist in my jeans. Yet she was so natural in the way she spoke; it made me realize just how much I didn't know her. How much older than me she was.

I hated that. I hated being a kid. After this walk there'd be nothing else. She must have already figured out just how dumb and inexperienced I was. Until she could get rid of me she was being kind and polite. Then I'd never see her again. Our thin connecting thread, the one going back to the fifth grade, would snap.

'Very male-oriented, though, that movie,' she spoke, party to not a single one of my doubts. 'And bad acting.'

'The music ...' I ventured.

'Awful.'

'Actually, it was a pretty bad movie.'

She said with a straight face, 'Wanker Ken Russell.'

So after a beat I said, 'With naked girls everywhere.'

Not missing the next beat she added, 'With great tits.'

And me: 'And great bodies.'

And her: 'Fucking everyone as they please.'

And me: 'And ready for more.'

Which she concluded: 'Vocking the lucky vockers all over the place.'

I couldn't imagine she'd be so profane, and now we were laughing, a release of tension, at least for me, but it might have been that way for her as well.

An older woman cluck-clucked at us while she walked past with her string shopping bags, having overheard the whole thing.

'It's good to see you, Eco,' Stina said, catching her breath.

'Hey, I play in a band,' I replied, searching for a way to keep her talking, to maybe even impress her.

'Is your band good?'

'Uh—no. No one likes us.'

'Maybe just not yet?'

'I don't know.'

'What do you play?'

It wasn't her thing, the type of music we tried to make. And I wouldn't have wanted her coming to hear us either. The moments of complicity were passing and we were close enough to our homes that I felt I was already losing her. Such an indefinable, irretrievable quality sometimes, this thing called connection.

We walked the decline of Brunswick Street and came to the glass storefront of a dilapidated second hand book shop. We were close now to the local cinema and several grocery stores.

'Hey,' she said. 'I found a beautiful copy of Hunchback of Notre Dame here, 1920s edition. You know how much it cost? Fifty-five cents. I always come back.'

A woman in a grim brown twinset was stacking paperbacks behind the large pane. This was Miss Pettigrew of Miss Pettigrew's Preloved Books. Painfully thin and with her hair in a tight bun, wearing very thick glasses and an expression of unnatural severity, she looked like the type of bookish librarian who wouldn't crack a smile for love or money.

Stina waved as the woman glanced up. The return smile was full of warmth.

Well.

I didn't move toward the door, feeling guilty. Of course I knew this place. Miss Pettigrew used to keep boxes and boxes of comic books on tables right here, out front, always beside some of her most interesting book additions. I used to come by after school. If she was occupied and busy inside, I'd slide a DC or a Marvel under my shirt or into my school bag. Livio would join me sometimes, even though comics weren't for him. He'd take a couple then pass them on to me.

One afternoon the boxes had disappeared. They never returned. Miss Pettigrew's severity increased.

'Let's go in,' Stina said.

'Oh no, not this time.'

'Actually she's closed anyway. She must be getting ready for next week.'

I was thinking how in the fifth grade Stina had been taller than me. She used to be a little pudgy around the middle, with baby-fat legs. Now I was the one too stocky, but at least I'd made a slight gain on her in height. Stina was willowy and graceful, her body lean, and for a girl of sixteen her breasts had a generous shape. I liked the way her dress moved, the way she moved—and just like that I received a moment of clarity, a shard of sunlight illuminating a dull place in my mind that previously had been left dark and untouched.

An artist might paint someone like her with a slow, loving brush; a musician would give the very idea of her a wistful melody; a poet might write lines full of longing ... and the fifteen-year-old me was simply overwhelmed.

We went back to talking about music. She wasn't against all music, she just didn't know very much about the things that were popular on the radio. Her preference was for soul and blues singers, mostly female, and from a long time ago. She mentioned names that didn't ring any bells.

We had a lot more in common with books. Writers like Wells, Heinlein, Asimov and Ray Bradbury. The collection S Is For Space had been a set text at my school but not hers, one of the few things the Christian Brothers managed to get right. After reading that I'd devoured the stories in R Is For Rocket. Stina had read his work far more widely. She told me she'd finished Fahrenheit 451 for the second time not a week ago.

All the books she mentioned I would find at the library tomorrow.

Then far too quickly we were at her house. I saw it was an old colonial in need of repair, small bits and huge chunks of paint flaking everywhere. Wooden boards, timbers, everything was wasting away. It was the type of house my father always rejected with contempt. He said they had no value: 'Who'd want one even for free?' Good for knocking down only, and, in his mind, replacing with a nice three-storey block of brick flats.

Naturally enough one day all these ancient wooden places would be worth a fortune. Pieces of heritage only the rich could buy. Even I could imagine that, but not my father. The worth of the world was in the new and the solid; then again, maybe thinking this way was how he kept his old world of hunger and zero prospects far in the background.

Stina's father was someone I remembered very clearly. He wasn't anything like mine, and worked in an office, a man with soft palms and clean collars.

The Vågberg home was set high to catch the river breeze and views. Stina and I stood awhile in the front yard, which was rough and unkempt. There was no sense of a lawn, much less of a garden. Ragged and neglected things grew amongst abandoned beds of weeds. My ma would have thrown up her hands in dismay and not stopped working till she'd created a pretty garden.

Stina didn't invite me in but she didn't run away either; I couldn't have stayed anyway. If I wasn't sitting at the family table for dinner there'd be new stinking-hot summer building sites to become acquainted with.

She half-hesitated. Something was on her mind.

I was expecting Mr or Mrs Vågberg to come to the door and call her in. Only a female German Shepherd appeared. A lot of years weighed on her shoulders and she loped straight to Stina, ignoring me. She sat at Stina's feet and looked up adoringly. Only after Stina patted, caressed and spoke low to her friend did the dog deign to come sniff at me.

'This is Gudrun ... well, looks like she approves. We found her at the animal refuge. She was already fully grown. Treated very badly, but she joined the family straight away. She had another name but we started her like new. You must smell nice to her.'

The dog's attention made me blanche; her nose was trying to rub into my genital area. She was probably getting a whiff of the tiny drops of semen that had accompanied my erection. I made a show of patting the dog's heavy coat while trying to keep her off me.

'So next time,' Stina said, 'maybe you want to come and listen to some of my records?...'

Was I hearing her right? I could hardly believe there'd be a next time.

'Okay.'

'And bring some of yours, that would be interesting.'

Gudrun followed her up the front stairs. The hem of Stina's dress swayed over her smooth, light calves.

Then Stina danced up those last steps and the old dog had to hurry to catch her.

6.

Well, she hadn't said anything about when this 'next time' ought to happen, so I tried the same time next week. It was another warm Saturday afternoon. I managed to get the day free even though my father complained that he needed me. I made up a story about having to finish a big assignment, a history project to be completed with some boy in class I'd been paired up with.

'Not bloody Livio,' Papà growled, ready to be angry. He knew that if I was meant to do anything in the least bit academic with Liv the result could only be bad. My father and even the teachers at school considered my friend good for carting bricks, pushing wheelbarrows and nothing else. They looked forward to his early exit from the school system, and the body he was growing into said he'd be a valuable day-labourer.

'No, it's this other boy … Steve. I don't really know him.' I tried to be vague yet convincing, saying he lived in a street far from us and definitely a long way in the opposite direction to Stina's house. 'His mother's a teacher and people say she's a real bitch.'

'Yeah?' my father asked, finally more interested.

And that convinced him. My father's veneration of the world's toughest teachers had continued unabated. Anyone who ruled a classroom with an iron list was just fine by him. He and the mad-as-cut-snakes Christian Brothers remained a perfect fit. Brother Baxter was as close to a personal idol as my father would likely get. Save for Benito Mussolini, of course, though he was dead.

'Okay, so you go dere I no want dat dis boy he comes here,' my father spoke, never one to welcome strangers into the home.

So he believed my story, and subsequent variations as well, because I'd never before made excuses for not going to work with him.

That afternoon I was excited and happy and even a bit scared as I walked to the river and the park. A half-dozen LPs were under my arm. Along the way I did subtle things like glance around and behind, stopping to retie a shoelace that didn't need it, all because my father could have faked believing me and might have been following to see exactly where this no-good, lying son of his was headed.

When I let myself into Stina's yard I'd managed to work my-self into a high pitch of anxiety. The little gate off the footpath creaked open and shut, rusted on its hinges. Old Gudrun picked herself up from where she lay in a patch of dead grass and shade and came slowly to greet me.

I went up the stairs and knocked on the weather-beaten frame of the weather-beaten door. Now I could hear a radio, a weather report maybe. The front door opened to the aroma of fennel. Something was cooking. Mrs Vågberg's pleasant, still very pretty, now slightly lined face greeted me. She must only have been in her mid-thirties, but to me as a teenager all parents were hopelessly ancient.

Except, I sort of instantly realized, for her. I could actually imagine Stina's ma dressed to the nines, looking glamorous. Just one step away from being a star in some big budget movie. The step that kept her away was something like tiredness, exhaustion—I couldn't quite put my finger on what it might be.

'Vell, the boy—the boy of the man.'

She studied me with a curious sense of interest. One eyebrow was raised. 'Christina sees you at the moofies, she tells me. Vy don't you come in? What do you wait for ... er, "Eco"? She says this is what I hof to call you.'

I nodded, trying to seem like a regular guy, but I was tense as a hungry cat.

'She vill be back soon you know. Take a cold drink. Put those in the liffing room.'

We went inside and I left the records on a side table in the small living room she showed me. Mrs Vågberg looked at them with some curiosity. Gudrun had accompanied us. We'd passed the kitchen, which had that pleasant aroma of good food, but in here things were different. Dust was everywhere. The curtains were closed. Ashtrays held many butts. The room felt like old cigarettes and arguments. There were dead incense sticks too, maybe to mask the ashy, closed-up smell.

We returned to the kitchen. Mrs Vågberg lit a cigarette. Now I noticed how yellowed her fingers were. There was an open bottle of vermouth by the stove. She gave me a glass of ginger beer and a piece of some kind of orange cake, and before I'd finished these little refreshments Stina was home.

She had some shopping with her, something in a pharmacy's brown wrapper. She excused herself straight away and while she was gone I waited with Mrs Vågberg. She added herby ingredients to her simmering pot and stirred slowly, something of a distracted air about her. Gudrun had followed Stina as if they had a secret to share. In a few minutes Stina returned and was brighter, face washed, hair brushed. Her mother asked her something in Swedish. Stina replied the same wav.

'Sorry,' she said, turning to me, 'I wasn't expecting my period, but I'm better now. The walk helped and I've got some pills. Let's leave mother to her cooking.'

Stina was dressed in black jeans and a small pink halter top, now barefoot. She carried a small tray of more cake and drinks. I followed her into that living room and she put the tray down and shut the door. Despite the dust, the room was nice and private. She took a look through my records then kneeled by the family stereo system and put the diamond needle down onto a track by a singer named Nina Simone. The first song was called Feeling Good.

First there was a lonely voice with no accompaniment, then a big fat band kicked in. It sounded great, not at all what I was expecting.

'Wow,' I said.

Stina gave that smile of hers, curled at one edge, then as she sat cross-legged on the floor with me her body couldn't help moving to the music and voice.

She asked me what I'd been doing. I said something about school. As we made small talk I watched her. It was almost a shock to realize how alone I was with her. This had to be a dream, right? She didn't seem to mind the way I looked at her. Her face was a little paler than usual. I knew as much about what happens to girls every month as I knew about the NASA space program. I wondered if there was something I ought to be doing to help. Didn't they say a warm water bottle on the belly was supposed to ease discomfort?

Against her white skin her lips seemed fuller and more the colour pink than ever. She reached back and pulled her hair out of its ponytail. It fell to her shoulders in blonde, natural waves. In a minute she'd plaited it. I had no idea how she'd done that. But I was—

Feeling good.

The record was a compilation of different artists. The next songs were more soulful, real heartbreakers. Stina turned the volume down a touch.

'Where did you get all your records?' I asked.

'My mother ... she used to be a musician. She learned the violin and viola, but she liked being a singer better. I'm talking about when she was a teenager in Stockholm. Her career didn't go very far. Then she met my father. She was just a singer in clubs, but she says her voice wasn't strong enough. Maybe she didn't really give it everything.'

'Do you sing?' I asked.

Stina said 'Nope' quite lightly, which I took to mean that maybe she could. She again considered the covers of the albums I'd brought over, more interested in the designs and the layouts than any of the music they might have held. I had the feeling she didn't want to talk about anything too serious.

'This one here ... "Alice Cooper" is a man?'

'Uh, yeah.'

'All ... right ...' she said very slowly, drawing the word out. Then as she considered the very androgynous, almost effeminate photographs of the next albums, she asked with a touch of humour: 'And this one and this one also?'

'Yes, David Bowie and Marc Bolan, definitely of the masculine persuasion.'

'Hmm, they make me think there must be such a thing as a third sex.'

'I guess that's right.'

'I've heard their names before. Are they famous? Nice furs.'

'Those records are a bit older. Have you heard of Led Zeppelin? This is Physical Graffiti. I had to wait a while to get it but it's still pretty new. See the way the inside sleeves come out? The little pictures through the cutouts? Clever, huh?'

I let her look it over, and she seemed to think the cover was indeed very clever.

'But this one, this is my favourite.' I showed her the ornate, grey-hued double album packaging of Quadrophenia. This took more of her interest. Stina turned the pages of the big book of photographs that came with it, carefully studying each one. Then she read Pete Townshend's short story inside, about a lost Mod named Jimmy. While she did that I flipped the blues record playing over to side two. Now it was Peggy Lee singing a song called Black Coffee, about as far from The Who as I could imagine.

'No one was buying this one,' I said. 'I got it for three dollars, my best bargain ever.'

'Well,' Stina nodded, 'this man can write. I like the story very much. And the pictures are beautiful. Black and white photography is always my favourite, you can make shading so interesting, you know?'

She turned one particular photo towards me; it was of the character Jimmy lying crumpled on his side, fully dressed in bed. His walls are covered with cutout pictures of nudes. Lots and lots of gorgeous breasts, girls out of magazines from the sixties.

Stina had that playful way again. Her face said she understood the corners of a boy's dirty little soul, and it was fine.

'What sort of pictures do you have on your walls, Eco?'

I had none and said so, and she poked me then gave my shoulder a shove.

Somehow we started wrestling. It was what she wanted. Gudrun got up and moved away. Stina's hair smelled of berries. I wanted to lick her neck, kiss her lips. I couldn't tell if she thought that would be good or if she would scream in disgust.

Her hands in mine were smooth and strong; she rolled this way and that, playfully, not too hard, and I went with her.

She was stronger than I would have expected. Her breasts briefly touched my arm then they pressed against my chest as I let her hold me down. I hated my soft belly. She felt as if she contained a kind of lean, concentrated power. She could have held me like that for a month, I'd never complain. And her eyes were strange, like they were laughing into mine.

Meanwhile a torch singer crooned something sad about her melting heart, then Stina's leg brushed my erection and she didn't quite move away.

'Children,' Mrs Vågberg said from the now open living room door, speaking with some humour. 'Something to eat.'

Stina gave me a last playful shove. She straightened her clothes and turned the music louder just as she half-skipped from the room. I sat cross-legged, there on the floor, alone with the dog. My prick was hard and sore. I felt as if the blood had drained from my head, actually leaving me giddy. Gudrun's sleepy eyes took me in. They held a wounded quality. Maybe she envied my careless play with Stina, after all, that poor dog seemed to hurt everywhere.

I gave her a long slow rub, which she liked. She lay on her back and spread her back legs. There was a half-grumble, a half-moan in her throat. I could relate to that.

The two Vågberg women were seated at the kitchen table. Mrs Vågberg had a late lunch of cold cuts, a few different sorts of cheeses, and bread she'd baked that morning. Her pack of cigarettes was by her plate and she was drinking a half-glass of vermouth, neat. What simmered in the pot was for the family dinner. There was a chair and a place for me. I sat down. A folded cotton napkin was waiting, and a glass of fresh juice that tasted as if oranges had just been invented. This had to be heaven. I thought I was exactly where I wanted to be.

'And how is your family?' Mrs Vågberg asked, and Stina shot her a look.

Somehow, instead, we started to talk about local politics, a subject a million miles from my thoughts, yet it was fun.

'These men they are cunts,' Mrs Vågberg laughed. Stina seemed even more displeased. Her mother said to me, 'Take a cigarette if you vant vun,' and I couldn't believe she was serious.

She was.

So I started smoking my first cigarette, trying to do it exactly the way I imagined James Bond might, even as Stina's sardonic glare told me I'd be a lot smarter to just put that thing the vock out.

7.

After that first Saturday I lived to hear Stina say Hey Eco, listen to this one as she played me another blues tune or a whole side of some lovely yet heartbroken torch song record. She loved her own, and her mother's, but gradually she took to more of mine as well. The artists turning her my way were David Bowie, The Velvet Underground and The Doors. She'd never like The Who or Led Zeppelin, but Jim Morrison might as well have still been alive; Stina just about stole the first Doors album and LA Woman from me. Roxy Music weren't at all to my taste but she purchased all their records up to Siren and soon she was trying to turn me onto them. Even Marc Bolan, who was well and truly in decline, just about a completely forgotten star in this country, could still make colour come into her face.

'I will have his children,' she said. 'You wait and see.'

I felt special for the way her musical tastes grew far more *au courant*, and I loved every minute of being allowed in her home and quiet rooms—yet we were an odd pair, me always so pudgy and bumbling where she was so graceful. Once when I held her by the hips as she showed me some dance steps I realized how narrow her waist really was. Long legs, slim hips, breasts growing larger. All before seventeen years of age. In my heart I knew someone like me wasn't going to entertain her very long;

she was made for more than friendly moments in a dusty living room. The world was waiting.

Still, for now, records were our connective tissue and we listened to as many as we could, some over and over. A pile of her mother's were hard and heavy 78s. Edith Piaf was a favourite, but there were blues and jazz singers like Billie Holiday, Bessie Smith, Etta James and the occasional more modern star like Janis Joplin, who'd died the very year Stina and I met.

Some of the recordings weren't all that good, but I often found that added to the raw emotion in the music. Hearts have been broken forever; the story of it always needs telling. For whatever reason Mrs Vågberg must have known it all, through these singers she adored, yet Stina herself was moving away from all this sadness—she told me she could play Roxy Music's For Your Pleasure and Stranded, or Lou Reed's Transformer, or T. Rex's The Slider, four times in a single night. While doing her homework and still getting As. It was strange and even funny to see how she'd gone from Mahalia Jackson to Mott the Hoople in such a small space of time.

'Listen, is this right?'

She was trying to whistle the little coda that comes at the end of Golden Years; the single had just started being played on the radio. I'd used my own money to buy her the little 45.

'Sort of.'

I did it myself, echoing that lovely but brief whistled melody of David Bowie's.

'Eco—but that's perfect.'

Yet she couldn't quite get it.

'This?'

'Not yet.'

'My number one challenge,' she told me.

Then, in a space of weeks, I sensed changes between us, the intrusion of half-secrets and things not quite said.

Of course, Stina turned seventeen a good year ahead of me,

and she was going out at night. The Vågbergs were far from
strict; their daughter could have her night-life. She did so well
at school and seemed so level-headed within herself that there
was no problem at all. My 'freedom' was made of more paltry
things: these visits based on lies; occasional Saturday afternoon
movies on my own; once-a-week band practices, which I had to
be home from by eight p.m. I was still being treated, and living,
like a boy.

Stina and I spent more afternoons listening to music but
when I was gone she was dressing up and hitting the town—or
wherever the hell it was that free teenagers went. It was clear to
me: I was a friend, platonic as her dog. Someone to talk to and
share records. I wouldn't move anywhere from that particular
space. She was too lovely; I wanted her too much; I didn't possess a great deal of the real Stina at all.

One midnight while my parents slept I climbed out my
window and loped all the way to her house. Like a spy I secreted myself in a clump of trees across from the Vågberg home.
Though two lights burned inside, no one seemed to be awake.
Then Stina arrived, maybe thirty minutes later, passenger in a
big red and black Ford with fiery speed-decals plastered all over
it. A guy with long hair smoked a cigarette behind the steering
wheel. He flicked the butt into the street. I saw his hair was longer and blonder than Stina's. He looked like a rock star—no, he
was the embodiment of a Marvel super-hero, the Norse god of
thunder transported to our town.

In the shotgun seat Stina was a dusky profile. Music wafted
from the car and I recognized it—On The Beach. That made
me crazy; my LP of it had been on her turntable, we'd talked
about Neil Young and played his records. Now I imagined I was
about to witness this guy making love to my Stina right there,
in front of her home, in front of me, while Neil Young sang his
Vampire Blues.

Instead they talked a little, then he gave her a long kiss goodbye. It all seemed so unhurried and natural.

I thought I would die; the world was made for people as free as these two. Me, I was one of the serfs and underlings of the world, someone condemned to read about finer and happier people in books, and watch them in movies, then be their waiter in bars and restaurants.

Stina slid out of the Ford and straightened her yellow mini skirt. Such legs; the sight was horny, obscene and depressing all at the same time. She went up the staircase to the front door and let herself in without a backward glance. That was it. No drama, nothing happening, just sweet life rolling forward. The same scene would be repeating itself in quiet streets all over the country.

I imagined a squeal of arrogant tires. The guy lit a fresh cigarette and drove away, nice and quiet. I went home and wept under my sheet. When I ejaculated I was biting down hard on a corner of my covers.

8.

Fuck caution, fuck acting like a child.

I took Stina to the movies. A Jack Nicholson rerun. Lots of swearing, fighting and roughhouse sex. The Last Detail. Even at a Saturday midday session, it was a blast. I came out of the theatre swaggering and joking like it had been me up on that screen.

'I'm gonna get a fat tattoo one day, Stina. It's gonna say "Free".'

For an hour I didn't feel so much like a serf anymore. I did feel free. I wanted to take Stina by the waist and bend her backwards, plant a big one right on her cherry lips. Nicholson was loose and crazy and terrific. Stina loved him. Maybe she'd like me better if I just went wild on her.

She said, 'You know, why don't we see more films?'

So my lies at home got bigger. We watched Liv Ullman and Max von Sydow in a slow-moving European movie. Sam Peckinpah's Bring Me the Head of Alfredo Garcia, which had a special weirdness all its own, made us leave our seats wondering what exactly we'd just seen.

'"I been here before and you don't know the way,"' Stina would quote, making her voice sound exactly like that of the prostitute–girlfriend in the movie who's about to be raped by an armed biker, and who wants to save her man from a hopeless act of courage.

'"There's nothing sacred about a hole in the ground or the man that's in it … or you, or me,"' I'd quote back from a different part of the film, trying to sound as weather-beaten as Warren Oates.

Soon we were talking about film people, not pop artists. They became our new vocabulary. There was Bergman, Coppola and this guy Scorsese. The young actor Robert De Niro, wow, in Mean Streets and especially The Godfather Part II he took your breath away. He got me strutting like a cocksure young gangster.

'You've got the same eyes,' she told me, trying not to laugh at my antics.

I looked things up. De Niro was fifteen years older than me. Al Pacino, eighteen. Sean Connery seemed super cool and ageless. I wanted to be all of these men and I wanted to be in their sorts of stories.

'But what do you want to do Eco, after school, after university—if you go there?'

I didn't have a clue. Be an adventurer. Be like Bruce Lee. Lose weight.

'What about you?'

There was something. It was in her eyes, even if she wasn't saying it.

'Come on, what?'

'I go to acting classes.'

'Huh?'

'Three afternoons a week, after school. It's been a year now.'

She'd never told me this. She'd never uttered a word about what she might want to do with her life.

Now I remembered that Saturday afternoon I met her at Lisztomania. Stina there on her own. Maybe it made sense now. The girl had been studying. That's why the film had her close attention, why she hadn't missed a detail. Sitting in the theatre she'd been soaking up that big-screen world, watching and analysing the way the actors did things. Me, I went to movies on my own because I didn't have friends who were interested enough to come along. She did it because she wanted to absorb cinema itself, transport herself in.

No wonder she knew so much about films and filmmakers.

'You really want to act?'

'Not just that ...' Her face came alive. This was a dream she couldn't dampen. 'Eco—I want to be big.' She started to laugh. She meant it.

There was so much excitement about her now, so much life, yet this part of Stina had been hidden from me. I'd never realized just how much of herself she'd been holding in reserve. I looked at the glow in her face and thought, Man, she will be. She'll get that. She'll get to be as big and famous as she wants, plus more.

How couldn't she? Even my heart beat faster at the thought. Stina's name up in lights, with her very own star in front of that Chinese theatre place. What was it called again?

'Grauman's.'

And then she pulled me by the arm and kissed me. Kissed me really, really hard, with all the enthusiasm of her dreams. But on the cheek.

'You're not making fun of me.'

'Why would I?'

'Eco. Thank you. Thank you.'

Still holding my arm, one more kiss, this time closer to my mouth. It was as if a light went on inside me. So this is what it feels like. This is what it's like to be Nicholson, De Niro, Pacino and Connery. To be on the other side of life. Not a serf, but a man.

'Hey Stina.'

I was going to grab her the way Warren Beatty grabbed Julie Christie in Shampoo.

She was walking away. Our bus was arriving. We sat together barely speaking. There were only two other passengers in there with us. We could have kissed and fondled all the way home. The driver was a woman with her hair in a net and a handy pack of Pall Malls at hand, one of which she was smoking out of the corner of her mouth, à la Bogart. She wouldn't have cared if I slipped a hand under Stina's skirt. Would Stina?

I itched to try it.

9.

We were well into '76 now, what a great era for new movies and to be discovering the old ones. Cinemas around town and in the suburbs were doing regular reruns of things thirty, forty, even fifty years old—of course, that brought us all the way back to the silents, to Georges Méliès. In the days before VCRs and DVDs these screenings were always popular and packed. Beside Stina, in darkened theatres with busted seats and rats or mice running amongst the wooden rafters, I was happier than ever.

So at home I studied extra hard, put good effort into assignments, compositions and maths tables, and especially into the subjects I detested, all to make it seem true that I benefited from this amazing free tuition I received from 'Steve and his bitch-teacher-ma.' I reasoned that if my parents didn't have to worry about my grades they wouldn't question my outings. Maybe I could even engineer a lot more. They still believed I was always at Steve's place for study and assignments. Sometimes maybe I went off to see a Sunday morning movie on my own. I'd always done it, so in their eyes nothing was different.

Goddammit, but they were actually proud of me. This mask I wore of the dutiful son and student was as convincing as a re-ligion. My parents mentioned something that would once have been unthinkable, of actually meeting this school mate and his bitch/saint of a mother. I made credible excuses for why this shouldn't happen, then fantasized I could make my lies bigger, maybe arrange a sleepover at 'Steve's place'. If I could get away with that, where could I take Stina—a restaurant? A motel? Could I ask her for so much?

All a dream.

I was nothing but a boy, and she had men.

10.

Still, Stina never said no to new films and reruns and many double features, which was what I liked best. Two films in a row meant double-time with her.

We ate everything up, and in those days it was a piece of cake to get into the movies we weren't supposed to see.

'How old are you?'

'We're both eighteen.'

That was all Stina needed to say.

Australian films had become better and dirtier, and we went to all the reruns, squirming through the stupidities that were Alvin Purple and Alvin Rides Again, not to mention The Adventures of Barry Mackenzie. Awful, but awfully great too. Then came Walkabout and Wake in Fright. We emerged from those sessions just about shaking. International classics were revived there was Gone With the Wind to see, The Wizard of Oz and Singin' in the Rain. Seven Samurai, The Seventh Seal, Bicycle Thieves, La Dolce Vita—man, it was an education into a world so much greater than the one we knew. We talked about Michelangeli, Antonioni, Vittorio de Sica, Vincente Minnelli and Douglas Sirk as if they were our friends. How many Charlie Chaplins did we take in? Marx Brothers films? Woody Allen became a favourite. After Play it Again, Sam we absolutely idolized Humphrey Bogart, then discovered Bogie was great in everything and anything.

'The Roaring Twenties or The Petrified Forest?'

'The Roaring Twenties,' I replied.

'Lauren Bacall or Ingrid Bergman?'

'Ingrid Bergman.'

'Bacall for me,' Stina said.

She was taking her cue from the screen. In my mind she was already transformed; she'd be before cameras in elegant gowns, with platinum hair, her lips full and red, every man sitting in the dark hopelessly in love with her. Stina's name would be the secret on their lips when they made love to their wives. Nothing could be more certain. She'd be the daring beauty her mother could have been; on the cover of magazines so that women would use her as the divine image they wished for themselves.

Where would I be in this equation?

There was no equation. I'd be the missing number in the long addition that ended up in her fame.

Often in the dark I'd stay close to catch the scent of Stina's hair. Some moments she'd slide her hand into mine. Scarlet and Rhett's daughter falls off her pony; Death moves close to the knight Antonius; Sylvia dances in the Fountain of Trevi; Brigitte Bardot, created by God to humble all men, pouts from the screen. My heart would hurt and sing at the same time. Stina was a friend who was something else; she wasn't a sister though she seemed to be. She was out in the world doing private and secret things without me, yet at the same time we shared this oasis.

It was confusing; something to love and hate. When we sat close in the dark I'd find myself wondering whose lips and mouth had kissed her recently.

By now she was well into her final year of school; I'd have one more year after that.

And then?

The answer came as we walked home from 1923's silent The Hunchback of Notre Dame. Stina remained just as silent too, which was unlike her. The river was still and few people were around in this early Saturday evening. The sky remained light and the heat was a death-shroud. Stina's house wasn't far.

She said, 'My parents are getting divorced,' and she looked ahead, looked at the river, and touched the perspiration on her upper lip.

'Are you joking?'

'No.'

'Why would they?'

'Well,' she started. 'Well.'

I waited until she could get it out.

'My father has had women for years. It's always been the same. This is the way he is. Once I overheard him encourage my mother to find her own lovers.'

I was stunned. Were adults really like this?

Stina kept her eyes on the river, but I could see how hurt she was.

'It's not that he doesn't adore her. He does, or he did. Now my father says he's fallen in love. She's French.' Stina spoke blankly now, as if on automatic. 'I've seen her. She's not much. She has a family with money and she's abandoned her husband. No children. Much younger than him. Twenty-six years of age. I could look up to her as an older sister. They're planning to leave Australia together. Forever.'

'You're saying that your father is going to leave the country with a new woman.'

'He has a sudden calling pour la belle France.' Even with her sarcasm, she seemed quite disconnected from what she was telling me. She was keeping herself that way. 'My mother has had someone too, but it didn't do anything for her. Out of spite for my father, I believe. No real passion. Or maybe physical passion and nothing else. So now she smokes and drinks and listens to songs that keep her miserable.'

I stared past her. The dust in that house. The ashy living room. This was incredible. It was a movie. A movie playing out in front of me that I'd been too dumb to recognize.

'She says she's fed up and wants the two of us to go back to Sweden. You know my mother never wanted to come here in the first place? It's true. This is one thing that makes her furious. All these years in a place she didn't want, for nothing. She hasn't made a life in this country. She's in the house. She used to sing.'

Now Stina pressed her hands to her eyes, had to squeeze hard before she could go on. She actually started to cry. but without sobs.

'We have family in Stockholm. My mother thinks it will be better.'

I put my arm around her shoulders. Her normally cool body felt hot, her skin damp. After only a few moments she pushed free.

'So do you hate him?'

'My father's an honest man. Honest about his desires. If that's what he needs, that's what he needs. It would be worse to live a lie.'

'But what about you?'

She wouldn't look at me.

The river wasn't still. There was the slow swirling of current. She seemed spellbound by that.

'I live too many lies.'

'What?'

Then she was silent.

So we sat in a nearby bench, the wooden slats old and peeling. In the pathway an incredibly fit mother with a huge bosom went by pushing a double-pram. She was in lycra and seemed to be telling the world she'd cracked this motherhood thing wide open. Meanwhile, a small wooden council ferry steamed a snail's pace across the brown river, travelling from the New Farm jetty to the pier across the way.

'But what are you talking about? What lies?'

Stina thought a moment. This time she didn't avert her eyes.

'Look what I do to you. To the sweetest friend I can imagine.'

'You haven't done anything to me.'

'Huh,' she half-laughed. 'Well put.'

The meaning of that was pretty clear, but I told her it was all right.

She was smarter. 'You don't have to be so kind, Eco.'

Stina's expression was sadder than ever, but her tears stopped. This thing with her parents had just about shattered the ground between her feet. I wasn't sure what to say, so kept my mouth shut.

After a while she cleared her throat. 'Well, I have to brush up on the language. I haven't lost it, but I'm rusty. We'll be home by Christmas. Just a few months ... I'm going to have to think about Stockholms universitet. I hear it's quite wonderful.'

She sat there. We were silent once more.

After a minute I had the slow-dawning impression that she was waiting.

A sort of blush came into her face. She took a long breath. She looked at me as if she was angry. Actually angry at me. Without warning she pushed in close and kissed me on the lips. The tip of her tongue touched mine. Her mouth was hot, lips moist and open.

This was my first real kiss, and it came completely out of nowhere. With Stina, older than me, lovelier than any girl I could imagine.

I was too shocked to react.

My lips barely moved; my hands didn't touch her.

Stina shifted away. Pushed herself. Almost to the far edge of the bench.

'Eco,' she spoke, looking down, breathing low and hard. 'You have to grow up.'

That was how she saw me.

Nothing was going to work again.

Part 3

I.

As if to make matters worse, Livio got sick and I ended up with no one to turn to. Just a few weeks of year eleven left and he never saw another day of it.

I went to his place afternoons and weekends but he was too ill to say much. Most times he wouldn't even come out of his bedroom. His mother would be in her usual black and red house dress, an apron tied over it. She didn't like me visiting and would lurk in the background like a stout shadow of gloom. There was no talk of hospitals or doctors, though I gathered these had been involved. No one wanted to say what was wrong with him. I imagined imminent death, cancer most likely. Inoperable, unbeatable, wave this life goodbye, Liv, you won't live at all. If I could get my head together, at his funeral I'd make the most moving speech imaginable.

Then, on the very day school broke up for the year, he reappeared, waiting for me at the end of a street where kids crowed with delight. The ones who'd finished year twelve had their shirts in tatters. School ties and hats were thrown into gutters.

'What happened to you?'

'It's ... I just can't ...'

'But are you all right?'

'... I guess ...'

Livio didn't want to say a word about what had been wrong with him. In the days and weeks that followed I understood he was different. Somehow quieter, almost reflective. Strangely locked inside himself. He'd lost something of his previous self and didn't laugh much, yet neither did he get angry. He seemed evened-out, but in that way of a long flat line.

'What you had, this problem, will it ever come back?'

He shrugged a no.

So it was the summer holidays. For me I knew what that

meant. Not just the fact that Stina would be leaving—if her mother and father remained true to their individual plans—but that there wouldn't be much holidaying for me at all; this was always the peak period of extra bricklaying work. Livio had to work with his father too, though it wasn't daily, just a couple of times a week. Because of the mystery illness his old man was taking it easy on him.

I began to see that others—female others—also would have liked the chance to take it easy on Liv.

Despite whatever had gone on with him, Liv had grown. He wasn't so much a kid any more. The year's difference between us was making, well, a difference. The local girls took notice of him; he was swarthy, he'd trimmed down, yet his arms and legs seemed bigger. Not just that, but a certain rugged masculinity had come into his features. You could even have called him swarthily handsome, or on the way there.

Man, we were changing—me just not fast enough.

2.

The summer holiday. It was hot, it was hell, and there was no escape. I couldn't make up handy excuses about studying with 'Steve'—there was no school to make up stories about. My father simply assumed I would be on hand to help him. That meant every day.

It bugged me that others were so free but it bugged me more to see the way they grew. Liv was just about turning into someone new. It was the same with other boys who'd been in our class. Like they'd lined up for some secret super-drug injection or something. Lined up without telling me.

I was working like a dog, but in terms of muscles and facial hair and getting taller, I was still at the starting block, left behind. I didn't look any different; I was still soft in the middle; I was the same.

Liv, though, he was even changing his thinking.

He gave his bass guitar to a teenage neighbour and didn't want it back. The next day I did the same with my pathetic set-up, though it was a ten-year-old who got it. With the school year done our band had ceased to exist. One afternoon I went to the singer's garage and the only things I found were a broken bicycle and a box of empty beer bottles. The boys were old enough for driver's licences. One had got himself a motorcycle. Another, a ute with fat mag wheels. These days they preferred to head up to the sand and surf of our northern beaches, which were populated by girls in bikinis. Who was going to blame them? The one thing I at least shared with them was that I understood how insane our hormones were going.

I stayed in my bedroom, indulged in long episodes of self-abuse while thinking of Stina, who already seemed a million miles away, and turned my records up more loudly than ever, trying to live in that world.

'Giovanni! Stuta sa musica! Turn off that music!'

'And get to bed! We're up early tomorrow!'

I could barely wait for school to start again. I realized I could have more freedom during a school term than I could possibly engineer for myself during a so-called holiday break.

With special consideration for all the exams he'd missed at the end of year eleven, Liv had been allowed to pass. If he didn't do something miraculous in his final year, though, that would be it between him and the education system. Not that he cared; Liv could only see his future in the bleakest terms. Or, maybe in some strange way, it was in better terms than me. Manual labour. A low-level trade was all he was good for—that's what he'd mutter in his deepened voice. Then he'd brighten a touch and say something about travel, of endlessly moving.

Unlike me, who never much thought about other countries, he had a will to see the world; he envisaged a sort of future life where he had no roots and could just keep backpacking, hiking, mooching from continent to continent and having adventures in every one of them.

'But what was wrong with you at the end of school?'

'Nothing.'

'It was really nothing?'

'It was up here,' he allowed, once, touching a temple.

I thought that if I put things into pseudo-clinical terms it might be easier for him to open up.

'The cerebral cortex?'

'Um.'

'What?'

'Sort of … it was my thoughts. They went funny.'

'How?'

'Um.'

What on earth was he talking about—depression, anxiety, hallucinations? The possibilities were exciting and scary to contemplate, things I couldn't imagine. What was Liv's inner life like, now that we were getting older? What sorts of thoughts and dreams did he have? The thing was, this guy I'd first met as a fetid lump of meat actually had these dreams. He was no beast. He possessed a heart. Maybe he was even more sensitive than I was.

'Come on, what sort of thoughts?'

'What's it called when you don't want to exist no more?'

I couldn't bring myself to say the words. He wasn't about to elaborate. His heavy Sicilian eyes took in the distance—and that very bright summer's afternoon two girls in nothing dresses, standing at the street corner, about our age, licking ice cream cones, giggled as they glanced our way.

His way.

Liv didn't even fucking notice.

3.

Before Stina's mother and father finally went their separate ways I managed to visit the house exactly three times. I knew why it felt like Stina was already a million miles away; she was keeping things that way.

I hadn't seen her since the afternoon in the park by the river when she'd told me about what was going on between her mother and father, and had kissed me. So the first time I collected my courage and actually went straight up to her home, no one was in. I hung around like a bad smell, watched by the old neighbour across the way. He was a pensioner named Mr Pattinson and his main interest in life seemed to be his dressing robe, which he always wore, and the weeds sprouting in his garden. Whenever these offences started to appear he was onto them like a shot.

The second time, Mrs Vågberg was there and she invited me in. She was in a fog of cigarettes, as if she kept one smoking in the ashtray of every room.

Though there was a For Sale sign out the front I sat with her and the topic wasn't broached. Stina was out. Her mother didn't say where. Instead, Mrs Vågberg served me a cold drink and snacks as if everything was the same, yet I could see how care-worn and tired she was. The house was dustier than usual and the kitchen was a mess. She looked fifteen years older than the last time I'd visited. We didn't have anything to talk about and she stared at me with her pale eyes, simply taking me in.

It was as if she wanted to ask me something. Something on the tip of her tongue. At the forefront of her thoughts. What-ever it was never came out. I felt uncomfortable and awkward, and when I left she nodded and forgot to say goodbye.

Then, late one Sunday evening in the dog days of that hor-rible summer, Christmas around the corner, I saw Stina in the street. My heart started to hammer. I was across the road and a little way behind. Stina was with her dog. Gudrun didn't need to be on a leash and Stina kept talking to her as they went along. The dog must have been in some pain; Stina gave encourage-ment. They progressed very slowly and I wondered what would happen to that poor mutt once the family home was sold. I wanted to cross the road, go talk to Stina, hug her, just see her—even if this sultry descending evening seemed to say that here was the hour for all good folk to be let alone.

Fuck that. I started to cross the steaming bitumen toward her.

The big Ford with red and black fire decals drove by, close enough that I had to step back to the footpath. It swerved to the other side of the road and a girl with long black hair was hanging half out the passenger window. She seemed all care-free smiles and boobs, a wonderful cleavage. The driver was that Nordic type, now wearing sunglasses, hair tied back and a cigarette dangling from his mouth.

Gudrun sat and took a rest as Stina leaned into the driver's side, laughing. The car engine ran, throaty as a locomotive, and this early dusk the guy liked revving it, filling the neighbour-hood. Meanwhile, an arrangement was being worked out. I heard something about pretty soon and tonight.

Claude Rains: I pictured him as the scientist William Griffin. Just like Griffin, here I was, right in the street yet an invisible man. I had the feeling that if Stina raised her head and looked straight across, even then she wouldn't know I was there.

By the time I was home clouds hid the moon and stars, plus strong hot winds troubled the heavily-laden arms of Abbott Street's massive deciduous trees. Cicadas called. There'd be a storm to soak this summer night, but nothing came just yet. Instead, there wasn't a spit of rain and the heat was driving ev-eryone crazy.

Including my mother, who wasn't well. This holiday season's constant high temperatures had sapped her. There was no din-ner on the table. I went into the garden with a flashlight and found some sprigs of rosemary and a few bunches of small-leaf basil. In the kitchen, without rousing her from the bed where she lay with a standing fan cooling her, I started cracking garlic and chopping a red capsicum and a few big field mushrooms. Had the pasta boiling, drained it, got tomatoes bubbling in the pot then peeled and de-seeded them. Added rosemary, pepper and salt. I was sweating like a pig but didn't care. Cooking sim-ple dishes was one of the few things that could give me peace. It was like that stupid piano in our dustiest room.

In a few minutes my father stopped watching television and came to investigate my industry. The aromas tormented him; he'd had his usual hard day on some work-site, this time without me, and he needed to eat. He opened a bottle of rough Stanthorpe red. My mother rose from bed and came to the table looking a little brighter. Between the three of us we finished every bit of my dish plus the wine.

By eight my mother had dropped back into a sweaty stupor, but not before holding me close and kissing my face. Her fingers entwined in my thick hair. In Sicilian she told me I was a good boy.

At the stroke of nine my father joined her.

'Come with me tomorrow?' he said in parting, his dialect extra rough with drink. He was drowsy and loose-limbed. 'Help me with some foundations?'

These were hardly questions. I knew I'd be up at five. I was going to be dead because when the continuous rumble of my father's snore came rhythmic as a train, and my mother complained once in her sleep, and I was certain it was the blue hour of one a.m., I dressed and used pillows to make the shape of a body under the covers. I formed a passable head by bunching a t-shirt up into a ball. In the dark, even to me it looked convincing.

I climbed out my window. The stifling heat was gone. Hot winds had abated. The clouds had parted and I could see perfect constellations. The moon hung heavy, sated as an old dog. It was a good night to be out. Our little neighbourhood streets were quiet and there'd be no trouble along the way—it just wasn't like that around here. The night would all have been so beautiful if I hadn't had the feeling that something malignant and cruel was eating away at my guts.

It was the third visit to Stina's place.

4.

I pushed myself into that crop of trees across the road from her house because three cars were already out the front. Their headlights were off but most of the car doors were open. A radio was on. First Rebel, then Gonna Make You a Star, then a Ringo tune. When Bob Dylan's Hurricane came on they changed the station and it was Rod Stewart.

They must have had a cassette of a T. Rex album because the music switched from the radio to three greatest hits in a row: Telegram Sam, Children of the Revolution and Bang a Gong.

I counted three boys and four girls. That included Stina. They were drinking, not making a big noise with their laughter and music, but having fun. Boys? Young men. Strapping lads, most people would call them, tall, well-built and sunburned. Only the girls looked too young for the scene. The Norse god's two friends had arms to carry boulders and close-cut hair, unlike his, which tonight flowed free. Stina and her girlfriends might have looked far too young and far too small beside them, but the starlight made Stina a goddess. Her hair was out too, hanging to her shoulders. Her skirt was short and tight. A strapless boob tube just invited your hand to pull it down.

Bang a Gong had the girls going. Man could they move and dance. I thought I would remember the sight of Stina dancing to this song all the way to my dying day. Their more direct audience watched with the hungry dog expression I knew so well.

Four of them chicks, three of us.

Yeah.

Obviously Mr and Mrs Vågberg weren't home, yet most of the lights in the house were on. The neighbours weren't happy. From the front verandah of his worker's cottage Mr Pattinson surveyed the scene. His eyes were hooded in wrinkled folds. Maybe he'd already called out for the kids to be quiet and they'd ignored him.

Then another neighbour from across the way—Mrs Black? Mrs Bates?—emerged in a pinky-purple dressing gown.

'Why doncha let people sleep?'

'In a minute Mrs Brookes, promise!'

That was Stina. Gudrun roused herself a moment, then curled up again.

Stina moved to the fence and said something to Mrs Brookes, then she was directly under a streetlamp. My heart ached so hard I thought it must stop beating. I had a memory of reading an interview with a famous Hollywood cinematographer, Gordon Willis or Sven Nykvist maybe, who'd said something like, 'You need to understand light before you can make magic'. Well, one undistinguished streetlamp down here near the river created magic all right—but of course it had a great subject. Stina was our little suburb's Garbo, Bacall, Bergman.

And this little gathering was her farewell. I heard it in the things her friends were saying.

Then, behind me, a voice spoke very quietly in plain English.

'We go home, darly, is not gonna work for you here.'

I turned and there she was, small and frail as ever—yet herself strangely beautiful in this shaded moonlight. Ma was standing there. Not shaking with rage. Just, I thought, being a mother. She came closer and reached for my hand. We spoke in Sicilian.

'Does my father know I'm here?'

'If he did, would I be the one standing next to you?'

She drew me away from the trees. I hesitated, looking toward Stina and her group. Stina wasn't by that streetlamp anymore. Now she was a perfect silhouette. I heard her laugh. I saw her drink. I felt like nothing would ever save me.

So I went with my mother.

'You can't keep a secret like this, Giovanni. If you did badly at school I would have stopped you, but you've been a good boy and you've been trying hard. And I know what it must feel like. This girl Christina, she's very lovely. And some friends know her parents. They all say it's a good family. The girl is smart and has a good heart. What happened when you were children we all should have forgotten. I begged your father to let it go, but he never did.'

'Why does he have to hate them so much?'

'He went there one day, you know. To tell the parents what he thought of them and their daughter.'

I couldn't believe it. 'Did you go too?'

'No.'

'What happened?'

'He never said.'

I remembered the way Mrs Vågberg had welcomed me that first time I'd come to their door, then all the times after. Never with any reproach, never with any resentment. Always kindly, and with just a touch of curiosity. She must have been thinking, So this is that angry Italian's son.

Wait—she'd actually said it out loud.

Vell, the boy—the boy of the man.

Then that last time I saw her, sitting there at the table in her fog of smoke and vermouth, looking at me so intently, as if she had something she wanted—needed—to ask.

If only she had.

We went slowly through the streets. I felt sick. My mother wasn't in any sort of hurry. Her steps seemed small. I thought of Stina slow-walking the pained Gudrun. Funny how it felt just the same.

'You're sure you don't know what he said to them? Did he yell and scream?'

Ma simply spread her hands. She wasn't lying. My father operated by his own rules, it was true. No one would ever know what went on in his mind or what sorts of things he'd done on the sly.

'But how did you know I went to see Stina?'

'I'm your mother. You've been going there a long time. And to the movies.'

Funny how I always thought I was so smart.

She protected me from my father. She knew there was no 'Steve' and no amazingly helpful teacher–mother; she knew I longed for this girl and followed her like a puppy. That I was crazy in-love with someone I could never have.

'The father is already gone, did you know that?'

'Ma, are you sure?'

'Nils Vågberg. His new woman's name is Alexandrie. They call her "Allie".'

This small suburb certainly didn't hide its secrets. My mother probably knew more about the Vågbergs than I did.

'Christina and her mother are going back home,' I said, my voice full of defeat. 'Back to Stockholm.'

'No,' Ma said.

'What?'

My mother stopped. We were near our place. I could see the long rows of those hulking trees, Abbott Street looming like some ancient forest. I heard the creak of branches, the constant motion, the rustling of thousands of leaves. It was the sound I'd grown up with, but here we were in the open, bathed in moonlight, that promised storm almost with us. My mother's face looked young and old at the same time. Tired, but somehow full of her old fire as well.

'Only Klara is going. Christina put up a fight and refused. Mother and daughter aren't talking. The girl has her eye on somewhere else.'

'What do you mean?'

My mother shook her head. She didn't know.

'She won't go with her mother. They say she's moving to another town or city. With her man.'

I must have looked completely blank. She didn't repeat it. There was no need to—I could take this as gospel. Stina was fighting with her ma and she had a man to take her away. Ah, of course, the Norse god: he had the arms to carry off any damsel. I didn't even know his name. How much more of an ugly lump and buffoon could I be? Stina wasn't returning to Stockholm, and she hadn't even bothered to tell me.

Ma tried to touch my face. I pulled away hard, as if this was all her fault.

Some of the softness went from her voice. For some reason she reverted to her broken English.

'So—you see how she is or no? Good heart and everyt'ing. Now we get home—and that's it.'

It was, and our house was just ahead, and a blustery wind kept rising, shaking our great trees some more.

5.

38 degrees Celsius, a few wisps of cloud, cooling wind gone. I was sleepy and distracted, moving like a dead man. These were the days you accepted any temperature under forty as a mercy.

Papà berated me like a herder trying to get the very last out of a mule. He wanted this job done and out of the way. It was in some new-estate development almost fifty kilometres south of the city, not a single tree for shade. Just brown dry earth that someday would be all brick and tile homes, carbon-copy gardens and green lawns fit for the pitter-patter of tiny feet.

Slept like a corpse that night, then came the disaster that was Saturday, temperature due to top 42 at that hell-hole we worked. A pre-dawn car radio report was all about train schedule disruptions because of track-buckling. People needed to ensure that any old or infirm people they knew stayed indoors with cool drinks. Dawn broke while we were driving. I could only think of Stina, and wherever she was now, and with who.

Soon enough the sky was a stark and unbroken blue. It hurt the eyes to look at it. We got to work. Hours dragged. I roasted in the heat like someone who couldn't quite believe the nightmare he'd found. By eleven a.m. 42 degrees came and went, I was certain of that. Midday the sun seared my face, the back of my neck, my arms and legs. In my mind I saw Stina and her man swimming somewhere to cool off, her in a bikini, him pulling her through crystal-clear water to take her sleek body into his arms. She'd lift her legs and wrap them around his waist.

It was as if I could feel Martian death rays scorching through my shirt, searing into my skull. I threw up. My father told me to drink some water and stop being stupid.

Sunday I couldn't move.

Dizzy; faint; threw up so many times there was nothing left but green-yellow juice. Dehydration and exhaustion, obvious as the sad pigeon that dropped dead from the branches outside my window and lay cooking on our concrete pathway. My mother brought me cool drinks all day, plus cold towels for my chest and neck. Whenever he showed his face she yelled and screamed at my father, despite the pulsing, pulsing, pulsing pain in my head. How could you have let this happen to your son? What kind of idiot are you? I actually felt sorry for him. Finally Papà stormed out of the house. My ma didn't care where he went. It took three days before I recovered.

That was when the street-gossip caught up with me direct. No need to hear it from my ma.

'You look like shit,' Liv said to the peeling skin of my forehead and nose. 'And guess what, all them Vågbergs have gone.'

It didn't cross my mind to ask how he knew or why he even cared, I just ran there. Well, it was a staggering half-run. I found open doors and windows, a home completely emptied, and a house painter being watched by old Mr Pattinson as his brush touched up the eaves.

I felt something go away from me. It just sort of lifted and disappeared.

6.

Simply hunt through my mother's pills and swallow all her valiums at once. The thought caught in my mind and wouldn't let go.

Day by day I'd open the bathroom cabinet and stare at those bottles and vials. I could do it last thing at night so that when my parents woke in the morning I wouldn't be waking up with them. No more images of Christina dancing under a streetlamp to sexy rhythms. No more guys a hundred times better than me leering at her legs and her breasts and her turning hips. No more thoughts about the way I meant so little to her she didn't even think to say goodbye.

My father would come home grey and exhausted, and I'd sit at dinner with both him and ma while they talked about this or that, but I wasn't there. He'd say something like, 'I need you on this job, how about you get up early and come with me in the morning?' and I'd rise from the table leaving my plate mostly untouched, and go to my bedroom, where I'd lay down. It would seem only a moment later that he was shaking me to come start the new day. Some mornings I went with him; other mornings I stood at my window watching him drive away, knowing he was cursing me and my stupid head and this country he'd moved to.

One early afternoon when he ought to have been off on some building job somewhere, my father's utility truck—overladen with a cement mixer, wooden and steel wheelbarrows, shovels, picks, mattocks, toolboxes, and all the rest—pulled up at the entrance to the creaking wooden pier where I sat staring into the mud-brown currents of the river. Even though I was somewhere else it was impossible not to recognize the particular rattling rumble of a vehicle I'd spent far too many sleepy mornings and bone-dead evenings travelling in.

How did he know I was there? Why was he so early from work?

Heavy footsteps. Work boots covered in the dust and dried speckles of concrete. 'Giovanni, get up,' he told me in Sicilian.

He could stand there or not stand there, it made no difference to me.

'It's enough of this bullshit. I told you to get up.'

It was funny. I couldn't remember how long I'd been sitting there, but now I simply wanted to lie back and close my eyes. Close my eyes and be that one thing Livio had told me, to not exist anymore.

'I know what's happening and you have to get it out of your mind. There isn't the slut on earth who's worth doing this to yourself.'

I slowly cocked my head. It was enough of a giveaway. He wasn't stupid.

'Ah,' he said. 'All right, so tell me. Who is she?'

Instead of infuriating him, my numb silence seemed to reach some place deep inside my pa, where he was still a young man cradling a new baby, a proud father helping his son take first steps, a man walking around the shops and stores of town with his little boy holding his hand.

Or maybe that place wasn't so deep at all.

'Giovanni.' There was a soft, almost understanding tone to his voice. I could barely remember ever hearing it before. 'Son. Just come home. Get your head straight.' He paused, waiting. When he got nothing, he said, 'At least tell me who it is.'

'There's no one.'

I looked up at him, a strong man silhouetted against the sun.

'Don't lie to your father.'

The river took my gaze again, and I said, 'You know all about lies, right?'

He wouldn't be baited. That didn't bother me. What I'd discovered was that when you stopped caring about things your own thoughts got out of the way and allowed facts to lie exposed.

This man above me; how many nights did he shower and wash his hair, shave if need be, dress into clean clothes and go stalking out of our house like a man on a mission? To play cards. Would a thing so innocent turn my ma into a woman of such quiet sadness?

I wasn't the only one who could read what was in front of him.

'It's that little Vågberg prostitute who ruined you in primary school, isn't it?'

'Don't fucking call her that.'

'You want to swear at your father?'

The sympathetic tone was out of his voice. There was partial anger, I thought, but more of a need to goad me, to get me to show a spark of life.

'Fuck off.'

'Get up and tell me face to face, don't sit there crying like a baby.'

'I'm not crying.'

'Baby.'

I tried to shut his voice out. How did he know about Stina? If he really did know. Was this place we lived in really so small?

'She's no good, Giovanni, just like the rest of her family.'

His words were needles under my skin. Even trying to ignore them made their effect worse. I could feel my blood rising.

'Shut up.'

Now he knew for sure. I couldn't have made it any plainer.

Well, what did it matter anymore?

'What did you say to her family? When you went to their house. What did you fucking say?'

My father's eyes bored into me.

Sicilian Death Stare.

'You swear at your father, you stand up like a man.'

I was up. I was facing him. Goddammit but I was taller than him. I'd never even noticed it had happened.

'What did you say to them?'

It had been another one of the things that went together like a jigsaw piece, an obvious fact that slipped into my mind without even realizing it. If I asked myself why Stina had so completely rejected and cut me off, I already knew the answer. It was because all those years ago my father had gone to confront the Vågbergs with his craziness. And with that sort of rage let loose in their home, how could any of them have wanted anything to do with a maniac's son? The seed of poison had been planted. The Vågbergs—Stina included—had entertained me out of civility, nothing more.

Vell, the boy—the boy of the man.

'Now tell me, Giovanni. Did you give her money? Did you pay for her body? How many times?'

'You're just so wrong about everything.'

'Did you steal money from your mother's purse to get that prostitute to open her legs?'

I grabbed him by the arms with no idea what I was going to do next. He flared up and took me by the collar, actually shaking me.

'Wake up, son! Stop dreaming of what can't be!'

The collar of my shirt tore away. He threw it aside, then pushed me backwards.

'You don't know,' I managed to get out, but then I was sobbing. 'You don't know what it feels like.'

He stared at me with no idea how to handle a son's tears.

In that moment I actually hoped he would rough me up, beat me into submission as if he held all the fury of nuns and Christian Brothers combined. Yet the truth was that my pa, for all the quivering trepidation he provoked in me, had never once struck me. Had never even come close. A voice to turn your blood cold, that patented death-stare, yet he'd never raised a finger.

He turned away.

'Come on.'

He went a few steps down the pier, then waited.

'Hurry up.'

I trudged behind him to the utility truck. We drove away. I quietly wept and couldn't find a way to stop.

'I know what you need.' My father's large, calloused hands gripped the steering wheel. 'This infamia finishes tonight.'

7.

The magic woman who came to the house was a strega, a witch, a sort of mystical seer and healer originally from the region of Calabria. She was at the front door, short, squat and so old her face looked like a prickly pear. Her hair was a stringy grey and hung around her gaunt cheeks. She had dentures and there was a herby smell to her, as if she lived on nothing but greens and leaves taken from a backyard garden. Finally her chin had a mannish shading of long sharp hairs like a beard, which only managed to make her look even more like that prickly pear.

We all sat into the living room. She asked me straight out if I was sleeping a lot.

'Yes, most of the time.'

My answer made her moan and sway with her eyes rolling back to reveal only their whites. When she came back from wherever she'd gone she immediately diagnosed a creeping sickness placed on me by someone who'd given me the malocchio. Both my parents started, because the malocchio is the curse of the evil eye. My mother and father reacted by making the traditional mano cornuta, which is done by extending the index finger and small finger of the right hand and pointing downwards.

This magical gesture will, of course, ward off such curses.

The woman smiled grimly and told my parents that in this instance things had gone too far for that simple gesture to work. She said she'd show them why. My mother should go get a plate of water and her bottle of olive oil. When she did, the witch set the plate of water onto the sofa next to me then poured in a little of the oil. It formed one large globule. This, she said, was the indisputable sign that I carried a most terrible curse indeed.

Then she started to moan again, and that became a chant.

My ma said, 'Look, look what's happening.'

The oil was breaking up into lots of little globules, or was I imagining it? No, really, it was happening. I heard my ma praying out loud about magic and miracles, and my pa was so moved he had to find a handkerchief and wipe his eyes.

'The bitch who did this to your boy is smart and vengeful, but not very powerful. I've already broken her spell.'

A minute later my father was counting bills out of his wallet, looking like he couldn't give them to the old lady fast enough.

The woman took a corno—the devil's horn—out of her pouch. It was on a thin leather strap and she told me I had to wear this at least a month, to make sure the curse didn't come back. The corno she pressed into my hand was made of a red piece of coral. I knew that sometimes people wore them made of gold or silver. With great solemnity she told me to place it around my neck. I did.

The woman closed her eyes, one knuckle rubbing her mannish stubble.

'There's one more thing. The bitch put her juice all over you when she fornicated with you. You have to take care to wash it away. If you don't, her possession will happen all over again.'

It was useless to try to explain that, contrary to the belief of anyone in this room, I was still just a full-throttle, stupid virgin.

'But how do we do it?' Ma pleaded.

Turns out I had to bathe twice a day, but of course ordinary soap wouldn't help. The strega was going to make a little extra money by selling my parents a 'special cake of soap', as well as a secret element I'd have to add to my bath water for ten days.

'Then all trace of the poison in this slut will be off of him. Forever. He will find that he will never think of her again, and, even if he tries to conjure her face, nothing will come.'

'What if she returns and looks for him?' my father asked.

'She won't. When I get home, I'll place a counter-spell on her. This kind of evil has to disappear from the face of the earth. Death is her reward.'

My ma's eyes widened in horror.

'No,' she gasped.

As if he'd taken an unimaginable responsibility onto his shoulders, my father straightened his spine and said, 'Si, it must be.'

And so he counted out the bills.

8.

No Stina, no band, no guitar and an empty feeling when I sat in movie houses. Aimless and floating, until Livio proved himself far more useful than bathing myself in water tinged with a concoction of what looked like menstrual blood mixed with vinegar.

He kept thumping me for being all droopy and stupid.

Honestly, he gave me black and blue bruises up and down both arms. It was just his way. The holiday period was over and in the first weeks of my final year at school I was relieved to be out of the house. Still, the year ahead looked like a long walk in a wilderness, with nothing worthwhile at its end. Hollow. At least Liv was well and truly back to life. The same kid in a way, but more reflective, though that hardly stopped him from using his fists when he felt like it. I still didn't have a clue what had brought on that period of his decline. Maybe it was just growing up that had happened to him, yet that didn't explain such utter lifelessness, or the question: What's it called when you don't want to exist no more?

He did want to exist now. Liv was growing into a new, big body and shaved every other day. Jesus, but sometimes I had to step back and look at him. My friend was just about a man.

Liking physical things, action things, Liv had started hanging around the school's sports centre. It didn't take him long to convince me into going with him. The musical aspirations he never really had were done with and instead he showed an aptitude for gymnastics and weightlifting. Like me he hated football, cricket and all other forms of team sports. Anything that involved strength and agility, however, well this seemed to be his direction. And finally changes were even happening to me. The secret super-drug had been administered; man, it was working.

I was happy to need to shave; happy my voice was deeper; happy at the thickening of my shoulders and thighs. All my clothes were wrong, tight in some places and too loose in others. Always about a mile too short. Nights it was hard to get to sleep for erections that wouldn't go away. As if that hadn't been bad enough before, but now there were copious nocturnal emissions to contend with.

'Prayers'll fix it,' Liv told me. 'Couple a Hail Marys and about five Our Fathers when you get into bed.'

As if.

The unconscious libido refused to be distracted. In daylight hours we imagined having sex with anything that moved and in our dreams we carried it all out. Whenever relatives asked me what I wanted to do with my future, the true answer I never spoke was: To fornicate as much as possible ...

The best part was the way excess weight melted away. Both of us had leaned up without even trying. Liv's once-squat body stretched for the sun and in the space of what felt like only a few months he was a head taller than me. All that work with our mutual fathers also had an effect: we'd developed biceps, strong backs.

My ma revelled in what she saw happening to her son and modified her kitchen accordingly. She was a woman who believed in the power of meat as much as she believed in the power of God and witches, so she filled me with steaks and chicken and fish and more steaks. Despite all this food, or maybe because of it, the soft and pudgy me was a memory belonging to the lower grades. Papà made stupid jokes—'Where's my boy's iron rod?' he'd ask; 'Tomorrow we chop trees. At first it's hard to get in, then it's nice and pulpy, you'll find out!'—but if the price of this new and improved body was that I had to endure his bad humour, plus erections every minute of every day, who cared?

It was Liv, though, who literally threw himself into weight training and gym. Come on, he said, just fucken try it. Music, books and films had gotten me absolutely nowhere with girls, so what did I have to lose?

Liv was the expert so he started me off slow. Short to medium-distance runs as an intro. I gagged, coughed hard, almost threw up every time—but when hard running started to become an easy habit, he had me using the school's weightlifting equipment. Not only that, but he had me learning how to tumble on the mats too. Liv could do some of the flips and handstands the gymnastics students were always practising; he put the majority of them to shame. The problem was that most of these white-bread sports-lovers didn't like two half-black Sicilians invading their space. They weren't about to invite us to join any of their groups or teams. On the contrary, they wanted us out. Liv always stood up to the biggest jerks and one visit he caught himself a black eye. So did that loudmouth rugby front-rower, plus a new mouthful of broken teeth.

Liv's temper was as good as ever; the sports master banned the both of us from ever returning.

So instead Liv made friends with a local named Shane, a muscly twenty-two–year-old who lived nearby. Shane was a welder, but he'd set up his garage with weights. He didn't mind letting us in for regular workouts. Shane even liked being our part-time coach. He wanted us to do things right and made sure our technique was good. Sets, reps, posture—it was his religion. He idolized Steve Reeves and Frank Zane. Their sturdy, steely faces and frames looked down on us from muscle-magazine posters on the walls.

It was good to see Livio so different to that angry fifth-grade kid who'd been hauled away from his known world. So different to the one who'd moped around with thoughts that weren't right. Soon he even found his first girlfriend, a toothy, mousy-haired, skinny and very smart little thing with the unlikely name of Sandy Beggs. Sandy was his age, she ate just about nothing, and school studies came to her as easily as weightlifting sets and reps came to Liv. She was a young friend of Shane's live-in girlfriend; she'd started hanging around the garage whenever we worked out.

Within a short space of time it was easy to see just how much Sandy adored Liv. She intuited that he'd never quite made peace with this new country, and it was true that he remained in the immigrant mind-set, mostly because he didn't command the language, didn't quite think in English. So she decided her mission in life was to give Livio Vida the lessons he needed, to provide a personalized tutelage into the quagmire that is language, grammar and writing—not to mention into quite a lot of fucking as well.

Because it all came from Sandy, this neighbourhood girl who let him do whatever he wanted to her—like the old Yardbirds song, over, under, upside-down—he took to this new education without complaint. Even with enthusiasm. Sandy managed to have him read a few books, mysteries mostly, and then they'd discuss little things like expression and nuance.

The kid was amazing. I wanted a 'Sandy Beggs' for myself.

No, I needed one.

Things were good between them, but Sandy's reward for her affection was to fall pregnant and have to watch two hysterical families come together in order to decide her fate. Between these two sets of idiots, one gloweringly Sicilian, the other pure redneck Aussie, there was a single way forward: forget school and get married, fast, before the baby's born. Livio didn't think about it two seconds.

'Sandy's my girl.'

That's all he said. He was ready.

Sandy Beggs didn't agree. It was the seventies. Punk hadn't quite arrived and glam rock, though gone, had sprinkled us with its glitter. A lot of it remained, even if it was all such wishful thinking: this decade's living was meant to be easy. Shotgun marriages were out and sex and sexiness were the ways to live, weren't they, especially for horny teenagers?

Sandy was practical and forward thinking.

After school she really wanted to travel. London was the place to be, because in her mind that's where all the hip happenings originated. Few could argue with that. Compared to the rest of the world our town was an embarrassing dump. She loved the idea of what adventures might lie ahead for her and none of these involved something called teenage motherhood. The families could demand whatever they wanted; Liv could agree to anything; Sandy ran away. She had money she'd saved and in short order she had the baby taken care of, then just kept on going. There was a postcard from Sydney; some weeks later Liv showed me another from Thailand; the last was a card from Manchester, England.

'On my way again. Bless you, Liv!'

Three kisses and that was that.

At least it was a whole lot more than I got from Stina.

9.

For God's sake, he fell into the Pit again. Jesus. Sick to his heart, broken in his soul.

First I had to contend with his mother, who wanted to block me from seeing him, then even my own father got involved; after all, there was this brilliant Strega he knew about.

Well, I wasn't about to let anyone stop me getting Liv out of that bed he was glued into, not like that last time he was sick. Shane came with me to his house. Signora Vida blanched: Shane had close-cropped hair and tattoos all down his hefty arms and legs.

We barged down the corridor and dragged the dead weight of Liv off his mattress. Just about carried him into the sunshine. There, we cajoled, we yelled, we abused and waved our arms around. A powerful intervention, 70s-style. All it did was make him cry. Every morning after that I turned up on Liv's doorstep to make sure he came to school. Finally, Shane and I were able to talk him back into that sweaty little weightlifting garage.

Oh, but the 'bad thoughts' were back. He'd learned two words that went together like black poetry: 'Personal' and 'Annihilation.'

Fuck that, I told Livio, get your fat lazy arse moving.

He wasn't fat and he wasn't lazy. He was dead inside.

And he wouldn't budge. He was mush. He pined for his girl.

So I loaded up the weights and goaded him like he was the dumbest lump of meat ever put on this earth. Don't be such a fucking baby. He howled at all that metal. Pussy! I screamed at him. Liv screamed back at me. He screamed at Shane, who tortured him worse than I did—and Shane's girlfriend in the rooms upstairs would start to bash on the floorboards with a broom, and her baby would wail, and then and only then Livio would lift, and how, his face straining, veins popping out of his skin, tears of shame streaming like hot rain down those blood-engorged cheeks.

If kindness wouldn't save him, iron might.

He was in so much pain that for the first time, the very first time, I realized: Jesus, but I love this stupid asshole.

10.

Meanwhile, against all expectations to the contrary, school was kinder to me, my grades were good, and when I started back at work with Papà it didn't feel like such a punishment after all. In some desolate hole in the ground, getting burned by the sun and coming home aching all over, I found I could be happy. I liked things that stopped me thinking. Bricks and concrete kept Stina away. My father's work was all so not of the mind. The present and the future didn't seem to mean anything to me anymore, they carried no weight, no promise, no threat—so just live in present moments and take things as they come.

The week I turned seventeen and passed my driver's test, I drove Liv in my father's washed and emptied utility truck to the big Centenary Pool complex. Livio was distracted, not talking much. While we were there the freckled redhead on a towel next to me struck up a conversation. Her name was Veronica.

We left Liv to lie back and turn an even darker shade of red-brown than he usually was, and went into the water. We cooled off together and started a game of grabbing and teasing. She wore a nice floral bikini. There were hints of coral-pink nipples while we played. Her finger and toe nails were lacquered very red. Little fake pearl ear studs. Before the afternoon was out Veronica pulled me into a storage room no bigger than a closet. Untying her top and pulling down her wet, chlorine-scented bikini bottom, she introduced me to her sex and to sex itself. She was on the pill, she said, blow inside me. She was a new girl at the sister school to ours. Used to live down Lismore way till her army-dad got himself transferred to the barracks up here.

Come the weekend Liv and I went to see the little rock band she'd put together. They were called The Kants. No one got the joke. Veronica possessed a unique sound, a high sort of cater-wauling that would have made a dog run for cover. Even that new songstress Kate Bush would have blanched.

Like I cared.

For about a month Veronica wanted me and for that month I was happy. Her gloriously well-versed sexual instruction opened a door. Who knows, maybe something in my demean-our changed. After her I found another girlfriend, then another, then another. Soon I stopped thinking in such Joe-average terms. These liaisons didn't last and weren't meant to. AIDS hadn't ar-rived and STDs were things you got rid of with a shot or a tube of cream or both. I didn't let my parents in on my new activities, but every so often I'd catch the silent gaze my mother was giving me; she would never stop protecting her son from his father.

It's a mystery to me who I was or what I was even thinking in those days. There was a physical world and a sensual world and somehow I'd entered the both of them even as an empti-ness inside gaped like a hole that was incapable of being filled. I had the vague feeling that one day I'd revisit all these grey areas of my life and discover the true colours inside them. I'd understand what my life was really all about: this blankness that somehow attracted girls; my mother's quiet sadness; my father's rages.

And a never-ending question: What's happened to you, Stina?

Part 4

I.

Then it was a first year in Law and Livio was on campus too. Sandy Beggs was living proof that a boy's education can certain-ly be influenced by the quality of his teachers. Instead of find-ing himself on an unemployment queue he'd managed to score the absolute line-ball minimum to enrol in Human Movement

Studies. One day, if he passed, and if he decided to rethink his idea of being the world's greatest itinerant adventurer–traveller, Liv might even find work as a school fitness instructor. In reality this prospect wasn't very much of a goal for him; he was discovering the allure of booze, recreational drugs, and assorted other means for polluting that otherwise incredible body of his.

He wasn't alone in discovering these lesser pursuits, and today a group of us, deadbeats to the core, weren't doing anything so tiresome as attending lectures. Instead we zoned out at some fellow student's little flat.

Liv rolled a joint to share with two other guys. I had a beer. It was a Tuesday afternoon and we lounged like Lords of Torn Couches and Broken Armchairs. Someone flicked the television station over from Get Smart to the children's show, Play School.

Two clowns are clowning in a park created by paper trees and hand-drawn bushes. A girl rides into the scene on a children's bicycle festooned with streamers. She stops. The clowns play pranks upon her that make her giggle in surprise. She teases them and turns the tables so that the clowns end up on their backsides. She gives the camera a huge wink and rides off to the accompaniment of kazoo music.

In red baggy pants and a yellow floral shirt with printed giraffes all over it. Flowers in her hair. Face painted.

Christina Vågberg.

Liv was sitting there, a tendril of smoke rising from a corner of his mouth as if he didn't know his tongue was on fire. Someone cursed him for taking so long with the joint. He didn't say anything back.

For weeks afterward I found ways to watch episodes of Play School plus every other Australian television program I could think of: dramas, comedies, more kid's shows.

Nothing.

2.

Just that one, tiny, tantalizing tidbit to create a new life story for my lost love. She had to be living in Sydney, because that's where most of our television shows came from. Somehow, even in this small way, she'd managed to get close to her acting dream. She was happy because she looked happy; big red pants, a giraffe-print shirt, flowers in her hair and a painted face all suited her.

What could I make of that? What did any of it say about the real Stina today?

It was a good twelve months before the next thing happened, and it involved another bicycle.

By second year Law I was a university veteran who'd learned to cram for exams like a crazy man, if need be. It always needed be. I was so close to failing every subject it wasn't even funny. I'd scraped through first year with undistinguished results. Repeating even that modest feat seemed unlikely. Rather than lectures, tutorials and law books, my mind was constantly preoccupied with finding ways to minimize study time and maximize do-nothing time.

Then when I was half-dozing on a patch of green grass waiting for a Contracts lecture to start, Stina flashed by me, her bicycle's rickety old spokes rapidly rolling, a knapsack of books on her back.

There was a sudden glance between us, a heart stopping moment.

She was in a laughing, loudly chatting group. Their bikes disappeared in a rowdy pack, heading into the treed pathways that led from these grounds to the surrounding streets and roads.

The campus was busy. I didn't think, simply found my feet fast and bolted through groups of students who wandered with their books and their bags. Ran downhill. Caught a glimpse of the bicycles. Now Stina and her friends were going different ways. Trees obscured their progress. I took a path, saw a set of bicycle wheels, cut the corners and burst into the street.

The guy riding along had mad red hair and little round glasses. I nearly made him jump out of his skin.

I looked this way and that way; huh, what a surprise. Nothing.

It was summer and by now I was covered in sweat. When I stumbled back up the tree-lined pathways towards the building where my lecture would take place my mind was ticking over.

Stina was a student here? Jesus—but she was around. She'd returned. Why? And for what sort of degree would she be studying, and where might I bump into her again? I'd have to, I told myself, despite the fact that there were upwards of twenty thousand students enrolled at this place.

So much for my lecture. This semester I'd maybe made three Contracts sessions out of seven. Attendance was mandatory. Failure was a hard promise.

In Great Court I threw my bag under a tree and threw myself down with it. Grumpy, hurting—why hadn't she stopped? Stina was here at university; she was back in this hot little town; she hadn't made any effort to see me, to reconnect. I lived with my mother and father in the same house as ever. I still went to our local cinema. I did my ma's groceries for her down at the corner shops. Stina could have found me in sixty seconds flat.

Lying prone in that grass, I looked around. Lots of students were doing the same as me, but in groups, some with books open in front of them. A few threw Frisbees; someone flipped a football to someone who sent it to someone else. To really drain the life out of you, worse than bad thoughts and summer heat is the easy happiness of other people.

The green ground invited me to put my head down. I was conscious of a footfall. I glanced over my shoulder. And knew the only things to have passed since 1976 were gusts of summer breeze and a few hits on the radio.

3.

Stina's bicycle, an ancient thing was propped against the trunk of a tree. Her knapsack of books was beside it. She stood looking down at me, the sun behind her, making her a cut-out of blue sky. Around the sun-drenched court university life went on. She took off her sunglasses and held them in one hand. I couldn't yet make out her eyes. She was wearing a striped, short-sleeved T-shirt with a V neck, a pair of old Levis without a belt, and brown sandals.

I wasn't going to act like this was a dream come true. I wasn't going to throw myself at her.

Getting to my feet was like trying to move while mostly drunk, a familiar sensation, but I needed to remember she was flesh and blood, not an image painted from memory, not some kind of angel. Whoever she might be these days, Stina was as earthbound, fallible and shitty as the rest of us.

I stood in front of her, eighteen-going-on-nineteen. She would have had her twentieth birthday five weeks and three days back.

Neither of us spoke. I thought there was something about her that said she'd seen the world, maybe even seen a lot of what makes people who they are. More than likely she had. Run off with a guy, living with him, they could have toured the entire planet by now, seen and done incredible things.

Now she was taller than I remembered, yet with the same pale blue eyes, and, man, how they were taking me in.

She seemed fit, even athletic. Her skin was clear. Hair a bit shorter but her cheekbones were as high and delicate as ever. I wanted to touch one cheek, find a way to kiss it; I couldn't imagine the man who wouldn't want the same thing. Even when she grew grey as a cat she'd still be young. A small, deeper crease was at the corner of her mouth where she gave her crooked smile.

'Hello, Eco.'

'Hey.' One long awkward pause. 'Are you still acting?'

She probably wouldn't have expected that as a first thing for me to ask, but she nodded.

'I saw you on TV.'

A shy smile: 'That must have been a while ago.'

'Last year.' I couldn't stop taking her in, as if trying to absorb Stina's skin into mine. 'How about the acting training?'

'Of course.' She tilted her head a little. 'Why do you ask?'

'You look sort of strong.'

'I don't know about that, but an actor's body is her instrument, right?'

'Right.' For some reason that one word came out like an insult. Made worse by, 'Yeah, it must be. Her body.'

She waited a moment, then said, 'You can't hold a grudge, Eco.'

'What grudge?' I half-laughed.

Tears welled up, but not in my eyes.

Huh, funny. Why would she cry?

'Well then how are you?'

'A little scared.'

Maybe I wasn't such a kid to her any more. She wouldn't be scared of a boy. Did she remember the very last thing she'd said to me? Those words were burned like a brand into my psyche.

Eco, you have to grow up.

Well, here I was, all grown up. I felt like saying it to her in a voice that dripped with sarcasm: Hey Stina, guess what? I'm all grown up.

'So you're on campus?'

'I'm doing—' she had to clear whatever might have caught in her throat. '… drama and literature. But it's only for the year. I'm on a transfer.'

'You still live somewhere else?'

'The northern beaches of Sydney.'

'Oh? That must be very nice.'

She didn't say anything to that.

'Then why come back to this shithole?'

Was she wondering now if she should say goodbye, walk away, ask herself why the fuck she'd ever doubled back to come talk to me?

'Well, there's a job,' Stina spoke.

'A job.'

'Come on, what about you?' Stina asked, clearly trying to lighten the mood. So I told her about Law. She said, 'Wow, your parents must be very proud.'

'They're too dumb to understand how bad I'm doing.'

Two automatons would have been capable of a more interesting conversation. As if with the very same thought we simply stopped. Stopped dead. What I felt towards this new version of Christina Vågberg didn't make sense. Not in my head and not in dead words. Who was she? What had she become? Why was she even bothering to talk to me? Maybe there wasn't a single real thing either of us could say.

'Where did you go?' I asked, and I couldn't help it, even to me my voice sounded cold.

She cleared her throat again.

'You know my father went to, ah, France?... and my mother was on her way back to Stockholm. I moved to Newcastle. That's, ah, where things were for me.'

God, but I remembered that slight hesitation in her voice, thoughts needing time to become words. But not since primary-school. Not since she was that slightly pudgy, hair-in-plaits kid with an outrageous scheme for the settling of scores. How had it returned?

'That's where he moved, then?'

She said, 'His name is William. Bill.'

'Bill? That's disappointingly average.'

'What?'

'Not Flavius or Hildebjorn or Hermund, or something?'

'What are you talking about? It's Bill Flood.'

'And Billy Flood was in Newcastle?'

'It's where a job look him. So we went together.'

Yeah, talk ruined everything. But what did Stina really owe me? What had she done that was so wrong, other than to take her life in both hands?

'Just like that you left.'

'It wasn't so easy.'

'And your parents, they went their separate ways?'

She nodded.

'I thought you were so heartbroken about going with your mother?'

'Can you please,' Stina breathed a slow sigh. 'Can you please stop?'

'Stop what?'

She tilted her head. A certain defiance came into her face. Ah now. This I remembered. The nuns had tried to crush that expression out of her. She wiped at both eyes and they started to clear.

'For my parents,' she spoke, 'it was like they were never even married. My father's in the 16th arrondissement of Paris, a suburb called Piteaux. My mother's got three sisters and they have big families. I made a trip last Christmas, first to see him. Thankfully Alexandrie didn't expect me to call her "maman". They seem happy. Then to Stockholm. My mother didn't ask me any questions about them.'

It was the longest she'd spoken so far. The hesitation that caught her words was gone; that soft, soft, almost vanished accent of hers sounded like music.

Stina paused, waiting for me to say something.

Then: 'You know, I saw you before, Eco.'

'And you didn't stop.'

'No, I mean around the campus earlier this year. The first time was just a glimpse, but I knew it was you. Not even my first week here. The next time I followed you for nearly ten minutes. I wanted to say hello but you were walking with a girl. I could tell she liked you very much. I was waiting for her to go, but she didn't. She has long hair and a very pretty face. Is she your girlfriend?'

'I don't even know who you're talking about.'

'Auburn hair. She was wearing a printed wrap-around dress, like a hippie.'

'Maybe … this girl Annie? From my Torts tute. We're not even friends. We were probably talking about some assignment.'

Stina nodded. What little breeze was around didn't bring much relief to this simmering day. Students laughed and went to the places they needed to be. Stina's gaze was almost unnerving.

'So,' she said, 'what do you want, Eco?'

'Not a thing.'

I guess my face was saying something different.

Stina turned and grabbed her bicycle and pushed herself away.

4.

By the time I left university for the day I was a mess. Didn't give Liv the usual lift to his place and instead stopped by a friend's and had three of his beers. Drank them fast. One of his flat mates was there, an exchange student in third-year vet. Her name was Padma and she wanted to stay in her room. Wasn't really in the mood, but we'd had sex before. She'd even told my friend she'd quite enjoyed those bouts of far-too-drunk fun with me. This time it couldn't have been all that much fun but she got off and when I came she kept me on top of her and half-patted me on the back like I was a champ, her mind already on something else.

I dressed and left before she was asleep. In the car I talked to myself, a simple conversation really, just a whole lot of dirty words about this stranger named Christina Vågberg.

When I came in it was well past eleven. My parents believed the fiction that I liked to stay late at the university library studying or doing assignments. Or maybe my ma knew better and just kept quiet. In any case, I never got any trouble from them. I was a young man doing Law who'd put previous difficulties behind him. One day I'd be someone worthwhile. I'd told Stina the truth, though: they simply didn't know enough to understand. To them university was going fine, and why would I want to tell them any different?

The light over the front door was on, as it always was whenever I was late. Inside, dark. I always found that the best way to come in at such an hour. My favourite thing at the end of a day was to flop into the couch and flick around the television stations for some old movie. In those days you could always count on a Cagney, Hammer Horror or Bogart. The ones with Bogie tended to hurt because I'd remember where and when I'd seen them with Stina, even to the point of recalling what she'd been wearing, or entire conversations. Near midnight those old black and whites always looked better than ever, though just last week there'd been The Barefoot Contessa and The African Queen, both in colour. I remembered younger days of imagining ejaculating onto Ava Gardner's breasts. Which became Stina's. I couldn't imagine picturing such a thing towards Katherine Hepburn.

Before turning on the television I went into the kitchen.

A plate of dinner waited for me in the refrigerator. It was a bowl of meat balls in my ma's sauce. I dug in with a fork. Even cold they tasted good. I had the kitchen light on while the rest of the house was dark, but something made me check the dining room.

There against the wall by the window a chair had been moved. A shadow was sitting in it, sort of slumped to that wall. I walked slowly to the wisp that was my ma. She smiled up at me from where she'd been looking out through the glass panes, and even in the semi-darkness I could see her eyes weren't right. She must have been sitting there a long time, waiting for me to get home. Maybe she'd nodded off into a deep sleep and in a second would laugh because she hadn't quite realized where she was or what she'd been doing.

I said, 'Hey ma, you better get to bed, huh?'

Then one eye shut completely and the other was still half open and she looked terrible and strange, like there wasn't any meat left on her and no blood left inside.

She said in a small voice, speaking Sicilian, 'Who do you love more, Giovanni ... your father ... or me? ...' and that was it, because she died before I could even bend down to hold her.

She was against that wall, wilted and neat, and that's where she stayed.

Just like that, what used to be my ma was as empty as a pile of rags. There was nothing left of her in this room, either. I knew it with one hundred percent certainty; she just wasn't here anymore. I touched her shoulder then backed away and went to the main bedroom door. It was slightly ajar. I called for my father. There was no reply, no sound, and so I spoke more loudly. Still no answer. I turned on the light and the bed was made-up and perfect and no one was in it. Ma hadn't been so much sitting up waiting for me as she'd been waiting for her husband to get home from wherever he'd gone.

Yet it was all a jumble of thoughts and feelings, really. When I had the telephone receiver jammed to my ear and the operator was asking if I wanted fire, police or ambulance I couldn't get a word out. My breath simply would not come.

That poor operator, who sounded like a woman my mother's age, just kept saying, 'Please, don't tie up this line, what's your emergency?' to no answer at all.

5.

Stina came to the chapel and I didn't know what to make of that. She was in a straight black dress with her hair done up under a dark veil that came halfway down her face. It was when I followed the gleaming mahogany coffin down the aisle that I noticed her sitting there, in the well-crowded back row. She was alone. My father didn't notice her. He wasn't noticing anything. All the way through the service his eyes had remained shut, as if he couldn't bring himself to see. Someone had to help him walk behind us as Livio, me and four others picked the coffin up and carried it to the back of a gleaming black hearse.

We all followed the hearse as it proceeded at a snail's pace.

Everyone who was there, except for the most elderly, took that short afternoon stroll from the chapel doors down to the hole in the ground selected for Ma. I lost sight of Stina and didn't look for her. Now I was walking holding my father's right hand in my left hand. Liv walked on my right holding my other hand. He kept whispering reassurances.

'This way'; 'Stay strong'; 'Soon it'll be over and we can get these suits off.'

My father said nothing. His hand had a tremor to it and his face was lined the way it'd never been before. He'd arrived home while the ambulance officers had been examining the deceased. One of them guided him into the next room and kept him there. What was left of my mother was sealed into a bag. Two police officers were present. They spoke to him and wrote things down. There'd been alcohol on my father's breath and the smell of cunt about him. Five days later we were dressed in cheap black. That's how life goes. Today the heat bore down. I wanted to get to my bedroom and sleep a week. I just couldn't imagine what my life was going to be like from here on in. I couldn't think what to do about my father.

When the day was over I finally did get to lay in bed. Ma's standing fan turned slow, cooling me a little. There hadn't been a wake. My father had made clear there wasn't to be anything like it.

'A funeral is for crying, not for celebrating.'

A few people had ventured to the house anyway, but his total silence and the absence of cold drinks, coffee, tea or snacks meant that within an hour we were alone, just the two of us, my old man and me. I almost wanted to tell him he might as well go out for more drink and women. He watched television. We hadn't thought of dinner so went hungry.

Then as I tossed and turned I heard a gentle double-rap of the front door's bronze knocker. Papà was in bed now. He didn't get up. The house remained silent. I cursed and pulled on a pair of shorts. Bare-chested, damp with perspiration, nothing on my feet, I went to investigate, ready to tell some do-gooder relative or neighbour that we'd had all the sympathy we needed, thanks all the same.

With the shadow of deciduous trees over her, Stina was just going out the gate. There was a large cardboard fruit box on our patio table and in it were two platters covered in foil. Stina looked back toward me. A glint of moonlight caught her hair.

'What the fuck are you doing?'

'I thought you and your father might need something ... but ... I guess you've had lots of people looking after you?'

'We got rid of all freeloaders.'

Stina didn't quite smile, but she was taking me in. I lifted a corner of foil, then checked the other. She'd brought two generous platters of food. I felt a yawning in my stomach, no idea when I'd last had something decent to eat.

'Leave it on this table and the ants'll get into it,' I said.

'Or the neighbourhood cats.'

'What did you make?'

'One is rice. The other's a beef casserole.'

'Come in,' I said. 'You've never even been here before.'

She shook her head, she wouldn't come inside. Either she knew the time wasn't right, or that my father was home, or both.

I walked down the short front steps.

The night was only several fractions cooler than the dismal day had been. A breeze sighed across my bare skin. Behind Stina was my street's beautiful and secret forest. Or at least the perpetual illusion of it. I was glad she was out of that black dress and that she'd let her hair down. She wore something cool and simple now. A car was parked under a tree, just a small cheap sedan, and no one waited for her. Without thinking about it I slowly walked toward her, stood close, but not touching. This was nothing like being kids. This was nothing like the easy moves on girls who'd consider sleeping with someone like me.

Stina didn't step backwards, but her chin went down.

'So,' I said, 'what do you want, Stina?'

She didn't have an answer.

Without a moment's forethought or planning, I told her just what we needed to do.

Part Five

I.

I'd never been in an expensive hotel but I had my own money and had read enough books, seen enough films, to know this was the way it should be. When it came to glamour and glitz this place wasn't any rock star palace, but the hotel promised to be clean and comfortable, at least a few good cuts above plain and ordinary.

Mid-morning I parked the small sedan I'd managed to buy myself after my eighteenth birthday. It was on HP and I wasn't missing any repayments. I left it alongside those of shoppers and city workers in the centre of town, then walked towards the Botanic Gardens and the Park View Hotel facing it. Not an overly imaginative name, and no reason for me to choose this one over all the others in the city district—it simply was the first to catch my eye in the telephone directory. The venue wasn't important, only what was going to happen inside it. I had no inclination to ring ahead and hadn't considered the possibility that there wouldn't be vacancies. There had to be—it was a Wednesday. Brisbane was a sleepy, tired mutt of a place. People always complained about the way the decade hadn't added any soul to our town; it had no zing, no excitement. You had to go to Sydney or Melbourne for that, and if you had any sense you never came back.

In a pair of corduroy trousers, a collared shirt and canvas sneakers that, at least, were clean, I fronted the teak-lined reception desk. With a lump of cash in my pocket I wasn't all that nervous, almost felt like I owned the place. That feeling lasted about eight seconds. The reception manager worked me and my clothes out at a single glance.

How long would I like to stay? Just a day. Standard or Superior? I chose the latter because it sounded good. An extra seven dollars fifty for the privilege. Your luggage, sir? Really, not a single piece? What about your vehicle to park? Now I did feel a fool. It hadn't crossed my mind there'd be an in-house car park.

The manager didn't smirk or make a comment, but he had the measure of my day all right. What should I have eared, anyway? He could try to guess how many condoms I had in my pocket. There were six. Youth and hubris go hand in hand. If he spied Stina on her way in he could go cry in a corner. The man needed the details of my driver's license even though I had ready cash. No need for payment in advance, he explained. Tomorrow, checkout by eleven a.m. When you leave we'll add your room service charges. I was too embarrassed to tell him I wouldn't be leaving the next day, but very late this same evening. I couldn't risk it with my father, staying away all night. He'd have my hide, and had been a bundle of jittery, jangling nerves since the funeral. More to the point, even if she'd agreed to meet me here, Stina had made sure I understood that she wouldn't stay.

Just the day, all right Eco? To be together again.

Did she mean she'd sleep with me or not?

Whatever, she was on a clock. Bitch had her man to get back to.

Well, if the chance really came, for this one day I would eat her alive.

Superior room, sixth floor. I took the elevator, found 601, went inside and it was clean and sparse—far smaller and not as nice as I'd hoped. You've lived too long in movies, I told myself.

Fabulous hotels are for James Bond and Matt Helm. Turned on the television and with a soap opera in the background stood stock-still at the windows. My heart hammered against my ribs.

The time? Too early for Stina. Another good hour to wait, Jesus.

I realized I was looking at a clear day, at a pleasant view of the spreading gardens and river. At least the hotel's name didn't lie.

Man, what if she doesn't show? What if Stina thought about it and came to her senses. Decided she simply could not allow herself to get locked away in any sort of hotel room with someone who wanted her so much. And I did. The half-erection in my pants beat steady as a pulse.

Even at this early hour of the day I helped myself to a beer because I couldn't think what else to do. The morning ticked on, the glacial passage of minutes. I convinced myself that she wouldn't turn up. So I took another beer and a packet of salty potato chips. That erection just got harder. What, from beer and potato chips? Maybe I should take care of business in the bathroom; I didn't. The hour disappeared, finally, but she wasn't here. Ought I run from this place and salvage a shred of dignity with someone like Padma, or just open a window and walk into open space? Sixth floor, that'd do it.

I watched more TV and thanks to two beers on a mostly empty stomach I even dozed.

Just before midday the room's telephone buzzed, making me jump out of a sort of self-inflicted stupor. Had to wipe the drool off my chin.

'Eco? I'm in the foyer.'

Her voice was small and tight, not her at all. She hadn't wanted to ask at reception so I told her where I was.

In the bathroom I washed quickly, rinsed my mouth, tried to come back to life. It didn't take long. The blood was singing—literally fizzing—in my veins.

A minute, two, three passed, and in disbelief I heard a tap at the door. Even more disbelief at the sight of her. In the next breath she was inside that room with me. Well, technically inside, but trapped in the small corridor leading into the main suite. It was as far as she got. I'd grabbed her and pushed her up against the wall, kissing her hard. Her lips were soft and her hair was fragrant and I held her there so tightly she might not have been able to breathe. Part of me wanted to cry and part of me wanted to fuck her senseless. If she'd allowed it I would have done both at the same time.

Stina let me kiss her, and she kissed me, but, I thought, with more kindness than passion. Her body was stiff, taut, definitely not relaxed. In a few moments she deftly slid out of my grasp. It was as if she'd learned how to avoid pawing hands when just a schoolgirl.

'What have you been drinking?'

She'd tasted it on my mouth. It didn't seem to repulse her.

'Just a beer.'

'Now that's an idea.'

Stina looked around the room, glanced out the windows, took in the view, opened the mini bar fridge and considered what was in there. I knew she was just marking beats of time while she got herself together. While she tried to loosen up.

I thought she succeeded.

The blush was already fading from her face, and that strange angularity that comes from being tight and uncomfortable.

'I'm really hungry—what time is it?'

'Twelve, I guess.'

'I know how late I am. One full hour. I also know I'm lucky you waited. It took me time ... to decide. I was in town. I just kept walking around.'

I imagined businessmen and day workers doing a double-take, staring in her wake. Stina's blonde hair was down. Today she wore a dreamy, mod-style blue dress with white spots and a back-tied waistband. Zip-up brown leather boots and small gemstone rings on her fingers. The dress was angel-sleeved with wide, lace-trimmed ruffles at her wrists. She looked like she belonged to 1969, or down there in the botanic gardens, surrounded by fields of flowers and chirruping birdlife.

Enough to double the ache in my heart.

'It's okay,' I said, 'let's just relax now.'

So the very first thing we did after that initial kiss and grope was to not take to the bed—which we never might—but to sit on the small firm couch and look through the room service menu. That was nice. It sort of melted the moment. I was sorry I'd tried to manhandle her as soon as she'd stepped inside, but was very conscious of how close we were sitting; her knees were together and she was as demure as a schoolgirl.

I was thinking of the wasted years that had passed, and of that lucky asshole, Bill or William or whoever he was, waiting for her at home.

And this was strange too: I wished my ma was alive to take a good second look at Christina Vågberg. Imagine Stina sitting at our table the way I'd done so many times at hers; imagine the idea of a family—me, her, a little one on the way.

Man.

Sometimes I liked to tell myself I was just so different to that great fat middle of the road everyone else lived in, but I was so ordinary. When I thought of my dreams they weren't very much. A bed and the sweet forever of the two of us; a Hallmark card.

We decided on the simple and obvious: burgers and fries. After we ordered we noticed that the midday movie on television was The Heavenly Body. From the forties. We'd missed about five minutes. William Powell never did a lot for me, but Hedy Lamarr was gorgeous, and Stina liked the both of them. I was okay with her wanting to watch the film. William Powell had been in all those Thin Man movies with Myrna Loy, and she'd been in one of my favourite old films ever, The Best Years of Our Lives, so Stina and I took this fluffy entertainment in and idly brought up all the connections we could remember.

'She's German, no, Austrian, I think,' Stina said.

'Hedy Lamarr? Yes. And like you there's still just a trace of her accent.'

'You can hear it?'

'You can't?'

'I mean with me.'

'The both of you.'

'Huh. Her nickname was "The Most Beautiful Woman in Films".'

'The both of you.'

The small line at the corner of Stina's mouth, deepening a little.

'I wonder what her real name was?'

'Kiesler … Hedwig something-something Kiesler.'

'That's a name.'

'The way she looks. Even her profile.'

'What?'

'She reminds me of you.'

'We saw this movie at the Astor. It was on with Wife Vs Secretary. Remember?'

'Certainly do.'

When our delivery came we put the tray on the coffee table. Stina unzipped and slipped off her boots, then took off the small white socks underneath. I reached for one. She looked at me. I couldn't help touching it to the corner of my mouth. Who knows what she thought about that.

We sat on the floor, leaning back against the couch, and munched away. Fun, all the silly machinations these fabulously stylish characters were put through. Hedy Lamarr, a twin pleasure to watch with Stina. The fries were good and the burgers were better, and in an ad break Stina crawled across the carpeted floor to the mini bar fridge.

'We can afford drinks? I've got money.'

'On me, it's no problem.'

She uncorked a half-bottle of white wine. I followed her and helped myself to another cold beer.

Thing was, that little hippy dress of hers was quite demure in its own way, at least when she was standing up or sitting down, but it was short and the way she'd crawled meant I glimpsed smooth upper thighs and the curve of her buttocks in soft pink underwear. I felt I'd been hit by a pink velvet hammer. We slid back into our places and I'd gone hard as a rock again. Now was the time to really kiss her. I moved close. Her lips were soft as ever, salty from fries. Stina put a tender palm to the side of my face, but eased away and said we should let the movie finish. I'd pressed to her, and had felt her the stiffened nipples of her breasts. I was faint. What would she look like out of that dress?

Even though the old comedy was a lot of laughs and had a predictable but good ending, the ad breaks went on forever. I'd stopped enjoying the food because of my churning belly. The credits rolled and rolled, and an evangelical voice spoke about the magnificent deodorant that had sponsored our lunchtime viewing. We should all come back tomorrow for Red Dust, featuring the romantic pairing of Clark Gable and Jean Harlow, and always remember to feel fresh and dry using the incredible Super Fresh 'n Dry!

Stina had lingered over her food, taking up time, but she was finished now and we cleared our things away. I turned off the television. She went to the door, balancing the tray in one hand and expertly sliding it out. She put on the latch. I liked that. It made my heart want to stop. She didn't come all the way back to me and waited in the short corridor, all vulnerable and young, the way she stood there.

'Come on,' I said. 'Come over here.'

'Let me ... please, can I take a shower first?'

If that's what she wanted, a shower was fine, but the troubled look in her eye certainly wasn't.

So I lay over the bed covers and felt odd inside because that tough erection had gone away without Hail Marys or Our Fathers. The day was already a rollercoaster. My head rested on two stacked pillows and the big double mattress was surprisingly firm and comfortable.

Stina was taking too long, or maybe I was too anxious and time only held the illusion of having settled into absolute stillness.

Her second thoughts must have returned. What had it been like for her, pacing around town trying to decide whether to actually take those steps to this hotel? To balance on the edge of what she might let herself do behind her William's back? Was this something she'd done before—to have others in secret places?

No, no, no. Stop thinking like this.

Pitching up from the bed, I tried to get interested in the view again. What view, I couldn't see anything but that white-painted bathroom door. The shower ran, still. An almost overwhelming image came to mind, the same image I'd seen in a million magazines. A beautiful girl is naked under streaming water.

Come on, we're here.

We've got this room. Whatever we do need never be known by another living soul.

My ma's in the ground and my father's a man I'd like to take to with a pitchfork.

The present and the future are concepts I ignore with easy pursuits and fake ennui.

What should I do?

In a minute Stina would emerge, fully dressed. With an abrupt I'm so sorry, Eco, this was a mistake she'd hurry the hell away from this hotel.

So what should I do right now?

Eco, you have to grow up.

I tried the handle. The bathroom wasn't locked.

Stina was behind the dimpled shower glass. There was a hint of steam, of condensation. I kept my eyes averted, then slowly turned toward her. Her body was shadowed and blurred but I could see how lithe she was. She was crying. Stina sensed my presence and looked toward me. She stopped moving. She didn't say I had to go away. She didn't say anything.

She slid back the shower door.

No books or magazines, no photographs or movies, revealed such a young woman. I was out of my clothes. The warm spray felt good. She felt better. Stina only wanted to be held and in a strange way so did I. She lay her head on my shoulder and we let the water run over us.

Stina didn't cry now. It was good to be strong for her. I felt her soft skin and warm curves against me, but right then, more than anything, I wanted to look after her. For once the raw, sexual stuff hardly seemed important.

When we turned off the taps we used the large cotton towels to dry one another off. Stina dabbed at my chest then leaned in and kissed me there. She looked up at me then put her hand behind my head, gently drawing my face down to her breasts. As I tasted her nipples she arched against me, then took my hand and placed it between her legs. As we moved out of the bathroom and into the bed, Stina said my name three times, then she arched her back again and clenched her teeth, one orgasm mad against my mouth.

She pulled me up and whispered, 'Push hard, push hard,' then, 'It's all right, you can go all the way, don't stop.'

I was licking and kissing her neck, then she clamped her lips to mine.

2.

On the room's not-very-good built-in radio, Magic Carpet Ride was playing, a nice piece of psychedelia but probably not right for a bedroom. I turned the sound down. We were sitting up in that bed now, wearing the room's complimentary bathrobes. I lightly towelled Stina's hair dry. The song segued into a Beatles tune, but I wasn't paying it any attention.

She nestled into me and that's when I saw it.

'Wow,' I said.

At the nape of her neck, hidden under her hair, in an unobtrusive yet nicely elegant script, the word 'Dream' was tattooed.

'Tell me truly, what do you think?'

'It's beautiful ... I mean it.'

She smiled. I touched that word, nuzzled her skin.

'You've become so ... I don't know,' she shivered. 'Just the softest touch, Eco.'

Stina shook her hair out.

'You gave me the idea, you know.'

'I did? How?'

'All right. Remember once we went to see a movie called The Last Detail?'

'Sure.'

'What did you say after it?'

It slowly came to me, and I began to grin. She knew I remembered.

'You told me one day you'd get the word "Free" tattooed onto yourself.'

'I'll still do it.'

'So I thought a lot about one word that makes me happy.'

'But you were crying before.'

'I'm sorry ...'

'Don't say that. This is great today. Everything about it.'

'I ... I want you to know, you mean a lot to me.'

'Really?'

'That's why I'm here.'

I moved closer.

Then she added, 'But please don't forget. I'm with someone.'

'Then how does it work—this, I mean?'

'I don't know.'

'Will we do it again?'

'Do we have to think forward and around corners? Can't we just be here now, Eco?'

'Do you love him?'

'Bill? Yes.'

Stina slowly brushed her hair with her fingers. Just before she spoke again, I noticed the colour that returned to her face.

'It must seem like I don't. Being here like this. It's traitorous, I know that. There's no way to make excuses.' She pushed a little away. 'Can I try to explain it by telling you about something different?'

'Okay.'

'The other day when I told you about visiting my parents, it wasn't the whole truth. My mother did move back to Stockholm. Once she was there she remembered she didn't like her sisters very much. Or maybe she just didn't fit anymore. She only stayed with my youngest aunt for two weeks. Then she didn't even try any of the others, though they offered. Instead she found herself an apartment. A shoebox, she wrote me, and started a job in a delicatessen. A few months later she called my father and asked if he was ready to try again. He wasn't. Alexandrie and Piteaux made him happy. He explained that to her. He told me she sounded well enough, but that night my mother swallowed all the pills she had. A prescription to treat anxiety. My father contacted me as soon as one of my aunts contacted him. Then I went over.'

But I couldn't believe this news.

Cigarettes and vermouth, kindness and sadness, and Now you beeches go vock yourselves.

'That's both our mothers ...'

'My father was too cold about the whole thing. He said, "It was her choice".'

'My old man's stupid and he's got a woman on the side. Or lots of women. I don't know.'

Stina clenched a muscle in her jaw, gazing at me. Thinking. I didn't like this new look in her face. She was light but that was dark.

'What?' I asked.

She shook her head. 'Nothing.'

We needed to get away from these sorts of topics, but before I could speak she went on.

'It reminded me of what scares me the most.'

'What's that?'

'My father has this saying. "This is the one and only life." My mother lived it, without, I think, living. She stopped herself from experiencing, I don't know, joy. All the things she wanted. And she knew it. I can't let myself be like that. I can't let myself miss everything that's beautiful. Or interesting. Or ugly. Or whatever.' She shrugged. 'Well, no one can have absolutely everything.'

'If you loved him, wouldn't William be enough?'

'Nothing ever seems like it's enough.'

I frowned at that. I wondered if it was actually true. It sounded a bit too pat; a bit too easy. Sort of beneath someone like Stina. But I understood what she meant about joy, about stopping yourself from having the chance to experience it anymore.

All I had to do was think about my father, and the way he used to stalk out at night; my mother with that quiet sadness, always waiting for him. Not so much waiting for him to come home, but waiting for him to return to her, to give them both something to have together.

'You think I'm just being too greedy, right?'

'I don't blame you for how you feel. There should be more of it. Joy, I mean. Especially in here.'

'Eco ...' Stina shook her head, but with a slow smile. 'When you talk like that, it's like I don't quite know you.'

'Then let's stay here a week. A month. Let's never leave.'

She let that lie, like it wasn't right to say anything back. Then:

'But my father is a nihilist at heart. This idea of the only life we get. I believe we do come from somewhere, and go somewhere too. Even if it's not to Heaven and listen to a choir of angels. Maybe there's something like a great spirit that our souls are always a part of.'

'And when we kick the bucket, it's like drops of rain returning to the ocean. Would that make you happy?'

'No,' Stina shook her head. 'I am too greedy. I want the chance to remember things. I want to remember my life. Why can't I be an individual always—with my own thoughts and the things I love? Instead we're meant to become a part of some amorphous blob, this ocean of something?'

'That way leads true contentment. Someone said that, or some religion.'

'The celestial blob in the stars. Yes, big deal.'

'You really think about things like this?'

'What if the exciting part of existence is right now? What if this is our only chance to live our dreams? To eat, drink, walk in meadows, see the world. Talk, watch movies. Make movies and write books. And have sex. To experience orgasms that shake you like an earthquake. How do ridiculous pastures of eternal contentment, compare? Cows are contented.'

'We become eternal cattle, grazing away on stardust.'

She laughed a little, though without a great deal of humour.

'Do you think,' I started, not quite sure of what I wanted to say. 'Do you think that when we go back, maybe we're smarter? And that makes the celestial blob just one tiny bit better? This life down here gives us some wisdom, and we take that with us and add it to everything else?'

'You know what my answer to that is?'

'What?'

'I'd rather make love just one more time than settle for eternal wisdom. I'd rather listen to one side of my mother's old records than make my contribution to the Great Spirit. I'd rather hear the sound of the rain at the beginning of Riders on the Storm, or Lou Reed singing the way he does about his perfect day, or listen to David Bowie whistle at the end of that song. That's how selfish I am.'

'If I could give it to you I would, but I'm not quite God.'

'The truth,' she said, 'is that I just don't want to die. Life's too good, even when it hurts.'

We thought about all of this in silence. I could not imagine, or picture, or even think of someone like Stina drawing her last breath. How could she ever be laid out pallid and empty in some coffin? Yet I'd seen my mother that way; Klara Vågberg was gone too; no one was about to miss their turn.

'The thing is,' I finally replied, 'I'm sure you're going to get to be really old first.'

'Am I?'

'Of course.'

'What makes you so certain?'

'Well, I know things. Not in a God sort of way, but enough.'

'Then tell me.' She lightly slapped the covers with her palms. 'Come on.'

Leaning forward, I kissed this new delight in her face.

Then I thought it over a minute, and in that minute I saw a clear picture of the future, and it was like what I'd heard people call a 'vision splendid'.

Stina waited, and in her expression there was that open and unprotected quality I remembered so well. Her air of being, well, full of the thing scrawled at the nape of her neck.

'Okay, if you're going to remind me about movies we saw together, what about this one? Little Big Man, the western with Dustin Hoffman?'

'He's like, 121 years of age? Recounting his entire life of love and tragedies.'

'Exactly. Well, you're going to be a female version of his character.'

'William Crabb, that was his name.'

'Correct. You'll narrate your life of endless adventures. One of the fullest lives imaginable. Beauty and tragedy in equal parts. The movie will follow your memoirs, which will have been a bestseller. In three volumes. Three bestsellers.'

'So who'll play me?'

'Some future version of Ingrid Bergman or Lauren Bacall. No. Of Hedy Lamarr, of course.'

'Pretty good.'

'So you'll outlive your first husband and see the sad end of a second. I don't like the third's odds very much either. You'll get old enough to be a complete witch to your children, and there'll be a lot of them. And to your grandchildren as well, who'll add up to something like the population of a small town. We might as well think of it as "Stinaville". Eventually you'll mellow out and just be so nice to your great-grandchildren that they'll remember you every day of their lives. You're going to see the rise of space travel and the way humanity moves out to live on amazing planets in other galaxies. You'll survive world conflicts, including nuclear war. After that you'll get first-hand experience of super-technologies that help everyone discover the new fountain of youth—and what's more your head will be cryogenically frozen and five hundred years in the future you'll be right back here in a body even better than the one you've got now.'

'Mightn't I have this one?'

'They'll probably have it saved for you.'

'This is very interesting. And I believe you. But where is Eco in all this?'

'Poor bastard went young. Drank himself to death, expired in a gutter … unless of course some good woman changes history and helps pull him back from the brink.'

Stina's eyes searched my face as she enunciated every word: 'You—have—changed.'

'Huh,' I said. 'About time you noticed.'

3.

Soon our talk subsided. It seemed silly to continue. Silly to go on with mindless prattle.

Lying back together we enjoyed the rise and fall of each other's slow breath. How much better than talk was that?

We entwined fingers, slowly made love again, then drifted to the faint jangle of pop songs and weather updates.

4.

'So it wasn't a mistake to come today?'

'I don't know, but Eco, I've loved it.'

'Can you stay another hour?'

'William's been away. It's not a nice thing, but that's why I was free. He's back tonight, so I have to be there.'

'What's he do, this Norse god of yours?'

'Norse god?'

'Well, I've seen him, you know. Back in the old days before you left. Those arms and long hair. Very subtle black and red Ford ...'

'Jesus, do you mean Erik Gustavson? God no.'

'But—'

'But nothing, that's not William.'

'Then who is he?'

'Well, you couldn't possibly know, Eco. I met him in class ... he was one of my acting tutors.'

'That's how it happened?'

'We got to know each other. We became quite close, and started meeting and doing things together, firstly just long chats, then movies and things.'

'Oh.'

'Jesus, I'm sorry ...'

'No, go on.'

'If you're sure.'

'I'm sure.'

'William's talented and he gets noticed. If you get noticed you have to grab your chance. His first chance came with an offer in Newcastle. He didn't force me—he's not like that. I wanted to go. The timing was right. Then once we were there we barely had time to make our new home before he had a better offer, this time in Sydney for a children's show.'

'That's how I saw you.'

'William kept helping me no matter how busy he was, but

he had more and more to do with other shows too. I had a few small parts in musical theatre, not very many dramatic roles. That's okay, there's a lot to learn. Then came the big thing.'

'What's that?'

'The reason we're here. Bill's written half a dozen screenplays and one's underway. With him as director. Talk about his dream come true. Half the locations are down the Gold Coast. You know, those amazing beaches? It's about this group of kids who well, it's a horror movie. But guess what?'

'You're in it?'

'I get to be sweet, smart and sexy. So rather than miss a year of university I arranged a transfer. William's on the movie fulltime of course, something like that eats into everything. So far it's all been planning, but now they've started shooting. This first week is without actors. Test shots, panoramas, waves, the sky. In one more week I go down.'

'So it's really happening.'

'It sure is.'

'Remember we watched all those great actors, Stina? I always knew it'd be you one day.'

'I get absolutely murdered halfway through. Literally slaughtered like a pig.'

'How could they kill you off?'

'It's important to the story.'

'Who's the cunt who does it?'

'Our monster. They've got this actor named Eli Tulloch who's genuinely seven-six, and I'm not joking, his face is terrifying. I get goose bumps just standing next to him. I don't even think he has to act all that much ... but let's not talk about this part of it, okay?'

'Why not?'

'What they're going to do to me. It's called a stunt piece. The thing will look brutal on the screen, but it's sort of dangerous in real life too. Do you want to hear the truth?'

'Of course.'

'I'm scared.'

'Of what? A movie?'

'Don't laugh ... I know it'll just be buckets of fake blood and make up, prosthetics, but to get to that point I'm going to be dragged backwards across the sand by my hair. It's a long, long way, and William wants it uncut, a single take. I have to kick and scream as much as I can, he says I have to fight like crazy. You know, trapped animal stuff. There's a trick to it, but this Eli's a giant and he's really going to have my hair wrapped up in his fists. If things go wrong I could get hurt. Lose some of my scalp. It's happened before. Simple as that.'

'But these guys are professionals, right?'

'Well, it's not the biggest budget film ever, so the crew's a bit hit and miss ...'

'Stop. Wait.'

'What?'

'Why don't I come down? Do you want me to be there?'

'No, no ... of course not.'

'But if you're so scared, maybe you could use some moral support.'

'You're sweet, Eco, but ...'

'I'll just keep in the background, then when you need me—'

'It's William's world. Do you get that?'

'Sure.'

'So it wouldn't be right for you to be anywhere near us.'

'I'll keep in the background.'

'No. I'm sorry. No.'

'Then when do I see you again?'

5.

Maybe never.

The crazy romance of that hotel room made me forget there was a line Stina wasn't about to let either of us cross. For whatever reasons of her own, she could let me kiss and make love to her while we were here, but to go past that just wasn't part of the deal.

Not yet nineteen—what did I understand about the negotiations people make with others, or themselves?

The next week I tried to make plans to meet up with her again. She was hesitant, unsure; I hardly heard or let myself understand that.

Okay ... maybe after my 19th Century Lit class?

It was a Thursday. Right on lunchtime Stina emerged from a lecture theatre with about forty other third-year students. We sat together on fragrant grass in a quiet shade.

'I've got this friend's place, it's close by?'

When I put my hand over hers she squeezed it once then folded her hands into her lap.

'Eco, it's too soon.'

Her lilting voice had flattened. Every action, every choice in life, has a price, and look how quickly she was paying hers. Soon she had to go, there was someplace she had to be. Stina held me tight, her palms slightly damp, and she touched my cheek with her lips. I walked away shaken by the amount of hurt in those pale blue eyes.

Though we hadn't spoken about it, I knew she had another class the following day, which was a Friday. Medieval Drama. It didn't take much searching on faculty notice boards to find out what time it'd be on, or where. Very last session of the week in the Forgan Smith Building next to Great Court. My mistake was to tell Livio I wouldn't be giving him a lift home, I was going to wait for Stina.

'Who?' spoke Livio Vida.

His eyes had the appearance of someone experiencing an impossible shock, and that got me. It was funny, because I'd never imagined that all these years Livio might have carried something of a crush of his own. Well, it made sense. Who'd been the first person to show him real kindness?

So I explained it all to him, leaving out the hotel part. That was mine.

He wouldn't take no for an answer. In an instant Liv was like a big dog who knows his favourite ball is just around the corner. I kept telling him I needed to see Stina privately, but he wouldn't listen. He wanted to meet her again. It was only fair, he said, after so long. He'd just say a quick hello, then leave us in peace.

The next day there we were, the two of us waiting, poor Stina expecting to see no one.

The theatre started to empty and she was amongst the very last to leave, speaking with a wiry older guy in a good shirt and pressed trousers. I took him to be the lecturer. Soon he'd go his own way. I held Liv back. Stina glanced up, her arms carrying books. She saw us and the look in her eves immediately made me wish I was somewhere else.

Late Friday afternoon, her fellow students had that half-harried, half-relieved look of people who can't believe they've made it to another weekend. Meanwhile the lecturer kept speaking low to Stina, leaning in even as they walked, comfortable and smiling at whatever clever thing he had to say to her. His obvious intimacy told me I was wrong about who he was, and now I knew I really had to get out of there, and would have if Liv hadn't been standing his ground like a great chunk of rock.

As they approached Stina took Liv in. Her brain probably performed some sort of double take; in her mind Livio Vida would have remained that rotund, squat, fetid beast of year five. Here he was standing taller than me, his sexy, floppy hair in natural waves, with a strong jaw and a physique that turned heads.

As if in opposition to this, the guy beside Stina had a small pointed beard, round John Lennon-style glasses, a helmet of tight curly hair, and he was skinnier than Jesus Christ. It had already dawned on me. This wasn't some lecturer or university compatriot. It was the man Stina had decided it was worth turning her life upside down for, worth running away with: enter the talented and budding auteur.

The rest of the class dispersed. We were right there and Stina was forced to stop and say hello. She was stiff with Livio, awkward with me. We were old friends, from way back in primary.

'William,' he said. 'William Flood. This is great. It's a reunion, then?'

He said he liked the idea that Stina would have some companions at this university that wasn't her own, to have some human contact while he was away, busy.

'I don't want you to be lonely. That would just break my heart.'

He adored her. He was completely unthreatened by the fact that we were Stina's age when he so obviously wasn't, or that Liv carried such a raw physical presence.

Behind the thick lenses of those glasses William Flood's eyes were small, amber and penetrating. He had a serious demeanour, but with a genuine intelligence and kindness about him. Whenever he smiled deep lines—grooves, really—were embedded along his cheeks.

It turned out he'd finished filming for the week and had returned from whatever beach they were working on. He'd come to collect Stina. Her star turn, he told us, was about to begin. He'd been happy to wait, to sit in on this class with her, and he'd even surprised himself by enjoying the lecture.

'Lord, it takes you back. I finished philosophy and fine art right here, what, '68? Those were big days. What are you two studying?'

1968? Jesus, how old was this guy? Forty?

No, I discovered it later on: Bill Flood was thirty-four—he simply seemed older.

For someone so desperate to see his old friend Stina again, Liv was incredibly tongue-tied. He remained little more than that great mute chunk of rock. I couldn't discern any bounce between he and Stina, any juice at all. Had the years really turned them into such perfect strangers? Well, none of that was my problem. I preferred it that way.

William Flood's inquiring gaze seemed to take this absence in. I had no idea at all what he was thinking.

As for me, I had an actual chill at the base of my spine. It hadn't taken me long to discover that I simply didn't have the resources to deal with this situation, to stand here and be so friendly and nonchalant with this man who possessed my Stina in every possible way. Suddenly the liaison in the Park View Hotel felt tawdry and small, something that could already fade into insignificance, and might have, if it hadn't been all so nasty towards its innocent party, this William Flood.

I wondered: how could anything I'd done or hope to do ever compare with the things this man experienced with Stina? Then I caught her glance. She was standing a little behind his right shoulder and she was giving me a look. No, it was a message, and it said, Thank you, Eco.

I knew why—I wasn't letting myself give her away.

Fine. I could feel sick and duplicitous later; when I had the luxury of time I could lacerate myself with this new, truer understanding of what to be two-faced really means. No wonder Stina had been so unhappy the last week. No wonder her pale eyes had lost their lustre.

And yet that silent message only succeeded in making me love her more; I felt the connection between us more strongly than ever: it was back. No, it had never left. The last week had been an aberration. It was as if we were in the hotel suite one more time, or at a movie house sitting alone within our little universe of complicity. That look from her made me decide that I wouldn't give her up, that I wouldn't let myself feel like a flea next to William Flood, even with all his wonderful achievements and potential. None of that mattered. To me the only thing making sense was that no differing roads and no passage of years had failed to break my connection to Stina.

The rest was just nothing, and that included this kindly, weedy, pale little genius in front of me.

He spoke up, affable as a priest, and very sensitive to the waves of energy around him.

'This moment is incredible, simply incredible. I can sense the ... the history here. It's a beautiful thing, but hardly easy, is it? Wow.'

His small eyes were bright as pinprick-stars as he mulled this and other matters over.

'Livio, right, and Eco?'

'Wrong way around.'

'Okay,' he smiled, those lines lengthening and deepening in his thin cheeks. 'If I could somehow use this old friendship ...'

Stina's eyes just about widened in alarm, yet none of us replied, waiting for this man who was in his own world of thought.

'You know what,' spoke William Flood, most especially looking over Liv and his solid presence. 'This movie I'm making, we could really use extra extras.'

What a calm and reasonable voice. You could follow that voice into a war, or be provided with a sense of peace in a time of battle. Again I thought of a type of priest.

'So you know what we're up to with Black Beach Killer, correct? I'm sure Stina's told you. Well, two great guys like you, how wonderful it would be.'

Liv came to life. 'What do you mean?'

'Come visit and be extras on my film. Come tomorrow.'

Liv was already nodding and saying yes.

'Just in the background, you understand, it's nothing very grand.'

'Man, that'll be fantastic!'

How could he have so much enthusiasm for this? Livio watched occasional movies, but they were hardly things he thought much about. Was it the idea of being up on a screen that suddenly appealed to him so?

Stina reacted to the suggestion, but William Flood was facing Liv and me. He couldn't see her face. She cast her gaze downwards, and I thought, Okay, that's it, this is the step she can't take, as soon as she gets the chance she's going to tell me to stop screwing up her life and never come back. Yet almost immediately she glanced up and found my eyes.

The very, very small twitch at the corner of her mouth seemed to be her smile of acquiescence.

After all, it was what I'd wanted, right?

And maybe what she did too.

6.

Jesus, but that meeting confused me, so instead of keeping myself together I gave up and stayed out drinking. I could hardly say why, maybe because I couldn't stand the complications I'd created, or had stepped headlong into, or that made my thoughts go in spirals that made no sense at all.

Around eight p.m. Liv caught up with me at a friend named Myron's place. Myron was crying, as he often did, because he hated his name. Plus a hundred other good reasons. Only kid of wealthy parents who funded his every activity, Myron's refrigerator was always full of beer and carrots. Didn't make any sense, but that hardly mattered. Tonight Myron and his closest friends were stoned legless. He had money to buy the best weed, and they all were partial to uppers as well. Liv stumbled through the front door from wherever he'd gotten himself primed, and in a too-loud voice joined this merry crowd. Thing was, something about him had been annoying me since the afternoon's meeting with Stina and William Flood. I couldn't quite put my finger on what it was. Maybe I simply resented the way he'd muscled in on us, or the sheer bullshit of his sudden enthusiasm for the movies.

I found myself drinking and studying his rock-hard frame, the way his sleeves were filled by swollen biceps and over-inflated triceps. None of that came without hour upon hour in front of a mirror. Sometimes I had to wonder, what drove him to all of this?

Soon he was smoking and drinking and floating in his own little piece of heaven, except that his cheer seemed forced and to me he didn't seem very happy at all.

'Hey Eco,' he kept saying. 'Hey Eco.'

I couldn't stand it and kept moving to different parts of the house, to rooms he wasn't in, but sooner or later he'd follow and find me.

'Hey Eco.'

When the beer and weed ran out, no one wanted to eat

carrots and people started to drift toward the assortment of cheap vehicles parked in the street. No one rang for a cab. I'd at least had the forethought to leave my own car at home, which proved smart because I was well and truly cut.

I recall a lift with some do-gooder named Gordon who drove an olive-green EH Holden and who'd let six other drunks, including Liv, cram into the front and back. We ended up tumbling through the doors of that ride onto the weedy footpath and gutters outside one of the busiest beer gardens in town. Khe Sanh yowled from a distorting speaker system. I threw up into the gutter. Livio patted my back to get the last dregs out and when he leaned down close I heard him say into my ear:

'We're movie stars!'

He was still so stupidly jolly it just couldn't be real, as if he'd dressed himself in a suit of lights topped off with a happy-mask.

At least heaving the contents of my stomach made me feel better. I straightened, using Liv's shoulder for support, and looked him in his curiously clammy face.

'What's with you?'

His smile was a grin so bizarre it was practically a grimace. Man, but he looked out of it. His eyes were just wrong—and then he started jabbering some story about a great movie he'd seen. I think it might have been The Betsy. His words and sentences came fast and mad, staccato-style, as if he simply couldn't control his mouth and had to get everything out.

How much had he been drinking? How many of Myron's pills had he popped?

'But what the fuck have you done to yourself?'

Liv grabbed me and dry-humped my leg, cackling.

I pushed him off and escaped at a stagger, getting into the teeming beer and cigarette stench of this university pub by a bend of the river. He was behind me, then he cut straight for the bar. The entire place was jam-packed. Liv pushed through a four-deep crowd where everyone was hassling to be served. Curses and shoves didn't stop him returning at a canter, a full pitcher of frothed-up beer in each hand.

Jesus, he was up for a big one.

Yes, a pitcher each; we sucked that beer down like dying men who've found water in a desert. The music was screeching and above it people screamed at one another. At least now I couldn't hear Liv speed-talking. As soon as the last drops of our beer were gone we wanted more, but the few coins in our pockets didn't add up to a single dollar between us.

We needed to find friends with money.

So we went hunting through that rowdy multitude that stank of fresh and stale beer combined, not to mention of sweat and deep-fried delicacies from a greasy kitchen. We searched through groups of Law, Psychology and Arts students mixed with trade apprentices and guys in suits. Everyone was yelling and hooting and spilling more drinks. I felt I was losing myself, sinking into the quicksand of squeezed backsides and pressing hips, of firm boobs brushing my arms and people calling each other names like Best Fucken Mate Ever or Stupid Asshole. I started dancing with girls I'd never met before. Liv was shouting like a goat-herder. The music swung from (I'm) Stranded to Stayin' Alive to something by Fleetwood Mac, then New Kid in Town and Night Moves, a song that everyone wanted to sing along to. Then I was in someone's arms to the vomity schmaltz of I'm In You and I Never Cry and Handy Man, then this chick let go of me when God Save the Queen somehow circled back to Khe Sanh.

I found her again a few minutes later, seated at a table with six guys I vaguely recognized, and three other girls. They welcomed me like a friend and poured me a pre-mixed Black Russian from a pitcher heavy with ice. The one who'd embraced me on the dance floor had deep auburn hair and seemed vaguely familiar from somewhere. I'd lost Livio. She started yapping in my ear about something and whatever non sequitur I said back to her she laughed at.

Then I had someone's beer or maybe Black Russian all down

my shirt and my face was wet and I was climbing into the back seat of a car, exactly whose I didn't know. That beautiful auburn hair started moving like gentle seaweed over my stiff cock. My new friend made slurping noises that made me giggle. Before I knew it, in that cramped space somehow I was licking a calf or maybe it was an inner thigh, then I was pounding into her. Abby? Adele? Alana? Alicia? Alice? Avril? April? growled in my ear like some enthusiastic porn star, then she was pounding back at me, but not in a good way, instead striking at my shoulders and slapping at my face, screaming, 'What the fuck do you think you're doing?' and 'You stupid bastard,' and 'Get the fuck off me I'm Annie from your Torts tute.'

I was out of the car, throwing up into a new gutter.

She straightened herself and said, 'What the fuck is a "stina" anyway?' and slapped at me some more.

Then Livio was there, rescuing me, laughing his head off at the same time.

Annie wobbled on her high heels like she couldn't get her balance and I fell to my knees with Liv in the way so that I couldn't even ask what had set her off. There was a big blank space in my mind as if a heavy curtain had been drawn. Next thing I knew I was in a park and the grass under my face was thick and moist, but sweet and comforting too.

Something floated in the current of the dark river and it looked like a man with one arm held out straight. I watched it disappear into the gloom.

Slowly, slowly, the quietude of this river bank quieted something in me, too.

Livio swayed and his heavy hand thumped me on the shoulder.

'Friend ... my friend ...'

There was a gurgle in his throat.

Then he croaked, 'She's never gonna forgive me.'

It took me a good ten or fifteen seconds to find a way to hold myself together, to reply without shouting, 'Forgive you for what?'

His brain had stopped fizzing, but his mouth moved as if he had a hundred things to say and no place to start.

Then he said, 'I must have hurt her so bad.'

Liv snuffled and started to cry.

'Eco, I'm sorry,' he started. Then he said Stina's name twice.

Something went so cold in me that those fat tears didn't mean a thing. The feeling inside only got worse, and if you take his stoned and stumbling and stuttering shit, and you put it all together, this is what it meant.

Part 6

I.

Eco, it was a long time ago. I was a stupid kid.

You know that.

One day I was doing something I don't remember, but it was down the local shops and I parked my Malvern Star and I bumped straight into Christina. She had a pineapple and a tin of peaches in a string shopping bag and she was eating a peach that was really juicy. You know what it was like, same as you I never saw her up close or far away or nothing for what five years, and even then she gives me this special smile. There was juice on her chin and she had her mouth wet.

Girl'd been playing sports must have been something like hockey because her hair was a ponytail and she had on running shoes and a tight top with the number six on it and a pleated skirt that was short.

She asks me Liv, how are you? and also about my language have I been able to adapt?

I told her that I was getting along a lot better these days, then she was walking home and I went with her all the way to her gate where this hundred-year-old mutt was waiting. Stina pipes up about how she's gonna see some new movie with you next

Saturday and so to that I say nothing, better to just keep quiet, I know she's your girl and all that.

She didn't ask me if I wanted to come along to the movies and then Stina told me goodbye. She went up her front steps moving so silky with her ponytail swinging.

After that I couldn't help it on account of the truth is I never forgot about her not since first day of school in this country, and sometimes when I was dreaming of doing things to girls the face they had was hers and the legs I got open were silky like Stina's too.

I apologise, I know it was a lie right in the face of you Eco because I never said nothing about it, but from then on I did my best to bump into her all I could. When it turned out I couldn't I wrote her a letter and put it into a sealed envelope and put it into her letter box when no one was home but that dog. The letter only said a few things and I know I write bad so I didn't drag it out. Just Stina, I told her, all of my life I remember how you was so good to me when I really needed some help and understanding, and I want to thank you which I can do because I used my savings and got you a gift that means a lot.

I never heard nothing back so after another week I got this locket I bought made of what the shop lady said was sterling silver on a chain of sterling silver too, and I slipped it into a little padded bag and that went into her post-box.

Well Eco I better tell you something.

Stina she came right to my house the next day. My ma opened the front door and Stina was someone she remembered of course and not favourably at all. I told Ma to go away and took Stina into the yard but Ma stood right on the landing staring at us. Stina was concerned and serious and she said in that nice voice she always had that she wanted to talk to me. I could see she wasn't comfortable about it while being stared at so heavy from the house. So she suggested maybe I could come over to her place later on when her own parents were going out, then we could talk about things?

Oh man I was so crazy-excited all day I even went got myself a haircut and a clean shirt from the laundry and locked myself in the bathroom when my ma told me I wasn't going anywhere near that girl's house. I took a scalding shower and washed my new-cut hair and when I got out I wanted to smash the mirror because that butcher the barber made my hair look stupid but at least my ma gave up her grumbling and was back to cooking.

I slipped out and it was already dark then down to Christina's I flew. She greeted me with this expression that was half nervous and half something I couldn't figure. Right at her front door I grabbed her, just grabbed her. We fell inside her empty place but with a tricky sort of twist she got me off her and said Just sit down Livio, all right, just sit down.

So we did and it was hard to make small talk but Christina gave me a lemon squash and there was some cake her mother made and we sat on the couch in front of the television which wasn't on. I wanted to kiss her straight off again and unbuttoned her blouse but she told me to stop and put her hands right against my chest so I did it, I stopped.

She explained things to me in simple terms so that I could understand and then she gave me back that locket and chain cost me so much of my savings.

Wow, okay, I said, I get it and I'm sorry. I guess I'm not Eco or anyone good enough to be your friend, that's how it is huh?

I got up out of that couch and she came too and she said, No no no that's just not true I like you I really like you a lot Liv.

Those words meant a lot and sounded so good because no one never said nothing like that to me before but then I don't know what happened. It was so fast and it was like someone else did what I done.

Somehow I managed to make the coffee table fall on its side and things crashed and also broke. I must have pushed Christina back into the couch and the dog who I never took much notice of was standing looking tense. I got on top of Stina and the dog started to bark and then it was biting the back of my leg at the ankle even while I had my pants open and was getting Stina's skirt up and my hand under it. I had to twist around and try to swat the dog away and I did I got a couple good smacks in but the dog never even whimpered.

Christina screamed at me to leave the house and so I did and the next day while I was sitting in my room feeling like the world must have cracked in two there was a visitor to our door and it was her father Mr Vågberg.

Fucking hell, even though they hated Christina for what happened in primary and even though they didn't think much of her parents, before I knew it my parents set him into a chair at the kitchen table and asked him what he wanted they couldn't imagine what. Ma even offered him coffee which he didn't want he wasn't staying long.

I told him Hey, why don't you leave now, no one here's interested in anything you got to say. Instead he spoke polite and started up with some shit about young people and their feelings and how sometimes those feelings need to be controlled or else things go crazy. I wasn't much listening but was looking at Ma who understood every word and at my pa who didn't, though he was getting the gist.

I said Look, okay great thanks, but Mr Vågberg answered me with No, my visit isn't finished yet, thank you, Livio.

My father stood up and said Get out.

Mr Vågberg spoke then with this thing that if it was a knife it would have been made of steel. He said I hope you can understand my English because I want to ask you something Mr Vida. I want you to ensure that young Livio here stays away from my daughter. Livio has your father seen where our dog bit you? Can you please show him?

I said No dog never bit me.

Well it all went to shit from there. I got beat by my father and screamed at by my mother but I got out of the house and went down to the park and tried to stop bawling. I tried to stop bawling because the truth is Eco when I told you I got a couple good smacks in at the dog it was a lie the one I hit was Stina because she wouldn't do what I told her to do to my hard thing and from that point in my life I've wanted to die a cold and absolute death and never exist no more and I still feel it now.

2.

I didn't speak, I hit him and then I kicked him.
 I hit him and kicked him hard as I could.
 I hit him and kicked him and beat him and kicked him.
 Livio cried out like I should keep on going.
 Then I got away from him and followed the riverside.
 The stars whirled and wherever I went next was really very nice because there were no bad memories and no more talking and just a long quiet river under a sky made of silver shreds.

Part 7

1.

To the hum of distant suburban trains and road traffic close by, I woke with a cramped arm and bits of grass and dirt in my mouth, product of having slept facedown. I pulled myself up from a lush stretch of damp grass along these banks and walked stiff and slow back toward the scene of the night that was, the beer garden. It was locked and desolate, of course, and the too-bright Saturday sunshine picked out a slumbering body here, an ill but half-comatose body there, and suburban streets beginning to fill with folk whose lives had nothing to do with getting trashed and legless.
 Returning to the river, there was no sign of Livio—not unless I counted the dried blood on my right hand. Two knuckles were split and hurt badly, but the amount that was dried there must have come from a gushing nose or mouth.

Not mine.

I squinted into an already warm summer's day. The shimmer and gleam that came off the otherwise muddy currents hurt like star fire. I needed water and lots of it; sunglasses would have been nice. I realised I was wandering aimlessly, no direction or plan. I'd need a bus to get home, but without money I had a long, unpleasant walk ahead.

Then I was passing the deserted beer garden again, and in the small grassed and weedy car park across the street I saw several vehicles that had been left overnight. One of them was that guy Gordon's olive-green EH Holden. I was hoping to find him sleeping off the excesses of the night in its back seat. I'd catch a ride or beg a loan.

No, he wasn't there.

The car was empty and two windows were halfway down. A crumpled, empty pack of Marlboro cigarettes and a bent pair of cheap plastic sunglasses sat on the dash. At least I could use the sunglasses.

With an emptying, dredging, heaving of guts into the weeds, I opened the driver's door and helped myself to his cracked bucket seat. Gordon's car keys dangled in the ignition. Well, well. It took me a while to make sense of that.

Hey, why not?

I kicked the engine over. Fuel tank at three-quarters full.

Then I had a thought: all I'd find at home would be my old man huffing and puffing about the way I hadn't slept in my bed. I had a car; Livio was out of my hair; William Flood had issued his invitation and Stina hadn't been able to stop herself from smiling because of it.

2.

If there was a dark poetry to the fact that I was driving long highways to Stina hungover, in a stolen car, I didn't quite see it. Instead, white lines stretched on and the roads unravelled before the bent hood of the EH, and my mind travelled just as far and wide. To things I did as a kid, to a bee-sting at a birthday party, to the answer of a test I cheated from a smarter kid in year eight. I pictured everything Livio had told me, in irrational scenes that played like a plotless movie and brought bitter tears to my eyes. My right hand stung and throbbed. I tried to understand what was in Liv's heart, how he felt inside himself, how this so-called love he said he felt for Stina made any sense to him.

To betray his best friend; to actually hit my Stina. No wonder, back in those days, he'd just about eaten himself up alive. He should have.

What's it called when you don't want your best friend to exist anymore?

Yet I felt an unwelcome wave of sympathy: it had to be awful inside those thoughts of his. Not just that, but there was the way he tried to conquer his very self by using barbells and dumbbells and skipping ropes and heavy bags, resorting to endless reps and sets of exercises that tore his body to shreds and made him reshape his body to the better image in his head.

His own vision splendid, I supposed.

Then Livio Vida was gone and I saw my ma and Mrs Vågberg, dead in their graves. Lost forever, their dreams and thoughts eradicated from this world. Why? Why did they have to be so dead? And what then of my father—my father and the lies he told, not solely to those who loved him, but to himself? What must his own life look like to him? Did he see it as a success, a struggle, an adventure of some kind? Or was it all just a grim march from moment to moment, from day to day, from exertion to pleasure to bills, to exertion to pleasure to bills, a roundabout without end?

And I thought about this William Flood too, author of some horror movie, a rising star with authority enough to bless Stina with a role that might make her name.

These meandering, aimless musings entwined, succeeding only to make my personal doubts worse. The stale alcohol in my guts, brain and bloodstream didn't help. Who am I? What good do I do? What do people see when they see me—if in fact anyone sees the real me at all? My name wasn't even my real name: 'Eco', a short, abrupt nickname for some kid who never deserved much attention.

Stina had been naked with me; the taste of her was something I'd never want to forget.

Life's too good, even when it hurts.

A tattooed Dream.

Oh man, but beside all of that I've got this stolen EH Holden, a godsend, and right ahead of me is the sun-blistered sign to the beach I need.

3.

There were small tents for people to take shelter from the baking sun; one makeshift dressing room; a covered area where coffee, tea and cold drinks were offered by a large woman in an apron smeared with a variety of sauces and chutneys.

She had platters of white-bread sandwiches containing pressed chicken and margarine. I mumbled something about being an extra and made a hog of myself, at the same time taking in the non-glamorous paraphernalia and mechanics of filmmaking. There were silver reflectors for whatever magic and shadows the crew would make of this plentiful sunshine, then there was the camera itself, a huge beast of a thing that waited silent and sphinx-like on a heavy metal tripod.

Cars, two motorcycles and a small truck were parked on the hard-packed sand behind the main filming area. The crew were in a break, though a few shirtless guys in shorts revealed their bum-cracks as they spliced connections between long cords of electrical coil.

In a patch of shade, there was Stina, wrapped in a beach towel and downing a drink.

Next to her was the director himself, thin and tan, shirtless as his workers, arms wiry and a thick mat of black chest hair already peppered with white. Snake-like hips. He must have been in the waves just now, possibly to cool off, because his curls tumbled and there were droplets of water on the thick lenses of his glasses. With his high-cut, frayed-edge denim shorts, nothing on his brown feet, he looked like a member of a soft-rock band, Boston or Styx maybe, ready to play an outdoor summer festival.

Stina saw me coming; William Flood was telling her something, then he followed her gaze.

'Hey, one of the boys, great you made it.'

'Sorry I'm late.'

Stina leaned in and gave me a friend's quick peck on the cheek.

Flood said. 'We're a little behind schedule, Livio.'

'I'm Eco. Liv couldn't make it.'

'Really? I was thinking my camera would adore those big muscles. Oh well. So it's Eco, right, got it. You haven't missed a thing ... but for God's sake,' he asked, with some humour, 'what have you been doing?'

I pulled at my soiled clothes. They carried the stench of a very bad night on the tiles. At least I'd washed the blood off me. I kept Gordon's bent sunglasses over my bloodshot eyes.

'Anyways, I was hoping for at least twenty kids to help fill out the beach. One more will certainly come in handy. Good to have such a reliable friend,' he told Stina.

She glanced at me; we were careful as spies.

Flood gazed over at the teenagers gathered around the long service table. The sandwiches had gone and the cold drinks disappeared fast. The red puffiness of their faces said they'd already been in the sun too long.

'What will you be doing?'

'See the waterline there?' Stina started to explain, but the director liked to answer for her.

'She's got three major scenes in the movie, and appears as part of the ensemble in a good fifteen others as well. Each of the big ones is pivotal, and this is the first we're shooting. We'll be popping her cherry today,' he grinned.

Stina shook her head.

'The walk-throughs have been incredible,' he continued, gazing at Stina with unrestrained admiration. 'In a few moments we'll do it for real. She'll take a long walk out of those waves down there and come across the sand, heading up this way—see? We'll keep going till we lose the light, then back first thing tomorrow to prep her biggest scene. It'll be in the big dunes over there, plus a few shots mocked up in the studio later on—if we can match this gorgeous sunshine. We've scheduled her character's death over three and a half days. It's with our marvellous monster Eli Tulloch. You might get to see him tomorrow, if you're staying. Why don't you? Anyway, Stina's got a good two and a half weeks' work down here, then she's free to resume her academic life. Until we hit the theatres, of course. From there, well, here's hoping.'

If he carried any particular burden from running this production, it certainly didn't show. Instead, William Flood appeared to be perfectly in his element.

'Hey,' I said with ridiculous brightness, giving my best acting job, 'how about we grab pizza afterwards? Once you're done for the day?'

'Great idea,' William Flood replied, 'but you go with Eco, baby. I'm busy.'

'Yes,' Stina nodded. 'All right.'

4.

The director decided he liked my scruffy clothes and appearance for the beach scene I was going to help populate—'Method actor,' he laughed—and he invited me to snack and drink all I wanted until things were ready. I had to see the costume person, Lucy, but she didn't have anything she wanted to add to me. I gathered that all I'd be doing would be lying in the sand, slowly getting up, and walking into the water fully clothed.

Meanwhile, Stina would come walking the other way and simply pass me.

An extra in the background, nothing to it.

Stina was called into the dressing tent and didn't re-emerge. William Flood got back to business. I hung around, aimless as a bird. More than an hour passed. Nothing happened. Flood conferred endlessly with his crew and there seemed to be some intense discussion or disagreement about the framing of sections of sea and sand. The other extras were young, spotty, and uninterested in me. They all knew each other so I hung back, keeping away from them. My stomach had more or less settled, though the direct sunlight seemed to concentrate the sharp pain behind my eyes. I ate more sandwiches, then found a corner of shade all to myself and curled up, drifting off.

It wasn't until mid-afternoon before an assistant rounded the extras up and took us through our series of steps.

'You'll lie right here,' the guy told me, using his foot to form an unmissable X-marks-the-spot in the hot sand. 'Pretend to be asleep. Wait to hear my voice.'

Today they weren't taking any audio, so instructions would come via megaphone. Ambient sounds of little kids calling, waves lapping, surf breaking, seagulls squawking, whatever, would all be added later. At the word, my no-good-sleeping-off-a-big-night would shake himself off and stumble down to the waterline. He'd pass Stina, but had to act as if he didn't notice her.

'Okay, friend? You can't go wrong. What's your name again?' He noted it on his clipboard. 'Again—do not look at the girl. Let her go by. And the other thing, don't actually go into the water unless you hear me tell you. Why? Because you'll dive in fully clothed. So if we need to repeat the take we can't have you all wet. Walk to the waves and if you hear me say "ENTER THE WATER", you're good, do it, have a ball. If you hear "STOP WHERE YOU ARE" then stop and don't turn around. Just look out to sea, think Zen thoughts.'

He consulted his clipboard again.

'I'm Barry. "Eco". Huh, weird.'

5.

Flood was ready and Stina emerged from that tent. She was wrapped in an even larger towel than before. Her hair was longer, straighter and blonder. They'd worked on her. She squinted into the sunlight and came down the sand.

'Hey,' I said. 'Finally.'

'Acting is waiting,' she nodded, and looked toward our auteur. He was busy with that gigantic camera and two assistants. Stina took a deep sigh, glanced at the cloudless sky, and said, 'I'm glad you're here. This is tougher than it looks.'

'But the killing part's worse?'

She nodded.

I said, 'I'm not going home till that part's done.'

I had Gordon's car. I'd use that to sleep in. Even reported stolen, who'd find me? I had no idea what I could use for money.

'It'll be good tonight,' she said. 'Just to relax.'

'Pizza?'

'Yes.'

'I got rid of Livio.'

Her glance.

I added: 'He told me.'

'Did he?'

My throat had tightened. 'Yes.'

'You never knew?' When I shook my head, Stina said, 'Please remember, it was a long time ago.'

Then the wind picked up out of nowhere, blowing sand in our faces. At the same time, William Flood was calling.

'Everyone! Places!'

Stina took a moment to look into the distance, eyes narrowed. As if to calm herself, she whistled low; it was a simple, lovely melody.

'Hey, you've got it perfect now.'

That little piece near the end of a great pop song.

She gave me a slow, slow smile.

Flood's voice was new, strong and deep. His man Barry with the clipboard gave all his extras the thumbs-up.

And it was a dream and a nightmare all at once.

The beach was sparsely populated with pretend-beachgoers, faces and shoulders already sunburned. I threw myself down onto the X-spot, stealing glances at where the crew were set up. Flood talked to Stina and helped take the big towel away. For a moment she stood there, long and creamy and completely naked. Most people stared. Well, everyone. Then she embraced her role and jogged down the sand toward her first position. I watched her flashing buttocks, the swing of her blonde hair. Her breasts bounced.

I felt a single dagger of hatred for Bill Flood.

You bastard, getting her do this.

Barry barked through his megaphone: 'Asleep, remember!'

The sand wanted to cook me alive. I pretended to sleep.

The afternoon dragged on for longer than I could have imagined, death by outdoor frypan. The megaphone voice told me to 'STOP RIGHT THERE' always at that moment before I was about to set foot in the water.

'Let's just try that again.'

Nine or ten times Stina passed me, walking beautiful and naked, at first turning shades of pink then a cruel hue of red. How was that going to look up on a big screen? Nine or ten times I had to fall back to my spot again.

'Let's just try that again.'

'GET READY,' Barry would shout, William talking into his ear.

It was a choreographed torture, meant to torment anyone who had anything to do with this stupid film.

William Flood's face seemed determinedly in control.

'Let's just try that again.'

I swore that if I heard that one more time I would get up and eviscerate him.

'Once more, friends.'

At least he started varying it.

The problem wasn't Stina but the rising wind, the sun, the extras—and me.

Each time we broke, someone was on hand to wrap Stina in the big white towel and put something over her head and face. It didn't help. She was becoming distressed. Even the tiny amount of acting it took to simply walk up the sand was becoming beyond her. She started making her own mistakes, getting her eyeline wrong, or she simply couldn't get the sort of expression into her face her director wanted. Up at the camera important and incomprehensible things were being discussed. William Flood was relentless and without mercy. The heat made me want to scream and that crystal water grew more enticing than Stina's nakedness.

After another failed attempt at whatever it was that Flood wanted to capture, he himself came down to address first the younger extras by the water, then me. All of us, at various times, were looking at the naked 'Stacey' when we oughtn't.

He crouched by me in the sand.

'A problem we're having is the eyes. Remember Barry told you not to look when Stina crosses your path, not even a glance? Maybe I should have explained. There's something serious going on with Stina's character. An important turning point is going to happen once she comes up the sand and lays down by that dune up there. Our monster is going to drag her away and kill her. Fillet her like a trout, get it? For today this little visual cue we're doing here signifies, in a small way, that she is about to become invisible. Meaning she's about to disappear from the world. Of course, it's a little joke too. An absolutely gorgeous naked girl walks along, but on a beach people don't even notice. So stop glancing at her. The camera doesn't miss that. In fact it magnifies it a hundred-fold, and so your glance becomes the focus of the scene.'

'Then why not just leave it like that?'

He kept staring, glasses shining.

'Sorry,' I said.

William Flood tried it two more times before giving up. Barry's megaphone told me to relinquish my position. Some other kid in board shorts took my spot.

So now I was behind the camera with a towel over my head and a bottle of cold lemonade. I drank it like a dying man on his last chance. Stina pulled herself together and did what she had to do, conjuring up all the 'innocent insouciance' she possessed. She had a bit of a wiggle this time, or a sexy swagger, it was hard to say what—it was just an extra something. Flood cooed like a bird. Barry called through the megaphone and the kid who'd replaced me shook a weary head, coughed nice and hoarse, scratched at his sand-filled hair and trudged toward the water like a zombie. Perfectly choreographed, angelic and sexy, Stina passed beside him then kept coming.

I looked over Flood's shoulder. In the viewfinder Stina was a vision.

The kid heard 'KEEP ON GOING' and threw himself into the waves. Stina was a naked angel approaching, filling my eyes and the eyes of anyone nearby. Then she passed out of view of the lens. I noticed she hadn't been looking into the camera, but at William Flood standing beside it. The gaze between them seemed electric. He was grinning. No—his face held a sort of beatific fulfilment. A fist formed in the pit of my belly.

What was I thinking? What was I doing here? This thing between Stina and William Flood, it was as real as real can be.

Someone ran forward and wrapped the salvation of a towel around Stina's body. She stumbled as if she might faint. Lisa the costume girl hustled her into the dressing tent. Barry said something to our director about electric fans, and a tub of cold water and ice they had ready.

'Get her into it. Don't forget the aloe vera for her skin.'

Barry ran off.

Flood and his main guys were already refocussing on the far

stretches of sand and sea. They filmed the incoming breakers until the stock in the camera was done.

Meanwhile, the sun slipped low into the yellow horizon.

6.

The ice bath was heaven. Later they lathered her in creams. Now it was eight in the evening and I perspired while she didn't, the two of us sitting in a small, crowded pizza parlour with big cold beers in front of us. This was my heaven, even if nightfall hadn't brought a great deal of relief from the heat.

I was wearing a clean shirt and a pair of black jeans kindly loaned to me by Lucy in costumes. Before meeting Stina, I'd showered under a beachside nozzle, rinsing my hair and my mouth as best I could. Pity I had no way to shave, no deodorant to use. I didn't feel anywhere near human, but being with Stina lifted my spirits, got my adrenalin going. I wanted to reach under the table and touch her legs in that loose cotton dress she was wearing. I wanted to take her to a dark corner and hold her against me, kiss her hard.

Stina's hair was pulled back in a ponytail. When she moved her head I caught glimpses of the word at the nape of her neck. People's eyes followed her. It would always be the way. She was tired; languid as a cat; still far too pink in the face and across her bare shoulders.

'It's funny,' she said, talking about the day, 'I didn't really mind doing that scene without anything on. First drafts William showed me, Stacey was in a polka-dot bikini. Then the character evolved. Or devolved,' she smiled, though I might have detected an edge of cynicism. 'Anyway, it wasn't me naked, it was sweet Stacey-Lee.'

'So next this monster's going to hurt her.'

'That's the kindest way to describe what he'll do.'

'Did a mad scientist create him?'

'Nope,' she shook her head, 'there's a mythology, but I don't quite get it. Far as I need to know, "Jebediah Vale" has an insane hatred of women, end of story. Mother issues, I suppose.'

'Huh.' I thought it over. 'People love movies about madmen who hate women.'

'And in books too,' Stina said. Then, after a slow drink: 'That bothers you, right?'

'I don't know.'

'You know, all right.'

When I shrugged it was as if she saw something extra.

'And you hate what William's doing.'

'Do I?'

'Tell me.'

'I wouldn't have stuck you nude on a beach for everyone to stare at.'

'It's the movies.'

'Is that what you really think?'

She gave me her crooked smile. There was something to it that wasn't quite right. A forced quality that I wasn't used to in her.

'Okay ... do you really want to know what I think, Eco?'

'Yes.'

'I couldn't understand it before. When we were kids, I mean.' She gazed at me, exhausted yet serious. 'Some men love and adore women, but they're scared of them too. Or somehow, deep down, they resent how women make them feel. Maybe they make them too vulnerable, too naked. Or they resent the things they have to do before women will do what they want. I don't know, but maybe that can't help coming out in different ways. It's just how people are wired. William, I'm not so sure what goes on in his head. To write something like this movie then put me into such a role ... But you, I've always known you genuinely love women. That's the feeling I get whenever I'm around you. You're sort of gentle, and you want to see inside their minds or something. Maybe into their hearts.'

She shook her head then, half-laughed at herself, and rubbed one eye.

'When I say "their" I mean "my". You know that.'

She sat straighter, pulling herself together.

'Jesus, I must be tired, talking like this ... but I mean it, Eco. Bill's created this thing full of blood and dead girls. Does it mean anything? Who can say. But you, you're different. When you get older, you're going to be fucking amazing.'

She realised it as soon as she said it, the backhand that went with the compliment. So I was still a boy and not quite amazing enough? Thirty-four–year-old William Flood, well, he must be a champ.

'I'm sorry, I didn't mean it like that.'

I shook my head. Nothing was going to upset me, not when I had her with me tonight.

'Tell me about this fruitcake Jebediah, then.'

'You've heard it, Eco. He comes out of nowhere and drags Stacey behind a dune. He eviscerates her. Cuts her open and pulls her insides out. It'll be very graphic. And, well, there's one other thing.'

'God, what?'

'Well, the fact of the matter is, Jebediah's a sexual monster. He rapes the dying girl before he does the rest.'

'That's so disgusting.'

'In her wounds.'

It took a minute to make sense. Then: 'You must be joking.'

'William says he's referencing this Warhol film, the Frankenstein one? I haven't seen it.'

'Flesh for Frankenstein. I know it.'

'He's not about reinventing the wheel if he doesn't have to,' Stina sighed. 'Who knows what'll make it onto the screen anyway.'

'You should be treated better.'

'If a horror movie treated me better, would audiences thank the director?'

There wasn't much answer to that.

'I'll be wearing a loose summer beach thing I'll have slipped on after my little Aphrodite walk. I won't have to be naked again, that's the best part. There's an intense lovemaking scene to shoot in a couple of days, it'll come right at the start of the movie. William says he won't have me revealing too much. He wants that saved for the beach walk and murder, which comes about halfway through. His idea is the audience cops a naked eyeful of this character they've already fallen in love with, then boom, she's ripped apart in glorious Technicolor.'

'Well ... it's not much like the old scary movies, huh?'

'Innocent days.' She sipped her beer, then slipped a hand straight into my heart. 'Karloff as Frankenstein, Chancy as The Wolf Man, Lugosi as Dracula, and your favourite, Claude Rains as The Invisible Man.'

I just couldn't say anything, hearing my own words echoing back to me across so many years, but in Stina's voice. How had she remembered that so well?

Stina took a longer pull at her beer, brightening a moment.

'Anyway, after today there's no more actual nudity. I can afford to cut loose. William says I can eat what I want. After we're finished this movie I swear I'll get fat as a pig. I don't care anymore. All this exercise and special dieting so Stacey looks fantastic, it takes it out of you. You start to obsess about food and more food, not on controlling calories. I've been fantasising about bacon and egg burgers, and I don't even like them.'

A waiter stopped by the table.

'Okay,' she said. 'Io voglio un Quattro Stagioni, poi, per desserto, tiramisu.'

'Subito, signorina,' the guy grinned. 'What about you?'

'Same. And get us a couple more beers, okay?'

As he went away Stina said, 'What about that accent?'

'Not bad at all.'

'I've been studying Italian with tapes. Never know when Cinecittà might call.'

'We need a new Anita Ekberg.'

'I'd need bigger boobs. And hips. But I'm learning the language because sometimes I'm too nostalgic about the old days. Our suburb and all the migrant kids and the families like mine and yours. I should think more fondly of my neighbourhood back in Stockholm, but somehow that just doesn't work. For me it's the Brisbane River and the broken-down powerhouse on the banks.'

'The rose gardens.'

'The river and old wooden ferries.'

'Your deciduous trees. Even that stupid school where I met you.'

'Yes.'

'Still, I do my best not to look backwards, at least not very much. But when I do I kind of see you, Eco. I don't know what you think about that.'

'Then why not just come back all the way?'

'And do what?'

It was written in my face, wasn't it? Stina cast her eyes down. Just be with me.

7.

'Hey, there's this trick we've been practicing for tomorrow's slaughter.'

'What is it?'

'The lead stuntman's been drumming the steps into us, it's pure choreography. Eli, or should I say "Jebediah", will have my hair wrapped tight in his hands. Like this, see? It'll look as if he's really dragging me backwards. My own hands will be up, holding him hard by one wrist. That's the key. It's the only thing that'll keep the pressure off my scalp and stop me getting hurt. If I slip or if I fight too convincingly, or if things just go wrong, I'll lose my grip. If I lose my grip, in the split-second before Eli can let go I'll have my hair torn out. That could mean a good piece of scalp too. Riiip. Deep down I know I'll be fine, but it's going to be intense. Remember I told you William wants me to fight like mad, go crazy, the way you'd do in real life? This isn't a love story. It's not like what you said, they're not going to let Stacey get treated better. She's too sexy and too wonderful and so she gets it worse than anyone in the movie.'

'Retribution for being beautiful.'

'You said it.'

And she flicked the plastic menu as if the waiter hadn't come for our order.

'You know what, Eco? William wrote this thing. He's either a genius or just—'

'What?'

'Hateful.'

The word sat there.

'Wait a minute,' I said. 'You're not so happy about this.'

'Well. Maybe. The truth is, at first I said no. And I meant it.'

'Really?'

'I told him I didn't think I could make anything of a role like this. William said, "Are you an actress—or a mouse?" He got that from what Billy Wilder said to Barbara Stanwyck when she didn't want to play the murderous, manipulating wife in Double Indemnity.'

'Then why did you change your mind?'

'How many chances do you get to work, especially in Australia? What did I train and do classes for? But to me this isn't a movie. It's William's worst fantasy, an exercise in how much men can detest women. So what good does it do?'

She didn't have her accent any more, the one from when she'd been a kid, but for a moment I saw Stina in her plaits, blue eyes shining, a little soft around the middle but her face hard and earnest as she'd put that exact question to our terrifying nuns of Grade Five.

'It's just a horror movie,' I heard myself say, defending William Flood when I didn't want to. 'Cheap thrills to suck audiences in. No need to make too much of it.'

Which was funny, really. I resented William Flood more for exposing Stina's body to all and sundry, than to tearing it to shreds.

'You're right, Eco. I can't ruin his moment, anyway. Or mine.' She stopped, then added, not without at least a touch of humour, 'I'm just wondering where all my wonderful acting training has gone.'

We sat there like that.

'Jesus Christ, but right now I don't know what I'm feeling at all.'

And our waiter arrived with two more beers.

8.

Stina wiped her wet mouth, carefully placing her drink back onto the table. It was only her second, but for what was supposedly an Italian place these things came in big, heavy German steins. The day, the beer, the conversation itself: her eyes were becoming glassy and she seemed to wind down, like a clock forgetting how to share the hours and the minutes of a day.

There was very little air-flow inside this place, even with the windows and doors flung wide. A ceiling fan turned directly above us, achieving nothing. The heat of other people's bodies only added to the sense of stupefaction. The beers were served ice cold and every table had its share.

'I don't think I've ever complained so much ... after this pizza comes, if it ever does, I'll have to go. What time is it? William said they'll be done by, oh, God I don't know. Midnight probably. Who even cares?'

If there'd been a Pacino, Connery, Nicholson or De Niro with her, I knew how they might have made her stay. I gave it my best, raising her hand to my lips. Stina tensed.

'I complain ... but I'm with William. You understand that, don't you?'

'Right now you're with me.'

'Where's this pizza?'

What made her mood sink so? Exhaustion? A summer's ability to suck the living juice out of you? Or the prospect of six-foot-six Jebediah Vale dragging her backwards across sand dunes by the hair? Her skin remained pink and bright. Her eyes, almost sunken into darkness. I'd never seen her this way. Stina regarded me with a vague expression of having more to say. As if, now she'd started, the rest needed to come out. Instead of letting it, she was indulging in that beer, big sip by big sip.

'And I want another one, even if it makes me sick.'

Our waiter was just this guy in board shorts and a t-shirt, sandals on his feet. I caught his attention and signalled for two more.

'I should probably mention I don't have a cent to my name.'

That made her laugh, but with a sort of weary resignation.

'William, William, William,' she shook her head, 'lord and master. He gave me plenty of money for tonight ...' Then she stared past my shoulder, at something behind me, maybe outside. A shadow crossed her face.

'What's up?' I asked, turning at the same time, but there was nothing out of the ordinary.

'I thought it was ... no, I was just thinking.' She pressed her eyes, brows furrowed. 'So, look, this thing about Livio, what he told you. Things are still okay with the two of you, aren't they?'

It was what I didn't want to talk about. I shook my head. Things weren't okay. They would stay that way.

'Eco, I never wanted trouble between friends.' That frown deepened. 'He's like a brother to you.'

'I don't know. And it's not your fault.'

'Maybe it is. I just can't tell anymore.'

'You should have told me he was bothering you. Why didn't you say something?'

'Teenagers, young men, old, they convince themselves of impossible things. That's what he did. Women are the same. They let themselves get carried away. Then the thing turns around completely.'

'I don't get it.'

'What I mean is, no one's heart gets broken more than anyone else's. It's the way we all are. Women and men ought to live on separate islands or something, just meet in the middle every now and then for a few days' fun, then go back home again.'

'What?' I half-laughed.

'Forget it. Livio just got things mixed up.'

'But he hit you. Liv admitted it.'

She reached over and grasped my right hand, holding it hard, turning it in hers, making me wince.

'What about this?' She took the left as well, showing me my own split knuckles and bruising. 'You think I'm blind?'

I pulled my hands away and hid them under the table.

'Oh to hell with it,' she said.

'No, tell me, how bad did he hurt you, Stina?'

'It wasn't anything.'

'Don't you ever say that.'

And I felt a flash of anger bright as a sun, and Stina's eyes stayed on me.

Then she finished her stein.

It was better to choke these feelings off. Stina was upset enough. My black, tortured knuckles gave me away. Maybe she'd decided I was the same as everyone else. Here she'd been, talking about William Flood's gory little movie, yet his violence was imagined whereas mine was real. It had come over me blindly, force of a tsunami. I'd kicked and beaten Livio without a moment's pity—and now, for the first time, I felt sick about what I'd done. About what I'd done, and the way Livio had absorbed it, as if he'd wanted more and more.

This had to be part of the change in her mood, but there was something else, I could just feel it, and our little dinner of beer and pizza wasn't going anything the way I'd hoped. Nothing was. Not since the moment she'd left the Park View Hotel: not since finding William Flood beside her at that last Friday class; and definitely not after last night's long spiral into Livio's story.

Stina kept looking straight at me. 'Let me see your hands again.'

Hesitating at first, I slowly lay them flat on the table, ugly and sore.

'Listen to me, Eco. The thing is, I don't have any right to get angry at you.'

'It's all right.'

'I have thoughts that aren't pretty, too.'

'Everyone does.'

'I sucked him off, did he tell you that? Right there on my couch. Poor Gudrun watching. Livio was so intense I was scared of what he might do. This voice in my head kept saying, "Make him get out of this house. Pick up a knife. Stab him to death. Break a vase over his head just like in a thriller. Do anything. Just make him go away." But in the moment—he kept pushing himself at me. I couldn't do anything. He wouldn't give up. As if he had to dominate me and once he did he'd have what he wanted. He even got my wrists together like this, in one hand, and he's so strong I couldn't break loose.'

'Jesus.'

'So I did it. I gave in.'

'Stina, please—'

'Disgusted?' She kept her breathing even.

'No.' I shook my head. 'Only in him.'

'Think again. All of it was revolting. I hated myself. Hated myself for being so powerless, then even more for being so scared. All because this stupid boy said he was mad for me. And when he came I held it in my mouth, and he looked so satisfied and superior and happy I spat it at him. Every drop. I spat it all in his face and then I hit him and tried to scratch his eyes. He went wild. Of course. Is that the way he told it to you?'

The smudges under Stina's eyes, the wisps of blonde hair falling across her forehead, the glaze of resentment in her gaze. My Stina, and look what's happened to her. Look at the way she's thinking.

It was what she'd been talking about all along: men with women, women with men, and the things they do to each other. The good and bad we make. The weariness in her face, and the sadness, and, yes, even the anger, said she knew clearly how love could mix with hate, and tenderness with rage, and how mad love can be one breath from violence too. There was the physical type and the emotional type. The former from Livio, yes, definitely; maybe the latter from our genius, Bill Flood. And something told me it had come from another place as well, meaning her father. With his indifference and cool distance, so little to feed a daughter.

Then what about me? Forget my hands, forget last night. Couldn't Stina see she'd never have a moment of any of these bad things from a boy who'd adored her since day one, Grade Five, those nuns tripping and spinning in the greatest reprisal a small girl ever devised?

I couldn't speak. I just kept taking Stina in, then the fact of those nuns struck me too, their complicity in this, how they'd left their mark on all of us, professing such devotion to the innocents in their care while at the same time using cruelty and intimidation to bend them to their adult will.

Add it all together and what did it mean, really—that none of us is capable of loving at all? Stina wanted the opposite of this, she yearned for it. She dreamed of living in a gentler world when that was just about the one thing you couldn't ask for.

'Whatever happened, Stina, just remember that it's over. I'm glad you told me. It's okay. All of it is. And none of it matters any more. Let go now. Just like that. Let go.'

I started to draw my hands away, to hide them again, but she reached out and held them where they were.

'Let me keep looking.'

'Why?'

'They're strong.'

'Maybe you're stronger.'

'Really? Black Beach Killer. I want to fight the monster and save Stacey. I want to stop the terrible thing happening to her. And I wouldn't mind breaking William's head for dreaming it all up.'

'Then do things this way,' I said, smiling at her, though I was serious too. 'Let William work out his fantasies on someone else. It is just a movie. A load of stupid fun. There'll be a line of actors happy to take your place. Leave it to them and come with me. We can go right now.'

She tried to reflect my smile, but wasn't quite getting there.

'It's not so easy.'

'Who says?'

'I'm going to make you hate me, Eco.'

'You can't.'

'I want you to understand how we got here.'

'I understand enough. I've got a car. We can go park somewhere dark. Then there's something I'll get you to understand.'

She straightened her back, look a deep breath as if she liked the idea, the picture of it, the possibilities and promise of a nice, spacious back seat. Then a sigh, just a soft breath, releasing itself from her lips and creating two words.

'Your father.'

I stared at her. She stared back.

'Stop,' I said. 'Don't talk.'

'He came to the house when he was so angry about the way you were expelled. My mother was alone that day. Take away the hurt and the anger, and they must have found something in each other. That's how it started.'

'No.'

'Afternoons he finished work early.'

I shook my head.

'Sometimes he came to the house before I was home from school.'

Yet I remembered a day in particular, when he'd been waiting for me at the old wooden pier by the river, and the way I'd been confused that he'd finished work by mid-afternoon. Most times I'd had to labour with him we'd gone on right until nightfall, but, of course, on his own he could work whatever hours he liked.

And did.

Languid Brisbane afternoons; that blazing summer sun and a shaded bedroom; one lonely woman with a husband who encouraged her to find comfort with anyone other than himself.

'When he had enough, it wasn't nice. She wanted to hold on. He ... he told my mother what he thought of her. He made his opinion very clear. Then there she was, worse than before, a piece of garbage.'

'Stina,' I said, though I didn't want to hear it. 'What did you do?'

'If you let people get away with things, with the bad they do, it eats you alive. So I left my mother weeping on her bed and I found him. See your hands? If I'd had those, I would have used them. Instead I told him what I knew. About his mask, I mean. I told him I saw through his facade. I told him people saw him for what he really was. While he was strutting around, people were whispering. About him and your mother. What sort of a woman can't keep her man satisfied? Horrible gossip. What sort of a wife turns a blind eye? It eats you to do that. Eco, it ate her alive. And you know that.'

'No, Stina.'

'He tried to stand over me. He tried to dominate me. When he couldn't he changed to being sorry. Of course. Just like Liv. Then he cried and it didn't make me pity him. Especially when he begged me to never tell you. To never tell your mother. And I said to him, "You're such a stupid man, you think your wife doesn't know?" and maybe it actually hit him. Until that moment, maybe he'd actually believed he was smarter than the whole world.'

I closed my eyes.

'And you, Eco, you. In the middle of all this you were always looking after me, and it felt so wrong to take your kindness anymore. I thought one day I'd grow up to be just as stupid and treacherous and self-justifying as everyone else, so I decided I had to get away or go mad. William from my classes, that very kind and polite tutor, so intense about this film world he loved so much ...'

The words died in her throat, and I realised she'd stopped

because she was looking over my shoulder, and that shadow came into her face again.

I twisted around, nothing was there, just strangers wandering by, but I had a crazy feeling it was my father, or hers, or the ghost of anyone who'd ever let her down, come to stand by those sea-salt–stained front windows to see what they'd made of this girl.

I turned back to Stina and she had nothing left to say, but the things she'd already said, they made me feel I'd been kicked in the belly.

So I breathed with great care, and tried not to think about what had happened, about what it must have been like for Stina, or for her mother Klara, who used to sing in little cafés and cherished her old long players of torch music and broken hearts. I tried not to see my father and his swagger, or the way my mother must have looked at him, believing yet not believing in him. Maybe I could have worked it out for myself, if I hadn't been so stupid, so lovestruck. Why hadn't I ever wondered about the way Mrs Vågberg gazed so enquiringly at me, through that haze of cigarette smoke and vermouth she lived in? Why hadn't I asked myself about her particular smile—especially when I had my own mother living with her own melancholy, sitting alone, sometimes taking to that empty room of dust motes travelling down through the air, her long hands picking out soft melodies on a half-tuned piano.

I tried not to think about any of these things, but I saw each of them again, sharp and distinct, all the way back to the first day I'd gone to Stina's house and her mother had contemplated me with that strange sense of curiosity, even of affection.

Vell, the boy—the boy of the man.

Stina hadn't liked her asking after my family. I'd taken that to be about the bad blood left over from primary school, but no, Stina knew he'd been there, that my pa had made himself at home in that place long before me. He probably knew the layout and felt more comfortable in the Vågberg house than I did. And what about those nights he stalked out of our home for card games with friends who didn't exist, sometimes did he go straight there, if Stina was out, if Mr Vågberg was off travelling again?

I'd never know. I wasn't going to ask. I wouldn't travel backwards. Somehow I was past caring. My mother had cared, and look where she was. Mrs Vågberg had eaten herself up and she was gone too. And Stina was here now, chewing her bottom lip, drinking so much beer, all because she'd needed to get this all out or die.

It didn't matter; sooner or later a son will learn his father is fallible and worse; lives in close little suburbs run on far better and far poorer matters. Only problem is, others are involved.

'How is your family?' Mrs Vågberg asks, and Stina shoots her a look.

Forget any of this. If I look toward something new, now and into the future, we can be new too, just Stina and me.

'Like I said, we can go right now. We'll drive and keep driving. Take it from the beginning. We'll live our own way. No one will ever tell us to do anything different. All right?'

She was too tired and too burned out and everything about her seemed to fall inward. Her hands shook almost imperceptibly. She tried to look up, half did, then reached for my face. Her fingers came away wet, and I didn't even know I was crying.

'I've become exactly what I hated. How does life trick you so easily? I went to that hotel to meet you with my eyes open. I dressed for you. Took a lot of care. I knew what would happen and I wanted it. Then when I was home I gave William the night of his life, to make amends, to make him mine again, to say sorry, but only inside my head, and to make myself feel better.'

'It doesn't matter.'

People at other tables were staring now; some kindly do-gooder actually decided to approach us, the crow's feet around her eyes saying that she would rescue this wretched girl from the silly boy who must be hurting her so.

What might I tell this intruder—Leave her be, this kid's vulnerability is a curse? She's open to the world and she's open to me, but none of it's brought her anywhere close to the love she wants?

The woman leaned in. 'Let me help you, dear.'

I wanted to push her away with my palm in her face.

Stina said, as if we were still alone, 'You're my best friend, Eco.'

Friend is not enough, friend is nothing. You can give me the night of my life. You can give me the life of my life.

I reached for her hands. She wouldn't let me take them.

Stina grabbed a napkin, held it to her eyes, then, in disgust, flung it down. By now the two of us were a hot and crowded beachside pizzeria's perfect centre of attention.

Before I could reach her, Stina's chair went backwards, she shoved past the woman, and she was running out.

Part Eight

I.

William Flood and me, we didn't need to keep in touch, though from time to time we did, now that we shared some history, no matter how unwillingly. The seventies and eighties, the early nineties, all an era before email and social media, before such strange new days of needing to update everyone you supposedly know and love with your latest shirt, watch or harebrained thought that just crossed your mind. In the long-gone past you either visited someone, rang them on their telephone, or wrote them a letter. If you weren't prepared to do any of these things, contact was over.

So we exchanged a Christmas card every now and then, sometimes a short note—me, perhaps, to write about one of his new movies I'd seen, Flood to return a word of thanks and ask how I was. Nothing much else, but it was a definite exercise in not letting go. His career was easy enough to follow, anyway. There was always a story to pop up somewhere, even if it was only once or twice a year, a few lines in the back of some entertainment rag or trashy magazine.

After Black Beach Killer he didn't make any other ghoulish slasher movies, nothing like it at all. William Flood had either been cured of his interest in viscera and human horror, or it'd never been real in the first place. The ready-made sequel implicit in the silly, open-ended closing moments of his first feature never eventuated; I believe he kept the rights to himself and wanted the thing to stay what it was, to become nothing more. Funny thing though: Black Beach Killer made money and acquired a reputation, especially with the advent of VCRs, then DVDs, then streaming movies. Still, he never followed that path so readily set before him—at least not until nearly four decades later, when he was into his seventies, and decided he wanted one last shot at a real career, and, perhaps, a chance to create something like the 'Christina Vågberg' that might have been.

2.

It was back in my early thirties that I had my strongest moment of reconnection with the man. This was a period when, not having found any opportunities in Hollywood, Europe or Asia, he remained in his home country making soulful, low-budget movies that worked, or didn't, on the intimate scale. Of course, this meant he'd gradually faded into insignificance, and was funding his work from credit cards and oddjobs, and sometimes not at all.

At that time, for me, life had mercifully picked up. I hadn't been able to forgive my father and never slept another night in our old home. He followed his direction and years accumulated with no contact between us. I felt it better that way. Instead I concentrated on whatever it was that I could make for myself, and somehow I found I could love the new avenue I drifted toward, which was school teaching. Hardly earth-shattering, but good enough.

I even managed to meet a woman I kept thinking of whenever I was away from her. She was slightly older, and happened to carry the unfortunate name of 'Tina'. I might have called her by some affectionate use of a middle name, but she didn't have one. She was simply Tina.

This spoiled many an early date, my mind always wandering toward the irony of having something of a 'Stina' in my life once again—yet without the S for sexy, or for sensual, or even for Swedish. But I got over that. Tina revealed her own strengths, which I quickly learned were an ability to be tough-minded when needed, to be practical when I was the opposite, and to treat me with kindness when my shoulders slumped to the weight of the everyday.

She's a natural brunette, short, quite bookish. At a beach she will wear large hats and sun-safe clothes.

A little after we'd decided to marry, we visited her extended family in Sydney. A day came when I found myself alone; an outing to Luna Park and the big zoo simply didn't interest me. Her extended clan of Norwegians mixed with Scots loved just these sorts of outings; I wouldn't be missed.

So I stayed back and found myself looking through a telephone directory. Of course, I was searching for a familiar name.

'Jesus, man, I'm two suburbs away. Climb in a cab.'

3.

He still had his hair though the curls were thinning, and he'd developed the sunburned, wiry frame of a long-distance bike rider. Not quite fifty years of age, I would have guessed his body fat at only three or four percent. He was affable and kindly; time had taken its toll on his lined face, as had three divorces and four children, each of which lived with their mothers and new fathers. His home was a small but neat flat where he made me a macrobiotic meal that featured mung beans, homegrown peas and organic brown rice. We drank an organic red wine that tasted a little too much of the dirt the grapes had been cultivated in. And we talked: that small bit of old times we'd shared, what we were doing now and might yet do in the future.

Of course, as it had to sooner or later, the conversation turned to Christina Vågberg.

'Do you want to see her?' he asked, eyes small and sharp behind his thick lenses.

He had something they'd done a long time back, he told me, with an old camera borrowed from the ABC. Filmed it in the kitchen of the flat they'd been living in. More recently, he'd dug the old film out and had it transferred to VHS; if I wanted, he could have the video-cassette in the player, we could watch it on his television.

'No,' I told him, heart pressing to my ribs.

But it was Yes. Yes to seven new minutes of Stina.

4.

What was that you said?

The voice belongs to a much younger William Flood. He's invisible behind the camera. The image is only of Stina's face. No black and white for this memory. She's in glorious colour and this film's done straight and plain. The picture isn't perfect and shows signs of the aging stock it was transferred from.

Huh? she replies. The girl looks a little sleepy and ruffled, but there's a hint of humour in her young features. A lightness. It looks like a morning and Stina has woken up happy.

I asked you what you just said. I was getting the camera ready, didn't quite hear you, baby.

Oh okay ... you asked me what my life's motto would be if I had one, which I don't, so I told you my father's.

She lifts a corner of toast to her mouth and takes a small bite, wiping crumbs off her chin. Looks like some sort of healthy grain bread with strawberry jam and cheese. Not only is her face extraordinary, but so is the sound of her voice. She's maintained just a hint and a touch of her Swedish accent. Funny how in primary school it had seemed so pronounced, yet in later years I'd barely noticed it at all.

Let's have it again, young William says.

Next she raises a cup to her mouth. Steam rises. Tea or coffee in a plain porcelain mug.

'This is the one and only life,' she quotes.

That's not a motto, it's a statement of fact. Or of belief, depending on your anti-religious views.

Stina smirks.

It can be a motto, Bill. Because everything you do has to come back to that one idea. You can't live like you're going to get another chance, right?

Hey, yeah, don't worry. I agree with that!

But, Stina frowns a little, why do you? I thought you believed in heaven and hell and all of Christianity.

Of course. I still do believe in God ... 'I believe in God and Mercy and all that ...'

Hang on, hang on, hang on. No paraphrasing. That's from The Third Man, you can't go all Harry Lime on me. It's what he says when he's up in the Ferris wheel cabin with Holly Martins. The next bit is about the dead or something.

'The dead are happier dead. They don't miss much here, poor devils.'

That's it. God, I love Orson Welles.

Me too ... but all the same, I do believe in God and the saints and so on. We all agree you only get one go-round on this crazy Ferris wheel of a planet. We're not Buddhists. What's next happens up there.

So for you there really is a 'next'?

Yep, enthusiastic William Flood replies.

Well, that's what I'm not so sure about.

Really?

I think this is it, actually ... at least for the psyches we have. I mean for our own individuality. That's what disappears forever, even if there is an 'up there'—get what I mean? So in that sense this life here on earth is definitely all there is. I don't much care about the rest.

Wow, such a nihilist in my house. Then what exactly do you wish you could hang onto?

Stina gazes ahead. She must be gazing at what she can see of her boyfriend as he films her. This would have been done sometime in her first year of university, maybe when they were living in Sydney and she'd appeared in that kid's show. A good year before she'd met me again; before Black Beach Killer was a go.

I watch the way she's thinking. God, how I remember that look.

After a moment she speaks again, to answer his direct question.

I don't know for sure what I want to hang onto, but I always get the feeling somehow everything will go away. But when you make love to me, Bill ... when you fuck me it's like even you think it's going to be the last time, forever.

No, that's the way you do it.

There's a momentary pause, then they laugh together in this young passion they're living night and day.

5.

Okay, let's try a different tack. If we were ever going to make a film together, what would it be about?

Oh, I wouldn't know that, you're the artist, right?

Just some ideas. What occupies your mind, Stina?

I really can't answer that.

Well—have you read any books that'd make a good movie?

Everything, she laughs. Just everything. Wait a minute ... let me think. Jesus, it's too early for these kinds of questions!

Come on, first one?...

The Invisible Man, then.

Done to death. Why?

Stina laughs. That wonderful line in the book: 'Drawbacks I saw none.' I love the idea of leaping into something so strange and amazing it seems like everything about it will be wonderful …

… before it turns to shit?

Well, she says, still enjoying herself, I guess that can be the way of the world.

Give me another one. The Invisible Man's for hacks.

Let me think. Could you turn that off till I'm ready?

Back so long ago, William Flood won't. It's unclear whether Stina realizes the camera is still going, because she carefully finishes a triangle of toast, actually slurps the last from her mug, and looks down at her hands. More than likely she must know it's running, surely there'd be the whirring of the camera's mechanics, but she seems to have switched off; she's not making any sort of performance at all. It strikes me that the expression in her face is far more naked than anything she will do with her body on that beach.

The lens remains focused on Stina and my heart has to break all over again, not just for seeing her like this, but for the small fact that a simple quote from a book by HG Wells was still in her mind.

She didn't forget her friend Eco; I think, somehow, I stayed with her.

6.

Okay, I'm not sure about a good book or idea, she says, but whatever we'd do together, it should be to add just one more piece of beauty to the world.

Wow, from nihilism to idealism in a single bound.

But not impossible. After you're finished with this monster–killer–slasher–horror thing, whatever it is you're cooking up, when you're a famous movie director and all, promise me that's what you'll do?

Add some beauty to the world.

She nods.

Sort of avoid eviscerations and bucket loads of blood.

I read something once, it was from Chekov—

Ah, excellent.

He wrote that the world and everything in it is beautiful, but the things that aren't come from our own thoughts and our own actions, when we forget the higher aims of our existence, and lose our dignity as human beings.

Whew. And so that's what you're saying.

I think so.

I get it, William Flood says a little less jokingly.

Do you?

Yes ... so listen, Stina. This movie I've been talking about, I'm approaching it as a calling card. That's all it is. People love horror and I want to get a lot of backsides into seats. You can't make a career in film without big money behind you, so this is going to be my way of getting noticed, of getting kick-started. But the real stuff I want to do, it's a million miles away from beach killers and teenage beach plots, believe me. And, you know what? It's not what I'll do next, it's what we'll do. What we'll do together, you and me. Understand?

Stina's face lights up, her eyes. She's so ... open.

Tell you one more thing.

What? she asks.

You're the piece of beauty we'll add to this world.

Here Stina is, immaculate and young, loved and loving.

7.

The camera pulls back as seconds tick down.

The wider shot reveals the kitchen Stina's sitting in. There's an old-fashioned gas stove behind her, kitchen utensils, a copper kettle and a coffee pot on a burner, a very low blue flame wafting. Not an expensive place by any means, just an old wooden flat in a far older world.

She turns her face, silken hair in plaits. Just a hint of that Dream tattoo at the back of her neck. She always liked plaits, could make them in five seconds, dexterous twists of her wrists and hands, done.

I see cheap, frayed yellow window curtains behind her. They're drawn shut, probably to keep direct sunlight out of the camera lens. Also to soften the scene. So she sits quietly thinking in the gauzy light of what I'm now certain is 1977, and probably very early in that year too, seeing Black Beach Killer seems so embryonic.

That was the year of pimples on my nose and Like a Hurricane. The year of my ankles always showing at the bottom of long trousers, and Aja by Steely Dan, but of Never Mind the Bollocks, Here's the Sex Pistols, too. Of movies like Star Wars, Annie Hall and Saturday Night Fever, plus Suspiria, Eraserhead and the very first in the 21 Up series. Anaïs Nin's erotica was published posthumously in Delta of Venus, and Stephen King had The Shining. Then there was The Thorn Birds, Falconer, Aunt Julia and the Scriptwriter, Love is a Dog From Hell ... I read them all that year, many I remember better than what I read last week.

An unforgettable time, at least for someone like me, and that's where William Flood's managed to keep her.

Quick, quick, film's going. Don't hesitate, just tell me—what do you like, Stina?

I beg your pardon?

What sorts of things do you like? Generally speaking.

That's a question! Everything. Books and movies and dancing. Lots of different types of music. And acting, of course. I love just the, just the physicality of living.

Physicality?

You know I swim and ride my bicycle and run. Yoga one day soon, you'll see. Also ... also ... uhm, more importantly ...

Yes?

Well ... I like making love. There, I said it. The intensity of literally having another person inside me. Of having you inside me, Bill.

She pauses.

And then I want to go into the world as far as I can, Stina says. See everything. Travel under every star.

Each and every one?

Yep, without exception. God, it's such a cheat, isn't it? Such a cheat that one day we have to—

8.

It cut off, but that night I visited William Flood he could still recall the word his camera failed to capture, the only word that made sense.

His TV screen was black now, and Stina was gone.

Part Nine

Then it was a long blur of motion.

I was on my feet too, but this guy who looked like he might have been the owner himself proudly brought over two large steaming Quattro Stagioni pizzas and set them down. I told him something I don't remember, like Go away, or We can't take them now, and he said, What? Okay, sure, but pay the bill, that's still two pizzas and, look, six beers, and he was not to be argued with.

So I had to watch a fleeting silhouette of Stina rush off outside while I fumbled for money that wasn't there.

Oh yeah, Stina was going to pay, courtesy of the auteur. Jesus, by the look in his face I could see this owner-guy was no fool, he'd probably seen a thousand stupid kids doing a thousand stupid things in his place, so I gave up and tried to heave him out of the way, and while he was solid as a rock and getting mad, out of nowhere Livio Vida was intervening, and I had no idea where he'd come from. He had bruised cheeks and a black eye and a lip just about three times its normal size, but also a twenty and a five dollar note in his hand. He gave them to the owner saying he was paying for his friends. I didn't have time to ask what he thought he was doing here because Stina was well out of sight, man, she was gone.

I pushed out of that place and ran into the street looking up and down.

Actually believed I'd lost her, which would have been typical of my luck, but even in teeming crowds you don't miss someone like Stina. There, the blonde hair in plaits. The loosely swaying white summer dress.

I caught up to her right in the hot central Surfers Paradise strip that the main highway still runs through to this day. We were surrounded. Tonight lots of people were outdoors, trying to stay cool, looking for some kind of evening breeze, still wearing summery beach clothes, fanning themselves on account of the muggy heat.

I managed to say Hey Stina, and it came out in this gentle voice I didn't even know I could have, and she stopped and turned. At first she looked tortured and confused, but I said Hey Stina a second time and she just stood there and said Oh God Eco.

Yes, this was how we'd always be, just sort of getting the best out of each other even when we were feeling our worst.

Stina's thoughts seemed to clear and she grabbed my arm hard and before I knew it she had me up against a wall in a corner between two arcades. It was quieter here than anywhere else. She pressed her long body to mine and her tongue was in my mouth and I felt her shudder all the way through, top to bottom, head to feet, one great tremble of I don't know what. I took her face in my hands and kept kissing her, sort of bending her too, arching her, making her breathless, me tasting her mouth and her tongue, and it was nothing at all like kissing her at the Park View. This was as raw as food and wine and life and death all put together.

Then Livio was there again.

She let out a curse, we broke away from each other, and Stina glanced at him and she said Eco one last time and then she was off.

Stina, I called.

She stepped away from the edge of the footpath, moving past a group of people who were standing there waiting, and that was because she went to take a crossing against the light, but she didn't quite realise it was against the light, and she sort of hesitated on account of that, and maybe too because of the sound of my voice.

But she'd made a new decision, and a good one at that, because I knew my Stina very well. In that moment, in my mind, I already entered a world where William Flood was left behind and Stina and I were living together somewhere, always sharing a nice bed, and one day we'd realise that we were old and everything we needed to do was done and we could just hold each other's hands as the dark came down. Maybe Stina saw all of this too because she looked right back at me, or into me, and I cried out

Wait

and saw a small boy who believed in protective force fields, and a big black bus full of black-clad nuns that screeched and swerved to avoid his innocent stupidity, but this time the bus was yellow, and a lot smaller, and who knows what the people inside were wearing.

The yellow bus hardly screeched or swerved and in the place where Stina was looking at me there was now a vacant spot and then the bus was a little crooked with one wheel up on the footpath and someone shouted and a lot of people made helpless sounds.

Livio was running forward and I didn't know where I was or what I was doing and that was a feeling to stay with me for years and decades, and is in all likelihood the same feeling that will one day make me have to write all this down or die.

Part 10

I.

Over the years I watched Black Beach Killer many times, of course, but maybe not on as many occasions as I might have expected. There was the initial cinema run that I frequented regularly, even though it killed me to do so, then small pop-up appearances in obscure suburban or regional theatres and drive-ins, some of which I had to drive two or more hours to make.

Come the age of VHS, I waited patiently while my new life of schools and dating strangers I barely liked went on; finally the thing was available. I watched the cassette tape I purchased a half-dozen times in the same number of years, getting good and drunk with every viewing, freezing the brief images where Stina appeared.

Really, what was the point of watching the entire movie when she was in it less than a minute? Less than thirty seconds.

A single scene. One.

Then I lost the thing in some period of moving house, and I tried not to think about it again. The era of DVDs came, however, and old movies were once again becoming available, all shiny and renewed. It took some distributor the better part of a decade to decide to do a new release of Black Beach Killer, so I watched it all over again in an amazingly pristine new format, going sometimes from start to finish, but mostly only for that beach walk. Of course it had been all William Flood had the chance to film—the rest of Stina's scenes had been meant for later in the schedule.

So there was no real character named 'Stacey-Lee' anymore, just an anonymous, naked blonde who strolls out of the waves and up the beach, with an off-screen murder and screams added in post.

At a distance of decades I could still marvel at Christina Vågberg, at how much a part of my life and memory she was, and at how I might have made it into that scene too, even as just one small woolly head pretending to sleep in the sand, then stumbling along the beach past her, if I'd been able to keep my eyes off the slight swing to the curve of her hips.

Still, there was something almost far too brutal about the clarity of those images; maybe William Flood and his team had done their job too well.

Celluloid, VHS tapes and DVDs—not to mention the very occasional appearance on late-night cable movie stations—kept Stina young and attractive, but it was the Stina inside me that always had the greater effect, for sometimes I would find myself in a mental one-sided conversation with her: the things I should have told her, the better way I could have framed things, or the simple new events that were happening to me that I thought she might like to hear about. And I pictured her face so close to mine: sometimes as a teenager dancing to pop tunes, sometimes as the child who had her head full of wily schemes to get even with those above her, and often-times just as she'd been lying back in that hotel room bed, her hair across the pillow and her eyes tightening with pleasure.

I kissed her lips then and I've kissed her lips for decades since; it makes no sense, but neither does the human heart.

Yet the strongest, the most powerful memory came in a dream that I had one night after making love with my wife and sleeping sated and happy, entwined in her arms. One baby was asleep in the room next to us, another was asleep deep in her womb, even though we didn't quite know it yet.

I can't say the dream ever recurred, at least not in any way that I understand consciously. It never presented itself more fully or in differing variations, taking on interesting new angles and steps.

No, it came just the once, on that particular night, and it was vivid as blood.

2.

Somehow I'm walking past my old Christian Brothers school, and Brother Percival Baxter's stalking around the playground, tolling his stupid bell, as is his way.

From there, I see once again Fortitude Valley's hole-in-the-wall Italian and Greek cafés, its corner stores, Salas Delicatessen, the Collosco restaurant, plus all the pizza parlours and cheap fish and chip counters I walked past almost every school day. Here's Palings, the record store, with its album of the week featured out front. Looks like this week's hit is Tubular Bells. There's Waltons, the department store my ma got most of my clothes from. And Monty's, the second-hand brokerage that robs its patrons blind. I even pass the second hand bookstore that will burn down in April, or maybe May, 1986. The owner, with her little old lady bi-focals perched on her nose, has her thin arms heavy with books she's finding homes for in her shelves.

'Hello Miss Pettigrew, you remember me? I used to come by quite a few times a week.'

She nods a reply and keeps at her work. I ask her about all the comics she used to keep in boxes out front, lures to draw potential customers inside. Miss Pettigrew tells me they're now well-protected in the back, because, '... kids steal 'em. Just lift 'em and walk away.'

'Did you ever know it was me?'

'You were never as smart as you thought, you pudgy little shit.'

Take care, I want to tell her, but she's gone, and entire blocks of the old suburb shift away because I turn my head to familiar music, and I'm in the park, where a group of kids have gathered by the river. Behind them there's the full spread of Camphor Laurels and Chinese Elms, of flowering shrubs, green plains and gentle hills. Endless rows of Jacarandas aren't yet in bloom, their leaves, for the present, all yellow. Flowers are everywhere and the roses are out; well, here's the place they always seem to be out. The brown snake of our river slugs along with an old wooden ferry making its slow crossing from one side to the other.

While some folk kick a soccer ball, and groups of children play games, and a professional Tai Chi ensemble practises near the rotunda, families and friends enjoy their picnics with baskets full of food and drink. Those who are on their own relax and watch the sights and feel the breeze and think their lonely thoughts; there's enough space in these vast acres for everyone to feel they own a special piece of privacy.

In a place so pretty you'd expect the music to be something like Fleur de Lys or my ma's creaky old Claire de Lune, but what's playing is the polar opposite.

Yet still fits.

Car doors are open and a radio, cassette or cartridge plays loud. The music's got a good solid beat, a nice, familiar, chunky Chuck Berry-style guitar riff, topped off by a singer's androgynous voice. The sound is almost unnaturally clear, as if my ears have been blessed with unearthly acuity. Within this sexy rock band interplay I hear a piano, another keyboard making a glissando, baritone and alto saxophones, and clever backing vocals. Each of the song's instruments is distinct, there's a wonderful separation to them all.

Two guys with long straggly hair, big arms and surf t-shirts drink beer out of cans. Rough, faded blue jeans. Three barefoot girls are in little tops and short skirts. Stina's one of them. Her eyes are closed, not so much as a smile on her face. The music's everything. The girls are dancing in the grass. The guys are watching with knowing grins—and here's something else: it's as if the girls are dancing in between the separation of the sounds. I can even see the music, and those young, supple bodies weave in and around and through its colours and contours.

Gudrun barks up at me. I bend to rub her fur.

When I look again Stina's on her own, the others have gone

away, and she's pure and crystalline, the music moving through her. This makes her so much more a part of the rhythm and the beat, of the guitar lines and saxophone notes, the vocal melodies.

In fact, it's as if she's living music: man, she's dirty sweet and she's my girl.

Stina opens her eyes and calls me to her with a glance, with the warmth of her bare skin. I go into her arms and her scent is fresh as a handful of berries. Stina wraps herself around me, still moving.

'Time is great with music,' she says. 'This song's from 1971 but it sounds like today and tomorrow all at once.' Then she ripples herself nicely in my arms. 'And time is good with people too,' she says, 'because you're with me.'

And I'm kissing her lips and eyes because I can't forget the way we used to sit in her house and listen to records, or how we sat close in new cinemas and older movie theatres, with our giant but very young imaginations transported a million miles away from this everyday life we've been a part of, in a little suburb of a not-much-of-anything town, in a country so far away from what we thought was the true centre of things it made our lives seem all the more insignificant.

'Hey,' she breaks the spell with a half-breathless sigh. 'Come with me,' and we take the ferry that's waiting, and sit up the back as it sails from one shore of our sad river over to the other.

Stina says, with a considerate smile, 'Well, here we are.'

3.

It's the exterior of what must be a historic, old world movie theatre. The building is very art deco, huge. Sort of a dream come true for two people like us. The outside walls are covered in bougainvillea. There are arched doorways with fine carvings and lattice work, iron balconies above, and front gardens of rustling trees and shrubs. A neat but thick row of hedges too, and

I think I can name these trees, even if I'm no expert: they're oak and beech. I've never been anywhere near a place like this, and definitely not with Stina.

She holds my arm and keeps very close, giving off a warmth and a scent that's all her own. Of everything I like about her, of being with her like this, what's best is that she's more womanly than I remember. More, sort of, herself.

We pass beneath an arch and it's a step into an older world. A world that's like thoughts and memories put together. The carpeting and rugs are thick, the walls have a velvety, textured quality. It's quiet and smells good.

Through this door, Stina says, and as we take it we enter the Park View hotel's 601, and a tray of hamburgers and fries waits ready on a coffee table in front of a television showing The Heavenly Body. The food looks and smells great. The beer and wine in the small refrigerator will be nice and cold. There's that bed too, and a pair of white robes laid out. Behind the closed door of the bathroom the shower is going. I'd be happy to stop here.

'No, not this one,' Stina says,

But I take a moment to brush the hair away from the back of her neck. I expect to see the word Dream, but all that's there is her sweet skin.

I kiss her there anyway.

When I draw away we're already in what must be the main part of the theatre, and all the seats look well-spaced and comfortable. The screen is enormous, a great view of it will be available from wherever you choose to sit. As we walk in the lights come down, and even though it's just the two of us I have the feeling we're surrounded by old friends, family, strangers, and their oceans of dreams.

Front row or middle? I ask.

But Stina's gone.

And I know what this means now, because the movie's already playing, and I sit back to watch the sun shining over the most vivid memory I possess, of an endless beach populated by spotty teenagers, where waves crash and rush to the shoreline, and an elegant Swedish girl walks over baking sands as she heads our way.

This time she stops and puts a hand to her cheek as if a breath of wind has touched her. She smiles at this, and maybe at some stray thought tinged with sadness. Looking at her I know that of everything I ever did, the good, the bad and the endless in-between, there's one thing that went right.

Thank you, Stina, thank you for letting me be your friend.

And now the dream is melting because the movie's done and at the same time the hamburgers and beer have tasted so good, and The Heavenly Body really made us laugh, and Stina lies back opening that white robe, putting out her arms.

Please come here, Eco, she says.

So I do, the feeling of weightlessness like music and love and midnight movies, and I know I'm lost, now and forever.

Hey, what's this? she asks. I thought it was going to be Free?

Well, in the end it didn't feel quite right.

And that's okay with her, because she bends her mouth toward the back of my neck, even gives my skin a small wet lick before she kisses what I've had inscribed there in blue ink.

My Eco, she breathes soft and low, it's my favourite word ever, Dream.

2016

ROMEO BECOMES MOONLIGHT

'La parole de Dieu,' the priest spoke into his heavy black beard, and the small congregation stood from the many rows of close-ly-packed wicker chairs. The choir's resonant voice again enveloped the Sunday morning's assembly.

The priest and his assistants were in layered vestments gleaming with satin, gold and silver thread. The high, barred windows shaded in a golden daylight sympathetic to their ritual. That light filled the small church in splintering shards and soft colours. As the High Mass continued, sunlight inched across the main altar. The singers paused and shifted comfortably.

'Elevons nos coeurs.' The priest's tone was slightly muffled by his beard and vestments. The congregation, excepting a small number who remained apart due to their silence, replied, 'Nous les avons vers le Seigneur.'

Romeo was one of the silent ones. He stood when others stood and sat when others sat, and he let his thoughts drift with the prayers and the incense and the singing. From time to time he glanced at the young woman in the choir's second row. She hadn't quite drawn him to the cathedral, but she was a part of the choir, and it was their singing that brought Romeo there from week to week.

Eight male and four female voices harmonised in Greek. To Romeo their voices carried a strange, strong Arabic inflection, long notes quavering and wailing. The sound reminded him of Muslim ceremonies he'd attended in Istanbul and Izmir, but the style fitted this Christian church too, with its clutter of Byzantine decorations and candles flickering behind red glass. He liked the way those red-glassed candles hung on chains from the beaks of a row of sculpted birds. The birds were faithful replicas of the

Maltese Falcon statuette in the old movie, well, at least to him.

Despite his wandering thoughts the voices found their way inside Romeo, wrapping his heart in a welcome embrace and swelling his blood in a way that made his cheeks shine. His stocky body relaxed into the fine wicker chair. His neighbour's shoulder pressed to his own. A wave of gentleness flowed through him, like a slow morning awakening, in stages, in a languid bed, first to hear rainfall against misted windows, then to smell coffee brewing on a stove, and finally to sense the welcome warmth of another body there with him beneath white sheets and winter blankets.

Romeo's eyes closed. He worked late at the small Sicilian restaurant in, appropriately, Rue du Roi de Sicile, where he cooked inimitable dishes for cash payments under the table. He slept little more than four or five hours a night—always an early riser—even when there wasn't all that much to rise to.

Incense wafted around the gathered parishioners. Inside, the air was heavy; outside, the morning was fresh after a night of rain and cracking thunder. Around Romeo people made the sign of the cross, and the reminder of a faith he'd never quite understand somehow succeeded in making his sense of peace all the greater.

It was like this most of the Sundays that he walked from his share-apartment in the Fourth to the small Melchite parish of Saint Julien Le Pauvre, on Rue Galande. It was near the infinitely more exalted Cathedrale de Notre-Dame de Paris, yet he preferred the smaller church because it was cosy and beautiful and unlike any he'd seen. He'd read that it had been completed in the thirteenth century and handed over to the Melchite order in 1889. Throughout the Middle Ages it was a hub for university political life, but that life grew too rowdy and was subsequently banned from the little church. Other than regular masses and ceremonies, it now offered a program of classical concerts; the ones Romeo attended were free, then of course there were these Sunday mornings of Greek High Mass, for which he'd developed an unexpected affinity.

For his lack of belief Romeo enjoyed the slight illegitimacy of his presence; he liked the way he could sit amongst large groups of parishioners who, in the main, would ignore him. Sometimes he was within a group of Greeks, sometimes a group of French. He liked to watch the heavy-set faces of his neighbours, or the fine-boned faces, or the many shining black faces. Most Sundays he could pick out American visitors, maybe a few German and Dutch tourists, yet he'd never overheard an Australian accent. Paroisse Saint Julien Le Pauvre just didn't seem to have that sort of attraction.

Then, recently, he'd noticed her, always in the choir's second row, with black hair pulled back from her face so that, weekly, the subdued church-light revealed the smoothness of her cheeks and the darkness of her eyes. He couldn't recall the day when she had first noticed him, but the way she blushed revealed that she had; so did her surprising way of sometimes staring straight into his eyes while her chest raised and her glorious voice poured out, echoing with those of her friends against the old walls and plaster ceilings.

He was aware of her gaze now, in the middle of this intoxicating hymn, Glory of Byzantium, her eyes so clear it was as if she saw into his heart. Romeo tried but couldn't maintain the contact; he glanced down.

The priest stood before the veiled sacristy and lifted his arms, praying aloud. The assembly, including Romeo, mirrored his actions, if not his words. While a lay assistant in a plain shirt and jeans picked up a staff crowned with an ornate silver crucifix, a second assistant kept the incense wafting so prayers might all the more easily reach Heaven. The priest raised the Eucharist chalice. Romeo understood the transubstantiation process was now to have happened. He remained in his wicker chair as others moved into the aisles to receive their Saviour.

As he waited for the final stages of the mass, Romeo noticed something out of the ordinary. It was the first lay attendant, perhaps mid-twenties, in that plain shirt and jeans. His Eucharistic duties were complete and he now leaned behind a pillar, out of sight to the majority of the congregation. He was chewing his way through a half-baguette crammed with cheese and salami. The young woman from the choir's second row came to stand beside him. They exchanged a small joke, then as she put her white hand on his shoulder he gave her the remainder of his baguette; she didn't refuse. Instead she ate with gusto, crinkling her nose in pleasure.

For the second time Romeo looked away from her, then he stood and left the church before the ceremony was complete, preferring the welcome bite of the morning's chill air.

He wasn't looking for her but she was in Square René Viviani, a quiet garden beside the church and set along the River Seine's quayside. Romeo was near the twisted and heavily propped old acacia that was said to be the second oldest tree in Paris, transported from North America and planted there around 1680. The city's oldest tree was in the Jardin des Plantes but he hadn't visited it; the second most aged was impressive enough.

The young chorister was off to one side of the park and was being sick into the grass beneath a row of shading chestnut trees. Romeo hadn't meant to linger, but he'd seen her make a rapid exit from the church almost straight after he'd left, as if she'd wanted to follow him. Instead she'd managed to reach a private corner of the garden before her stomach gave way. Now she was on her knees in the lush grass, doubling over. Her friend wasn't with her and made no appearance. At a distance, Romeo watched on. In the church she was a vision; in daylight, a stranger.

The sun disappeared behind a thin layer of clouds. Toward the park's centre young children kicked a ball. Nearer, an older man in a grey, frayed suit adorned with medals and badges sat in contemplation, smoking a pipe. Past a couple embracing and kissing, a young mother pushed her pram. There were shaded pathways and fragrant nooks and crannies at every turn; many folk strolled, others sat in benches reading newspapers. The chestnut trees were in neat rows abundant with very green leaves. Romeo reached for one of those leaves. In his rough hand it felt soft and smooth. He looked ahead. No-one had noticed the young woman's distress. The air was sharp, but carried the drifting scents of flower beds. Romeo couldn't make himself move.

She sat back on her haunches and took a deep breath, hands on her thighs. Now her hair was out, falling across her face in a way that made him think of lost nights in smoky bars, never-ending kisses in darkened corners. He liked the way that hair was so dusky, yet in this gloomy daylight he saw previously hidden threads of silver and gold—curiously reminiscent of the threads in the priest's vestments.

She turned from where she kneeled and Romeo felt her glance like a kind of heat that went into the pit of his stomach. Her eyes glistened and might not have reflected illness at all, only loathing, or desire, then she leaned forward and was sick one more time.

Romeo forced himself across the grass. He kneeled beside her and held her hair away from her face while she was copiously sick again; he gently patted her back. The odour was nauseating. To the left he saw flourishing beds of red and yellow tulips he could concentrate on. The young woman coughed. Tears ran from her eyes. She wiped her mouth with the back of her hand then was pulling a lace handkerchief from her sleeve. She said something in French.

'Je ne parlez Français, je suis Australien.' It was his familiar introduction. 'Si vous parlez lentement, peut être je comprends.' Romeo knew his sentences were mostly incorrect verbs and convoluted tenses, but it was the best he could do.

'Australie?' she said, cocking an ear. 'You speak French with an Italian accent.'

Romeo thought about that and couldn't think of an appropriate reply. Funny how many other people had mentioned the same thing.

She put a hand to one eye and applied some pressure, sniffing at the same time. 'What brings you to this quartier?' she asked, as if they were sitting in a bar, sharing drinks.

There was no chance for conversation because a park warden was strutting toward them. Romeo recognised the expression in the man's face: it was outrage. He probably assumed they'd come there after a long party night of drinking; that they were full of drugs; that each of them held no regard for this city's pockets of beauty. Romeo had seen the smallest to the largest Parisian dogs shitting or urinating in Parisian boulevards and avenues, yet a young woman didn't seem to be allowed to be sick in a park. The warden marched down a tree-shaded pathway, his demeanour already attracting attention. A fortyish fonctionnaire in an official blue suit, he arrived gesticulating and barking orders.

Romeo wanted to speak up but felt a burning in the pit of his stomach, a familiar flare of anger he knew he had to contain. The young woman spoke quietly in his stead, in French, a studiously even and polite tone. For all her submission, whatever she was saying only infuriated the man more. Spittle shot from his gummy lips and Romeo watched her shrink from his increasing admonitions. It was difficult to understand what the warden actually wanted them to do. Romeo saw complete humiliation in the young woman's face.

He rose to his feet. With no intention of doing it, Romeo slapped the park warden twice across the face, as if challenging him to a duel, right cheek and left cheek. Then he turned to help his new companion up. Her humiliation hadn't lasted long. She was smiling, if not almost laughing. Romeo looked back to a small crowd that had gathered—then he saw the battered silver whistle between the fonctionnaire's lips.

A screeching-peel filled the air. The onlookers jeered in derision. Three uniformed police officers came into the park. The young woman tried to raise some defence; the park warden spoke rapidly and pointed at Romeo. The officers had Romeo in cuffs and held his arms. As they led him away, the warden following, the crowd gave greater voice to their disdain. The police ignored them. They weren't interested in the young woman either. After they'd pushed Romeo into the back of their black sedan she was left behind, alone in a narrow street watching their departure. It had all happened so fast it felt like the blink of an eye before he was being bustled into a local station. On their way in Romeo looked up. It was 34 Rue de Rivoli, a place he'd passed many times without realising what it was.

The preliminary procedures were minimal. He gave his name and had his wallet confiscated. He had no other belongings, other than coins and his front door key. These were taken from him, as were his shoes and belt. No one spoke English. In another moment he was locked into a holding cell shared with two very large skinheads, both of whom shouted what Romeo took to be political non-sequiturs. The cuffs had been unlocked from his own wrists but this pair, twins, apparently, remained handcuffed together. Their wet red eyes and spitting mouths accused the police officers, and turned on Romeo too. He moved as far away from them as he could, which wasn't much. The cell smelled of stale urine and stale blood, though to the eye it seemed clean enough. There were no bunks, only a short concrete bench cemented to the wall. Romeo did his best to ignore his companions, to be patient, to not let their shouting and anger inflame the hatred already twisting and turning in his gut. Soon enough the park inspector would have recorded his story; Romeo would have a chance to give his side. There had to be someone in this station who spoke at least a little English.

He sat and leaned his back against the stark cold of the concrete wall. His feet, in his socks, were already numbed. He closed his eyes and tried to conjure the serenity of Byzantium chants. Saint Julien Le Pauvre was a long way off; he saw silver and gold thread in the hair of a sick and humiliated young woman.

Sitting at a bus stop outside the police station, she was lighting a Lucky Strike. Romeo came down the front steps, cold, dishevelled, now too tired to be angry. A good eight hours had passed.

He saw that at some time during the long day she had changed out of her austere church clothes. She was waiting for him in a tight white top and a loose printed skirt that reached her ankles, only just revealing the careful lacing of small black boots. A leather jacket was over the back of the bench.

'Are you feeling better?' he asked.

'Me? Dieu. What about you?'

'They decided I'm not quite a criminal. Sent home with a warning only.'

'I rang. They would not let me speak with you. "What is his name?" I could not answer.'

'That's okay.'

'I have been home. I have been to a doctor. He has given me medicine. Father Epaminondas, the priest from our church? He wanted to come when I told him the story. If you were still here tomorrow morning, he would have been at this door.'

'Thanks for the support.'

'You do not know half. My brother has come and waited here with me. He gave me that stupid food he has no sense to keep safe. He is sick too. Then his wife came, but she had to take him home. Some friends arrived and sat with me one hour. They wanted to meet a real romantic hero but they became bored and went to see Jean Reno in an American movie. They said to come with them.' She shook her head. 'No. For today I am here.' She looked toward evening's last rays of sunlight, glimmering through a pollution haze. 'Did you have a wonderful time in there?'

'I made some new friends. Two brothers I should have to dinner, them and their neo-Nazi cadre.'

'I want to know why you hit that man.'

'I've just been through it ten times.'

'Once more?'

'He was mean to you.'

She said, 'And now?'

'Go home and uncork a cheap Bordeaux. I don't need to go to my fabulously entertaining night-job tonight. I'll probably doze off in front of the television. It's agreeably humbling that in your language even cartoons are a mystery to me. If I have to, I'll make pasta for my flatmates. I'd give anything for cable.'

'You will better come with me.'

'I thought you'd miss the subtlety of my comments. I will better come with you?'

'Bien sûr.'

'You've got cable?'

'Not to my home. My parents are not good with strangers.'

'Okay.'

'My name is Isabel.' She flicked her cigarette into the gutter. 'The officers in there finally told me yours.'

'Finally?'

'I went into that office many times to ask your progress. My brother and my friends were very impressed. Romeo. It gave me butterflies.' She didn't smile. 'You are a romantic hero today.'

'No.'

Isabel kept looking at him.

They walked along streets and quaysides he knew well enough from three months alone in Paris, but with Isabel holding his hand everything looked different. He'd never really noticed how the cobble-stoned streets of Île Saint Louis seemed constantly in shadow; he'd never walked by the innumerable little restaurants and wonder what it would be like to go there with a woman and drink too much; he'd never bothered to look up the sides of house and building façades.

'That is where our history is,' Isabel told him. 'High up, not on the street. You see the way these houses are slanted at the top? This is the way they are built in the seventeenth century. The passing eras, you see? These here are completely different again, and so are from a century later. It is easy to understand. The shape of the windows holds many of the secrets. At doorways all you see are renovations for tourists and families with new money. One day I will be an architect. But in the suburbs. I want to create good living for the poor and migrants.'

A strong wind came coldly off the Seine, but her hand in his stayed warm. She didn't seem to mind the mess of him; he needed a shower, a shave and fresh clothes. He was aware of his own body odour. The cell had been putrid, the twins delighting in urinating onto the bare floor as frequently as they could. Yet, despite all that, Romeo now felt the same kind of peace inside that his visits to the church always gave him. All that anger, gone. Useless and self-destroying. He breathed in the chill air. This day and evening were like a dream. There was the bad and the good, one indivisible from the other. You had to live with that, always. Tonight he'd rediscovered his feelings from inside the walls of Saint Julien le Pauvre. Or he'd been given them, by Isabel.

The sky had darkened considerably; soon the girl would want to go home. She'd mentioned parents; he imagined she'd also want to protect her voice from the deepening chill. Isabel led him to an alley where a vendor with a cart still served sweet crêpes and roasted chestnuts. Isabel purchased him a hot snack and watched him eat. He was ravenous. She didn't want anything for herself.

'Sundays are so busy here,' she said. 'The weekends. Our streets are so crowded with foreign buses you can't move. We stay away from these quartiers in the spring and summer.'

Isabel put her arms around Romeo and pressed herself against him. She was his height, but slight, and so warm it was as if she had a fever. By the streetlamps and headlights of passing vehicles she seemed to glow. It was the same effect he'd seen in the church, her in the choir's second row. There was so much youth about her, so much that was unmarked by troubled years.

'You keep looking at me,' she told him. 'When you think I will not notice.'

'How old are you?'

'Seventeen,' Isabel replied. 'You thought I was older.' She kissed his cheek and when he didn't respond she pushed him away. 'Stupide.'

Romeo looked into her face. Yes, despite himself, he'd

guessed. She was young. Too young. Church lighting and desire had made her seem older.

'Don't be,' she said.

'What?'

'Stupide.'

She took his hands and kissed his lips. For that moment Romeo didn't care that Isabel was half his age; people would relish informing him how wrong it was to want her—yet who were these people and what had they ever done for him? How had he ever benefited from the counsel of others? He was an outsider, and an outsider was what he would stay.

'Sometimes,' Isabel said, close to him, 'sometimes you look so angry.' She pressed her chest to his. 'I feel your heart. Are you angry for my age?'

'Sort of.'

His voice as too gruff; indeed, he was angrier than he realised. He wanted something to be easy, at least just once. For someone to be easy to deal with. No one ever was. He wished he was the romantic hero she'd mentioned, or at least a man with a little more wisdom than the donkey-king of fools he was.

'Don't be. And please don't send me away.'

'You don't want to go away?'

She shook her head, then looked down, letting go of him and expecting words that would hurt.

'I won't send you away.' Romeo did his best to make his voice gentle. 'I promise.'

'Then come with me,' she said.

River cruise boats that followed each other up and down the Seine shone their great lights over the Left and Right banks. Romeo watched the way their spotlights crawled and flickered over the houses and buildings, painting them a brilliant white. Isabel led him from dark streets to a darker waterside. It was the quay between Pont Marie and Pont de Sully, and it was even colder by the river, but there were quiet places to sit and watch the city's reflected lights in the river. Isabel pulled Romeo's arm around her shoulders. She was wearing her leather jacket and gave a shiver. They walked toward a bench half-hidden by the shadow of a high wall. Other couples were in their own shadows.

On the quay, at the water's edge, homeless men were gathered in a group and were singing. Romeo watched them pass a bottle. The river cruises were incessant, flat observation decks crowded with spectators. Isabel seemed happy and relaxed. Something told Romeo this was her spot. He tried to remember the kissing places of his own youth, but the memories felt as lost as all those desperate yearnings.

'What is it?'

'I think I like it here,' Romeo said.

Isabel smiled at him. They were standing by the bench, eyes adjusting to the darkness. The song the clochards made was bawdy and rough; Romeo recognised a rude word or epithet here and there. Isabel wasn't bothered. In fact, she liked it. He thought she'd enjoy translating it all for him, if he'd asked. They listened to rasping voices, hoarse, throaty laughter.

'You know,' Isabel touched his cheek, 'you are a dreamer.'

'Maybe sometimes.'

They sat close to one another. Isabel put his arm around her shoulders again, then rested a leg over his thigh.

He looked at her. 'Comfortable?'

She thought a moment. 'I liked you in the park. I liked what you did to that arrogant man. You did not think. Though I have seen you sitting in a church week by week, in that moment you did not let yourself hesitate for one second.'

'More fool me.'

'This is wrong. We are a country of sleepwalkers. Nothing makes us wake up to what is around us. I am the contrary. I think too much. Many nights I cannot sleep at night for my thoughts. The things I will want to do, how can I name them. I have told you one. To be an architect. To be a help to other people. But this is one idea of a thousand. The only moment these thoughts disappear is when I am singing. You know what?

When I take the communion, I think of the body and the blood of Jesus Christ coming into me and it makes me so excited I can faint. Like the butterflies you give me. I do not think this is what the church asks.'

Romeo watched the shadow across her face.

'Now like this,' Isabel said, and she put herself gently into his lap, facing him. She slipped out of her leather jacket and slid her bare arms around his neck. She studied the black places of Romeo's eyes. As she did it was as if she was thinking too much again; deciding a thing or two, maybe deciding between more of this, or less.

Whatever she wants, Romeo thought.

Then he held his breath as Isabel pulled his head forward, taking his mouth to her throat. He couldn't help himself; he ran his hands under her long skirt, over Isabel's slim thighs.

She said, 'No, not this far,' but Romeo felt the heat of her in his lap. She pressed down into him, her breath heavier. She held him more tightly. Romeo wondered what her thoughts were. Then he tried to imagine what she dreamed for herself, and what she saw in those dreams of helping others.

And what do you see when you look at someone like me?

Isabel put her hands to both sides of his face, her touch warm and careful. Her eyes were closed and her lips were very red. Romeo thought he perceived a brilliant white moon shining behind her, but it was another river spotlight and then he was lost.

Her friends turned up, drinking and popping pills, still excited by the movie they'd seen. There were three boys and two girls, laughing and crowding over one another to get a look at Romeo. Some seemed a lot older than Isabel, but Romeo didn't pay them enough attention to care. There must have been some prior agreement to meet; Isabel didn't seem surprised. The shadows hid him and Isabel's arched body did the rest. In the darkness of the quay her friends were like young, playful dogs. At first they goaded the homeless men, who goaded them back. It was all so good-natured it might have been a nightly ritual. Isabel didn't mind that her friends had arrived. Maybe she even liked it, for she kissed him with greater ardour, whispering to him and pressing into his lap. Sometimes she called back to her friends.

One of them was doing his best Jean Reno, whipping out an imaginary gun and shooting the others, who died, hid, or fell to one knee and fired back. They were in their own dreamland. Romeo wondered if they'd offer Isabel their pills, and if she would take them; he certainly wouldn't. He wished they'd disappear. He heard, 'Bang!' and 'Blam!' and 'Aaiiee!'

The men drinking and dangling their feet over the quayside swore at them without rancour and cried, 'Arrête!'.

'Do not mind my friends the clowns.' Her breath remained warm on his face, and her lips were swollen with kissing. 'They make themselves crazy.'

'They're pretty funny, really.'

He felt her fingertips touch the hard line in his lap.

'What are you doing in Paris ... my Romeo?'

'I got sick of home. I got sick of familiar faces. If you really want to know.'

'Tell me.'

'Well, spent some time traveling Europe, mostly on inter-country trains. When I got to Paris I was going to stay a night, but I met a Sicilian guy and he had work going in a restaurant. I like to cook. No training except in the home. They pay me cash and that makes it worthwhile. So, no plan. When I get bored I'll go.'

'As heroes will.'

'I slapped a man in a park. That's nothing worthwhile.'

She went closer to his ear, whispering, 'Is this worthwhile?' and caressed him with her index finger.

There was music. One of Isabel's friends had a portable cassette player. After the lapping of the waves and the voices of the clochards, the sound was too loud and too intrusive. Isabel lifted herself from Romeo's lap. She joined her friends and they were shadows dancing along the quay with the river behind them. He saw her putting her hand to her mouth. Pills. Then she had a bottle and was drinking. Except for one who stayed behind, the homeless men decided they'd had enough and staggered away. Their remaining friend stretched out and made himself comfortable where he was, a small mound of rags. Isabel danced in silhouette, her lean frame turning circles and her skirt billowing. Her jacket was beside him and he took it in his hands. When he lifted it to his face he inhaled her scent. The others were leaping around Isabel, high on Jean Reno, drinks, pills, the night, youth.

Their bottle went from one to the next. Isabel's head tilted back as she drank again, her long neck a soft line against the surrounding dark. As they danced they called out, the music a frenetic mambo with an insistent beat. Romeo knew the band, Les Negresses Vertes, and their exuberant, shouted chorus echoed across the Seine:

'Li lo li, Li lo li le, Li lo li oh le!'

Isabel's body seemed to understand the rhythms of the world; she danced without inhibitions, graceful within that circle of leaping shadows. Watching her filled him with a greater desire than when she'd been sitting in his lap kissing him, rubbing him. Now he longed to hold her again. He felt as drunk as if he was drinking from that bottle with the rest of them. The song changed to something with a slower semi-rap beat, another French group, he thought, but one he didn't know. Towards the end there was one sentence in English:

'Life's a bee-tch, and then you die. Voilà.'

Isabel returned when a different song started to play. Her face shone. She fixed him with her look and stood before him, serious-faced yet playful. He pulled her back to where she'd been. Jazz-cool filled the air. Portishead. Isabel entwined Romeo with her legs. Her friends were far away. Isabel's mouth was hot and he had a sense that she gave in to herself first, him second. Romeo's hands went along her warm legs. Her mouth tasted of whisky and perspiration. He stopped kissing her. Isabel whispered to him in French—or maybe it was to herself—and now her hands trembled as she reached down. The melancholy call of the music surrounded them, and Isabel found a way to undo Romeo's buttons. She shifted and shifted. He felt her strain against him.

The singer from Portishead, what was her name? Romeo heard her sing, 'Give me a reason to be a woman, I just want to be a woman—'

Now Isabel made a small gasp as her flesh gave way. Her breath and tongue were on his neck and he thought, No, I won't, I better not, but she moved slowly now, and when he looked he saw a tear on her cheek. She kissed him, mouth quivering. Her voice came from far away.

'This means you have to be good to me. And always.'

'I will. I promise I will.'

No church, choir or wafting incense was ever going to make him feel as good as this. He let his fingers dig into Isabel's back, and when he looked past her shoulder what he saw wasn't the moon, or the searching lights of the passing river barges, or even the low skyline of the right bank's buildings, but the silhouettes of Isabel's friends now bored with dancing and play-acting. They'd discovered the remaining clochard and had set upon him. Even as the jazz-cool music wafted, he realised he'd missed the muffled cries and moans as fists rose and fell, as feet kicked and crushed.

Isabel said, 'What is it? What?'

He couldn't articulate it, and pushed Isabel's light frame away. He stood, and straightened himself, and did up his buttons.

'Stop,' he said. No one heard him. 'Stop it!'

He heard Isabel say something, but what came over him wasn't about to be restrained. He rushed in, overwhelmed by rage, and he pulled and pushed the young boys from the blood-ied clochard, plus the two girls as well. The old man struggled to an elbow, blood on his face, in his hair and dripping along one arm. Romeo felt no blows either to himself or through his fists, and then Isabel was beside him and she was screaming.

He saw he'd already beaten two boys bloody. The third whimpered on the ground. There were the red marks of thick fingers, of a slap, across one girl's face. The other comforted her. Romeo looked at right hand; the knuckles were bleeding.

Isabel wept. Romeo wasn't sure if she was crying for what her friends had done or what he'd done to them. She didn't seem to notice the clochard making his way into the distant shadows of the quay, crooked as a broken crab. For a moment Romeo hesitated. He'd take Isabel with him. They'd make a secret life. Then he realised he didn't know a thing about the girl. She was a child and he was the donkey-king of fools. For a moment he put his hands to his face, and felt a shudder go through him, then he left Isabel to her friends and caught up with the old man.

When Romeo propped him with his shoulder the clochard resisted, then let himself be half-carried along.

In the Paroisse Saint Julien le Pauvre he saw Isabel again, but it was many weeks later, the Saturday night of Easter. As he stepped inside, her choir was already singing a Byzantine hymn. He'd worked eight nights straight, but his cash-under-the-table had ended up being less than half what it should have been. The restaurant was closing down.

'Fratello Siciliano, I gotta go,' said the owner.

The atmosphere inside the small church was comforting and familiar, all heavy incense and candles burning. He found a vacant seat and sat quietly, staring at the choir, at Isabel. Her hair was pulled back and her clothes were black. Christ was about to rise from the dead and in a few minutes Isabel would take that sensuous idea of Him into her body. The idea of her had given Romeo endless sleepless nights. He'd accepted a crazy work schedule without complaint; if he wasn't able to empty his mind, he could at least have it deadened.

She saw him, of course, and continued singing. They watched one another. Even after so much time had passed he again wondered what she saw when she looked at someone like him. Their gaze, one to the other, remained steady. Neither needed to look away. Her voice, at a higher pitch to those of her fellow singers, was clear and glorious. He wanted to close his eyes and be taken away. Romeo wondered if he could speak to her after the service, but, in a moment, and very, very slowly, Isabel gave a shake of her head. It was the gentlest of moves, from left to right, one not to be read by anyone but himself. Yet it was the most emphatic no Romeo had seen.

Was she telling him he shouldn't have turned up here to disturb her? That he shouldn't make the further mistake of coming near? What if it was a message that of course there was no baby to worry about? Or was it simply that she needed him to believe she wasn't the same as her friends?

Moonlight shone through the bars of the windows and the choir moved on to a new hymn. In that pale light Isabel's image seemed to grow stronger, shimmering, and he felt that in the crowded gloom of the congregation he was receding.

No, that wasn't quite correct.

He wasn't so much receding as being absorbed into the incense and prayers, into the voices, where real peace resided. He might as well have been melting into the moonlight that illuminated her.

Now Romeo thought he had an inkling: with that shake of her head Isabel was making him invisible; she made him fade away. The romance of his name wasn't real. He was as much a hero as her friends were. All of it was true, and he felt no pain— he only wondered how a young woman might find her dreams. Isabel's no meant she'd never let him find out.

He'd made Isabel two promises—the first to not send her away, the second to always be good to her. Well, he could only be true to one.

Romeo took a deep breath, found his feet. Others moved aside for him. He knew the timetable; there was a night-train to the Italian frontier.

1995

SUGARBABY

One

Duvall wiped his eyes as he concluded this, the final transaction for Sandy, surprised at just how great his sense of loss was. He'd always expected that making a last payment would hurt, but he'd hoped he would be able to contain it to a minor twinge; like the sting of a blood test's needle at the local surgery run by Dr Laine, or the small sadness of lifting a stiff pet bird from the floor of its cage. But the girl had finished her degree and that was that. She'd never made any pretence about being available to him a moment longer. Her eyes were set on that year of travelling she'd planned: Asia and India, then on to Europe, the Caribbean islands and the Americas. After that she wanted a steady job in a city like Sydney or Melbourne. Now that her mother had passed away and her studies were done, Sandy was clear about having no desire to return. He of course didn't come into the equation.

John Duvall knew he didn't have to give her so much, and maybe shouldn't, but he'd always been a generous man. He transferred a nice round $2,000 using their regular method, PayPal. Let her upgrade to nice hotel rooms and not rely on so many backpacker hostels, buy herself better dinners, clothes she wanted, whatever pleased her best. She'd given him so much solace and so much satisfaction that it actually hurt to imagine her doing these things without him, or with some boyfriend, the existence of whom he'd sometimes suspected but didn't have any right to ask about.

As the transaction receipt arrived in his email account Duvall clicked on a picture gallery he kept of her. Nothing salacious and not too many, just everyday snaps she'd let him take here in his quiet little suburban home. These could have been photographs of a favourite daughter, granddaughter or niece. Something ached deep in his gut. Maybe this was a good thing, a sign that even at his age he could feel the hurt of needing and wanting someone, that the well-furnished but still-empty rooms of this place didn't define him. Yes, he was alone, nine years now since Mary had died, but he didn't necessarily want to be alone.

The pictures showed Sandy as she was. Not a tremendously pretty girl, and the snaps somehow even managed to suggest that she might not be overly bright or creative, but he knew she was warm-hearted and kind. She'd always managed to treat him with a certain respect and deference for his age that had been married to a natural gift for tenderness. One day she would be a good wife and a good mother, no doubt about it. He imagined Sandy was already a good friend to anyone close to her. He'd miss the scent of her hair, the sound of her voice, her young body's smooth skin, and the unexpected complicity of the handwritten notes she sometimes left him—not to mention those myriad textings of hers, composed in an ispeak perfectly matched to her personality:

ZZZ, when Sandy had wanted to let him know she was 'sleeping, bored, tired' and wanted to come over;

VSF, 'very sad face', when, for whatever reason, he didn't want her to;

i h8 it, when something hadn't quite gone her way, or the best one,

G2CU 2nite, 'going to see you tonight'.

There were a hundred others of course, but he could barely remember them for their hieroglyphic quality. Yet, in some small way, those textings from a person of the current dominant generation had always done something to lift the spirits of John Duvall, a man most definitely of a generation on the way out. He'd come to consider her messages a small connection to this world that age and circumstances had distanced him from, that he could barely find a way to live in anymore.

Whenever he'd texted her back, he'd used the impeccable language taught him by his schooling and extensive business life, never succumbing to the tempting shorthand of his tiny telephone's buttons, or the special weirdness of predictive text:

Dear Sandy, by all means, if you would like to arrive by eight I will have supper ready for us. Sincerely, Duvall.

It was funny, from the start she'd used his surname only and he'd accepted that, Sandy moving from 'Mr Duvall' after she'd first come to help her mother do his weekly house-cleaning, to 'Duvall' after she'd sent him that first almost incomprehensible mobile telephone text message—the one inspired by his old-man's longing gaze, something even a girl with her innumerable outside interests couldn't miss.

Sandy's mother Glenda, now the late Ms Glenda O'Connor, had been coming to his house for almost two years. She'd done a neat job of keeping his rambling old timber home clean, and had always managed to liven it up with sprigs of flowers placed in pots or vases at strategic corners of various rooms. He'd liked the feel of the place after one of Glenda's visits; she opened curtains and shutters his indifference normally kept shut, letting in the sort of friendly daylight he rarely even thought about. While Glenda was cleaning, mostly Duvall would sit with a book beneath the heavy, shading branches of the trees in the garden, or he would leave her alone and drive down to the shopping centre for a bag of groceries and a haircut. If he wasn't going to be back soon enough, he'd place her pay in an envelope on a counter by the telephone. She would leave a short list of any cleaning products that needed to be purchased for the following week. For almost two years things had progressed this way, quietly and without incident, and he hadn't noticed her slowing down or doing any less of a job. Yet, one day, as she was leaving, Glenda had struggled to get a few unfamiliar words out.

'Mr Duvall ... so you know ... I'll come as long as I can, but I need to cut my working hours ...'

'Is something wrong?' he'd asked, genuinely concerned. Now he'd seen the tiredness in her eyes, the way one shoulder seemed a little stooped, a trace of frailty he'd never noticed before. How had he missed all that? She was fifty-five, always slender, but he realised she'd become thinner and much more lined in the face.

'It's osteo ... and when they did more tests, they found some lumps ...'

The next week she'd arrived with a girl she introduced as Sandra. As she'd presented her, there'd been the gleam of both pleasure and pride in her wearying eyes.

'My youngest, Mr Duvall. She's going back to university to finish her final year and she needs a little holiday income before it starts ... and I can use the help.'

'What are you studying?'

'Psych.'

'And it'll be your last year?'

'I should have finished two years ago but I took a break.'

Duvall wondered how old she was. Early to mid-twenties? Her voice was soft but not submissive, her eyes were very clear, and she gave the impression of a person who could handle just about any job that was handed her.

'Well, fine,' Duvall had nodded, trying not to take any special notice of this young woman who, despite making no attempt to impress him, already seemed like an extra ray of light in his home. 'I'll give you the hourly rate each, is that good enough?'

'Oh no ...' Glenda protested, 'she's just here to help me ... we'll share ...'

He paid double, of course, and as each week passed he continued to do so. With Sandra's help the cleaning didn't seem to take any less time, but it was much more thorough, and he would have found it unconscionable not to provide this extra pair of hands their due—and that had nothing at all to do with the almost physical pleasure he found himself taking in the way she moved around his rooms. Duvall could hardly discern what quality of hers attracted him so: Sandra would come to the house in baggy jeans, even on hot days, never revealing her legs in shorts or a skirt, and always wearing something like a man's cheap checked work shirt with a t-shirt underneath. Usually there were old joggers on her feet and her hair would be pinned up in a bun, keeping it out of her face. Practical stuff. She never spoke to him beyond the basics—'Mr Duvall, where are the bigger garbage bags kept?'; 'Would you like the bins moved out for collection today?'—and there was not the slightest hint of attraction or sexual tension. Nothing that spoke of a man and a woman. How could there have been? He was a sixty-eight-year-old developing a longing ache for a girl who was entering her prime. Duvall knew he would have had only slightly greater a chance with Glenda, who had divorced, she'd once told him, more than ten years back and would never, ever, ever marry again.

After the holiday period—which was of no great note to Duvall, for he no longer had any family close by, and who for a decade had spent every Christmas eve and day as a volunteer serving lunch and dinner to the dispossessed of the creaking old boarding house down the road (in truth, after the first couple of years he'd started to do this by rote, but preferred the activity to the solitariness of his own Christmas alone)—Sandra arrived without Glenda, and after a friendly-though-mostly-noncommittal greeting had set straight to work with her bucket, detergent and sponges.

'Is your mother unwell?'

'Mr Duvall, it hit her hard over Christmas. Then the therapy, and the, you know, the drugs she has to take ... The doctors say she shouldn't work anymore. We've got help at the house now, three days a week.' Sandra spoke quietly over her shoulder, not making a big thing of this news, but he understood that the situation with her mother must have caused her unspeakable grief. She paid great attention to polishing the porcelain wash basin in his bathroom. 'I can keep doing this till uni starts if you want.'

'Then you'll concentrate on your studies ... and looking after your mother?'

'She won't let me do that,' Sandra almost smiled. 'You know my mum. The worst thing she can imagine is to be responsible for stopping me from doing well. I never thought I'd go back to finish my degree, but now I really want to. And it means a lot to her too. So it's easier on her if I move out. Lived away lots before, it's okay. I'll find a share house. My two sisters are married, got kids, but they don't work. They'll go over pretty often. All together mum'll get everything she needs.'

So, in-home care for Glenda, then the inevitable move to some sort of nursing home, Duvall thought, unable to stop himself from feeling the weight of his own mortality. Maybe Glenda had years, maybe only a few months. He decided he'd send her something disguised as a severance pay, a tidy sum that might be helpful, his thanks for the quiet way she'd gone about caring for his home, and, by extension, him.

'Are you certain you'll be all right to keep coming?'

'Unless you want to find someone else now, Mr Duvall?'

Now she was looking up at his reflection in the large mirror above the basin. He thought that she'd been able to read the answer in his face long before they'd even started talking.

'No.'

'Well, first semester classes are about five weeks away. I guess that's five or six more times I can clean for you, plus everyone else on mum's list,' she said, dipping her sponge into the soapy water of the bucket at her feet. 'Would you like me to make you a cup of tea first?'

'Oh, I never expected that of your mother.'

'Got a big long background in waitressing,' she half-grinned. 'Cafés, restaurants, everything. So I don't mind ... I noticed you were sitting in your garden just before.'

'I had a book.'

'Then go back, I'll get you a cup, it's cool.'

He'd been about to protest, but immediately reconsidered. Let this girl bring her own touch to this house, he thought. So Duvall had returned to the warm sunlight of his small garden behind the house and had tried to concentrate on the pages of the thriller he was halfway through. Ten minutes later, Sandra, in those baggy jeans and red checked shirt, her dirty running shoes and pinned-back mousy-brown hair, brought him a tray. She placed it on the white wrought-iron table by his chair. He watched her use a strainer to pour him a cup of tea brewed in a pot using leaves, not a bag. She let him add his own milk and sugar. By the teapot was a small china plate with two cream biscuits from the tin in the kitchen.

'That's all I could find, Mr Duvall.'

'Sandra, this is heaven.'

'Only my mother calls me that, I'm really Sandy. Now you take it easy and I'll be done in an hour.'

'No rush.'

He meant it. Duvall found that what he really wanted to do was to sip his tea then go back into the house and make some excuse to talk to 'Sandy' some more, find a way to engage her before she finished for the day. It had never been like this with her mother, of course, but he felt something inside himself being constantly drawn to this young woman. He glanced at his left hand, wrinkled, thinning skin and veins showing, a hint of a coming liver spot. He remembered Sandy's as the sunlight had caught it just now, gently touching the vines of some cherry tomatoes he'd planted and which were coming to ripeness: her skin was young and supple. He knew what some of the attraction was: further decline lay ahead for him, but for her there was just about anything. Dreams of youth and the excitement of trying to capture each and every one. Don't dying things always edge toward the light?

She was mopping the kitchen floor when he brought the tray inside and placed it on the counter.

'Tell me—what do you plan to do after you graduate?'

'Travel,' she said easily, no thought required, still mopping carefully. 'I'm saving up.'

'Good to have a goal.'

Sandy smiled then. He liked it when she did and wished she'd do it more.

'That reminds me too, Mr Duvall. If I'm going to keep working a few more weeks, would you mind if we don't do the cash thing? When the money's in my pocket it just sort of goes ... Have you ever tried PayPal?'

'For online purchases ... not a lot ...'

'Could you do that with me too? I'll leave you my email address, that's all you'll need. I'm all set up and then the money goes straight into my savings.'

'If that's what you'd prefer.'

Later, it felt strange making that first payment, and when he'd used her email address (sandythesuperkittenbaby@gmail.com which left him both bemused and curious—'super-kitten-baby', did that signify anything in particular?) to ask if she could come to the house and clean for him twice weekly, he'd received an almost immediate response: TGTBT, Yes! and was versed enough in technology to understand that she'd used her mobile phone to email him a reply, even though he had no idea what the acronym was supposed to signify. He carefully wrote, Excuse me, Sandy, but what does 'TGTBT' mean? and pressed the send button. The explanation was instant: Too good to be true!

Her enthusiasm for the extra work pleased him. Duvall had started to wonder if there was some way he could keep her services into the start of the semester and beyond, for the entire year in fact. He decided to email Sandy one more time and ask her if she could anticipate any hours during the week or weekend that might suit her once university really started, hours that she would want to come to his house for the extra cash. He could be flexible, he carefully composed, hoping not to sound desperate. She needn't even conform to a set schedule. Sandy could clean for him whenever she had a free hour or two.

Lifting his hands from the keyboard, Duvall reflected that surely this sort of arrangement would be perfect for her. She would need money anyway, wouldn't she, living away from home, needing a job to help pay her share accommodation and general living costs, not being able to rely on her mother?

The thought of losing her had already started to hurt. Sandy was as good as Glenda in the cleaning stakes, but if she hadn't been it hardly would have mattered. And it hardly mattered that he was doing something he'd never really considered in all these years since Mary had passed away: paying for companionship. It wasn't even a real companionship, only the opportunity to let his old eyes move over the half-graceful, half-functional movements of a young woman, of a girl, yet it was what he wanted.

He could have been an uncle to her; more likely, a kindly grandfather. With a combination of anxiety and desperation, Duvall sent the email anyway.

Sandy came to the house the following Monday, looking a little tired and drawn from her weekend. Well, what young woman wouldn't, given a normal social life? Then she was there on the Thursday and the following Tuesday. She missed the Friday because of some sort of engagement that had slipped her mind (Omg 4got v sorry!) and made up for it straight after the weekend. Two weeks or so of modest cleaning, but each time Duvall had asked her to do a little more and more—nothing at all strenuous, just simple tasks to keep her in his home ten, fifteen, thirty minutes longer. She was always willing, and this had pleased him, but he was more than a little disconcerted that Sandy hadn't offered a word of reply to his email. Nothing.

Dear Sandy, I'd like you to consider working for me into your university year. Is there some kind of flexible agreement we could come to that might give you ample time for your studies, and to care for my home? It would be such a pleasure to continue your employ. Warmly, John Duvall.

He wondered if maybe he'd pushed things too far, if he'd revealed himself so much that now she was uncomfortable answering. Perhaps things were going from bad to worse for her mother, and Sandy simply didn't have the emotional wherewithal to contemplate future plans. He berated himself for that email, and began to resign himself to Sandy's imminent departure from his life—the start of the university year was just a week away—when, the following Monday, Sandy arrived to clean at the appointed hour, but was dressed differently. No baggy jeans, nor that mannish work shirt, her battered running shoes. She was still extremely modestly dressed, but her clothes were fresh and clean, new even, and they emphasised her figure. Nor was Sandy's hair up in its usual severe bun. It hung over her forehead in a sideways fringe and was tied back in a ponytail. Her hair shone, with a little extra colour and highlights added. The mousy brown had been lifted with sun-tinged streaks. A few light strands fell across her cheeks, softening her features and making her look, well, what she was. Twenty-four years of age; she'd told him one day when they'd had a brief chat about what it was like to return to university life.

Duvall was physically taken aback. There was no hint of cleavage, no hemline to indiscreetly rise when she bent and worked (she was wearing ash-grey trousers, though these hugged her legs and hips more pleasingly than those old jeans had), and no explanation, of course, for her new appearance.

Duvall couldn't help himself. The clothes, her hair, this softening difference, all of it gave him an ache, a physical ache in the heart plus an even more pressing ache somewhere behind his left temple—in his mind, Duvall imagined, deep inside that part of the brain which attempts to manage the conflict between bleak certainty and wild imagination. For him, it was the awful pain of desire married to the simple fact that Sandy, not to mention any young woman like her, was far beyond his reach.

Decades and decades beyond his reach.

In a sort of swoon Duvall lingered close to the rooms where Sandy cleaned, making what must have sounded to her—it did to him—inane small talk. Once and only once Sandy raised her head and gave him a direct look. An absolutely direct look that cut through him. What did she see? What did she perceive in him? The truth?

It only lasted a moment, and far too soon she was collecting her things and leaving. Duvall had the distinct impression that she'd wanted to say something to him almost as much as he had wanted to say something to her.

Sandy, come closer.

Mr Duvall, don't you know that you are a disgusting and stupid old man?

That's what was unspoken, he knew it for certain, then Sandy was gone, driving away a little too quickly in the battered Ford Escort she shared with her mother—if poor Glenda could even drive anymore—and Duvall collapsed into his most comfortable over-stuffed armchair, feeling the walls of his clean home suffocating him.

Just ten minutes later his life changed. He heard the single-note tone of an email arriving into his inbox, and it took some not inconsiderable will to leave the armchair and see what it might be about. His heart sank a little further when he saw the message was from sandythesuperkittenbaby. Duvall simply expected the worst: Not coming back, or some variation.

Instead, he read something incomprehensible: cud uz xtra oo or 2 per.

It was sent from her mobile phone of course. Why? And why just ten minutes after leaving the house? He knew the suburb where Sandy still lived with Glenda was at least double that time away.

She must have contemplated things, pulled over somewhere, then dashed this off to him before she could change her mind. Was this what had seemed to be on the tip of her tongue when she'd given him that naked gaze?

Duvall had to scratch the message out on a piece of paper using a pencil. She'd sent him something of a puzzle. Some of it was simple to decipher, some not.

cud=could

uz=use

xtra=extra

oo=two zeroes, meaning what, Duvall wondered?

or=or

2 per=two of something per week? per item? per action or activity? per month, day or year?

All right, let's see.

Sandy could use an extra something or two per something.

Two zeroes. Did that signify the number 100? It would make sense. Three zeroes would be 1,000, and so on. All right.

Sandy could use an extra hundred or two per something.

Well, Duvall transferred her wage on a weekly basis. Was that it? Perhaps Sandy was saying she could use an extra hundred or two per week.

Meaning?

Duvall slumped back, the beat of his heart heavier than he could imagine.

Meaning she had read his puppy-dog gaze correctly.

Two

So he'd done it, John Duvall had transferred two hundred dollars to Sandy's account even though nothing was due and she hadn't yet worked for it. Ought he to consider it payment in advance? If so, for what exactly, more cleaning?

No, it was extra. Something beyond the cleaning.

He received a text on his mobile phone, not his email account, the following day: Thx, when? Duvall sat almost the entire afternoon through considering this. Then he replied, carefully typing it out with the blunt tip of his index finger, Dear Sandy, do you mean to ask when should you come visit next?

He couldn't tell if there was any irritation in her reply: When u want me. The regular shorthand, those stilted sentences of hers, and now this lack of a question mark—if the message needed a question mark—were all doubly frustrating. He didn't know if she meant to say, When do you want me to come over? or I am available to you whenever you want me.

Almost exhausted by this process (he wished she would simply telephone; he wished he felt free enough to do so himself, but he didn't) he tried to be more direct.

When would you be free, Sandy? earned the curtish response of: w/e.

All right, that meant she could come at either the 'week's end', or 'on the weekend' itself. Wanting to inspire a little more clarity in her messages, he texted something very exact: Friday evening would be lovely, Sandy, and I can make us dinner.

Duvall soon read: F ok no dinner will be 18, which at first glance he thought meant 'Fuck, no dinner' plus something else, but, on reflection, he soon saw it for what it was: 'Friday will be fine though not for dinner. I will be late.' Duvall thought he might be getting the hang of this. It was as if Sandy had drawn him into an interesting word game, and he found he liked the complicity of it. These direct messages: her to me, me to her. It's a conversation. No wonder the young exponents of this new art had so much fun with it.

What time should I expect you on Friday, Sandy?

10–11.

All right, let's make that firm. Between ten and eleven in the evening. I will be looking forward to it very much.

A final reply came more than three hours later, as if she'd had something better to do in the interim. Duvall was sure she had.

WEG

He didn't have the faintest clue what that one might mean.

When he was very small, John Duvall had grown up in a green rural area, an expansive chicken and pineapple farm his father had inherited from his father before him. Little John had only eleven years on the property. His father was forced to sell up by the shrinking economies of trying to make a profit from a family-run farm in this new world of imported goods and mass-production.

His parents used the money from the sale with clear-eyed precision. They moved to the inner-city and purchased a number of run-down houses in good locations. It was well before the property booms of the later decades. Together, they set forth on a program of renovation and sales. After all, the only skills John Duvall's parents shared were those that had to do with early rising, a tolerance—indeed, a predilection—for hard work, and the tremendous fear that one failure will generate of future failures to come. There would be no more.

Duvall didn't very often think about his early years. His parents had worked tremendously hard, they were distant, and they prospered. As their only offspring, his inheritance at the age of thirty-nine—when his mother passed away just two years after his father—was very good indeed. By then he'd been running his own small business in land and property development, and though he'd lacked the ambition and hard-nosed cunning required for truly stellar success, Duvall had felt he'd done well enough. He and Mary were comfortable. They had a nice, expansive timber home in a leafy suburb, a penthouse on the coast that overlooked the crashing waves of the ocean, an annual vacation overseas, and private school education for Steven, their sole child. Steven had always demonstrated a head for figures and now worked on Wall Street no less, a wife and three children of his own. Duvall was proud of him, and was pleased he'd done so well, but their regular communication had always been through Mary. After she was gone they seemed incapable of anything but the most perfunctory small-talk. Weather; sports scores; the latest scholastic achievements of the grandchildren. It had almost been a blessing when Steven had taken that first overseas transfer.

If there was one thing of the past that Duvall remembered with the greatest fondness, and sense of loss, it resided in those very early years. He didn't dream so much about Mary, their first date, their wedding day, her final moments in a hospital bed too sedated to even return the pressure of his hand; he didn't yearn for that first sight of their baby after it had been pushed out from its mother and lay all swaddled, crumple-faced and bawling in Duvall's arms; and sometimes he barely remembered the way his grandchildren had so quickly changed from infants to toddlers to pre-teenagers with strange transatlantic accents.

No, what most often appeared in his mind's-eye was that wide, almost never-ending expanse of rural landscape his family had once owned. He remembered being five years of age, then six, seven, eight, nine, and ten, finally eleven, standing on a hilltop with their dogs, quietly surveying the open country surrounding the farm. The forests at the edges of the fields and meadows. The irregular but beautiful line of blue-tinged mountains far in the distance.

And that's where he was when he was dreaming of Sandy. Somehow this dream of her walking towards him, her hair loose in the breeze, was taking place back there. And he knew he was just a boy, and Sandy was as she was now, a young girl entering the prime of her life. The dogs were moving against his calves. He could actually feel them pressing to him, just as they used to do. He could smell the warm scent of meadows in bloom. Young John Duvall was on a precipice overlooking the long slope of the descent beneath him, a hillside running down and down and down until it met the start of hundreds of acres of untilled land.

And as Sandy came toward him with that serious-but-not-un-kind expression on her lips, he'd felt that he would fall, he must fall.

So now it was the Friday night and he was too keyed up to make himself supper. He'd forced down a piece of grain toast with jam, but had been unable to touch the pot of tea he'd made. The hours seemed to tick down without mercy; he'd wanted time to slow so that he could take hold of himself, reason with his own thoughts, try to deal with the uncontrollable fear that made his blood into mercury. Duvall couldn't sit in one place and think; he couldn't read; he couldn't stand the jabbering of the television. He simply couldn't be.

What on earth had he set in train by depositing that unearned money into Sandy's account—and who was she anyway, who was she really? Why did she want or expect an 'extra hundred or two per week', and what did she think she had to give in return?

For that matter, what did he want in return?

His mind kept moving to thoughts and images of sex. The idea of sexuality, a part of being so far removed from his life as to be non-existent. It pained him to recall that he'd ejaculated perhaps a dozen times in the nine years since Mary had passed away, and each instance had not involved the presence of another human being—except on his computer screen, where he'd let himself become inflamed by pornographic images of such lurid and breathtaking clarity that he'd felt his consciousness actually shiver. Duvall hadn't enjoyed those images and he hadn't enjoyed his ejaculations, either, for he was a man who'd lost the only woman he'd loved or wanted. It was true. There'd never been anyone else, he'd even lost his virginity to Mary, and now he was entering and quite bitterly embracing his twilight years. This material, this stuff so freely available on one's computer screen, it was for far younger spirits than his own, wasn't it?

Younger spirits such as Sandy's. Younger spirits such as her boyfriend's, if she had one—or ten.

That day he'd constantly checked his little phone for texts, his computer email for a new message. There was nothing from Sandy to say she was too busy, that she couldn't make it after all, had forgotten something important.

It was only with a shot of Tullamore Dew whiskey, taken neat in a shot glass, that Duvall could find a way to take stock of himself. A second shot glass of the stuff burned pleasantly in his stomach and down into his legs. His own anxiety had left him weary, but at least now he was calming down. Three or four weeks back he'd reflected that he'd soon be paying Sandy to come to the house not so much for the cleaning but for the company. Now he had to tell himself that this 'companionship' simply was being formalised. Between them there would of course be no funny business. None at all. He wasn't capable of it and he was certain that Sandy would not be offering it. He'd let his imagination and fears go; all right, he could relax. They would talk. Maybe she liked chess or Scrabble; Duvall certainly did, and he spent many nights with friends—friends his own age—over a board, or with a deck of cards, playing without aggression or too much competitive spirit, chatting and sharing a bottle of good port or Muscat.

So much calmer now, Duvall put ice into a tumbler and splashed in three fingers of the good Irish whiskey, then he took his chess set, the checkers board and the Scrabble game out of the cupboard. He placed them in clear view on the formal dining table, his immediate signal to Sandy that he neither expected nor wanted anything untoward. It had moved past 9 p.m. An hour or so to go. He sat down, he drank, and he waited. Duvall even felt himself nodding off from time to time—and yes, when the sound of a car door slamming came from outside, and there was a rather hurried knock at the door, Duvall's chin was on his chest and his mouth hung slack, and he was transported away from that hillside once again, coming back to reality. He'd touched the edges of his dream of being ten or eleven and about to fall, then the whole thing was gone.

As he blinked awake, Duvall was aware of just how heavily he breathed. Sleeping. Panic in his sleeping. What a thing.

Duvall tried to straighten himself before he approached the door, but the combined effect of his slumber and the whiskey had left him slightly disoriented; as he opened the door to Sandy he barely noted that she didn't much look like the young woman he knew.

'Mr Duvall, could you pay the cabbie?'

He trudged automatically down the path to the dark street, where a taxi driver was keeping his light shining on the front of the house. Duvall felt in his pockets.

'How much is—'

'Thirty-three seven-five. You want receipt?'

By the time he'd returned inside Duvall was more himself. Sandy was standing by the kitchen table moodily looking down at the chess and checkers boards still in their boxes, plus the Scrabble set. She knew his home well enough to understand these games weren't always so openly displayed. Duval thought that in the set of her shoulders there was an arrogance he'd not seen before. She was dressed for a Friday night out and her hair, previously only streaked with highlights, was now fully blonde. It wasn't pinned back or tied in a ponytail, but hung loose to her shoulders. When she turned her head the curling locks caught the light. Duvall thought she had made herself into an attractive young woman without trying too hard. Her eyebrows were finely drawn, and as she looked at him, for the first time he thought about the colour of her eyes. He'd never contemplated this before, but he saw that Sandy's eyes were grey-green and rather sad. At least for tonight.

She wore a sleeveless golden tan dress to the knee that looked both classy and retro, something modelled on the Carnaby Street days of the sixties. He couldn't help wondering if she would even be aware of the era. On her wrists were thin golden chains, and a pearl or its imitation in twisted gold showed at each very fine ear lobe. She'd done her eyes with a heavy mascara and her lips were red, but she didn't seem to be wearing any other makeup. What spoke most of a new side to this young woman, however, was all contained in her attitude. There was a certain scornfulness to the way she stood there, the way she looked at him, and even in the way she spoke.

'Would you play one of those records of yours?' she said, tilting her chin toward the collection she regularly dusted for him.

'Anything but country.'

Duvall contemplated playing her something to match her Swinging London dress. Not early Rolling Stones or The Kinks or The Beatles, these would hardly match a Friday night mood, but maybe Nancy Sinatra's record with Lee Hazlewood, or an old collection by Sandy Denny, Marianne Faithfull or Dusty Springfield. Still, he reflected, this was all too literal. Instead he chose a special rarity, an album he liked by Cesária Évora, the Morna and Coladeira singer from Cape Verde, nicknamed the 'the barefoot diva' because of her penchant for performing without wearing shoes. He enjoyed the mood of all 'Cise's' records, and Duvall reflected that it hadn't been all that long since Évora had died. She'd been just two years older than he was now. As he was bringing the diamond stylus down onto the opening track of her 1988 debut, La Diva Aux Pieds Nus, Sandy spoke behind him.

'Can I help myself?'

Duvall turned. She had the bottle of Tullamore Dew in one hand.

'Do you like it neat?'

'I'd prefer some soda.'

'There's a bottle in the fridge.' He was about to go get it and mix her a drink, but he picked up the cover of Évora's album and pretended to study it. Something in Sandy's attitude was unsettling, and he didn't want to give in to its call. 'Do help yourself.'

She soon came over to where he was standing. Perhaps her scorn had softened, for Sandy had mixed him a similar drink. She passed it into his right hand. They didn't clink glasses.

'I like the music,' she told him, 'very earthy voice,' and at this proximity he caught himself looking at how soft her lips seemed to be, even in their deep red. It was hard to reconcile this young woman with the person who'd been coming to clean for him. Sandy would never be out-and-out pretty, but Duvall thought that she had conjured more than enough allure to attract any male she might want. Add her ironic and rather moody gaze into the equation, and you had someone special.

Duvall drank. It was his fourth or fifth of the evening, but now he didn't feel drunk. They remained standing by the record turntable and vinyl collection, which stretched to over a thousand long players. Though he didn't really want to know, he needed to make conversation, so asked, 'Well, where have you come from, what have you been doing tonight?'

'Drinks with someone,' she replied, and didn't elaborate. A thought was in her mind, Duvall could see that. Then he saw the colour rise into her cheeks, even as she lowered her eyes. 'Mr Duvall,' she started, now not meeting his gaze, 'what do we do?'

He said, truthfully, 'I wouldn't know.'

Sandy drank. She contemplated the carpet and rug and furniture that she cleaned, even the curtains that she dusted.

'I want someone to help me,' she spoke.

Duvall was sure she had rehearsed a special speech, something, some approach, but he wasn't certain that she felt it was coming out right. The colour in her cheeks intensified.

'I was hoping ... that you might. You did pass me some extra money, that was very much appreciated. And I didn't have to ask very hard ...'

'What exactly is it that you want help with? Is it your mother? Is the insurance not covering—'

'No, all that's fine. I mean, it's as fine as it can be.'

'So?'

'It's nothing much. I took a few loans the last couple of years, just from my sisters, my mother. It'd be good to pay them back. I travelled a little too long ... India mostly. When I ran out of cash I settled in Goa, hardly spent a cent. Now there's university. And general costs,' she shrugged. Now that she'd started her story, it was as if it needed to come out. 'I've been a waitress since the age of sixteen. Nice places, dumps, everything. An assistant nurse too, since nineteen. I've had old people step on me and spit on me and swear at me, and in nursing homes I've had people shit on me too ... I've had to clean up residents who died, give them a shave, use wads of tissues ...' Sandy closed her eyes. When she opened them she said, 'And I've done everything as well as I've known how. But I've sort of had enough.' She tried to smile at him. 'I've even been a housecleaner.'

'I'm so bad?'

Her eyes showed how much she appreciated his small attempt at self-deprecation, at lightening the mood.

'When people can't take any more of one sort of thing, they make arrangements for something else. Something that suits them better ... that maybe they can live with more easily ...' Sandy let out a sigh and seemed disappointed in herself. 'Now I'm babbling.'

'It's fine, just go ahead.'

'All right ... I've found out as much as I can about something different. It—' Sandy took a long sip from her glass. 'Do you want me tell you?'

'Yes.'

'Can we sit?'

They moved to the sofa. Sandy slipped off her flat shoes and tucked her feet beneath her, sitting sideways so that she could look at him.

'I've seen sites set up for arrangements between men and women. There are women who want looking-after and help, and there are men who feel safer, or more secure, or whatever, with a relationship clearly based on needs and fulfilling them without fuss. Very, very few strings attached, if any.'

'Yes?'

'I mean, these are financial arrangements.'

'Oh,' Duvall said, absorbing her meaning. 'You mean men who pay women a weekly wage or something? And in return they receive the woman's favours? That's prostitution, isn't it?'

'One man, one woman, in a mutually satisfactory negotiation,' Sandy said with a shake of her head. 'It's got nothing to do with prostitution. If it did, then that's what everyone does every day of their lives.'

'What?'

'Don't I prostitute myself to come here and clean for you, to make you pay me for my time, my personal time and effort that is spent to your benefit? Do you see?'

'Well—it's not my place to belittle whatever people arrange between themselves to be happy.'

A certain confusion had clouded Duvall's thoughts. Was it what she was saying, how she was going about saying it, or the simple fact of her presence and proximity? He couldn't tell, and drank some more. Sandy took the opportunity to freshen their glasses.

When she returned he said, 'But how do you know about these ... sites? You're talking about Internet web sites, am I following you?'

'I joined one. I gave myself a name. I asked for help with studies. I posted what I would be willing to give and what I wanted in return.'

'An extra hundred or two per week.'

'At that stage I was asking for more.'

'More. And in return?'

'Me.' Sandy paused. 'On something of a mutually agreeable timetable.'

Duvall had to think. Words failed to form in his mind. This was overwhelming. The purity of her idea, of what he took to be her offer—for why else would she be here, why else would she be telling him all this?—stunned him. He'd been content to pussyfoot around with notions of conversation and companionship, just look at those ridiculous games he'd put out. Could he really imagine Sandy sitting at his formal dining table moving chess pieces or creating triple-word plays while sipping Muscat? Here she was giving it to him straight. Straight as straight could be. Quiet in her tone, but unapologetic, speaking with a sort of take-it-or-leave-it attitude; Duvall found himself admiring her all the more.

'Did you have any success?'

Sandy's grey-green eyes looked at him levelly. 'There'll always be plenty of takers. Plenty of suggestions. Great ideas. "Why don't I book us a penthouse suite for the weekend, I'll drown you in champagne and film you on your knees"; "Come over and strip, my best friend and me will give you a party you'll never forget"; "Let me open my trousers while I drive, you can get your head down there and work."'

Duvall cleared his throat. 'The tenor of the times,' he said, trying to sound worldly even though he was shocked to his core. Just imagine saying any of those things to a young woman; imagine this young woman actually telling him about it.

'What else should I have expected, right?'

'So you changed your mind.'

'I decided that route wasn't for me. Maybe a change of approach.' She gave him more of her plain and straight gaze. 'I … I think I've known for a long time what you've wanted, Mr Duvall …'

'… oh no, not at all …'

'You follow me.'

'Sandy … please … you have to remember, I'm getting to be a very old man …'

'And you watch me.'

Now he didn't reply.

'I feel safe with you, Mr Duvall.'

He still couldn't say anything.

'I don't feel safe with anyone else … I mean, not in this sort of a situation.'

Duvall tried to muster some response, find a way to muddle through. Things were going so fast he couldn't quite understand his own reactions. A part of him was titillated, true, but a far greater part was in terror. A healthy and vital young woman like Sandy could not dream of the type of problems a man his age might, and most likely would, experience. It was almost laughable.

'Then … perhaps … best to keep it that way …'

'I know you won't hurt me.'

'I wouldn't. I—' Duvall shook his head. 'I couldn't.'

'That's what I want. Someone who won't hurt me, no matter what,' Sandy spoke more softly.

When she was certain he wasn't going to say anything else, she waited a few moments more and quietly finished her drink.

'This is the longest conversation we've had, and I think it's enough now. I—I'm going to go in there.' She indicated the subtly-lit corridor, but he knew she meant his bedroom at the end of it. This was a room he always made sure to tidy before she came in with her own cleaning to do. 'Tonight I drank a lot of vodka, and I need to lie down. I'm not drunk, I don't do that. But what I am going to do is close my eyes. Close my eyes and relax. If I'm alone, I hope you won't mind, but I'll go to sleep. If I'm not alone, then—then I won't sleep.'

Sandy put her hand to the side of his face. He couldn't believe it. This young woman whom he'd desired week after week, who'd even begun to inhabit his dreams, actually put her soft hand, with what he saw to be lightly sunburned—or should he say sun-burnished—skin, against his cheek. There was no pity in her gaze, not even an appeal, but most shockingly of all Sandy then slipped her arm around his neck and her face was against his and she kissed him once, hard and on the lips, then she was gone and her footsteps went lightly down the corridor.

Duvall sat where he was.

The side of the record finished and for long moments the needle squelched softly against the empty vinyl. Duvall forced himself to stand and turn it over. The needle came down on the start of side two and Cise's voice, so earthy, yes, as Sandy had found it, filled the room with a lovely Morna ballad. But it was his own face that now caught his attention, reflected in one of the windows where the curtain was sashed back, and in that softening glass he wasn't a man of sixty-eight but someone younger, perhaps in his early fifties. Well, that seemed young to him. What he would have given, tonight, for just this one night, to lose two decades of deadening. To heed a siren song sent out—just this once—to him.

Évora had the voice of someone who had lived. He'd read that even though poor health had made her need to end her career prematurely, right up until the end she'd continued smoking her favourite cigars and cigarettes, and drinking her favourite alcohol, and had received friends and guests in the Cape Verde home she never kept locked. The woman had lived.

And what of him, Duvall?

He found his drink where he'd left it, and swallowed the cold remainder. Then Cise's voice followed him down the corridor to the half-open door.

Three

Duvall had the most curious dream. Or the most curious extension to his dream, because he was on the breezy hill overlooking those meadows and woodlands once again, and his dogs were beside him, pushing against his calves. No one else was present, and when he looked down he first saw that there was an immense drop into empty space, and, second, that there were no dogs with him at all. As for Sandy, or some beautiful reinterpretation of her—no. He had this countryside to himself and this countryside had him to itself. Nothing and no one was going to intrude, and he wasn't a boy, he was simply Duvall, as he saw himself reflected in his mirror every morning while shaving and every evening while cleaning his teeth before bed.

Then he fell into that vast abyss, but it wasn't falling, and it wasn't fast either. The dead-drop beneath him had once again become the more familiar decline of a wildly overgrown hillside, nothing more. There was no chance of a plummet into oblivion. On the contrary, Duvall found that if he filled his lungs with sweet clean country air, and stretched himself out nice and straight, he could float down the side of that hill and follow its gradient at a gentle pace. This wasn't some sort of tremendously impossible act of flying, of soaring off into the sky. Instead it felt natural and perfectly in tune with his abilities. Duvall glided. He was aware of long stalks of grass brushing his cheeks, against his throat, his chest through his shirt and his legs through his trousers. He sensed a wind rising and moving through the distant forests, then it arrived to cool his forehead and face in the bright sunlight of this summer's day. I'm really doing this, he told himself, it's really happening—and a feeling of happiness and fulfilment the likes of which he hadn't experienced in decades went through him, something like those good strong shots of Irish whiskey burning in his belly and warming him all the way down his legs.

It's lifting me, he thought, lifting me, and for long moments he felt the old, long-forgotten stirrings inside, the very juice of him.

Duvall awoke with the morning light streaming into the bedroom, falling across his face. With everything that had happened the night before he'd neglected to draw closed the curtains for sleep. He couldn't see the bedside clock, and with the weight of the girl's head and arm on his chest, he didn't want to make her stir or wake. This time of year, with that sort of light, he knew it must be somewhere between 4.30 and 5 in the morning.

Duvall's dream was already fading, though the sensation of I'm really doing this lingered. Far more pressing was the fact of Sandy beside him; across him, actually. Extraordinary. He was on the cusp of becoming a septuagenarian. She was so young. He wanted to ask her what she was doing here; he had a second more inane question that he'd forgotten to ask earlier in the evening: What is 'WEG' supposed to mean?

He marvelled at what he could see of her long, smooth body. Golden-brown where the sun had warmed it, a hint of white at the curve of her hips. Young beauty, he thought, no wonder I've stared at her so. At least he hadn't allowed himself to go to fat, but his skin was looser, of course, and his chest was matted with grey and white hair. His waist hadn't thickened very much, though below that, well, the kindest he could say was that he had chicken legs, the bane of most older men. A weekly tennis game with a revolving list of acquaintances, and twenty-five laps of the Olympic-sized public pool several streets away, performed three times a week, come rain, hail, or shine, did well to keep him in trim. But he'd given up riding the expensive Italian mountain bicycle he'd once been so proud of after a silly tumble in a public park had dislocated a shoulder; after that, he'd become a little too worried about broken bones. Still, he maintained a good diet, and was judicious with his intake of alcohol—yet time will have its way, this is a given.

So, Duvall wondered, what must it have been like for this poor girl to be so intimate with his decaying body; how would she recoil when she remembered what she'd done, when in the light of day she would see him all too clearly?

Duvall tried not to allow these thoughts to intrude, to spoil his mood. For he felt surprisingly good and clear-headed, somehow strong too. He had no idea how the many vodkas Sandy had said she'd drunk last night, and the large whiskey and soda nightcaps, would leave her this morning—but for himself, well, today seemed to be a good day indeed.

I'm not soaring, but I am floating, he found himself thinking.

The most surprising turn of all, Duvall reflected, which was even more surprising than Sandy's naked body splayed against his, was that last night's lovemaking had actually happened at all. Fear, anxiety, the sheer inertia of an old body that hadn't even attempted such a thing in a decade—all of it had promised embarrassment on his part and resentment on hers. Instead, Sandy had been gentle and practical in her approach. And it had been her approach indeed, because she'd done everything, everything and anything to stir and coax him, and he'd been a lamb, easy and passive, shy, only willing to follow her firm lead. He couldn't recall how long it had taken, but to Sandy that hadn't seemed to be a problem. She'd done a good interpretation of enjoying the process. Either the girl was one of the finest actresses he could imagine, or—as he most suspected—her generation's sexual life was so utterly foreign and incomprehensible that he ought to stop trying to divine its source and reach and simply enjoy its consequences.

After she'd made him penetrate her and come she hadn't been satisfied, and she'd asked him to hold her as she'd then gently, then more boldly, brought herself to orgasm in his arms. The shuddering of her long tan body together with her soft cries were things he thought he would carry to his last breath. The only woman he'd experienced anything similar with had left this bed nine years back; she'd been the sole woman to occupy it, until now. And until last night Duvall had never experienced an orgasm, much less watched an orgasm, with anyone but Mary.

Then Sandy had lain close to him and they'd talked a little, but not much, and neither of them had felt any real need to. Lying still in the half-light, Duvall had quietly waited for Sandy to move away from him and gather her things, dress and make herself presentable, then call a taxi to come collect her. Instead she'd nuzzled her face to his chest and said It'll be good when we do this again. A light kiss on his chin, her hand over his heart. You should get some Viagra or something, it'll help us a lot.

Always practical, always pragmatic, that take-it-or-leave-it attitude, yet whereas the words should have cut him to the quick, a terrible underscoring of his diminished powers, the way she'd said 'us' and not 'you' had melted him.

Us.

As Sandy's university year unfolded and made its demands, Duvall and his surprising new lover found an unexpected symmetry. For Duvall, things fell into place so easily that this so-called 'financial arrangement' seemed like the most natural means for a man of his age to find happiness and solace. It also felt like the simplest way for a studious young woman like Sandy to finish her degree. And she was studious, which was something that he very much liked about her. At first he'd thought that, despite the serious way she'd gone about his house-cleaning, in her private life she might be one of those silly girls you read about in the papers who lived for weekend nightclubs and endless social networking-via-technology. A candidate for having nude photos or videos of herself taken by a boyfriend, while drunk, and circulated all over the Internet. Her many texts both sent and received, the Jean-Shrimpton–style dress, plus the numerous vodkas she said she'd drunk that first time she'd come to his home after nightfall, had certainly encouraged the view. Yet as time passed Duvall found that even though Sandy appeared to have a good enough social life, this wasn't as important to her as he'd first imagined. She rarely, if ever, turned up hungover. She rarely, if ever, cancelled a visit they'd arranged. And she never spoke about shows, clubs, sports matches or music festivals she'd been to. New movies were things she liked to tell him about; his extensive vinyl collection with its myriad eras and genres of music was something she liked listening to Duvall explain. As it turned out, she was most attracted to his blues albums, and old songs by Bessie Smith were at the top of the list. Duvall could not imagine any of her friends' portable music players being loaded with anything similar, but Sandy sought out the digital versions of the ones she liked the most, and there they were, the little album pictures of things by Blind Willie McTell or Howlin' Wolf or even Robert Johnson flicking past on her compact iPod Touch.

More often than not she would come to the house with her laptop and psychology texts in her backpack, and he would play records and settle down and read certain key chapters of some important book of hers as she read others. Though he had no background at all into studies of the human mind—much less the manifestations of illnesses so bizarre he was almost beyond comprehending them: the multiplicities of schizophrenias, plus sexual deviances in any form, amongst the most confounding—his experience of life and its vagaries helped him to help her. It was a curious thing, all right. He would never be a teacher, but he could be something of a guide; in turn, Sandy hadn't introduced Duvall to sex, but she'd certainly rolled away the stone from the tomb of his desire.

She told him she found it easier to read and study and write her papers with him, there in his home. The share house which she'd moved into a few weeks after starting the university year, was, she said, a nuthouse. Fun, but distracting. And her own home, where her mother Glenda suffered, well, that wasn't much of a place for studying either. Sandy said she visited her mother as often as she could, and when she was there far more important things needed doing. Such as sitting and holding Glenda's increasingly frail hand, and listening to her mother's stories of her life long ago.

One night when Duvall asked Sandy how her mother was, as he always remembered to do because he'd genuinely liked Glenda, she said, 'It doesn't seem long now,' and later in the darkness of his bedroom at 2.17 a.m., after he'd helped her structure out a particularly tricky assignment, and they'd eaten a light supper and made love twice, thanks to the 40mg Cialis tabs his doctor, Maurice Laine, very cheerfully had prescribed him, a text had buzzed into Sandy's well-used Samsung. After she'd read it, he'd needed to hold her for more than an hour before the trembling stopped and she'd been able to summon the strength to go face what had finally happened.

Sandy returned the next night, which wasn't usual, not two nights in a row, and this time she didn't have her knapsack. No books or laptop, and she didn't want to hear the blues or any sort of music at all. Sandy had stopped along the way to purchase an ice-cold bottle of Smirnoff. What she wanted to do was to sit with Duvall and drink and talk. She turned the living room's lights down low. She told him about her mother Glenda, from her earliest memories as a child. It wasn't a terribly sad evening, somehow not even mildly depressing. Instead Duvall knew he would remember the night the way he thought he would remember Sandy herself, as a sort of light in his life. For all the love-making and erotic activities she encouraged in the bedroom and other parts of his house, Duvall felt these quiet hours in particular would always be the most touching.

She asked him about his son. By then the level of vodka in the bottle had descended considerably. Duvall swirled the ice in his glass.

'My boy Steven,' he started. Sandy listened. It wasn't until almost the dawn before they'd slipped into the double-bed, both of them now mumbling and wet-eyed with booze. After that, Sandy hadn't returned for more than two weeks. Duvall understood. He didn't go to Glenda's funeral or send flowers. He didn't want to intrude into Sandy's private life.

CICO, which by then he knew meant Can I come over?

Yes, by all means, I'm so looking forward to seeing you again.

When Sandy arrived she was a little quieter, but more herself. All her assignments had done well; she showed him the grades and he was so proud of her that the next day he purchased a collection of compact discs of old music she liked but still didn't have. By some form of alchemy he knew she would transfer these to her tiny machine. Sandy kissed and kissed his weathered face. Duvall's heart surged for her—she'd stopped being his cleaner (he did all that himself now, and successfully, he wondered why he'd never thought to be self-sufficient in that regard), he gifted Sandy a very decent weekly payment for what they'd agreed need only be a single visit per week, but which she always turned into two or three visits, and he couldn't imagine ever wanting anything but absolute happiness for her.

He also couldn't imagine any question of morality that could taint what they were doing. He questioned the harm to himself and to her and couldn't think of a negative. Since Mary had died he'd managed to go on even though he'd been certain he never would, and nine years later he'd progressed to a point of being more or less fine. Yet he'd been existing and not much else. Here he was now, living.

And for Sandy—was she really selling herself? Was she really a young woman who'd taken the easy way to get along and so had ended up corrupting her own soul? He had no illusions that without the weekly payments he would ever see her again, but in terms of damage inflicted to herself, he thought sincerely that there was none. How could there be? She wanted this and had asked for it. She'd tested the waters, had discovered the route she didn't want—those men with their revolting ideas—and she had decided on a route she did want. So how was Duvall exploiting her; how was he taking advantage? Once, early on, then many times after that, he'd made sure Sandy was clear on one very important point: 'If this ever gets uncomfortable for you, just say, I'll understand.' She'd told him she would definitely say, and, if it got that way for him, so should he.

'One of us says it,' Sandy had spoken with her quiet smile, the one that made him always need to kiss the corners of her mouth, 'and that's the divorce.'

As far as he could tell, she had never come close. He certainly hadn't. The thing just seemed to work. Maybe all relationships are a transaction, Duvall reflected, a sort of negotiation. We're programmed to long and to want and even to expect some ideal of romantic love that will sweep us away into endless bliss, but, in the end, even if it's at the most unconscious level, we work out our terms and conditions with the person we think we can bear to be with: I give this, you give that. I don't like X and I'll never do Y. Would you make sure to do the same?

It had been something like that with Mary. Until the illness took her, they'd been happy. Duvall thought about this often. I'm not romanticising it. If she was here to be asked, Mary would say the same thing, for the few problems that came up, between us the whole show had been lovely.

Of course, he hadn't told any of his friends about this new side to his life. More and more Duvall had been feeling that these good people weren't very much like friends at all, not really. For all their fine points they were just nice folk he used to spend the grey hours with, and no one had made too much of a fuss about his increasing absences. There were always others to fill the chair at the chess table, to pour the Muscat or port, to regale them with humorous stories about their funny and strange offspring. Individuals came and went from such groups; few questions were asked because the answers seemed always so manifest; a new medical treatment needed undertaking; an accident or infirmity had occurred; in one or two cases there'd been something of a late-blooming romance. Last year there'd even been a marriage: both over seventy-five, his second, her third. Not many of Duvall's male friends had—at least as far as Duvall knew—taken on a sugarbaby.

Now that was a word to make him half-smile and half-grimace. Yet the word that made him laugh out loud wasn't the exact opposite side of the coin, 'sugardaddy', but the truth of the entire matter: 'sugargrandaddy.'

The extent of Duvall's pleasure was completed by one more thing, and that was the dream that now came quite regularly, usually, he noted with interest, on the nights when he was alone, Sandy not with him. He would be in that countryside again, sometimes with the dogs, sometimes not, wind rising through the trees in the distance and a blue pall smudging the long irregular lines of the mountain range. From up high, standing at the peak of a hill, he again would see an almost infinite fall, a direct plunge down into nothingness, but when he took that deep breath and filled his lungs and leaned forward into space, the dead-drop became the grassy hillside's gentle decline. He would descend, floating, enjoying every moment yet not being particularly shocked by the wonder of his ability.

One night the dream changed: Duvall didn't float downward, instead he rose up. He ascended with the power of his own volition, and from up high, there with the spreading clouds, he saw the entire reach of his childhood home. The old house, the farm, the pastures, the fallow lands and rolling meadows.

Just over there were the other farms—in reality long-gone, of course, but they lived forever in dream-memory—including the cow pastures owned by the Wiseman family. He remembered Mrs Melly Wiseman riding over on her chestnut mare pulling the wooden cart that carried the vats of that morning's fresh milk. Little Mary used to come for the ride after milking; she'd been four years younger than him. When he was ten, she'd been six, and when the local community got together on Sundays after mass and members of different families played each other in one-set tennis matches in the school grounds next to St Patrick's chapel, Duvall used to walk with Mary down to the nearby creek and they'd watch the tadpoles and frogs, and wet the soles of their feet still aching from their good Sunday shoes. Then, one by one the families sold up and moved on, the old community evaporated into the air, and it hadn't been until the funeral of Walter Wiseman sixteen years later that Duvall met Mary again. He'd seen the obituary notice in the newspaper and had decided to go pay his respects, and to see how time had treated all the old faces—the ones still alive, that is. There Mary had been, now in her early twenties and lovely, wiping her eyes and holding her sister's arm at the loss of their father.

'Aren't you—?'

'And you're—?'

When he awoke, the memory of the dream remained so thrilling that the next time Sandy came to the house, he said, 'You know, I'm thinking of going back to visit the area I grew up in ... would you like to come? We can drive out, it's not far. Then we can stop for lunch on the way back. A bit of a country outing, it'll be fun and not too long a day.'

Sandy didn't quite stiffen. She was silent a moment, then said, 'I come here ...' and that had been enough.

So with the memory of young Mary and the dream of soaring over the hills and lands of his youth still fresh in his mind, Duvall had taken the drive on his own. He hadn't been this far into the outer western suburbs in thirty years, and of course things were so changed that at many turns he hardly knew where he was. Most of the old farmlands had become housing estates; quiet country laneways were now roads that intersected with myriad highways. The new houses were magnificent; expensive vehicles had taken over what had once been dusty tracks.

Amidst these new enclaves that dripped of such affluence, he had to search hard to find what had once been his, then there at last was one significant piece of it: Duvall found his hill. They hadn't had a name for it way back, but now it was signposted as Summerland Heights, and was populated by a handful of new mansions on what looked to be symmetrical two and a half or three acre lots. Still, driving carefully so as to not get lost in all the cul-de-sacs, no-through-roads, and little roundabouts, he found a section right near the top, at the north-eastern face, where the land was still being developed. This particular sub-division wouldn't be available for purchase and building upon until the middle of the following year.

With relief Duvall climbed out of his Lexus. Here the road was gravelly and ungraded. He stood on the side of this hill he remembered so well, facing away from the homes and all the development, and he saw, first, the distant forest, and next, the outline of the mountain ranges. His heart lifted and soared. He felt the years melt away from his shoulders, and he imagined that here was his dream and soon he would float.

Duvall sighed and let out his breath with contentment, then he filled his lungs as deeply as he could.

A wave of nausea shuddered through him. A slight tingling at the left temple became the toll of an iron bell. When he picked himself up, Duvall found that his shirt and trousers were stained with grass and there was a graze on his cheek that throbbed. He couldn't recall what had happened; he certainly hadn't floated. The only thing he could tell himself was, Good the girl wasn't with me to see. He dry-retched near his car.

Duvall drove with the radio silent, remaining well under the speed limit. He wasn't entirely convinced he'd make it all the way home, though he eventually did, and then he slept twelve hours. When he awoke it was as if the entire experience had only been part of that self-same dream, except that this time he bore some marks on his face, as if to show where he'd been.

Four

So now this was the day and it was the end. The university year had passed too quickly; it was as if only yesterday Sandy had come to his home in her golden tan dress and newly-blonde hair falling to her shoulders. It was early December. For her there'd already been last lectures, last assignments handed in and graded, last examinations sat and marked, and fond fare-wells made to lecturers, professors, classmates—innumerable folk Duvall had heard mentioned and would never know. Her graduation ceremony would take place Friday midday of the following week, and he hadn't been invited nor had he expect-ed to be. The world outside his front doorway remained com-pletely hers. Duvall hadn't imagined he would ever intrude into it; the only slip he'd made, really, had been to invite her on that short sentimental journey.

Duvall's regret, if he had one today, was that in the last little while study demands had kept Sandy from visiting as often as she usually had. The thing had turned into the originally-ne-gotiated once-per-week. If she'd needed even more space than that he wouldn't for a moment have considered holding her to the contract, but he did wish that these closing weeks of their friendship had been easier. The last few times she'd been to the house Sandy had been her kind and tender self, but a slight undercurrent of absence had intruded, as if her mind had fi-nally moved on to other things. Exams, final papers, those all-important results, yes, but also her plans—all that travel, all those bookings she must have carefully researched then made, the glorious moment she must have been holding in her mind when she would finally sit back in an economy class chair, ear buds transmitting some favourite music (Bessie Smith? Howlin' Wolf? Something more contemporary?), close her eyes and feel her flight surging into the sky. Soaring, yes. It was her turn.

Duvall transmitted the money plus the extra two thousand he wanted her to spend on herself. The electronic receipt arrived into his email in-tray. He closed down his Internet connection and contemplated the photographs he had of Sandy on his computer, then he sat where he was, holding his head in his hands and wondering just how vile the plunge back into mild existence and the grey nights of board games and drinks with folk not too unlike himself would be. He didn't quite feel the urge to weep, but that might have been because he still had this one night left to look forward to; after that, well. One night to say goodbye, the rest of his years for remembering. A single night to make her remember him, too.

2nite TE, as she might write. 'Tonight, the end.'

Duvall lifted his face out of his hands and checked his watch. He had a couple of hours. There was a pain in his heart; that was Sandy. A small tingling ran along his left temple; that one he wasn't so sure about. Something like an embolism or aneurysm would be a sure-fire way to have her really remember him the rest of her life: 'Right at the end I had to call an ambulance and watch them take him away, he was pretty old after all.'

In reality he was sure there was nothing wrong with him. He was simply suffering from sadness edged with tension. Duvall had been naturally healthy all his life, no major incidents at all, and the minor ones had been irritations at most, nothing worth remembering. At the beginning of the year, before filling out his ED prescription, the good Dr Laine had given him an in-surgery medical examination, which included an ECG, and had sent him for a full-spectrum blood test. All fine. After that dizzy spell on the hillside, Duvall had asked for the same to be done again; the second round of results pleased Dr Laine even more. He was confident that Duvall had experienced only a mild attack of vertigo.

'Good cholesterol up, bad cholesterol down, your resting heart rate is lower than it was at the beginning of the year,' Dr Laine told him, sixty-six years of age himself, with a protuberant belly and the broken-veined nose of a drinker. 'Whatever you're doing, keep it up, John. I wish I was in your shape.'

Duvall opened the top left drawer of his desk and found the blister pack. Popping out one of the pills, he considered cutting it in half as he sometimes did, what with the renewed confidence these little miracles had provided him with. Instead, he decided on the full 40mg. His nerves were at him so he wanted the drug's full insurance. Instead of swallowing his pill with a glass of water, he snapped the seal on a new bottle of Tullamore Dew. Into his glass he added three cubes of ice. Well, it was an occasion. He didn't care if he woke the next morning with a headache—and for tonight Duvall had already planned a couple of things he hoped Sandy would like. Not that he knew a lot about champagne, but there was a bottle of vintage Veuve in the refrigerator, plus a platter of cold seafood he'd driven all the way to the bayside fish markets to purchase, produce taken in that morning straight off the trawlers. Would she like these touches?

He cursed his nerves, then tried to laugh.

When Duvall heard the familiar sound of a cab door slamming he couldn't contain himself any longer. Nervous as a boy, he opened the front door and stood half-shadowed by the porchlight, chafing to see her. He was dressed in a new cream-coloured cotton sports shirt and chinos. A casual look he hoped she'd like. Sandy had never mentioned any preference at all for the type of clothes he should wear, but he just didn't want to dress old. He didn't want to dress too young either; hopefully tonight's attire was something of a happy medium. He wondered if Sandy would have thought to do or bring anything special for this, their last meeting, then, at the first glance of the elegant shape moving toward the house out of the taxi's bright searchlight, he thought she must have decided to change her hair. The colour, too. What was that called—a pageboy cut? Sort of Audrey Hepburn-ish, and darkened?

She came up the unfamiliar pathway and approached the unfamiliar home and the unfamiliar old man standing there waiting. The porch-light gave her a good view of Duvall, and Duvall a good view of her.

Duvall's eyes tried to penetrate the darkness behind her, looking for Sandy.

'Who are you?'

'My name's Britney,' Britney with the Audrey Hepburn hair and hair colour spoke. 'You're Mr Duvall?'

'Yes.'

'Sandy asked me to come along tonight.'

Duvall had to get the idea into his head and in a straight line. 'Sandy asked you? Why? When's she getting here?'

Now he pictured something completely inappropriate, some sweet idea of Sandy's gone completely awry, a surprise as misdirected as a missile without a gyroscope. She'd meant to make weight and meaning of this occasion. She'd decided on a very special farewell gift for him. If the thought hadn't so sickened him in the belly, he would have had to laugh at the irony. Two women for him, Duvall, who needed to rely on big doses of special little pills? He wanted to ring Sandy straight away and try to shake this misdemeanour off.

You're so well-intentioned, he'd say, but so off the mark! I just want to see you, no one else. Hurry over now, please.

'Sandy's asked me to say something to you, it's sort of a message. And, uhm, I guess that's what I've got to do, is that okay?'

'No ... no, it's not okay. Who are you and what are you doing here?'

She stood there facing him and didn't reply because she'd already given him the answers to both questions.

What was her name—Belinda? No, Britney. That's right, Britney. And she had something to tell him that Sandy, for whatever reason, wasn't able or willing to do herself: not in person, via a phone call, or by email or text. Extraordinary.

Duvall didn't want Britney in his house. He wouldn't let her in. He didn't want her anywhere near him, and the squirming in his gut told him that he didn't want to hear what she had to tell him either. He wanted to see Sandy. His gaze again travelled past Britney toward the dark of the street, where he was certain a second taxi was just about to arrive.

'Mr Duvall, she's not coming. That's part of what I have to tell you.'

'You're serious?'

'Yes.'

'And what's the other part?'

'Could we please do it inside?'

'No,' he said.

'Okay, uhm ... but Mr Duvall, it's what Sandy asked me to do.'

He was deflated, displeased—yet somehow still ridiculously hopeful. All it would take would be for the blessed cab to pull up ...

'All right,' he relented, standing aside, 'but it'll have to be quick.' He indicated the way through the front door with his open palm.

'I appreciate it,' Britney said.

Duvall nodded, and couldn't have cared less. As Britney passed he caught a whiff of classic Chanel, and it couldn't help but turn his stomach even more.

'All right,' Britney spoke from the sofa, hesitating.

She watched Duvall where he was seated in the large armchair opposite her, then she looked down at her white hands neatly arranged in her lap. He could tell she was uncomfortable—and who wouldn't be in a situation like this?—but was determined to press ahead. She had a nice pert body, he could tell, for the light blouse she wore and the figure-hugging knee-length skirt, and she was prettier than Sandy would ever be: dark-eyed, dark-haired, beautifully shaped eyes. She wore simple silver ear-rings, something like an amethyst ring on one finger of her right hand, a couple of plain bands on her left, and was otherwise unadorned. The pageboy hairstyle looked natural and unforced, nicely suiting the delicate bone structure of her face and cheekbones. It didn't seem as if she'd had it done for some special occasion. This occasion. Duvall took her in and found himself despising her; despising her for simply being there in that sofa when it should have been Sandy, with him pressed comfortably beside her, that stupid bottle of Veuve open.

'Could you please hurry up?'

'All right, I've known Sandy awhile. We've become pretty close. She asked me to come here tonight, I know you were expecting her. I know this must be disappointing. She said to tell you that now she was saying it.'

She said to tell you that now she was saying it. Duvall had to run the ridiculously constructed sentence through his mind before he grasped its meaning.

'Saying it? Saying what?' he almost spat.

'Sandy told me you'd know.'

Duvall was about to hurl something cruel and accusatory at Britney, but immediately had to hold himself back.

Of course. Of course he knew.

If this ever gets uncomfortable for you, just say, I'll understand.

One of us says it, Sandy had spoken with a quiet smile, and that's the divorce.

But this was so unfair. There was no need for Sandy to take a step like this. The thing between them was over because they'd negotiated it so. She was finished her studies and she was heading overseas. He knew she was going. Their textings earlier in the week had confirmed this would be the last meeting. It had been coming a long time, they'd both anticipated it, and now the moment had arrived. What was the problem? Duvall raked his mind for instances where he might have given Sandy some indication that he wanted or expected more. Had he? He honestly didn't think so. Yes, this ending hurt him more deeply than he'd anticipated, yes his sense of loss was far greater than he'd imagined it would be, but what was she thinking—that somehow he'd keep after her? Pester her forever with his unwanted presence, with a hundred texts a day like some callow youth?

Duvall almost felt the urge to pour this out to Britney, to express the utter unfairness of this step, but who was she? Why should she care? And why would he even want to speak his secret thoughts to this utter stranger—an interloper?

'I understand,' he forced himself to speak evenly. 'Though the message is unwarranted. Please pass that thought on to Sandy when you see her.'

He breathed hard through his nose, keeping himself together. The things he was most conscious of, however, were the twin aches in his heart and temple. He already knew that she'd managed to hurt him immeasurably.

He wouldn't offer Britney a thing. Not a drink or a simple cup of tea.

'Is there anything else?'

'She just wanted me to tell you that.'

'Is there any particular reason a phone call or a note wouldn't have been enough?'

'I don't know.'

'So, thank you for your time. I hope you have a pleasant evening wherever you're headed.' Duvall started to rise. Britney didn't move.

'Sandy said you'd be upset. She didn't want it to be like that.'

'Upset? It'll pass. Now—'

'Sir? May I speak with you a little longer?'

A lifetime of politeness toward others made him have to slowly sit back down in the armchair. He didn't quite lean forward to listen, but even now, tonight, the way things were, he found it difficult to be rude.

'All right.'

'Sandy and I, we've become friends, like I said. And she's spoken about you ... she told me you're a very nice man, very kind. A really great companion.'

'What on earth are you talking about?'

'Sandy suggested I should take her place. She wanted me to come here so that we could start to get to know one another. Uhm, Mr Duvall, Sandy knows how much she's meant to you. She said she hated the thought of you being sad—'

'I will not be sad.'

'—or lonely—'

'I will not be lonely.'

'—and I know I could never replace her, but, uhm, here I am, sir.'

Duvall felt his breath a little hard in coming. God. So this was it. This was the game. Sandy's game. Britney's game. Their game. He was a lonely old man of means, so why not make the most of him?

'You're a prostitute, I take it?'

'No—I'm just like Sandy.'

'Studying? And you just need an easy way to get by.'

'It's a little different.'

'You said you were just like Sandy.'

'I mean, what I want is. And what I can offer. I don't study. I do work part-time. I have a little girl. She's three. Tonight she's with her aunt. That's my sister. And my sister is looking after her more and more because it's hard to find good work and it's hard to make ends meet.'

Duvall noted that Britney's eyes had started to glisten. Was this an act? Even if it wasn't, why should he care? He felt an unfamiliar coldness rise up inside him, something that was hurt and angry, and—unbelievably—might even edge toward violence.

He needed to grip his hands together.

'So you're prepared to sleep with someone like me and indulge my pleasures in return for a good wage, and this will help you pay the rent and feed your darling little daughter. I understand well enough.'

Britney didn't speak.

'Well?'

'Mr Duvall, I—there's no need to react this way ... Sandy thought—'

'Sandy thought? Or did you think? Did you think there's a carriage of the gravy train going empty, so why don't I find my own seat? Correct?'

'Sandy never told me ...'

'Told you what?'

'... she never said you were like this ...'

'Oh I am, you silly girl. And my needs are monstrous. I'm like a satyr, you'll be on your back and on your knees and standing on your head your every waking moment, and even when you're asleep I won't leave you alone, all those gorgeous little holes to fill.'

For a moment Britney was stunned silent. She stared at him, lips parted. Then she whispered, '... just horrible ...'

'Then why don't you go? Get up and go if you feel so affronted. But sluts don't become affronted, do they?'

'... I've never, ever, been called that ...'

Britney lowered her head and started to weep. The hurt seemed so shocking that she couldn't move. She wasn't wearing much mascara, but what she did have started to run.

'So if you're such a lovely prize that I'm going to be paying my good money for, let me see what I'm getting. Come on.' Now he ungripped the tight hold of his own hands and leaned forward, and he felt as if he had a knife, and sentence by sentence he was plunging it more deeply into Britney's flesh. 'Your blouse, unbutton it and take off your brassiere. Shimmy your skirt up to your hips and do open your legs, would you, a man likes to know what he's buying.'

Britney's shock was now interlaced with fear.

'... cruelty ... such cruelty ... I'll ... go ...'

He saw her hands trembling. Her bottom lip. Spittle had gathered at the corner of her mouth. She finally got herself to her feet but couldn't seem to go further, couldn't seem to make herself back away from him sitting forward there in his armchair. It was as if some animal instinct told her that if she tried to break and run he would lunge forward and bring her down. The features of her face had broken, and now one hand covered them. Her shoulders shuddered, the sobs like great rents in the fabric of the room.

Duvall perceived all of this, and he perceived himself too, and a great wave of sorrow had him standing next to her, pulling Britney close with his arms around her shoulders, and she resisted, tried to struggle away with wordless cries, expecting the worst.

'My God,' he said, 'I'm so sorry ...'

She fought against his arms, hard, but he was stronger. Too strong, even at his age.

'I'm so sorry, my God I'm so sorry, you poor girl ... I didn't mean a word, what came over me, please I beg you to forgive me, like a monster, I didn't mean a word—'

She managed to pull back.

'I apologise, with all my heart I apologise, let me make you a drink, I'll give you anything you want—'

Britney looked up at his face, one hand now free, and she slapped him hard, but she also saw how genuine his sorrow was, his own alarm and utter disgrace at himself, then she seemed to lose strength completely, and her cheek went onto his shoulder, and there she wept and shuddered for all her years that were so wrong, and Duvall felt the great fall inside himself for his own years gone wasted, and he was sobbing too.

Duvall spent the days in his home, mostly with the curtains closed and without any need or urge to go out. He slept a great deal and also lay in his bed or sofa and didn't sleep a great deal. He picked at the food in the pantry and the refrigerator with no particular hunger, and neither drank alcohol to excess nor completely avoided it. He was existing, and that was the sum of things. Sometimes he heard his harsh and hating words again, and sometimes he saw Sandy crawling naked into his bed, extending her arms to him with the sheet pulled to just below her navel, the gorgeous swells of her white breasts and pink nipples waiting for him to lay his face and lips against them. Sometimes she was serious, sometimes she was smiling, and sometimes she was Mary too.

If he had one most prominent activity, it was inspired by the short exchange of words he'd had with Britney after they'd both calmed down and she'd let him make peace with her, just before he called for a taxi to come collect her.

'How did you become friends with Sandy?'

'We were signed up on a dating site. We saw that we'd both gone out on a date with one particularly horrible guy. Real sadist, couldn't even hide it over a first cocktail. Sandy IM'd me and we ended up chatting online a few weeks, then we met for a drink. The friendship struck up from there.'

'What dating site?'

Duval had signed himself up to sugarmoneyhoney.com and once his account was active he was free to search for whatever type of woman he wanted in whichever hemisphere, country, geographical location or postcode he most desired, the age range she should be, her weight, height, body shape and proclivities, what she should be able to offer and what her requirements were from him as prospective financial supporter. He sent messages to absolutely no one, but he received at least ten to twelve requests for further information about himself on a daily basis. These requests were from pretty young women and far more mature women, and usually had a photograph or two attached. There was a lot of nudity, smudged faces, and a great deal of innuendo or direct solicitation. He had no idea if these profiles were real or not, whether the emails were computer-generated scams or the real thing, and he didn't care to find out.

Where Money Meets Honey
Are we a call girl service?
NO!
Are these financial arrangements prostitution?
NO!
Do we support mutually beneficial arrangements?
HELL YEAH!
Come join the dating site for men who love to spoil their
women, and for women who need a little more help and excite-
ment in their lives.
Trust us, these arrangements are
AS OLD AS MANKIND ITSELF!

Though he looked far and wide—quite literally, there were
thousands of women of all ages, creeds and colours, in coun-
tries and cities both near and far, ostensibly desperate to be
supported by men such as himself—Duvall was only interested
in one person's profile. He glanced at Britney's page because she
had given him the moniker she used:
Brit4U
Age: 26
Asking: Email for details
Body Type: Slim
Height: 157cm
Ethnicity: Caucasian
Last Visit: 36 hours ago
But the one he went back to daily, if not hourly, belonged
to SuperKittenBaby. Admittedly, there were six SuperKitten-
Babies listed, in locations as diverse as Stockholm, Alabama,
Athens, Lucca, and Kenya, but the one he wanted was the local
incarnation.
Age: 24
Asking: Help with school
Body Type: Athletic
Height: 170cm

Ethnicity: Caucasian

There was her picture, the face slightly blurred so that one wouldn't quite recognise her in the street, or sitting next to you in a university lecture. She'd written a small introduction about herself, and though it was the standard sort of guff repeated in an infinite number of the profiles ('I'm a friendly and positive girl who loves the outdoors, looking for a friend who can …') she hadn't told any lies either. Sandy described herself as practical, focussed, friendly and warm, and without demands. She made a thing of asking for someone who was kind, and, in general, all she wanted was help with paying her way through her degree, plus a little extra money to put towards her big adventure: a year's backpacking the globe.

Last visit: ten months ago

Though he checked regularly, that information didn't change. Ten months ago; that was probably soon before or soon after she'd come to him in her golden tan dress. Something about that squeezed his heart; plus the fact that the information remained the same. She hadn't returned to the site, looking for another man.

Friday morning Duvall shaved carefully and showered, then he dressed into the powder-blue Italian two-piece suit he'd purchased for that late-in-life wedding the previous year. It had been, he recalled, one of the happiest weddings he'd ever been to. Duvall had already pressed his white shirt and polished his black leather shoes, and as he stood in front of the mirror making an expert Windsor knot of his woollen tie, he reflected that he was doing exactly what he'd promised himself he would never do. For Sandy, the world outside his front door had always been hers, but today he was entering it.

It had taken one short telephone call to find out where the graduation ceremony was being held; the receptionist who'd picked up the phone was even willing to email him an attachment containing the day's running sheet, but he told her that wasn't necessary. He knew the layout of the campus well enough, and in the shimmering midday heat he quickly found a spot to park on the third floor of the multi-storey car park. As he walked across the beautifully maintained grounds and gardens he wasn't perspiring, despite the humidity. His temple thrummed a little but his belly was quiet.

Soon he was sitting toward the back of the great theatre and he enjoyed the choir that sang two hymns, the vice-chancellor's address to the hundreds of friends and families gathered there, and the non-political and mercifully brief, if not out-and-out humorous, speech the premier of the state made, which was aimed at the graduands themselves. It took an eternity for each graduate to walk across the stage in their outrageous gown and hat, collect their rolled piece of certificate, shake the premier's, then the vice-chancellor's hand, and descend via the opposite stairs. All applause was to be held off until the end, and though there was an inappropriately enthusiastic smattering here and there, Duvall restrained himself when Sandy took the stage and demurely did as she was supposed to do. He felt tears prickle his eyes. A shudder went through him. Joy for her, sadness for him. Someone was pressed too close to him on the right, and as Sandy left the stage Duvall excused himself and made his way down the crowded row to the centre aisle—annoying many who had to get out of his way—and went and stood outside in a patch of shade, but near the main exit doors.

Within thirty minutes everyone had emptied the theatre. Discreet groups filled the grounds, taking photographs, shaking hands, hugging, plenty already leaving. Duvall had his eye on Sandy; she was with what he took to be her sisters and their husbands. There were several small children with them, a couple of younger girls too, and three or four male adolescents. No boyfriend that Duvall could discern. He moved on the periphery of these groups, not interacting with anyone, but when Sandy finally saw him, he noted the concern that came into her face and the way she quickly extinguished it, so much so that despite the smiles and laughter of those around her, she became something of a blank. Duvall gently eased through the crowd, politely made his way past the sisters and their children, then reached out and took both Sandy's hands in his.

She simply stared at him.

He wanted to tell her, I'm sorry to break the boundaries we set, but it's just the once, and despite what an old man like me wants, or tries to want, the human heart's a little too treacherous, and boundaries are really things it refuses to understand.

Instead he caught his breath and said, 'God bless you.'

By the time Sandy replied, Duvall had driven the Lexus all the way out to the stretch of land that used to be his childhood home, the once-upon-a-time countryside that was now variously labelled 'Meadowlands', 'St Patrick's Chase', and 'Summerland Heights'. He had his coat and tie off, and had unbuttoned his shirt collar. It was seasonably warm and, on this hilltop, as a sort of grace for anyone considering the purchase of a two and a half or three acre block, a cool and very sweet breeze from the distant forest made the long fronds and carpeting of wild grass sway and bow. Maybe he could buy one of these patches of land, he was thinking, right at the peak, and whenever he looked out a window he'd picture having once lived around here with his family, and all the years in between.

Duvall was taking a deep lungful of that sweet air when his mobile vibrated in his pocket. It was a text message, not a call. He squinted to read the screen in the bright daylight.

GodXU2, which he deciphered as 'God bless you too'.

He contemplated the small screen a moment, then composed: Always meant to ask what WEG means?

It took her a heartbeat.

Wicked evil grin.

He had to smile of course; he would remember that grin. Wicked, sometimes. Evil, not that he could recall.

Remake a life here—or he could simply go back to his home,

Duvall reflected, where he was already comfortable, because whether he fell or rose up didn't have to do with this place, or any other.

2012

THE SLEEPING STRANGER

One

When Moggill Road was dirt and the timber getters had given way to farmers, yet freshly cut trees still floated down the river to the sawmill in Toowong, well, that was when her Sundays meant the church service and a best frock, and one-set tennis matches in Indooroopilly's yellow heat. In those young days they called her Grace because Graziella came off their tongues like ash and iron filings, so now when she found the stranger curled up and sleeping with her dogs, the first thing she wondered was what his name was, and how it might sound in his new country.

She knew something of what had happened but nothing about the place he came from. Women in black with their faces covered and men in crumbled streets shaking their fists. Who wouldn't run away? Her own home country hadn't been any better. War makes no comforts anywhere. Paper stuffed into the holes in your shoes, soup with no meat and a single potato to share among a family. This man sleeping with her dogs probably the same thing.

Nice to be able to escape to somewhere else.

The big news had started over the last few days. The surrounding region, and a lot of the land that Graziella and her husband Filippo had once owned, started to appear on the television too. There on the screen with searchers striding through: the forest, the valleys, those nearby manicured hills dotted with the new century's dream of perfection: mansions, swimming pools and tennis courts. It was a long time ago since they'd worked the hundreds of acres of chicken and pineapple farms that only drove you bankrupt. After Filippo died, all she managed to hang onto were three acres for herself, the old house,

one machinery shed and a chicken coop. Bills and debts gob-
bled up the money. Now everything here was worth millions.
Millions and millions and millions.

Yet a stranger was sleeping with two old dogs in her shed.

People in the area were excited. Some were scared, expecting
to find fugitives in their homes. The police had set up a special
number to call if you had any information: if a fugitive was running through your back paddock, for instance, or was on the
kitchen floor making breakfast of your Affenpinscher. In this
area, when it came to pets, people leaned toward the exotic. As
for these very exotic escapees, well, Graziella wasn't about to
join the hysteria. Where would they turn up, people asked one
another in the Kenmore Woolworths and the Bellbowrie Coles
supermarket aisles, where were they hiding? Popular opinion
said they were more than likely up with the rapidly diminish-
ing number of wild deer left foraging the state forest, soon to be
clubbing their fawns to death for food.

'Smoke'd give them away,' the newsagent said. 'And if they
eat them raw they'll be dead before they're recaptured. Vermin
in deer, of course.'

The gourmet butcher, at odds for twenty-three years with his
neighbour the newsagent, ridiculed such predictable ignorance.
'Deer eat grass, last time I looked. Cleanest meat you'll ever see.
Now, if these fellas go killing wild pigs, then they'll see vermin.'

'Wild pigs? And where do you see wild pigs, genius?'

It was that sort of neighbourhood.

All three of Grace's sons were willing to move home for the
duration, to protect her. 'Ma, these guys are animals,' said Joe,
the middle one.

'They could turn up anywhere,' warned Sam, the youngest.

'Even if they're not animals they're desperate enough to try
anything,' the eldest and most reasonable, Charlie, said, switching television stations for the weekly game.

Joe even joined a group of searchers for a day, but returned in
a state of acute boredom. 'The creek's dry,' he told her, referring

to the winding stream flowing through the lowlands that had provided his boyhood years with untold hours of adventure. 'When's it really gonna rain, hey Ma?'

'Now, you see a man in trouble,' Graziella ordered her children, 'you give him water and food and you think twice about calling the police. What do you think we did in the war when the Germans started getting slaughtered? We hated them, but we fed them, and let them go too.'

Her sons harrumphed, knowing better. Germans died like hunted sheep in Sicily. Graziella gave her boys their dinners and told them to get home to their families, she didn't need protecting. When they were gone and the television was off, she cursed her husband—bless his departed spirit—for sticking so much of his small mind into the brains of those boys. Sometimes it seemed that the force of his personality had been a barrier to the wisdom that should have come to a better educated new generation.

Graziella wasn't concerned about desperate men on the loose. If she had been, then she might as well have been concerned about desperate men all her life. Her father, the one truly good man she had known, had taught her to pass through the failings of all things masculine. Three uncles martyred themselves in the second world war, believing the fascist lie to the end. A fourth, her favourite uncle, was a small town mayor, and even he had managed to cause the end of his own life. He'd ordered the summary execution of three American GIs for the alleged rape of a local girl. No evidence against them, but he hated all Americans as marauding devils. A trial? Forget it. Shoot them in the main square. A week later when the American army arrived in force, they filled him with bullet holes. Equally illegal, but there you go.

Then the worst. Right here in these once-sleepy rural outskirts, a long time ago, Filippo had taken part in the beating of a black man caught stealing from people's larders. Filippo and a few of his Australian cronies had taken the man, whose name Graziella had never known, to the river's edge. She did her best to believe that they hadn't intended to kill him, but his body was found downriver, lodged in a tree-root near the outflow of the cement works—and of who had done it, no one of significance was ever the wiser.

Protection on her remaining tract of land was left to a pair of lethargic dogs and a nice double-barrel shotgun. The younger dog was twelve years of age, a Great Dane called Sylvia who hardly ever barked. The other was Prettyboy, seventeen years if a day, an ugly mongrel she'd found in the street as a puppy. All his life he'd been friends to any and everyone. Half-blind and half-dead, Prettyboy already looked like a corpse, only capable of scaring an intruder if the intruder believed in ghosts.

It didn't matter that her dogs were useless. Graziella knew she had her wits plus nerves of steel. If she could survive the pre-war disintegration of an entire social fabric, and the poverty and famine of war-time, not to mention a post-war economic collapse, she could handle anything. If she could survive coming to a new country and making a home, and spending a lifetime managing and assuaging the personality of a man like Filippo, she could survive any intrusion a group of scared, skinny, exhausted refugees might make.

But what a remarkable thing had happened: first the big pile-up on the Ipswich Motorway that saw endless heavy traffic re-routed through—of all places—the slow-going Moggill Ferry; then, as lost as lost can be, a transportation bus slid down an embankment while trying a u-turn up on Rafting Ground Road, not far from the Brookfield Produce Store.

The police rounded up eight of the refugees but some were still on the loose. Grace couldn't remember how many, maybe the same again. Maybe only two or three. One. None. Hysteria can't count. SES workers, volunteers, neighbourhood children and their pets tramped through the hills combing the area. From her bedroom's crumbling balcony Graziella had seen a group of searchers on a distant ridge: they looked like picnickers on Easter weekend unable to find a good place to lay their blankets and baskets.

Now she looked at the stranger sleeping in her shed and wondered, Are you alone? Where are your friends?

This sleeping man—his skin was entirely, deeply black. It seemed rubbery, malnourished, loose and unhealthy. He was ugly. Even in perfect health he would be ugly—and he was so still he might as well have been dead. The dogs had accepted him during the night. All three were exhausted and didn't stir.

As Graziella watched, a stone of apprehension settled, not in her heart but in her stomach. Apprehension, or would it be better to call it sorrow, because she knew that this man's freedom was momentary and would come to a bad end. He would be found. Sooner or later he'd have to emerge, and that's when the chains would fall on him, just when he tasted the sun and told himself he was free.

Graziella decided, without needing to decide it, that she would help him.

The hay and straw softened her step as she back-stepped from the shed. The sun hadn't risen. The orange on the horizon was minimal. Mist hung amidst the trees and filled the valleys so that the length and breadth of her property seemed to exist in space, surrounded by nothing. At least for this hour, until the sun did its job and burned away the haze, this place was its own world as it used to be.

She wished Filippo had never been forced to parcel up and sell the vast quantity of their land-holding, but debts had mounted and his health had gone. At one time they owned most of the region but land taxes, wages and fuel costs skyrocketed at the same time as the price of pineapples and battery eggs fell like stones. Somehow, farming land became worthless beneath them, but developers kept coming to tell them that residential acreage blocks were the modern world's new gold. Well, her new gold went to pay bank bills, government loans and endless debts; there was nothing in her account now, that was for sure, and there hadn't been for years.

Her sons told her even these three acres were too much for one old lady; agents of course waited for her to sell up or die— go somewhere cheaper, smaller, more practical. But the view wasn't too much for her; neither were the crowds of cockatoos who came each morning; or the deer and the giant white stag she still sometimes saw, despite the acreage fencing that kept them out of gardens.

Not quite so alone as she was most mornings, Graziella left the stranger where he slept like a sack of broken bones and went to feed her chickens.

Two

There were three new eggs in the coop. They went into the pocket of her apron for the walk along the pathway back toward the house. Mist remained heavy and not even the birds had started a new day's song.

She pulled her knitted jumper more closely around her shoulders. Last week, wild hail storms had ravaged the city but it was the type of inexplicable thunder, rain and trouble that didn't put a drop of water into Brisbane's dams. The roofs of three nearby homes had disappeared. Here, she'd spent days sweeping and mopping, and clearing her vegetable plots of fallen debris and flattened stakes. The tomatoes, ruined. Joe would help. The work had left her exhausted, yet mornings like these were moments to be happy. Even if her thin legs ached and she unexpectedly had to sit down on her way back to the house. Graziella instinctively put her hands into the big pocket of her apron in order to feel the warmth of the just-laid eggs. She caught her breath. Her lassitude was physical but was also a sort of depression, she recognised it, and in recognising it her heart sank a little further. It wasn't for ruined trees, plants or vegetables, and not even for herself, but for the stranger lying in the straw, the breath and body-heat of two old dogs keeping him warm. She'd better bring him a blanket. Maybe she should have nudged him awake and invited him into the house for something hot to drink and warm to eat. How much had he already endured?

Joe, who had a voice you couldn't forget, was already answering the question.

'Listen, Ma, you take each individual fella from these crazy countries and maybe you'd say he himself isn't an animal, but the whole lot of them put together—they just got a violent way of life. You seen them on the TV? What about when they go stupid through those religious festivals? Smacking their own heads. Now that's stuffed. So better watch out because, you come from a place like that, you're desperate and capable of anything.'

Graziella would let the man rest, and he could take as much food and water as he could carry, but he would have to go. Where? Straight into the arms of everyone hunting him. There was no alternative. She couldn't drive a car any more and she certainly didn't have the young woman's energy she'd had in war-time. There was no underground Resistance to protect one running man; there was no network of 'safe houses' agreed between neighbours that could create a sheltered passage for an individual fleeing trouble. That was the old world and different times, an old-fashioned way of seeing things.

She turned her eye to the rising light, yet that wonderful mist persisted.

Graziella forced herself to her feet. She tottered. It was like this lately and she made sure nobody saw it. She knew she was the relic of a bygone era; her body was frail and her way of looking at things was as useless as ancient laws chiselled into stone but displayed in the corner of a museum. Was that reason enough to let go of what she believed in? She would never forget how at the end of the last war, when the worst of human nature was loose, mercy had still found a way to blossom. Her father. He passionately hated the fascists but he'd said no to exquisite revenge and had instead assisted the escape of a half dozen party officials. He had little Graziella bake bread for these men, pack them food and water. Why? It was either that or see them slaughtered. Justice was not in the wind, her father said, only the mob.

She couldn't forget another of her father's actions. A German soldier, no more than a boy, concealed in a cupboard during an American army search. When they could finally bring him out his uniform's trousers were soaked at the front. Her father laughed it off and said they'd imprisoned him with the pasta and grain for longer than the human bladder could endure, but she knew the German's shame came from terror and nothing else. Her father gave him a pair of his work trousers and tied the waistband with twine because he'd been a heavy man. He helped him escape, hidden in their cart, while in the town's nearby avenues and alleys other German soldiers were being chased into corners and stoned, stripped naked of their uniforms and pierced with pitchforks, strung up by the neck.

In one street, the mob; in the next, her father.

There was no one she could ring on the stranger's behalf. No one she could trust. She looked up at the hoop-pine treetops as the first birdsong of the day peeled across the sky. A new thought struck her: her father, the terrified German boy, and her father's cart.

This morning Joe was coming in his truck to deliver her weekly groceries. Part of his inheritance had allowed him to open a big fruit and vegetable store in Aspley, and even though that was away on the other side of town, he liked to deliver her groceries himself. He was a hot-head, that was true, and she had to admit he wasn't very smart, but in the main he had a good and considerate heart. At least to his family. Today they'd arranged that he'd stay an hour or two to collect the masses of dead branches those storms had strewn everywhere. He would fill up the back of his truck and dump the lot at the rubbish tip.

Grace contemplated it. Joe was a man with whom there could be no reasoning. She would have to make il straniero—the stranger—hide in the house. It was probably something he was used to, anyway. Then, well, the truck was huge and rickety, and always packed with wooden boxes and cardboard cartons.

Joe even used it to help family members move furniture. Add that to the fact that the fruit and vegetable store was so far away from this area. Add that to the fact that Joe would be going to the largest rubbish tip, which was even further. What if she could make the stranger secrete himself in the truck while her son was working? It wouldn't be difficult. He could cover himself in rags and sacks, and slide right in the back behind the biggest boxes. The man could be transported far away then jump off when the opportunity arose. He might even wait until after the rubbish was dumped and scurry off unseen across the tip. From then on, well, from then on his life and his luck would be his own.

For a moment Grace even contemplated the impossible—talking Joe into actively helping—but the timbre of his voice and the quality of his hostility stayed with her.

'The bastards know they got no chance. You make sure you keep the bloody shotgun handy, all right? I checked it for you. You know what Pa would do.'

Three

Yes, she knew what Pa would do. And she knew what she was capable of doing too.

So long ago, when youth was such a welcome fire in the veins, her conscience made her call the local district police chief. In a soft, soft voice she told this officer what had happened to the black man. In the old country, informers were the vermin of the earth. She turned herself into one such hateful organism and gave the names of the men, including Filippo's. Though she trembled for a week straight nothing happened. Ah, but wisdom comes too late in life. Now she knew, of course, the local police chief had been in on it too, but when Filippo finally came to her in the knowledge of what she'd tried to reveal, it hadn't been with rage and violence but with a broken man's tears and discontent. But I didn't touch him, I stayed back, I never even saw what happened, who was there at the end.

Lies? It wasn't up to her to decide any more. She made him go to the priest and confess; he did; it was never spoken of again, yet remained hard and cold in the deepest shadow of her heart.

Graziella put water on the stove to boil the fresh eggs. She had to admit that there was one thing out of all the confusing things Joe said that might be worth listening to. The stranger was a man in trouble. So would he understand that she was there to help him, had already devised a possible means of escape, or would desperation make him do something stupid? She despised the doubts that ran through her mind, but the seeds were planted and nothing she could do or think stopped them taking root. She was an old woman. A woman alone. Her father would have done the right thing, but he would also have made sure to be careful about it.

She knotted the food she'd prepared into a tablecloth and placed it all into a small wicker hamper. Fresh bread rolls filled with leftovers of Sunday's roast and her home-made tomato relish. Boiled eggs, peeled carrots, tomatoes, cheese, several mandarins from the orchard. A bottle of water and a thermos of coffee.

But what did he really eat? What did he really drink? What did his religion and customs not allow him to consume?

Out of all this she hoped something would please him. Then, when they were understanding one another, before Joe turned up, she would make him whatever he wanted for the next part of his journey. Graziella slid her wrist through the hamper's curved carry-handle and let the thing dangle from her forearm. Not wanting to, with regret, she took the well-oiled shotgun from its spot behind the pantry door, cracked it in two, and saw that Joe had left it loaded with two cartridges.

At least he had half-a-brain enough to leave the safety on.

She drew a deep breath and snapped the shotgun shut.

Sylvia and Prettyboy were not moving and il straniero was gone. It was as simple and cut and dried as that. Somehow he had quietly killed the old dogs and disappeared. Maybe they'd started to make a fuss; maybe in his country dogs were the Devil.

Her legs trembled, the ground moved and Graziella wanted to fall down. She put the hamper in the hay and clutched her shotgun. She touched her dogs to see how they'd died. Something about their necks, that was all she could tell.

If only she hadn't left him sleeping there. If only she'd helped him straight away. She wondered where he was, which direction he was headed. She pictured him running through the undergrowth but quickly losing the cover of vegetation. The wilder plains around him would turn into the well-ordered and neatly patterned suburban landscape that this area had become. In order to get into what scrublands still existed around Anstead, Pullenvale or Brookfield, and possibly make it into the immense state forest, he would have to start jumping fences, would have to start avoiding housewives, children, pets. He would discover that between him and any good hiding place there was neat suburbia and dogs not so easily dealt with. He would learn what the deer had learned: in civilisation there's not a single place to hide.

Tears pricked Graziella's eyes. Poor Sylvia, poor ugly Prettyboy. What a way to end.

Maybe, she tried to tell herself, he would find it a relief to be caught. There would be government food to fill his growling stomach, water to parch his dry throat. There was always the awful safety of incarceration. Or maybe neighbours' dogs would tear him apart; some local husband and father might hit the escaping man too hard on the back of his head with a shovel; instant justice would arrive for the simple, stupid killing of two dogs already half dead.

Graziella thought, and me half dead too.

Her legs ached. Her chest was tight. Just like that, the adventure and promise of do-goodery was over; she wished the stranger murdered or maimed. In the shed where the two bodies were inert and asleep before her, she stood leaning on the shotgun for support, listening for the telltale barking of dogs down in the valleys. There was something, all right, echoes floating on the wind, reaching her cars. Dogs. It might mean the stranger was in trouble straight away—or it might mean nothing. The neighbourhood mutts barked at tradesmen, the postman, their own shadows.

And as she thought it a shadow moved inside the machinery shed. Graziella half-turned but couldn't lift the shotgun high enough. A tremendous shove pushed her backwards. Her ankles hit some protrusion and she twisted sideways. Her torso wrenched right around and now she was on the ground, crumpled, and the shotgun, safety switch on, was out of her hands. Not that she could feel her hands.

The man who emerged from the dark looked down on her. There was the grime-stained face, dusky features. He seemed streaked with sweat and dirt. In his wiry hair were shreds of hay. His features had a deeply lined, slept-in appearance.

He spoke to her, softly but with urgency. Graziella couldn't understand a word. He looked down on her for long moments, then he was out of her view. When he reappeared he was holding the shotgun. He turned the barrels to his hands and with a howl smashed that long sleek body against the wall and the floor, again and again. It was as if he dared the gun to fire. It didn't. In a sort of furious ecstasy he broke it to pieces and threw the pieces away, then collapsed on his knees beside her. Despite his violence, his voice was so soft. Maybe he was urging her, or begging. All the same, incomprehensible words tumbled out. Graziella thought the most ridiculous thing: once upon a time she and Filippo had tried keeping turkeys, and this man's language sounded just like their gobbling.

Then what seemed to be one word: Jassim, Jassim, Jassim.

It could have meant anything. Don't die. I'm sorry. I will eat the food.

Or it could even have been a name.

Il straniero's eyes wouldn't leave hers. It was as if that gaze kept her in this world. His gaze had something of the compassion she'd seen in her father's face. Maybe then this was a man like him, in another guise, in a changed circumstance. The stranger touched her cheek. She couldn't tell if his fingertips and palms were soft or callused. Had he been a field worker or some kind of doctor or scientist? Who could tell. Where did he come from? It didn't really matter. Instead she was curious about the way he gently felt for the major vein in her neck. At the same time she had the sensation that all the blood of her body was coursing away into the ground, even though she was certain she didn't have the slightest cut. The man slowly lifted her arm. It didn't hurt. Her wrist came into her eye line and was without sensation, like the wrist of some other woman. Added to that, those liver spots and the mottled skin belonged to someone else. She wasn't ancient; she was a young woman, a girl baking bread for grimy-faced men because her father had asked her to.

The stranger felt her pulse.

Now Graziella could no longer see the large clay oven with the burning wood and the dough baking. She could no longer smell the bread being made. What she saw was not the familiar outline of her father's big shape. Instead, it was the machinery shed's doorway and the sky past it, the way a new day's sun was burning away the persistent morning mist. A burst of screeching white cockatoos swept across the clouds. They screamed to wake the dead; last month, a neighbour in the valley had been given a fine for shooting at them.

After the cool of the morning it was going to be a hot day.

He'd moved her. Then he wasn't a doctor. Though she didn't feel anything at being carried and set down, she knew only too well that injured folk were always meant to be left where they fell. Or perhaps he knew better, knew that a woman such as her would not care to close her eyes in a machinery shed, but instead upon a soft bed of grass in the shade. The shade was created by the hundred-year-old hoop pines behind the old farmhouse, planted long before even she and Filippo had made this place their home. There were poinsettias nearby. She smelled earth and lichen. The stranger's face was stricken.

Graziella wanted to tell him that it was all right; she could have named twenty, thirty, forty friends and relatives who'd been given nowhere near the number of years she had had. Not to mention that from her had come three big sons with families of their own. Seven grandchildren and Sam's wife Jenny was pregnant again. Over decades you learn to understand how things fall away and manage to go on all at the same time. If there was one thing to regret it was her husband and what he'd done one day by the river. If there was a second thing then maybe it wasn't this moment but what had led to it; to come to the stranger carrying a shotgun. To let suspicion take root and grow. That was something to be ashamed of. Her father, now that she thought of it, he wouldn't have done it this way. His hand would have come out first, in friendship.

Close by, dogs started barking. Il straniero turned his face toward the sound. She saw apprehension flow into his torment. Graziella knew what the noise signified: the closest neighbour's Staffis were baying at a vehicle pulling up at her gate. In a moment the driver would get out to open that gate, tell the dogs to shut up, and if they knew the driver they would. If they didn't, they would go even more crazy, trying to jump the fence. The driver would open the gate, drive the vehicle through, stop again, shut the gate, then come on up to the house.

Moments passed. The dogs settled down, stopped barking. They knew who had arrived. It had to be Joe.

Graziella would have told this man, Run now, for your life, and though she commanded him with the last of her will—Go, please, you don't know what my son will do to you—what she saw was a man falling into the river under a barrage of blows.

The stranger had to know that he had only seconds to escape. Instead, he took her hands in his. She tried to fix her vision on his face but somehow the great branches of the Hoop Pines were closer. She knew the stranger was kneeling beside her, and in her mind she gave her words all the imperious swagger she'd been famous for: Save yourself.

Despite this, the stranger stayed with her and spoke low, in what Graziella thought was a good voice for a prayer.

2008

COTTON YEAR & CLOCK

Whenever Eddie Drinkwater's mind drifted into the colours of his endless highways, he saw a white cotton dress on the floor of Room 355, Hotel Mayfair. He saw Nathalia trying to cover the green and black bruises of her cheek, and the one blood-reddened eye, with the curls of her thick black hair. He heard her ecstatic intake of breath, and felt her warm mouth cover him in kisses. The images, those memories, kept Eddie on all the country roads Nathalia Valenzuela now followed.

Eddie imagined that Nathalia and her no-good husband, a certain A-Grade mechanic and one time petty thief by the name of Joseph Bell, wouldn't have kept track of just how long this chase had been going. To each other they would probably say something like, 'How long we been running?' whereas he knew the answer. Today it was three hundred and sixty days. It gave him a thrill to think that the anniversary was just five days away. He'd make that anniversary mean something.

Driving out of a glowing plain, this mid-morning Eddie reached yet another new town, quite large, a mining community by the look of things. He parked the old Ford, took Leroy on his leash, had two cold beers in the front bar of a corner pub and purchased from a store on the main drag a slim book called Wedding Etiquette. This would be helpful. What gifts should a lover offer on a first anniversary? The answer was on page nineteen: cotton, clocks. That seemed odd. What possible romance could there be to cotton and clocks? Where were the precious jewels, the sapphires and diamonds that you'd expect to celebrate real love? The book told him: at the forty-fifth and sixtieth anniversaries respectively.

Eddie didn't find it curious that in the eighteen years of marriage to Big Janey, whom he'd left far behind in a white stucco family home, he'd never purchased anything that this little manual advised. Well, life was different now and so was he. Thank the good lord above. At a bus stop bench he took his time and headed a fresh page of his notebook The Cotton & Clock Year and that was all it took to make him realise the meaningful coincidence, the perfect synchronicity of things. The clock ticked toward the first anniversary of pursuit; the cotton referenced that white dress on the hotel room floor. The realisation made him smile so widely that a passing family of indigenous folk all smiled back at him.

Eddie took Leroy back to the Ford, tied the leash to the bumper and went shopping. With a shy but manly smile he purchased the best perfectly white size ten cotton dress he could find. One hundred percent cotton, he made certain. The dress cost him sixty-three dollars. He recorded the sum, together with the name of the saleswoman who'd served him, plus the name of the shop and the name of the town. One day these little details would be important. The children of Eddie Drinkwater and Nathalia Valenzuela would want to know the love story, so his notebooks collected it all.

In fact, in the course of the three hundred and sixty days he'd filled five thick A4 notebooks with his thoughts and his facts. This sixth one was already a quarter way through. Mostly he wrote at night. There were other times when he wrote in situ, watching Nathalia and Joe through his old police-issue binoculars. Whenever he could get close enough he left the binoculars to hang around his neck and observed them with the naked eye.

The funny thing was that neither of his quarry, whether sitting in a park, or buying pieces of fruit, or making love in a hotel room, ever noticed him. This made a grim sort of sense. To them he was a ghost—a ghost with a pen and a notebook and a trained eye that saw everything. A ghost with an aging travelling companion—wet-mouthed, tongue lolling, ever-faithful Leroy. Always ready to curl up beside Eddie's thigh. For those few ecstatic weeks when things had been so good between them, after

Eddie had rescued her from her plight, Nathalia would fight playfully with Leroy for the privilege of being curled beside Eddie's leg. This was yet another good memory to keep him on the trail. He believed one thing with absolute certainty: those good times would return.

In this year-shy-five-days Nathalia and Joe had probably convinced themselves that ex-Officer Edward Drinkwater wasn't even on their trail anymore, so it was their mistaken conviction that rendered them incapable of perceiving him. One afternoon three months back, breezy, half-raining, leaning against a lamp post with Leroy carelessly urinating against a wall, Eddie had bent his face to his cupped hands in order to light a cigarette. That very bad man, Joe Bell, had walked straight by with his own hands sunk deeply in his pockets. Eddie watched Joe walk right on down the main street whistling the chorus of some popular song.

Shaken by Joe's apparent inability to see him, Eddie had rushed back to the room he'd taken. Because he couldn't think what else to do he performed one hundred and fifty sit-ups and one hundred and twenty-five push-ups. Then it came to him: he should affirm his existence. He checked his passport, unstamped in a decade, and expired, yet it still told him he was 'Edward John Drinkwater, Australian citizen'. He rifled through his clothes and his shoes and his toiletries. He held his shirts to his face and smelled his own odour behind the vague chemical sweetness of laundromat soap. He read through pages and pages of his notebooks and relived their stories. He even stood in front of the mirror and observed himself holding his loaded .38 to his temple.

'If I pull the trigger I am no more,' he wrote. 'Therefore I am real.'

This procedure continued into the evening, then in the later dark he kneeled by the bed and counted to the last dollar how much of his police union payout he still carried in his leather satchel. It was over five thousand dollars. His pockets relinquished three dollars and sixty-five cents of loose change. Eddie wrote in his journal,

'But Joe's a fool. How can a woman love such a fool? I am Edward John Drinkwater. I exist. I have entire journals full of thoughts. I am only an invisible man because I choose to be an invisible man. I have $5,061 in notes and $3.65 in coins. Tonight I'm going to eat half a chicken with potatoes and gravy and peas, and save the breast for Leroy.'

It had taken some doing, yet he'd come to terms with his ghostliness.

So now his most recent notebook was ready on the front seat between his thigh and Leroy's resting head. The book was open at the newly-headed page and held the information about his anniversary present, the cotton dress. Sooner or later he'd write one sentence, which would become two, two hundred or two thousand. The steering wheel felt good to his grip and he pressed the accelerator to the floor, leaving yet another town behind. It was raining. It was after midday. As so often happened, the morning glow was gone and the countryside had turned bleak under heavy clouds. As he left the more developed environs behind, the open highway spread to an undulating landscape of dirt, sometimes there were hints of scrub. The rain that fell was a sort of watery pink. This didn't surprise him. Eddie pushed the speedometer's needle to over one hundred and thirty kilometres an hour, his features without expression. A passing motorist might have imagined a Ford being driven by a mannequin.

Late in the day there was a sign:

Merivale

Population 53,000

Serving a community of 70,000

Eddie Drinkwater's battered '63 Ford veered off the main highway and out of the persistent rain, travelling fast toward a town shimmering under rainbow colours.

Just on closing time he learned from a man who ran Orchard Street Hardware that a couple in a rented silver Mazda had come in about two hours earlier. The man knew the car was rented because the company's identification label was hanging from the rear vision mirror. The couple had purchased a corkscrew. Eddie put away his badge and thought about that. He spoke to a group of school children waiting with their mothers outside a hamburger store. The most vocal little girl told him a lady with dark hair had been wearing cut-off jeans and had been licking an ice cream cone. Another child said the lady had asked about the weather but the man with her hadn't asked anything. Eddie thought about this information as well. He was so good at his job that if he'd wanted he could have found out the flavour of ice cream Nathalia had been passing along her tongue. He wondered whether Joe had taken the opportunity to kiss Nathalia's ice-cream-cold-lips. Eddie didn't ask the children, or their mothers, but he saw it in his mind anyway, one long, luscious, cold-tongue-kiss.

Had Nathalia and Joe purchased a corkscrew and ice cream before blowing straight through Merivale, or had they stayed? At the outskirts of the town he studied the highway disappearing north-west. The late afternoon had settled a dusky glow over the countryside. There was no rainbow. Despite his thoughts Eddie felt good inside. Whenever he was actively on the hunt he knew his life held purpose. Once upon a time, married, a father of two kids, an automaton trudging off to relentless, ever-lengthening shifts and coming home beaten at their end, his life had held no purpose whatsoever. Except maybe for the paying of bills. His neighbours had lived for weekend barbecues and excursions to the beach; he was supposed to be like them. Meeting Nathalia Valenzuela had changed his life; it was a change for the better, even with the tears involved.

Now a road sign told him that the next town, Thornhill, was almost three hundred kilometres away. He watched the fall of night from the Ford's bonnet, his boot heels hooked over the dented front bumper bar. Leroy slept close, just under the grill. Eddie decided to find a room. Instinct told him his quarry had remained in Merivale, but if they hadn't the next day or the day after he'd pick up their trail. Once he'd been right behind them all the way into Newcastle, only to lose their scent for five and a half days. Eventually he traced Nathalia to a down market Italian coffee shop and Joe to a service station where he'd found work at his old profession. A-Grade mechanic, Z-Grade human being. Soon after, the couple abandoned their jobs and were driving west. Eddie Drinkwater was a half-day behind.

A slow tour of Merivale revealed a handful of motels. Each looked as dismal and unclean as the next. He chose one with a sputtering neon sign, not because of the colours in the sign but because of the year '1947' etched into the motel's sandstone. The year of his birth. Edward John Drinkwater signed in as Edward John Drinkwater. He'd reverted to the use of his proper name sixty-six days earlier. He found he liked to leave a trail. It was a touch of spice, even if the Missing Person file on him was already filed away. He suspected it was; he'd left just enough scattered clues for any police investigator worth his pay to understand that Eddie was lost because he wanted to be lost. There was no crime in that. Then, to underscore the thing and remove all doubt, he'd even rung a station, had provided his name, had told the duty officer to relay to all and sundry that Edward John Drinkwater had undertaken a journey of self-discovery. He was travelling, meditating and seeing the 'real' Australia. If there was any crime in that, sure, come find him—but if there wasn't, well, why not save police resources for serious matters?

That made him smile into the motelier's face, which was well-lined and unwelcoming. Her lips were white, indicating kidney or liver trouble, he couldn't recall which. The woman took his registration card and read the information he'd printed.

'A policeman. Well, excellent. I'll feel safer tonight.'

'There's something you're concerned about?'

'Only the hours between night and day.'

'What in particular?'

'All things in particular.'

'I'll keep an eye and ear open.'

'You do that, Mr Drinkwater. Driver's Licence, please?' She read it and handed it back to him. 'That's expired.'

'It is.'

'What brings a city cop all the way out here?'

'A love of the outback.'

'You mean you've got some poor bastard on the run.'

'That's for movies.'

'You can't stay here on an expired proof of identity.'

Eddie smiled and drummed his fingers on the counter. 'Is that a padlock on your fire escape door?'

She coughed and put the registration card into the front pocket of her apron.

'Twenty-five dollars. The dog stays out of the room and breakfast's at seven.'

'I'll be gone before dawn.'

She handed him a key on a heavy ring. 'Top floor.'

'A view?'

'Lovely view.'

Eddie took his belongings to the unadorned room that twenty-five dollars purchased him. He returned downstairs quietly, and when he was certain that a back room's television had the motelier's attention he put Leroy on his leash and brought him up with him. They relaxed together, Leroy instantly up onto the foot of the surprisingly wide bed. There was one window and the view was of a narrow back street, a broken brick wall and a leaking drain pipe. His twenty-five dollars had also bought him a hand basin without a hot water tap and a clothes closet that had lost its door and mirror. Eddie had a quarter bottle of whisky in his satchel. He contemplated tonight's quarters and took a pull from the bottle. The whisky made a welcome burn down his otherwise parched throat.

The bed was very hard. The doorless closet contained three

mothballs and a dry mouse. In the hand basin someone had left a razor blade. Eddie opened his bag for fresh clothes and spread them out over a chair, then stripped naked and washed everything he'd been wearing save for his watch and canvas shoes. Eddie used a sliver of soap from his shave kit for the task. Behind him, Leroy remained curled up and comfortable, at first panting, then breathing heavily, then softly snoring.

After hanging his washing over various corners of the room, Eddie stood naked at the basin and, as best he could, soaped his entire body. He didn't mind having to use cold water but the sliver of soap was now the size of a thumbnail, and transparent. When he was dry and neat he peed long and hard into the same basin, then ran the tap for a minute, then stretched over the bed cover. Leroy didn't stir. With his eyes closed Eddie pictured Nathalia giving Joe a cold-tongue-kiss, and he couldn't sleep at all.

So he dressed and drank more whisky and went to the public telephone in the corridor downstairs. He searched through the small Merivale book for two numbers. The first was for a pizza restaurant. The second was for a massage parlour.

During the second telephone call he asked for a small woman with long, dark lustrous hair, if that was possible. She should come within the half hour, stopping by George's Pizza 'n' Pasta on Merivale's main street. At that establishment she'd find a Quattro Stagioni waiting in the name of Drinkwater. Then, if the small woman with dark hair didn't mind, she should stop off at any bottle shop and buy him a 750ml bottle of Johnny Walker red label.

The person at the other end of the line asked if he was the Sultan of Brunei, or if he had two recently broken legs, or if he thought that he'd dialled the Blue Nurses, but when Eddie mentioned the amount of money he was prepared to pay for the conjunction of these services he had an agreement. Back in his room Eddie looked down at the rusted drain pipe and the narrow street, and thought he heard children laughing. Leroy came to look with him, paws over the window sill, tongue lolling. He gave Leroy a few drops of whisky then leaned there drinking the last from his bottle, thinking about Nathalia and Joe driving almost three hundred kilometres to the next town, either tonight or tomorrow.

Five days to the anniversary? What was time, anyway? Maybe the idea of the anniversary clock was to say that time is endless yet recurring, a construct of ideas and perception. Why bring things to a close in five days—why not five years or five minutes? In his mind he'd given Nathalia the chance of a year. A year for the chase, a year for her to change her mind of her own volition and come to him. His money wasn't limitless and neither was his patience. He had a white cotton dress. Why not ask her to wear it now?

Eddie ran the tip of his tongue around the mouth of the empty bottle, then went to the hard bed and flicked through the first volume of his chronicles. His words were reassuring. At an early page:

'Her name is Nathalia Valenzuela. She's from Brazil originally, a recent émigré to our country. I was the Duty Officer when she came in to make her first report. Her lips were cut and swollen and the left side of her face was bruised. Her left eye was blackened both under the eye and over the eyelid right to the brow. She was lucky to escape corneal damage. The bad eye was red and weeping. Her good eye was green. She went through the story with me and I took it down in the official way. Officer Irene Sanderson was with me during the interview but halfway through she became tired and it was the end of our shift so I let her go home. Nathalia Valenzuela claimed that her husband Joseph Rupert Bell had beaten her after being dismissed for drunkardness from his job at a place called Hackett's Motor and Panel Repair. We had a couple of screens on Joseph Bell, 1986 and 1988. Two counts of housebreaking. He did time on one occasion and community service on the other. Nathalia Valenzuela said that on this particular day of his sacking Joe Bell had continued drinking into the afternoon. In the evening there was a quarrel. Nathalia Valenzuela, who is also Mrs Nathalia Bell, claimed she and her husband had quarrelled many times in the course of their eighteen month marriage but where there had been one or two incidents of mutual face slapping, there had never been anything as serious as this. Which was a beating, long and almost methodical, in her account.'

Eddie turned the pages and read another section. Here of course the usually precise script was erratic, round and loopy, more like the work of a child than of an officer of the law:

'I found it hard to put distance between a professional demeanour and the fact that I enjoyed Joe's blood. It was everywhere. He proved himself a bleeder, and a squealer, so it's true to report he bled and squealed like a stuck pig. The butt of my service pistol bounced off the side of his head and it was good enough to open up his temple. A man's skull will bleed to excess, it's true, but it was as if Joseph Bell had a monopoly on the idea. He thought he was being murdered and that's why he wouldn't be quiet. Most wisely, I'd picked him up and driven him in cuffs to a remote area. He was free to make all the noise he wanted. When he fell to his knees I started kicking him. He cried and moaned and in the end I had to keep going at it just to make him quiet enough to hear what I had to say. Which was this: 'Joe, how about you never hurt your wife again? And don't try to report this, because I'm only one, but if you upset my good friends, they'll take you someplace like this, and they'll be three or four. And we'll always be on to you in some way. We'll never leave your tail. Understand? Tell me one thing that you think that would save you from me.' A nice raw pulp, Joe listened attentively. Little bubbles of blood popped from his nostrils. I used a towel to dry them up, then wipe him down. I uncuffed him and he sat dreaming in the back seat while I took him home.'

Eddie wished he'd spent less time on that section and more on the one that followed.

'Big Janey couldn't understand why I put up this stranger Nathalia Valenzuela in our spare bedroom. She said that face would scare the children. Our children consume a steady diet of movies where men's faces melt like wax off their cheek bones and human eyeballs pop out on their stalks, and a poor woman who's been beaten by her husband is supposed to scare them? I'd never done anything like this before, and when I told my wife to keep quiet that was a first as well. In the morning the children went to school and Janey went to work. I'd told her that Officer Sanderson would come collect Nathalia Valenzuela and drive her to the welfare people but that was something I didn't arrange. The house was quiet. A pot of coffee was brewing and when Nathalia Valenzuela came down from the spare bedroom she was stiff and sore and the bruising had really set in. I didn't say a word about what I had taken it on myself to do to her husband, and we sat quietly talking over coffee until she was hungry enough to ask for breakfast. We talked all day. At first inside my home. Then on chairs in the shade of the garden. Then at a lookout with the city in front of us. The poor thing should have been in a hospital but she begged me not to take her, not to force her. That was okay. It was a day to remember. I felt like I'd never talked or listened so much in my life. Hours melted. When I asked her how old she was she said twenty.'

There was a loose creaking in the corridor outside the room, then a knock at his door. Eddie closed his notebooks and put them into the satchel with his money.

'Service with a smile,' she said. There was a man in a black t-shirt, black jeans and black boots standing behind her. They came into the room. She asked, 'Washing day?'

The woman was a redhead. At a pinch a dark redhead, but nothing like what he'd asked for. She seemed polite enough, kindly enough. Her musky perfume mixed with the garlic and meat of the pizza she delivered into his hands.

'Money,' her companion said. Despite his size he had an affable, even neighbourly demeanour.

Eddie set the flat cardboard box on a small table beside the window. Leroy looked at the visitors but was more interested in the aromas from the box.

'You visited a bottle shop?'

She reached into her kangaroo skin handbag. Eddie took the new whisky bottle and set it with a glass next to the pizza box. Steam made curlicues from the round hole at one corner.

'Both of you, please wait outside.'

He closed the door on them and counted cash from his satchel. Then he opened the door and made to pass the money to the woman. Her friend intervened and flipped through the notes.

'You won't be staying,' Eddie said to him.

'Stick to the rules. Nothing rough. Want me to take your dog?'

'He won't be a problem.'

'Lucy?'

'I don't mind.'

'All right. You, friend. Don't make me have to come back. If Lucy complains, I will be.' He slipped the money into a back pocket. 'I'll be down the hall. On this floor.'

Eddie let him out and closed the door. He sat at the small table by the window, Leroy attentive and hopeful beside him. Lucy took off her clothes and lay on the bed, face down. Eddie ate slowly and thoughtfully. He fed Leroy a piece. The pizza was warm and the whisky was warming. Warmth spread from his abdomen to his heart. Soon he'd had enough and gave Leroy the last two slices. He dribbled whisky onto the dog's tongue.

Lucy said, 'That's one lucky mutt.'

'He's old and deserves a bit of special treatment.'

'Will he stay in that corner?'

'He's not interested in us.'

'You know that for sure?'

'Yes, I do.'

Eddie took off his shirt and trousers. Lucy asked him what he'd like. She didn't mind slipping the white cotton dress on for him. She was neither pleased nor relieved that his further requests were perfectly straightforward. After he was finished he wept. Lucy patted his back several moments, then cleaned herself with tissues from her bag. She washed her hands in cold water, then changed. She gave Leroy a pat, who'd indeed curled up into a corner and was almost asleep.

'You know, if it upsets you so much you shouldn't do things like this.'

'Help yourself to a shot of whisky.'

'I'm not a drinker.'

He lay with his head against the hard pillow, watching (he ceiling, tears abating.

'Then pour me a glass, thanks.'

The door was already closing behind her. Eddie waited several minutes then pushed himself from the bed and poured the whisky himself. After two glasses he found that he needed to weep again. He did it quietly. Then he found that razor blade that had been left in the basin by a previous resident, and slowly cut the cotton dress to shreds.

In his notebook he wrote:

'When a woman cuts a man out of her life she also cuts out the memory of him. She then can eat, drink and make love without any influence from the man she said she loved. When a woman stops loving a man he's no more than a ghost. He has no sway or hold over her and never will again. This makes her strong. He may die. The trick of the thing is to work out just how exact the situation really is. Has she definitely cut the man from her life, or does she only say she has?'

Eddie moved his gaze to the window. The night-time fall of rain was wetly pink once more. He liked that, though he knew that if the shade turned more deeply into red it would forebode trouble. He went to the mirror over the hand basin and studied his face. His eyes were changing colour. So was his face. Many nights he was a chameleon blending with the turquoise, emerald or sea blue around him. Any colour, really, primary or secondary. Eddie returned to his notebook.

'Love started a long time ago. Love started in 1947. A new-born baby is all love. Later, there was an adolescent with a pornographic magazine. Then a fool in a church aisle saying I will love you forever, you stranger. Love always is, but will change. I've just destroyed a cotton dress that this morning meant so much to me. Nathalia used to kiss me with her warm mouth but today her kisses were ice-cream-cold for a Z-grade human being. Love is a woman in my arms then it's a woman escaping. It's a room of the Mayfair Hotel and it's driving across country toward the dry dead sex of a sex worker. Let's call that a form of love as well. Love keeps one man alive and puts paid to another. For three hundred and sixty days the former has been Joseph Bell and the latter has been Edward Drinkwater. The situation is close to being reversed. It's a matter of timing only.'

Eddie went to his satchel for his .38, safety on, always loaded. With it on the bed beside him he reread what he'd written. 'A matter of timing only.' The idea of the clock proved this. He went back in time, to close to the start:

'For my wife and my children I have done my level best to shut out Nathalia Valenzuela, for my wife and my children I have attempted to deny every blessing she has placed in my soul. She tells me she loves me and she needs me. She uses the word "adore" as if it's a natural part of everyday language. Nathalia tells me that if I take her away she will never go back to Joe Bell. I have dreamed of her and I have listened to her, but for my wife and my children I have not allowed myself to love her in return.'

Eddie look a swallow from the bottle, and that crawling warmth travelled into his heart. He hated his moments of weeping; he loved them too. He wept again, for what came fifty pages later.

'The price of loving Nathalia Valenzuela is to have her for moments yet lose her forever. She says it's over. I believe Joseph Bell has an unnatural hold on her. Yet it doesn't need to be so. If I can make a life with Nathalia love will never again be the loneliness I've known before. Love will never be an arid marriage. Why did I let myself believe it was? Love is the white cotton dress Nathalia wore the first night she waited for me. The dress she slipped from her shoulders for me, the bruises still in her face. I kissed them. She asked me to. Love therefore is Nathalia and a white dress and Nathalia in every colour she's worn. She never chose black. She came to me in violet and yellow, turquoise and maroon, burgundy and a burnt-sunset orange. I lived again in those colours. She described them to me as she removed each one, piece by piece. She made me know them just as she made me know her.'

Eddie held the first notebook and new notebook together. He placed them on the bed beside one another and reread the old lines about Nathalia bringing love and colour into his life and the new lines about the dead sex of a sex worker. Such a gulf. He put his hands in his hair and then he tugged at his hair. He pulled at his hair and he ripped at his hair. When he was finished with that he returned to the bottle. After a fifth he was ready to lie down and sleep. He didn't. Another fifth, and he thought he would stay up an hour. Eyes heavy, he couldn't write anything more. A television would have been nice, even an old portable black and white to distract his thoughts. Eddie drank another fifth. Now Leroy didn't like all the movement in the room and muttered and buried his head more deeply into his fur, wanting sleep. Eddie stood at the basin's mirror and held the muzzle of the .38 to his temple. He sat down, drank his bottle dry, swayed, moaned, checked the time by his watch and saw in three blurred images that his watch had stopped.

A matter of timing, then, when time has said it's done.

Brown hiking boots, blue jeans, a white T-shirt, denim jacket, and the revolver tucked into the back of his waistband, just the way his police academy training and on-the-job experience had taught him never to do. The streets were dark and empty. The ground moved. One and two storey buildings seemed inordinately tall. His spinning mind estimated an hour before dawn. The heat of the day and days before remained like a shroud. Eddie wandered into a place called the Town Motel; in the square courtyard car park there were six vehicles, none of them a Mazda, none of them silver.

He vaguely pictured trying at least four or five more motels. He'd navigate his way through this country town's geometric grid with thoughtful precision—yet his steps mostly stumbled and he found himself back in the main street three times over. His hands felt disconnected from his body. The previous kindly warmth of whisky was now a poison that his system worked to expel. He retched more times than he counted, each shaking moment like a small cataclysm inside.

The silver Mazda was in the front courtyard of the very next motel he visited, and—even better—it was parked in a slot with a large white-painted numeral that corresponded to the door it sat in front of. Number 7. Eddie checked the vehicle. Its hire company tag hung from the rear vision mirror. There was no luggage inside, nothing to attract a smashed window or forced lock. The car's panels were grimy with red dust and flecks of dried mud. The pounding of his heart needed time to subside. So here was the way to finish this journey; he'd start the new day with a fresh page of his notebook, one whose sentiments would match his very first notebook. No more stuff and non-sense about absence and longing; no more self-pitying assigna-tions with paid women to have to record in coruscating honesty. No more in the ongoing history of pursuit. He wanted to write about love and colours and Nathalia's caresses in real-time, not past-time. Love needed to return where love belonged, and the image of this brought him a gasping sigh. He contemplated room number seven's door. He could knock politely; he could kick it down; he could crawl through the sliding window at front, a quarter open for the night air.

Eddie contemplated that window. He saw a doubled, moving image. Imagine if every single night Nathalia had left a window open for him. Come take me away. Rescue me. What if, Eddie wondered, what if I've been blind? Blind and stupid and too much in love with the hunt, too afraid of its end?

He started to climb through. As he lifted himself to the sill the revolver dropped from his waistband and thudded dully to the ground. He picked it up and held it in one hand as he slid the window to fully open and tried again. He recalled training and practice. He'd excelled when needed. Now he pictured entering in a swift smooth motion; he crashed through the window in a clutter of limbs. Eddie brought the small aluminium Venetian blind down with him, plus a short curtain.

Crawling in the dark, trying to get to his feet, fingers scrabbling at the walls for a light switch, a small bedside light came on. Eddie stopped. He was looking at the couple now taking him in. He levelled the .38 into their faces, unaware of how their eyes bugged, or of the horror in their expressions. He felt himself in a world divorced from this situation. He felt himself in a room that wanted to spin on an unknown axis. His heart hammered and it was as if he watched himself and Nathalia and Joe from the window of a hurtling train. His stomach heaved and fought to expel poison; his head needed to shut down; his finger wanted to squeeze the trigger over and over again, obliterating all sight and sense.

And there were no colours. He wanted to scream for the absence of any real colour at all. Room 7 was a portrait of flat grey. The cut-off pair of jeans Nathalia had been wearing today—at least according to those kids Eddie had spoken to—were over the back of a chair. They should have been some shade of blue, just as the jeans he wore. Instead, they possessed a negative image. His arms and hands trembled. He'd steady the revolver with both, take the half-crouching position he'd learned so well. When he tried to do that his knees quivered, as did his shoulders, as did his lips.

'Honey?... What is it? What are you after?' Nathalia asked from the bed, her black hair far shorter than he remembered, and sleepily mussed. 'You want money? That's okay. We'll give you what we've got. Everything. What else? What else do you want? We can let you have the car keys. It's not our car, but you can take it.'

She nudged the man beside her, who said in a voice gruff with sleep and fear, 'Anything you want ... will you let us up?'

Eddie could barely get the single word out. Lips and mouth still quivering he said to Nathalia, '... You ...'

'All right. Okay. I'll get up. I'm halfway decent. Just be ... just be okay. Okay?'

He felt his finger's pressure on the trigger. When Nathalia was out of the way he'd plug Joseph Bell good and proper, but he didn't want to get blood and worse all over her. He wanted Nathalia to be—

—Nathalia?

Skinny legs protruding from a short black slip. Wrinkled knees. She never wore black, even under normal clothes. Was this her way of mourning the fact that she'd lost him? But her arms were skinny too, and mottled, and her skin all over seemed loose. That hair, far too short. And dyed black to hide white and grey, for sure. Nathalia, no more than twenty-one now, at sixty-one or close enough.

'What's your name, baby? Tell me your name.'

'I'm ... it's Eddie. Don't you know?'

'Eddie. That's a nice name. Edward. I'm Helen. This is my husband Ben. We're ... you know what we are? We're grey no-mads. Isn't that a funny thing to be called? But it's perfectly correct. Tell me how we can help you, and, uhm, why do you keep lifting that thing at us? Do you want us to drink? I'm not a whisky person. I think it's empty, anyway, isn't it?'

Without thinking about it, he tightened his finger a little more.

'What do you want? If you've had a little too much to drink, maybe you'd like me to put the kettle on?'

'Do you ... do you see colours?'

'Sure. There's, well, let's me think about this. Colours. You're wearing a sort of Hawaiian shirt, right? That's very colourful. Your shorts are, um, slightly brown, I think you'd say. And your sandals are black. The walls here are white, but that's not a co-lour, no, maybe they're cream and—'

He backed to the door and found its lock. The room had no axis and neither did he. Eddie dropped the empty bottle of whisky. He watched the two blurred strangers who watched him go, then he ran.

He ran the geometric pattern of the town all the way to his own motel, but he lost one sandal along the way and tore off his colourful Hawaiian shirt and threw it into a nature strip.

Almost three hundred kilometres later, still in shorts, no shirt, the other sandal gone, his mind fizzed with a single question: How could he have let himself go so wrong? To be on the tail of the wrong car, the wrong couple. It wasn't so much a rookie mistake as an act of out and out stupidity. So they must be somewhere far ahead, Nathalia and that man, out on the long highway in another rented car—or maybe they'd doubled back on him and had joined some new artery of outback roads. He shook, he wept, he pulled over. Sitting behind the wheel of the Ford, by the dusty side of the road, and squinting hard for the glare of the crushing sun, he wrote in his notebook,

'The preternatural leash that tied me to Nathalia is broken, for so long it held us together. I have to remake it. But how?'

He'd never felt so lost, or so wrong. The alcohol leached from his pores and its residue was in his head like the red dirt all around him. He threw the book and pen aside and contemplated that dirt, then the flashing amber of the car's petrol gauge, then that amber reflected all through the heavens and into the smudged horizon. Trouble. Where was the real .38? Pulling himself together he checked his rear vision mirror, then the road ahead.

'Some drunk broke into our room and threatened us with an empty whisky bottle.'

Eddie could hear that grey-army-couple now, prattling away. The officers in some country police station would have to investigate. He pictured the expression of tedium with which a couple of cops would receive this task. They'd do a sweep of the town and radio it through to the highway patrol. There'd be his description but no information about a car. Still, he was a man travelling alone. Somewhere out here he'd be stopped just to be asked a question or two. That would be it, the end, but the sort of end he didn't want.

Eddie patted Leroy's warm head, always against his thigh.

He tried to imagine how he might bluff his way out of trouble. Break and enter, threatening actions, he'd be in a holding cell until he could get bail; at some stage there'd be a court case. Lawyers. Time wasted. Nathalia Valenzuela would keep Joe Goodman and vice versa. He might even have to go home. Eddie wondered if in his absence Big Janey had taken those fitness classes she'd always talked about. She might have sought out the help of a nutritionist as well. In the space of what this morning made three hundred and sixty-one days, she might well have created quite a change in herself. He imagined his wife a woman renewed. Healthy. Fit. Some man would love her that way. She was definitely nice, always pleasant, never some awful suburban harridan. He tried to picture himself beside her but couldn't, not with the fact of Nathalia up ahead, or behind, or circling off in some wide desert arc he was yet to understand.

He kicked the engine over. The car's petrol tank needed attention, probably the oil and water as well. Leroy let out a grunt and a whine. The dog was hungry and thirsty. Eddie held back his need to retch. He wasn't sure if a good breakfast would make him feel better or tip him over the edge. He drove another kilometre and before the engine had a chance to sputter he turned into the blessed relief of a service station's huge commercial plain. After that, Thornhill, less than three kilometres away.

The place was a combined truck and car stop, with acres of concrete and tar, rows upon rows of sleek bowsers, and, within squat, interconnected buildings, what appeared to be a restaurant and newsagent, an auto shop and even a small grocery store. He saw chalkboards advertising the prices of fresh fruit and vegetables. There was another smaller structure for the rest rooms. Delineated areas marked where eighteen-wheelers should roll in and park.

Eddie drove to the closest bowsers. A half-dozen cars and a couple of caravans were making use of the station. A veritable conga-line of freight lorries had called in. He pushed his aching body from the front seat. Standing in the midday sun he glanced through the glass of the restaurant building. Truck drivers were sitting in booths listening and laughing to the antics of a man in a baseball cap, standing before them and gesticulating wildly. Breakfast trays were coming out from the kitchen. His stomach grumbled and growled.

Eddie pumped leaded petrol into the Ford. He washed and wiped down the windscreen of dirt and squashed bugs. He opened the boot and slipped on a pair of tattered joggers, then felt around in a bag for his .38. The real thing. He ran his hand over the butt to make certain, then quickly pulled on a loose shirt. Just as quickly he slipped the pistol into his waistband beneath it. If trouble was coming he'd give it a run for its money. When he walked across the stinking-hot tar to the glass walled nerve centre of the station he paid his money and purchased cigarettes, chocolate and three packages of ham sandwiches. After that he drove to the motor vehicle parking area. He put Leroy onto his long leash and clipped it to the bumper. There was grass and shade nearby and the dog could do his own version of what Eddie needed to do. He fed Leroy the sandwiches, which disappeared in a flash, and left him with an old plastic ice cream bucket of fresh water.

The men's rest room was cool and smelled of antiseptic. Eddie dug around in the front of his shorts and urinated long and hard into a shiny urinal. He had to lean with a hand against the wall for the feeling that he was on a listing ship. At the basin no amount of lanolin soap and hot water seemed able to shift the oily sheen from his face. He opened his shirt and doused himself, then plucked white hairs from his chest. There was a forest of them. Curious. In the rest room's mirror he saw deep lines etched around his mouth and eyes, lines that he couldn't recall seeing before. It was as if the night had been obscenely long; as if one bottle of whisky had managed to wear him down by years. Again the idea of a clock seemed to take precedence over the more agreeable and loving idea of cotton. He didn't have his latest notebook with him in the rest room, but when he was back at the Ford he'd write something like,

'What does our looming anniversary really mean?'

He checked more closely and there were no untoward colours or hues to his face—though when he glanced through a small window the sky, the countryside and horizon had turned a deep and deeper trouble-red. The shock of colour made the ground list hard, and he blinked rapidly, and as if by a spell of magic he was feeding his pocketful of change into a pay telephone by a shaded corner outside the rest room building.

A pre-recorded operator message told him: 'For the area and service you are dialling you will need to add the numeral "three" to the start of the number. Please try again.'

His coins were returned to him. How curious and strange that message was. Something like that only happened, Eddie seemed to recall reading somewhere, when the telephone company had to expand its available numbers due to population growth. Not understanding how this could have occurred in the space of twelve months, he tried the number again, but as advised. Almost immediately there came clear STD pips.

'Hello?' Big Janey said. To Eddie the voice seemed to echo from some primordial cave of the past. 'Hello? Please, who's on the line?'

She hung up.

Eddie's coins clattered down. As he dug them out of the change-slot he dimly perceived truckers leaving the restaurant, men filing through the doors in a grumble and gaggle of camaraderie. Rigs already blew black exhaust into the shimmering day. The earth trembled to the rumble of eighteen-wheelers. Eddie heard Leroy barking. He knew his dog would be excited by those trucks, but on his leash he was safe. Eddie fed coins back into the telephone.

'This is Jane speaking. Hello—have we got a bad line? Who is it, please? I can hear something. Aren't you going to speak?'

A coin dropped. STD charges must have sky-rocketed overnight.

Eddie sensed the line was about to go dead again. Janey would slam her receiver down and who could blame her? His throat was dry. He didn't know why he'd chosen to call, and now that he had he couldn't bring himself to say anything. Maybe he was after something like the simple reassurance a mirror and expired passport could give him: I'm here. I exist. Here's a woman who'd loved and married me. So I'm not quite invisible yet, and somewhere in the world echoes of my life go on.

He listened to the emptiness of the line, and, closer, was forced to hear the convoy's noisy departure. Then Big Janey's voice returned, unnaturally subdued.

'I can't believe it but I know it's you.'

Eddie pictured two words in his notebook: preternatural leash. Jesus, he thought, there are ties that bind you in all directions.

'I don't even want to say your name. I will. Edward. Edward. Won't you say something if it's you?' Pause, pause, pause, then: 'Are you sick? Are you hurt? Can't you talk? No ... after all this time, after so long, I'm certain it's you. Please. I won't hang up. Say something. Say anything. My Edward.'

Big Janey was crying. The trucks were gone. Leroy continued his barking and Eddie wondered why.

'If you won't talk, then ... then just listen. Stay on the line. Listen to your wife.'

Coins dropped one after the other. Eddie pressed the receiver against his ear to catch the sound of his wife's breathing. He tried to picture her in the white stucco home they'd shared with the two children, but he saw only Nathalia in Jane Drinkwater's place, sitting in her favourite chair. Wearing yellow and gold. He shook his head to try and clear the image away. He saw the convoy of cloud-belching monoliths blowing waste into the distance.

'Your son … he turned twenty-one without you. Your daughter, she has two beautiful children. Two. You're a grandfather. I nearly remarried, but … couldn't. And, you know, I … I made friends with that woman. Before she left. You know who I mean. If you didn't hear her news, she left that horrible husband of hers. She moved home again. I've had postcards from Brasilia. Just one every now and then, usually around Christmas. "Feliz Natal". She gives me a little update. She's studying—or was. Maybe she's finished Law now. Twenty-six or twenty-seven, still so young, a life ahead of her, but her own woman. So right for someone who suffered the way she did. Hear me. Are you listening?'

Poor Leroy, barking. Maybe Eddie had misjudged the length of the leash and the poor dog was stuck in the sun, cooking. He'd go to him in a second, as soon as the coins ran out. But this stuff Big Janey was saying, was making up, such a fantastic mixture of lies and desperation, it mad him so sad for her.

'Edward, you helped Nathalia. You were the one who got her free. She was lovely. She was young. She needed someone to rescue her. That's what you did, and once upon a time I hated you, but now I don't blame you. Not really. But Edward, she's gone. I'm here. Will you come back?… is that why you're calling?'

He rubbed a hand over his damp face. Lucky he had his diaries as reference points. Every thing and every day were faithfully recorded. He'd left one back, so little Peter was fourteen now, not twenty-one. Sally was far, far too young to have children. Come on! Even Big Janey couldn't believe he would fall for that. The desperation in the woman, so tragic. And Nathalia was with Joseph Bell, and was most definitely in this country, and did still need saving. Eddie had white hair and deep lines, and poor Leroy had aged tremendously, and the telephone company needed to add more numbers to cope with an expanding population, time didn't lie. A clock is a clock. Colours appear when they need to and people lie when they have to, and Nathalia is making Leroy bark.

Sure, of course, that stupid dog had loved her so.

'Edward, you must know that we're waiting with love for you to come back to us. Please say you will. Let me know where you are. Tell me what you're thinking and what you want to do. Tell me you're all right because I love you, Edward, I never stopped—'

He'd left the receiver swinging and the words to end in a burr of a broken line, coins expended.

For there she was, Nathalia Valenzuela, at the Ford. On her haunches, caressing happy Leroy. Joe Bell was at the back of the car as if inspecting it for details, then he spoke some words to Nathalia and started to amble toward the station's glassed nerve centre. Eddie was coming from the other direction, behind him. He'd seen that Joe's dark features were, as always, evil. He looked a little more wiry than Eddie remembered. The endless road must have worn him down and here he was in a uniform tricking the world. Nathalia was tricking no one in exactly the same way. Her blue hat hid her hair; she must have bundled up all those lustrous black locks. In fact she was all in blue, such a pale shadow of her better colours. The sky was lower now, in a red that was close to black. Eddie started to hurry, reaching into his waistband as he ran, then he stopped, adopting the stance, so much good training in him it almost forced him to call out a warning.

The first shot cracked the enflamed carapace of the day and caught Joe Goodman in his right shoulder blade, spinning him around. Eddie fired again and he saw the slug enter Joe's throat and blow out in a mist of red behind him. Joe didn't drop straight away. Instead he stumbled a long way backward, eventually lost his footing, rolled once on the hot ground and was still.

Eddie heard a shout and felt an angry hornet buzz past his left ear. He turned. Coming forward from the car with the sky bleeding down over her was Nathalia. She was holding something out to him. He imagined it a white cotton dress, but it was too small, and not white. He smiled, feeling the tears that blurred his vision, so much love inside him he felt he must burst. He walked across the asphalt to meet her. He wanted to tell Nathalia what he knew about their cotton year and the clock; all of time would be their own. Soon he'd even read her his notebooks. Nathalia could hear everything she'd been and still was and would be to him.

Then there was another shout and her hands flared and he was on the ground. The red of the sky was a red in his eyes, and Leroy broke his leash and pounded to him. Eddie felt that thick tongue on his face, and he thought of the many forms of love a man is blessed to know in his life, and his eyes fixed, not on Nathalia, whom he now could not turn his head to see, but on what must be the air conditioned cool of the restaurant beneath its red pall, and within its red booths, where travellers had stopped eating eggs, toast and chocolate, and their cups or mugs of coffee rested unmoving against their open mouths.

1989

WHERE BREAD IS SWEET

It was a balmy morning.

I could see through the open bedroom windows just how balmy it was. The heavy branches of our front garden's palm trees moved listlessly. There was a bit of a breeze that carried the scents of suburban flower beds and freshly laid blood and bone, but no relief came with it. The breeze was warm as tepid water. It was going to be the balmiest day Brisbane had experienced that summer season. Normally I would have liked that, but the fact that the windows were open drove me crazy. They should have been closed. The mosquitoes had been getting their fair share of me during the night. Mosquitoes like to attack human systems that are low in vitamin B, that's what I read once. My body must have hoiked all its vitamin B ages ago. Despite the night-time attacks, I hadn't been in a position to get out of bed and do something about nature's cruellest insects. And somehow it had been cool during the night too. Hot during the day, cool at night. Nice, but unexpected. No wonder Johanna and I spent the night tossing and turning and fighting for the blankets.

The root of all last night's evil stood on the bedside table. It was a bottle of Teachers', with a film of whisky at the bottom. That was all that was left, a thin film of whisky that wouldn't wet my whistle. Two very sticky glasses also stood on the bedside table, whose flat surface was once polished mahogany. Maybe it still was, but all I could see were sticky glass rings.

The first thing Johanna said when she opened her eyes was: 'You were snoring all night.'

She already had this look in her face—this look and a pouting lip, and my headache making her good and ugly.

'And you had the covers. I couldn't sleep with you stealing the covers and me freezing to death. Why didn't you shut the windows like you're supposed to? I've got bites all over me.'

I had this look in my face too.

Johanna turned away as if she was switching me off, but when I made her look at me her eyes were wide and green behind the tangled mess of her seaweed hair. The alarm clock told me it was past time to get ready for work, but I didn't like the way Johanna could be so many millions of miles away from me. So I stayed in the bed and hassled her with my hands and my bad breath and my elbow until she gave in and we made love. I did my best. Johanna had a lot on her mind. So did I. Maybe it was the Teachers' hangover, for both of us. Johanna smiled at me once and I smiled back, but it was a bad performance on my part and wasted anyway. Mostly, Johanna had stayed the millions of miles away.

'That was good,' I said when I was dressing.

'Can you pick up some milk and bread on your way home tonight?' Johanna said from the bed.

I liked the look of the day.

All Brisbane summer days are easy to like. You can spend your life bleating and whining about the heat or you can open yourself up to the scents of flowers in full bloom, to the sounds of cicadas and birds calling out from great jacaranda or deciduous trees, and to that pure vision of sky that can either warm your face or turn green with amazing hail storms. I like the heat and I like the sweat and I like my open collar shirts and open car windows. I'm a Brisbane boy. Better than that, I'm a Nundah boy. I like to watch television in the afternoons, bare-chested, barefoot, tousle-haired, wearing only boxer shorts. I've never wanted to go anywhere else in this world, and that's my strength in life.

While I sat in the garage it crossed my mind that it was one of those silly days when instead of driving off to work like a good boy I could just as easily have kept the car's accelerator down all the way to Dicky Beach at Caloundra, or Muller's German Restaurant high up on a cliff face of Mt Tambourine. Yet as I eased the Commodore down the paved driveway my head was hurting again and I was thinking about all the things Johanna and I had frittered away since my money had come through. There'd never been so much red wine in the shelves or so many bottles of whisky on the sideboard. We liked eating out a lot these days too. That bonus from the yard really made the difference, but while the coffers were full it seemed like the hearts of Johanna and me were good and empty. Or maybe I was doing what they said in the advice columns of Johanna's magazines. Maybe I was projecting. Maybe my heart was the only problem.

When Johanna found out about Sandy she took it standing, all things considered. It was good Johanna found out about it. That brought things to a head and now it's all over, and as these things go, the money's just about all over too.

The Moorooka Magic Mile of car yards had been the happy hunting ground of my working life since I left school. There's hardly one shonky used car yard, or one thoroughly professional new car dealership, that hasn't earned a good buck from the fruits of my silver tongue. The thing is, I like the people who come into the yards and have a chat with me. I couldn't care less whether I was selling cars or cobs of corn, I just like all the different interactions. So people bought their cars from me, and then, out of nowhere last month, I scored a very minor fleet contract with a local BHP office, and the money came tumbling in. Life can be so sweet and surprising. Johanna and I just went wild, even with Sandy's fading shadow still at our shoulders.

The dealership was up ahead and I pulled in off the main road. I was about an hour and a half late. The gravel and dust in the driveway scrunched like a mouthful of broken teeth, and I stopped beside the little pre-fab office that stood in the middle of our colourful sea of Japanese cars. I didn't get out. Sandy was at her switchboard and Mr Simpson was right beside her. Sandy slid open the side window of her stuffy little office.

'I'm not coming in,' I said. The sun was high and bright and making me squint. I kept my sunglasses on but my headache was developing quite an edge. I liked the way Sandy's very red lips parted when she smiled at me. She could read me like a newspaper. 'Come on,' I said, 'I've got heaps of clients to chase up today.'

Mr Simpson leaned over Sandy in just the same way I must have done all those Fridays before, at the start.

'Making house calls now? Wonderful innovation.'

The tone of his voice told me that despite my winning ways with clients of all shapes and sizes it wouldn't be too long before I had my severance pay. The true art for me would be in predicting Simpson's timing, and resigning the day before. I had a pretty good record in that regard. And when I resigned, maybe I'd take Sandy with me on to the next Magic Mile car yard, and really give him the shits.

'I'm asking you if you're making house calls, Doctor.'

'House calls,' Sandy said without batting an eye. 'At the Travel Lodge.'

That was my cue to leave. I had to hand it to Sandy. Despite the way I'd treated her, she was still pretty sweet toward me. But she was no fool. Her red-lipped smile was all too knowing. Mr Simpson leaned further over her and his mouth was opening for one great bellowing admonishment. My reflexes were fast. I had the accelerator flat before he could utter another sound.

In the rear vision mirror I saw all the dust flying around the driveway. That would send Mr Simpson into a tail-spin. He'd have little work experience Bobby hosing and buffing those Japanese cars down in no time at all.

Sometimes a hangover can be the most peaceful of experiences. It's like some other slightly dazed world that you just float around in, full of blank spaces and personal revelations that stun you with their insight, then just get forgotten.

The open window of my car gave a good breeze in my face.

There was the smell of very fragrant wood smoke, as if somewhere nearby someone was burning a hell of a lot of eucalyptus branches. I took the bypass to the freeway. When I got onto the city streets I stopped at an intersection and let a mother and her kid cross the road in front of me. They were holding hands. The kid was a little red-haired, freckle-faced boy in drekky brown shorts. My hangover made me focus right down onto the way the kid's mother held his hand. It seemed to take forever for them to cross the street. Their joined hands just made me want to weep. I felt a regressive ache in my head and chest, and needed a drink or a shoulder to cry on. Or someone to tell me they loved me—and I had a bottle of Teachers' whisky to thank for these mawkish sentiments.

Maybe that's what made me drive to a place I wouldn't normally have thought of visiting. It wasn't to the coast or the mountains or anywhere I could have made the most of the balmy day. It was to that retirement home on Gregory Terrace, 'Canossa', run by the Sisters of Mercy, which is as fine and as true a name as you're ever likely to get for a holy order. My great-aunt, my father's mother's sister, was spending her last years there. Her last years were running on a bit. She was ninety-three years of age and at the last count the Sisters of Mercy had been her family for twelve years. Recently my Zia Angie had an operation to give her a pacemaker. She got through that okay, and that pacemaker would probably keep her going another twelve years. Zia Angie was strong stuff. She was the old world. She'd seen the old world and its people fade away, but she was going to stay in the new world as long as was humanly possible.

And I never visited. Until now.

I walked down the corridors. The place was old and smelled the way hospitals do. I passed nurses and nuns and wardspersons. There were a lot of old people, most of them in beds or sitting up in wicker chairs facing posters of the Antibes, the Whitsunday Islands, or Santorini. I found Ward 2c, and there was Zia Angie lying in her bed. She was dressed in a pink nightie and there was a yellow ribbon tied in her hair.

Her eyes were right on me.

'And you?'

'It's Joe. Little Joey. You remember me, Zia Angie.'

'Joey? But you're the son of Claudio. How you've grown, how you've grown. What a man you are. You were such a good boy when you were in short pants. Where is your mother? And where is your father?'

'Not here,' I said, because they'd been dead as long as Zia Angie had been at 'Canossa'. 'And how are you keeping?'

'Have you got your father's car?'

'I've got my own car.'

'Is it outside? Is it a nice day? Will you take me for a drive?'

I hadn't expected that. 'Sure,' I said.

Zia Angie's face was so white she might not have been in the sun for a lifetime. I went out of Ward 2c and found a nursing sister, and she was good and pissed off that I didn't know better than to get an old woman's hopes up. When I went back to the room Zia Angie had forgotten about the drive and instead had an old cardboard shoe box resting on the covers of the bed.

She was like a skeleton under the covers, almost transparent, almost no longer there, propped up with pillows and with that yellow ribbon tying back her wispy hair. Alone in her little room with no television and no radio and no magazines. What did she do all day?

When I sat by the bed again I moved to take her hand, but Zia Angie wasn't having any of that.

'So, little Joey,' she said sharply. 'This is Maurizio.' The shoe box was full of old photographs and her frail hands picked carefully and lovingly amongst them. 'He was born on the nineteenth of August 1889, and he was the smartest and the strongest of all the children. So everyone thought, but he died unhappy because from the time he was a little boy he was lazy and never had work and never made any money. He was my middle brother. Did you ever meet him?'

'No, Zia.'

'This is the eldest, Franco. He was the shepherd of the family. He was strong too, but he had no head for common sense. The Germans shot him. I don't know what for. Here he is with his flock.' Zia Angie was smiling at the grim face of her brother Franco. And then she did take my hand.

'What's this photo, Zia?'

There was a light in the old woman's eyes as she turned the next photograph around and around in her hands.

'But this, you don't know who this is? It's Maria, your grandmother, and that's me beside her. And don't you see who those two are carrying all the bread?'

It was so long ago, in times that are recorded in dusty books in forgotten library shelves. The photo showed a wide, cobble-stoned street, two older women—my grandmother Maria and Zia Angie as two middle-aged matriarchs—and a much younger man and woman.

Well, of course.

'Not married yet, your parents. Just courting. They used to bring the bread every Sunday for lunch, and then they were married and they came to Australia, and they brought me with them. We made a life. Your father liked to work.'

My courting mother and father looked like two skinny kids suffering their way through a war, but they still managed to be laughing in that cobblestoned street of Piedimonte. The funniest thing about the old photograph was the strange loaves of bread that filled my mother's and my father's arms.

Those loaves were huge. Wide and round, there was a big hole in each of them, making them look not like bread at all but car tyres. My father had three fat loaves laced up one arm. My mother was laughing at him and by the look of her it seemed she wanted to lace a few loaves up her own arms, but the two matriarchs watched sternly on. The photograph forever captured the oppression of their united gaze, as well as the happiness of two young Sicilian kids who would soon get married and head off for another country.

I was especially taken by my father's face. He'd never seemed the most happy-go-lucky man to me, but here he was laughing like a clown. The first loaf of bread was right up his arm, up against his armpit, and he was only wearing a singlet. I bet that when the time came to cut up the bread he would have made sure to give that particular piece to someone else—stern-faced Zia Angie, maybe.

'Here you cannot get this bread,' Zia Angie now spoke as if she spent all her days in grocery stores and bakeries. 'This bread is the best Sicilian bread in the world.'

I looked from the photograph to the liver spots on her hands to the loose creases in her face. It was only then that I realised her eyes were as green as Johanna's. I did my best not to stare.

'In this country the bread is sick. It is dead before you get it. You cannot eat it. They just do not know how to make it the right way. There's poison in everything. The bread here tastes like it is dirty and old. Do you know it is like this?'

'How should the bread be, Zia?'

'Dolce! Dolce come il zucchero!'

'Sweet like sugar?'

'Sweet! When we made the bread it was sweet without putting sugar on it. The farina must be the best, or you will be sorry you wasted your time baking bread.'

I was looking at Zia Angie's green eyes and I was thinking of Johanna. I was thinking how we had a nice house and how we lived in a quiet street and how we lived under blue skies, and how our bread was wrong.

Zia Angie was telling me that during the war her brothers used to risk their necks to buy contraband grain, and how they would bicycle the illegal sacks down from the storehouses in the mountains, bringing them to the village for the family and their neighbours to share. The dough they made would be baked in big wood-burning ovens right in the home.

'Now you will take me for a drive in your own car,' she said. 'Little Joey, in the long pants.'

I took the cardboard shoe box from Zia Angie's hands and slid it under her bed, where there was an old thin suitcase that looked as if it hadn't been opened in a decade. I helped her on with her slippers, which were fluffy and mismatched. One was grey fluff and the other was pink fluff. That made me angry at the Sisters of Mercy. That made me as angry as I'd been at Johanna for leaving the bedroom windows open. Why does nobody care about the right things anymore?

I wasn't about to ask permission to take Zia Angie away for the day, but as it turned out we didn't get more than ten steps down the corridor before she lost heart and started tugging on my sleeve to take her back to her bed. So I did, and as I helped her to lie down a muscle in one of her saggy, lined cheeks was twitching and would not stop. I held her hand as she fell asleep. It wasn't yet midday.

The bright, hot sun was a welcome sign after the antiseptic semi-dark of the home, but it was a little too late to think about driving to the beach. I felt lost. I didn't know what to do. I could have gone into the city and had a haircut and sat through a Hollywood movie, or I could have bought some fish and chips and gone down to New Farm Park and sat around watching the river. The truth is I was tired and dreamy, a younger incarnation of Zia Angie. So I followed an old habit and drove to the Travel Lodge, and it was good to be there again because they remembered me.

They gave me a room on the twelfth floor. There was a great view of the Botanic Gardens. I went straight for the Room Service menu. When Sandy and I used to encamp there, we'd drink beer and eat burgers and take lustrous oil-baths and watch crappy in-house videos.

In the cool and quiet of my room I opened one of the mini bar's little bottles of whisky, and had it with soda and ice. I took the next one, and the one after, neat. By the time my deluxe burger 'n' chips arrived I was feeling all loose and languid and happy. On the shelves above the mini bar there were all sorts of treats: hand-made chocolates in a small wicker basket,

Australian macadamia nuts, water crackers with little packets of cheese and chives, and a good half-bottle of Johnny Walker Black Label.

I opened the Johnny Walker and felt an oozing sort of satisfaction in the pit of my gut.

But it was the hamburger I really concentrated on. After a few more slugs of that whisky, the hamburger was the most important thing in my world. The hamburger bun in particular. I was just giving it the once over when there was a light tapping at my door. That annoyed me. It annoyed me more that I hadn't thought to put the Privacy Requested sign out.

Sandy was standing there and she was smiling. She looked good. She was smiling in that way of hers, and she'd changed into a little dress that showed off a lot of her legs. She smelled good too, and her lips were red.

'How did you know I'd be here?'

Sandy came inside and she put her handbag down. She didn't kiss me or touch me. She sat on the bed next to the room service tray, and she picked at the hamburger bun.

'You're pretty easy to read, Joe. I just knew you'd come back here and spend the day. I thought you might have found yourself another woman. I'm a sticky beak. I just went to the reception desk and asked for your room.'

Sandy poured herself a healthy slug of the whisky and sipped at it. Like me, with no mixer or ice.

'What about Simpson?'

'I left at lunch time and I'm not going back. He stinks. Stuff him. He can get Bobby onto the switchboard.'

'It's good to see you, Sandy.'

'I'm glad I'm not in love with you, Joe.'

She put out her arms and I went into them, and it was just like it used to be when we'd retreat to a room in the Travel Lodge and indulge our every human sense. Soon the languid voluptuousness in my gut poured out of me and into Sandy, and she soothed me and stroked my hair and whispered in my ear.

Later we drank the rest of the whisky and stared at the cold hamburger and chips. The red was gone from Sandy's lips and she was wearing one of the room's soft white robes. I hung around in the altogether. My head was heavy but whenever I leaned my head on Sandy's shoulder I felt better.

'Let's order some more food,' Sandy said. 'I'm starving.'

'Yeah.' I fiddled with the cold hamburger. 'Take a look at this, Sandy.'

'What?'

I took the butter knife and carefully scraped everything I could off the bun. I was drunk, I'll admit it. Sandy might have been as well, but I couldn't be sure. I scraped every last bit of butter and grease off that bun, then held it up for Sandy to look at. I don't think she saw what I saw. I don't think she fully appreciated the textures, the scent, even the inviting pores of that bun.

I said, 'Take a bite, Sandy.'

'It'll be cold,' she said. 'Let's order more.'

'Go on.'

'No, Joe.'

Sandy looked pretty pissed off. She left the bed and closed herself in the bathroom. Soon I heard the toilet flushing.

So I took a bite myself.

Was there sweetness in that soggy bread? The whisky had killed my palate—then again, maybe it had enhanced it. I took another bite of the bun and chewed carefully, slowly, not swallowing for as long as I could. But Zia Angie was all wrong.

Taste, texture, smell—and sweet as well. That soggy bun had it all. I felt so happy I went hunting in the mini bar for more whisky. There wasn't any so I opened a little bottle of rum and drank it with coke.

'Sandy,' I called, 'come and have a drink.'

The shower was running.

The headache from my hangover was fading away. I stood at the room's large picture window and watched the beautiful green spread of the Botanic Gardens. It really was something else. It seemed to sprawl out, a huge strip of nature that you could walk through and take shade in, and contemplate your life in. It was a good day. This is why we live and work and love each other until we're all crazy inside and the knots in our guts can never be undone, just for fine days like these.

I couldn't drink another drop. The bed was wide and comfortable. A clean pillow was under my head and I lay with my hands over my heart. Soon Sandy would emerge from her shower, all cool and fresh, and when she lay down with me I would nestle myself into her shoulder, and dream away.

That night Johanna was in a temper.

She started in on me as soon as I walked through the front door. I headed for the bedroom upstairs and she was at my heel the whole way. The dead bottle of Teachers' was still by the bedside, as were our glasses. The bed wasn't made and the room was full of dropped clothes and strewn bath towels. Johanna had a half-full glass of whisky that she kept pulling at. As I undressed she sat at the side of the bed, her straggly hair covering her face.

'Could you ever have imagined that things could get this way? I never believed they could, not in my wildest dreams. I rang you at the yard and that Mr Simpson said you wouldn't be in. Not for the whole day. He was fuming. Sandy wasn't there either. So then I rang the Travel Lodge, not believing for a minute that you could have betrayed me like that again, and they were ready to put me straight through to your room! Can't you even use another name? Are you a complete idiot? You're lucky I didn't come and drag you out! I waited for you all day while you were in there!

Johanna breathed deeply and then drank deeply. She was slurring her 's' sounds really badly. She would start lecturing me about morality while she couldn't even stand on her own legs. I was certain I'd heard that idea in an old song somewhere.

'And of course I assume it was Sandy that you were with. It's too much of a coincidence that she wasn't at work either. Or was it someone else? Someone I don't know? Someone you sold a car to with a big discount that you got lots of gratitude for?'

I was glad Johanna was too drunk and too angry to be crying. I was pretty sure that come the morning she would pack her bags and leave. My head was too fuzzy for me to focus on what she was saying. It was all so sad and sorry that with a bit more effort we could have made a real comedy of the scene. I wasn't feeling cold towards Johanna at all, I was just feeling distanced and disconnected generally. I wanted to reach out and touch Johanna's hair. That was the real truth. I wanted everything to be all right again too, but I couldn't remember the last time everything had been all right and I didn't know where to start.

'There's a leak in the roof, do you know that, and do you know the paint is peeling on every wall outside and that the front steps are rotten through so that one of us will break our neck soon? Do you know the grass hasn't been cut for three months and that you can't see a single flower for all the weeds in the garden?' Johanna showed me her hands. 'I've been on my hands and knees in the dirt for hours and the garden still looks like it hasn't been touched. This entire house looks like it belongs to two people who went away and forgot about everything and never came back. Not one cent of your precious bonus has gone into this place.' Johanna swigged her glass, finishing her drink. She blinked heavily. 'But the Travel Lodge has got plenty of your money, hasn't it, and your girlfriend. Have you bought her anything sweet and silly yet?'

I could see Johanna was getting herself more and more worked up. If she could find her feet she would try to hit me. Her wet bottom lip was out. I changed my clothes and went downstairs and Johanna came after me. That surprised me. I was certain that with a bit of quiet she would have collapsed on the bed. I went through to the kitchen. Not only had she done the gardening, and some detective work, but the grocery shopping too. She'd known I wouldn't come home with the bread and milk.

I had to pour myself a glass of water because my headache was back. I thought about the knots in my stomach and how they would never be untied. Johanna reached out and she touched my shirt, and at her slightest touch I started yelling.

And then stopped, because of the look in her face.

Johanna didn't say anything for a minute. Then she said: 'What is it, Joe? What is it—tell me. Please.'

All the grocery things were beside the sink, in a pile. The brown paper carry bags Johanna had recently taken to using were crumpled on the floor. A tin of tomatoes was also on the floor. Near the stove there were packets of rice and pasta, coffee, a bottle of milk and a carton of cream, and a loaf of bread. I was staring at that loaf of bread, at its plastic wrapper, at the use-by date.

'Look at this, Johanna,' I said. 'Just look at all the ingredients in this thing. The list goes on forever. What do you think this bread tastes like?'

Johanna didn't think anything.

'"Wholemeal bread-making flour, kibbled whole wheat",' I read from the packet. 'That doesn't sound so bad, does it? But listen to this: "wheat gluten, salt, yeast, vegetable fat, wheat germ, glucose, emulsifier, preservative, wheat malt flour, enzyme (amylase), and water added". I wonder what's even in the water these days.'

Johanna looked at me like she was going to be sick.

Somehow I would have to try and explain to her that everything that went on between us was important, but that this was important too. I was happy at all the good things in our lives and I was angry at all the bad, but when it all boiled down, the good and the bad were all so inextricably entwined that sometimes neither Johanna nor I had a hope of working out which was which. For instance, sometimes Sandy seemed like a gift from heaven, and then other times she was my idea of human hell personified. Sometimes the money that came in seemed like the very river of life, and other times it was just pure grey ash in my mouth. And Johanna, watching me with green eyes that were exactly like Zia Angie's, what was I to make of that?

It was just too hard, especially when the two of us stayed half-pissed. Everything of our lives was all tied up together, and we would have to do our best to live with that, even if none of the good things or the bad things could ever be untied, much less understood.

I just wished that I could have found the words to say that.

So I smiled at Johanna the best I could. She poured herself a glass of water, and drank it down with one gulp. I was very conscious of the cicadas buzzing in the garden outside.

Then Johanna turned, and that ache came into my chest again, because I liked the look in her eyes when she stared at me through her seaweed hair.

1989 (this revision 1995)

I ASKED THE ANGELS FOR INSPIRATION

Last night I dreamed of Rebecca again.

She came in a storm of falling angels. There was a little thunder and a lot of fat rain and the scent of wild roses. The rain pounded down. It beat on my iron roof and made cold waterfalls from the age-rusted holes of the guttering. It made my hands shake when they touched Rebecca's face. She lay beside me in my bed and she comforted me and she said, I heard you this time. She cradled my head. This time I had to come.

And there was that scent of wild roses again.

I looked at the river, at the sea of roses, at the angels falling from the black sky and into the white river. The wind blew me cold and Rebecca reached out for me. I brushed her hair from her forehead and she closed her eyes.

I said: 'I better answer the telephone.'

Don't, Rebecca whispered, and her voice was as gentle as the song of a choir of Christmas angels. Don't, it's supposed to be a secret, you'll spoil everything again, and she was gone into the two-thirty morning.

Through the din of the rainfall, the telephone. Again.

Stumbling through the cold house, wondering why it was a sin to feel such longing, I navigated the darkness—badly. Forehead against a door jamb, knee against a coffee table, and none of it really necessary for the kitchen light was on and Paul and Magda were in there squeezing oranges. Why hadn't they saved me from this; why hadn't they left me to sleep with my Rebecca? Fuck the casual cruelty of those who help us pay the rent. Paul and Magda were in T-shirts, their bare arms and bare legs brown as cow-hide. Amongst not many other things they shared a passion for beaches.

Sour in the mouth and crabby in the heart I stood by the telephone and stared at Magda's legs—which I do a lot of.

Tall, foreign, dirty as an unwashed potato, I'd had a werewolf's desire for Magda since the day Paul had taken her from a Noosa beach to his New Farm bed.

'Why don't you answer the phone?' I asked.

Four hands ran with orange juice.

'Leave the thing,' Paul said. 'They'll give up in a minute.'

But I can never leave it.

On its spindly supports the old house was rocked by rising winds. The wooden walls trembled. I trembled. The place was about to be blown off its ridiculously high stumps and out into the Brisbane River, where we would be washed away until we met the sea. I put my hand on the thrumming receiver and Paul said, 'Go back to bed you fucking idiot, you know who it is at this time of the night. Why do you encourage them?'

The house quivered.

Why do I encourage them?

Because of the dreams I have, Paul, because I know I carry a stone in my heart, Paul, that's why.

As if I could ever explain that to him—but Magda smiled at me and then she returned to the hand-juicer and a mountain of valencias. Oh, Magda could look into a man's heart as easily as into a stinking garbage bin. Her gift was to look without curling her lips in disgust. How had Paul managed to keep her so long?

The ringing ran out.

I said, 'Well, I forgot to take the receiver off the hook before I went to bed.' Lingering, watching Magda's legs. She came into better focus. Legs the colour and texture of expensive magazine photo essays. I was no longer sour. But hardly sweet. 'Sorry it woke you,' I said.

They came by with their glasses of juice.

'The telephone did not wake us,' Magda said. 'We have been sleepless.'

The rain fell hard but the noise was not enough to drown the new ringing of the telephone.

'Tell 'em to be fucked,' Paul said.

They smelled of stale sex and oranges, the sleepless Paul and Magda. Why couldn't I squeeze oranges with Magda while Paul was left to dreams of a ghost named Rebecca? There were goose bumps along Magda's thighs. She knew I was looking. I moved to the windows and pulled them fully shut.

'Go on.' Magda smiled at me again. 'No need to be ashamed. Answer the telephone.'

So I picked up the receiver.

It was as it always was. Silence. Space. Nothingness or eternity in my telephone line. No sense of a Being, but there was a Being. Two-thirty in the morning was this Being's time of day.

'Goodnight,' I said, and put the receiver down.

Magda walked by and put the two empty glasses in the sink. She poured a generous glass of juice and handed it to me.

'This was your stalker?'

'This was my stalker.'

I wanted to lean close for the scent of her hair, for the scent of oranges, for the scent of spoiled sex.

She went to the couch and she and Paul cuddled there. They might very well have been about to copulate there. I took the glass into my bedroom, bolted the door and bolted the juice. I turned out the light and lay down. Outside, the elements howled. I waited under the bedclothes for Rebecca to return, but the bitch wouldn't return. I tried to lure her with randy thoughts but only the rain kept me company. Its insistent fall against the iron roof lulled me. It is a lie to say I am lonely. I am only alone. And as longing as my stalker. With every passing night and day, the same sin.

Those two-thirty telephone calls had started a few months earlier. Whose life had I crossed back then? I had no idea. Who was it who wanted me? I couldn't imagine. Was it Rebecca? If only. The rain cried out.

Rebecca. Rebecca.

Holiday mornings. The telephone won't ring. Coffee and news-papers and the sunshine of a Brisbane day. Sit, waste time, watch the minutes drag. Fester alone. This I like.

I have a bad habit.

I like to video-record Rage most nights. With the Long Play option you get six hours of old and new music videos. I like to put the tape on when I vegetate around the house. It's my soundtrack for reading the papers, cleaning the toilet inside, sweeping the path outside.

The morning was humid. From the rear windows of my house I could see the river. Ferries quietly steamed against the current; off a jetty a man angled for catfish; at the closest bank a group of kids stood with their bicycles and smoked cigarettes. In a neighbour's weedy yard a fat black cat rolled onto its back and exposed its belly to leaden clouds. I sipped my coffee and read claims about Bill Clinton's sexual appetite.

I blame the endless funk feature on Rage.

The house started to sway, this way, that way, this way, that way, just like in the old Smiths' song. Ten metre supports at the back of the old wooden house will let you feel most vigorous movements. Sylvester was singing in his curiously appealing falsetto and I was at the dining table swaying as if on a rocking ship. The house was moving, moving, moving to an insistent funk beat. Why the fuck was I surprised?

For Paul had the libido of a randy mutt. He was always ready to mount a willing schoolgirl, a tree trunk, any available shin bone. I'd known love once but my house mate had known enough copulation to keep a cricket eleven happy into their dotage. Or was it in fact Magda with the unquenchable fire? The house rocked, the table rocked, my eyeballs rocked. Gener-ations of Funk passed. We dabbled in the sixties and the seven-ties and the eighties, even into the Reverend Al Green's current piece of gospel-drenched funk, but the rocking hardly abated. I turned the television volume louder and went and stood in the furthest removes of the house.

Nothing worked.

But I guess I had to admire Paul and Magda's dedication. Paul's even more so. Why is it that only the most worthy and undeserving of men suffer from PE? Paul must have been as numb as a gum shot full of novocaine. Even as that thought crossed my mind the screaming started. I know not to be fooled by this. Experience has taught me this only signals the end of Paul and Magda's foreplay.

I packed together a few things and fled before I lost my mind. From a corner telephone booth I rang Henry.

And he arrived at the street corner, at the top of the cul-de-sac that went down to the New Farm ferry jetty. Where I cowered from life and libido.

Henry said, 'G'day!' and I scrambled in.

His ugly Cressida was rotted through with rust, like the guttering of my house, which the landlord couldn't afford to fix. Neither could I. I lost my last job for stuffing up one too many times a Pearl Jam lead break and ending it with an unhappy ker-plunking of strings. Now no other band wanted me. Somewhere, sometime, some prick had called me Leadfingers, and of course it stuck.

End of a career.

Henry's car picked up speed along Brunswick Street—no prostitutes were out yet—but had to slow down in the Valley. The mall and the streets and the shops had long-since been festooned with lights and coloured streamers and Christmas bells. Families were out in force; where the families prospered the prostitutes failed. As we rattled by the market-day mall we saw crowds and heard music and saw children with their faces to the glass of art school Christmas displays.

'Boy,' said Henry. His contacts were giving him trouble and he worried at his eyeballs as he drove along.

I was glad to be out of Fortitude Valley but then there was the City. Ann Street to the bit of freeway that leads to Coronation Drive. The City was busier with Christmas lights than I could have imagined. The world was out shopping. What do you do when you're broke and the three-to-five year olds in your extended family have no idea what the word 'dole' means?

'Drive faster,' I said.

'Fuck off,' Henry said, and worrying at his eyeballs like a dog at a flea he nearly swiped a grinning pedestrian. 'Should have hit her,' he said.

And what can you do when the marketing men have your name and number, what hope have you got when a database remembers better than you what it is you love?

We went to the RE beer garden and festered the day through.

People came and went from our table, mostly to talk to Henry. Self deprecating, almost nauseatingly sincere, and the only person I knew under sixty-five who could do the rumba and the tango, he had the knack of making young women at parties fall in love with him in five minutes and contemplate marriage in ten. He was taller than me, funnier, better looking, and when we played tennis could hit a backhand. He didn't have a regular girlfriend. That levelled us a bit.

'Do you know what date it is today?' I hinted, always between drinks.

Henry popped his lenses and put on his glasses. His eyes were big and startled. 'Close to Christmas?'

We sat in the beer garden and listened to a fucked acoustic trio and at intervals rubbed suncream over our arms and necks.

Magda had met Henry once at drinks. During the evening when Paul was out of earshot and Henry was within earshot she had said to me, 'Your friend Henry Carter is a man I will very much like to fuck with.' Maybe I'd envied him since that night. A little later and with a little more vodka in her Magda had said, 'But you are not very old and yet you are very soft in your stomach'. Maybe I'd wanted to smack Henry in the head since then, who knows?

As the sun went down and my head went similarly, inexorably, down toward the table, I remember asking again: 'Do you know what the date is today?'

Henry gave me a strange look. 'What's gotten into you?'

'Too much beer,' I answered.

And both our heads went down and we had a nap and because it was Henry, nobody even thought to throw us out.

By nightfall we were propping each other up in the busy bar next to the Rum Boogie café. I can't remember how we got to Fortitude Valley all the way from Toowong.

'What you don't see,' I was telling him, 'is that tennis is a metaphor for Life.'

Henry was watching a young woman in a black dress. Her dress was one or two sizes too small. Her lips were incredibly red. A gaggle of stockbrokers circled her. Because Henry is a polite man he nodded at my meanderings.

'John McEnroe, the Australian Open, 1992, against the German goliath, Becker. Becker was number four in the world at the time and he'd beaten McEnroe in all their previous encounters. You with me? McEnroe was thirty-three and feeling it and Becker was twenty-four and just about on top of the world. McEnroe, all touch and not much power. That fluidity, that anticipation, that magic, but against the German? Not a chance. But he beat Becker in three sets. That night Becker left the court a humbled man.'

Henry looked pained to have to listen. He said hopefully, 'Want another drink?'

'Wait. Wait. You see, the magic was with McEnroe again. He kept fighting. He refused to die. He couldn't win but he did win. Then he went on to have that fucking amazing five-setter against Emilio Sanchez. And he won, but it took just about four and a half hours. How did he do it? Wasn't he supposed to be worn out? Wasn't he supposed to be at the end of his career? This is what I'm saying. When you're down and out, why do you have to stay down and out? When you're dead why do you have to stay dead?'

Henry's big eyes shifted from the shark-encircled young woman to me. 'What's the matter with you today?'

I looked into my glass. 'I used to play in a rock and roll band. I used to take drugs and write songs and dream about making love to Jean Seberg.'

'Why don't you just find yourself a girl?'

'You find yourself a girl.'

'Okay.'

It seemed a decent idea. So we moved on, but first all we found was some old friend of his.

The bloke was maybe thirty and drunk enough on beer and vodka to see past a man's blood and bone, just as Magda could without booze. We were in The Beat and the electro-dance thump was as it had been since 1985. What had changed was that many of the men in their leather shorts and singlets and muscles now had girlfriends. It wasn't a predominantly gay club any more. Anyway, Henry's friend leaned against me, slurped vodka, took one look into my face and said, 'You're the unhappiest soul I ever saw.'

'Who the fuck is this?' I asked Henry.

Henry said to his friend, 'Today has a special significance for him but he wants to be mysterious about it.'

His friend said to me, 'Tell us about it.'

I said to him, whoever he was, 'Why don't you get fucked?' And to Henry, 'You too.' And to the girl standing by me, 'Want to dance?'

So we danced.

She was wearing a sweet white dress that matched her sweet white hair and she looked a little like Madonna from the days when you wanted to cover her with kisses rather than run a million miles. But later when I was in the toilet the blonde was in there as well with her dress hitched up around her hips and a quarter-pounder pointed into the urinal. You take your chances. When I emerged Henry and his friend both said, 'Look, just tell us about it.'

I said, 'I'm not telling you a thing.'

Henry said, 'Okay, I've had enough of this,' and he and his

friend exited The Beat. His friend fell over once but caught up. I caught up as well. We stopped in at another busy bar. Henry had a job so he said, 'Okay, I know it's up to me. What are you having?'

I said, 'Crown Lager.'

His friend said, 'Stolly. Get 'em to give you a double.'

Henry disappeared.

Henry's mate said, 'The problem is you like to carry your problems around with you, but they're only baggage that you can choose to lug or leave behind. You don't want to leave 'em behind. You love 'em. They're what make you, you. Still, you coulda left your baggage at home just tonight.'

I stared at him, not inviting him to continue.

'You have a choice, a clear choice. You can be weighed down—or not.'

'Thank you.'

'The problem is too many people associate depression or sadness or misery with depth of character. Can you believe it? But you're no deeper than your average check-out chick or grave-digger. This misery of yours is an open invitation for someone to come out of the crowd and save your fucking life. That's why you love it so much. But nobody's gonna save you. Especially not a girl. Unless she's fucked in the head and that'll be where your depression really starts.'

'Who the fuck are you?' I asked as Henry returned with our drinks.

Henry said, 'This is Gordon. Gordon's kind of a poet.'

'Kind of a poet,' I said. 'Kind of a fucken drunk. And he smells.' I drank my beer and Gordon drank his vodka. He tried to roll himself a cigarette but it went on forever. I rolled it for him and jammed it in his mouth and lit it for him. I said, 'I had a girl and she left me three years ago today. I met her three years before that, on this day. Six years ago this day I met her and three years ago this day I lost her.'

'That arithmetic is crazy,' Gordon said.

'She was the first and only girl for me.'

'So?'

'From tomorrow I'll have been without her longer than I was with her.'

Gordon said, 'Count your fucken blessings. How old are you?'

'Nearly twenty-four.'

Gordon started to laugh. And Henry, expecting me to pour out my heart, or thump Gordon, moved on. We trailed him down the Brunswick Street mall and he couldn't lose us.

It took Henry ten minutes in The Site to find a girl. She was no older than twenty and was a friend of Gordon's. So it wasn't Henry's pulling power, anyway. Through the cigarette smoke and the smoke machine smoke, and through the neon-lit dark as well, Gordon and I watched the blossoming of nightclub romance. Dancing with the million other dancers, drinks at the bar, covert conversations with each leaning towards the other's ear-hole—Gordon and I drank with heavy bitterness.

Gordon said, 'You know, you should get yourself a new girl-friend. You might lighten up.'

I said, 'I wish I was Henry.'

Gordon said, 'I've never heard so much shit.'

I said, 'Well, what about you?'

Gordon said, 'I don't know about sex. It never made me happy. Sometimes I get obsessed and sometimes I die for a root but most of the time I know it won't make me happy. Women complain with me. Women get pissed off with me. I just come too soon.'

'My house-mate could probably give you lessons,' I replied. 'He never comes.'

The name of the young woman with Henry was Helen. She had long brown hair and very trusting eyes. She wore a black halter top and a brown skirt and out-of-date black Doc Martens. She seemed most comfortable with her arm around Henry's waist.

I asked her what she did, and in the electro-beat she must have mis-heard me because she hollered back, 'Oh, Curve and

Suede, really. I think the Pet Shop Boys have always been fun but this latest one, it's just the pinnacle. I still love Died Pretty though Peno shouldn't enjoy showing his dick so much. Chris Bailey's made a welcome return and who would have thought that after so many years REM could make such a beautiful album? I hate Guns N' Roses and Nirvana more than anything. I didn't go and see U2 but "Lemon" is the best David Bowie song David Bowie never did. And I definitely didn't buy tickets to The Girlie Show. How can that woman have any allure left? And that diamond in her mouth. It just looks like she's got a really rotten tooth.'

We all agreed that was true.

I said, 'I saw U2's concert. It was a stormy night. Brisbane summer, after all. All around, all that technology and all those screens, all those people and lightning strikes in the distance. It was like armageddon. I remember thinking, "Gee, they really are big". And the duet with Lou Reed, that was really something.'

Henry said, 'U2 supping at the cock of corporate rock.'

Helen looked at him with the beginnings of that thing that happens between men and women on nights like these. We got onto books. Helen said, 'I've been reading a lot of Nietzsche lately. And Henry Miller. Do you think it's funny they go together so well?'

Henry was smiling. Well he might. I wanted Helen so badly I could have thrown up there and then, but he had her all right. A recurring nightmare I have is that one day I'll really fall head over heels again, only to find the object of my desire's favourite albums are Bat Out Of Hell—I and II.

Henry said, 'No, Helen, I don't think that's funny at all.'

I guessed it was love, then.

Everyone wanted to go back to my place.

Gordon said, 'Any beer or vodka at your place?'

'No,' I said.

'Fuck,' he said.

We counted out our money. I had seven dollars, Gordon

thirty-five cents, and Henry a twenty and some change. Just enough for a cab fare and one bottle of cheap fire water. Helen looked at us as if we were the world's greatest losers, but Henry was already somewhere near her heart. So she came with us.

Out in the street, hailing a taxi for us, Helen's eyes glittered when she looked back at me and said, 'You should cheer up. Think happy thoughts.'

She smelled of roses.

Gordon carried around the odour of beer taps and dolour, Henry the sweet scent of success, me the whiff of death, but Helen, sweet Helen, she just smelled of the world's most beautiful flower. How had we latched onto her?

In the street, with sloping drunks and sad-eyed cops and sloe-eyed whores, we all latched arms and waited for a taxi.

Magda and Paul were screaming in their room. This time it was the type of screaming normal people do. The house wasn't swaying at all.

I said, 'Let's put Rage on.'

Everyone wanted to do that. We turned it on and turned it up loud and over the The The retrospective we heard Magda and Paul re-defining the terms of their relationship. It went like this:

'This Is The Day' and Paul was a worm who bolstered his piteous ego with a fat bank account;

'The Twilight Hour' and Magda was a slut;

'Giant' and Paul's BMW was an all too obvious extension of his (tiny, she shouted) dick;

'Infected' and Magda was a Polack slut;

'Sweet Bird of Truth' and Paul had never come to terms with his emotions or his sexuality. To him love was sex. Sex was life. Life was an epic search for a root. A root gave his life meaning and substance. A good root made him his own personal deity.

'It's the truth,' Henry said.

'You're about to know,' Gordon said.

I said, 'I quite like The The,' yet I was only speaking to Gordon because Henry and Helen inexplicably vanished. A blink of an eye and they were gone. The bottle of fire water was down to less than half. Vodka. Very fine. My ears were ringing and there was a discomforting sense of other-worldliness about my own house. How much time had passed? I said, 'Where are—?' and Gordon tilted his head toward the bedrooms.

'Maybe she's giving him a blowie.' Then, very politely he said, 'Got any beer?' His rollie had gone out and he was having difficulty getting it going again. I lit it for him.

'No beer, Gordon. Drink your vodka.'

'... 's making me sick in the tummy. I smell coffee.'

'You're imagining it.' But I smelled coffee too. I stood up, swayed, staggered. Gordon, lotus position on the carpet, put out his hands and propped me by the thighs until I had my balance. It took a while.

Meanwhile—

'Slow Train To Dawn' and Magda told Paul the worst thing she had ever done was to give her body to him (this was a line from 'Cruel' by Public Image Ltd—I never knew Magda was a music fan; yet again, an interesting woman with someone else. I couldn't be more depressed).

—and I was falling toward the kitchen.

Someone had indeed made a fresh pot of my Lavazza. I poured a mug of it for Gordon but Gordon had gone to sleep on the carpet. His rollie had dropped out of his mouth and was burning a small secret hole in that carpet. The bottle of vodka had overturned and the carpet had sopped most of it up. I hated that baby-shit coloured carpet anyway. On the television—'The Mercy Beat' and

I was just another western guy
With desires that couldn't be satisfied
So one day I asked the angels for inspiration
And the devil bought me a drink
And he's been buying them ever since
—and I watched a while and straightened the bottle and

picked up the burning butt. In his sleep Gordon muttered Cynthia, my darling, my darling, or maybe it was all just in my romantic imagination and he was nothing but another boozy *disparu* of this world.

I thought of Henry and Helen and the many bedrooms.

The wind was up and the house rocked ever-so-slightly. This meant he was probably giving her a gentle one in my bed. It was two-thirty in the morning. I knew this to be so because the telephone started to ring. I went down the dark corridor and threw open the door to my own bedroom. There, there, there they were, in my bed, except that they were over the covers, they were drinking coffee, and they were playing cards.

Helen said, 'Join us for some rummy.'

Henry grinned up at me, 'Come on.'

I pulled the door shut and leaned in the corridor.

Why should I be so threatened by one man who proves himself better than me? Once upon a time Rebecca and I had lain on that bed late into the night, had listened to music, had drunk coffee or coke or champagne, had played mah jong and scrabble and chess. Now—the corridor belonged to me.

And the telephone.

The ringing was insistent. This Being who seemed to understand longing and loss needed me.

I went to the telephone. I knew what would be waiting there. Through the windows I could see the river. I said, 'Hello?' For that's the game we liked to play. I liked also the familiarity of the emptiness and of the silence and of the breach in time and space. It seemed right. Henry and Helen playing cards in my bed, Gordon asleep in front of 'The Violence of Truth', Paul and Magda fighting or fucking their way into oblivion, and my Rebecca, lost forever in lovelessness for me.

I said into the receiver, 'Come on, Rebecca. It's you. It has to be you.'

Silence, and for the first and last time a breath, and the line was dead in my ear.

We went down to the river, Magda and me, because we were the only two left in the house who might communicate. Paul had thrown on some clothes and had slammed out of his room and had driven to parts unknown in that powerful German extension of his penis. Henry and Helen were two sleeping angels in my bed. Gordon, rudely awoken by Paul's departure, was drinking cold coffee, bleary in front of the television. I doubted if he took in very much. My last sight of Gordon, at least for that night, was as he tilted in front of The The's elegiac video to 'The Kingdom of Rain'. Only the lotus position stopped him from once again falling sideways onto the carpet.

And then there had been Magda, in the dark, in the corridor, crying.

So we walked together in the windy night.

New Farm Park smelled of roses. No wonder, for the southern hemisphere's largest rose garden grows there. Under a fat moon all the roses were in bloom. Only that moon lit the rolling hills and the sweep of the vast parklands. Magda and I walked amongst the rose beds. Magda ran her hands along the fat blooms and petals. Over the reds and the pale pinks and the whites, Magda's hands danced. Then she picked a rose and stepped on it and led me down the green banks to sit by the winding river.

The surface of the river glittered. The day made it muddy but the night gave it magic. The air was sweet and the river was enchanted and the moon was the colour of snow. There were no stars. Here and there came the sounds of the slapping of water, as if some sad muddy mermaid was climbing from the river to sit on a polished rock and lick herself clean.

Side by side, Magda and me, under a huge tree. I've never learned the names of trees. We leaned together. To me Magda would always smell of stale sex and oranges. She took my hand and she put it on her breast and I took my hand away.

Magda said, 'You know of that song that speaks to Montgomery Clift. That song that tells him to "just let go". This is what you must do.'

I said, 'If I let go, I'm alone.'

Magda took my hand and she kissed it and I took it away again. She said, 'Just let go.'

I leaned my head on Magda's shoulder.

Why does it take as little as a look to make me fall in love and as long as a lifetime to make me forget it?

Magda wouldn't take no for an answer so I let her hold my hand. No sad-eyed mermaid sat on any rock, yet in the space and the silence we watched the dark glitter of the river for a long time, as if we believed she was there. Or about to appear, our mermaid, full of grace, out of the black waters.

A fruitbat flapped overhead and screamed.

1994

PARK GÜELL

Barcelona, España, 1984

'The dead man was found at Park Güell, and a sight he was too. Will I tell you what they found when they found him there, in Park Güell?'

'For another cerveza?'

'Why not?'

I was waiting for Chiara to arrive in the Bar Zurich but what I found instead was an old man with a barrel chest who wanted free beer. He had come to my table and imposed himself on me. There were other free chairs in that busy bar yet he had chosen the empty rickety one beside me. We had sat long minutes in our silence, with him casting me odd sideways glances when he expected I wasn't looking, then we had our beer. Somehow a halting conversation in Italian followed, and I realised I was starved for Italian in this country where I barely knew a word of the language, and so I let him drink another beer, this time with me.

He was slack-jawed and watery eyed and hunch-backed, all this from thirty-three years of driving a taxi cab around the ever growing, ever throbbing, ever filthy streets of Barcelona. Now his rough brown hand signalled the waiter who served at our corner. This waiter was in both a dirty coat and a dirty temper, an abject figure himself, who could have done with a few good meals and a few less cigarettes, and so he suited the bar. So did the old man, and so, somehow, did I.

The atmosphere there was close and heavy and grey with cigarette and pipe smoke. It was difficult to hear the old man's words amidst the laughter and the shouting and the clashing of beer mugs. The old man had to lean close to that grey-faced waiter and then he had to lean closer to me. He wanted me to know he had secrets I could persuade him to tell, if I parted with enough money to buy him enough beer. Around us, yielding bodies crowded over strong bodies, slender arms draped over muscular shoulders, and the fresh secrets of youth were shouted from beautiful mouth to attentive ear and my aged companion tugged at the leather coat of a handsome boy in torn jeans and a torn white T-shirt, and he begged a cigarette, a cigarette which that young Spanish blade reluctantly produced from a soft packet of Lucky Strikes and lit for him with his battered Zippo.

My companion inhaled deeply and the belly under his flannel shirt quivered.

'You have not been long in Barcelona, or you would know of this dead man.'

'What was that place they found him in?'

'Park Güell. You've not been? You must be the only visitor to Barcelona who hasn't. It's one of Gaudí's—the revolutionary architect and artist, in ease you're ignorant of him too. I know we Italians like to believe we produced all the great masters. The park was one of Gaudí's great works. Some people say he was a genius, other people think Gaudí discovered hallucinogenic drugs too early in life. If you look at his work you can see he discovered something early in life. He could transform anything he touched, from the Casa Batlló to La Pedrera. They're both evidence of his genius. Go for a walk tomorrow and see those houses, they're easy to find. Or I can guide you—there's an idea! Those are two houses unlike any houses on this earth. You will look at them and your reality will change, if only for five minutes. You have the look of a young man who would like his reality to change very much, very much indeed, do you know that? That's why I sat down with you.'

'Excellent,' I said, and looked for another table I might move to.

'Gaudí had such magic. He touched the street lamps—even street lamps!—in Plaza Real and made them something not of this world. You've seen the spires of the Sagrada Familia, the

Sacred Family Church? Unfinished, and it seems like a monument from the dream of a deranged genius, yet look at its symmetry, at the way it flouts the laws of religion and architecture and art—yet somehow stays true to them!—and you understand the sweep of the man's vision. Sadly for us, the Sagrada Familia will probably be destined to remain unfinished. The terms of Gaudí's bequest say that only public money can be used to complete it, but the public have better things to spend their money on these days. Well. It was a street tram that killed Gaudí. Just as a road accident killed Camus. Isn't it amusing when the most uninteresting of events snuffs out greatness?'

'I've never thought about life in those terms.'

'You're too young, of course. One day you will understand the banality of this world. However, despite the intrusion of so commonplace a death, our architect from Reus had many profitable years in which to make real his visions. Twelve years before that terrible accident Gaudí finished Güell Park. He changed the very landscape to the shape of his own mind. It has the sense of—ah, but it's useless for me to try and describe such a place if you haven't seen it. I will show it to you. Yes, would you like that? Tomorrow. You can hire my car and I will guide you. Very reasonable rates. A discount for a countryman. Yes indeed, you see I was born in Verona. The north of Italy. You too? It's your accent. Very cultured. Are you a young man of letters? Once upon a time I had aspirations for learning but circumstances brought me to Barcelona where, as you see, I've remained one of God's most pitiful creatures. Still, I am a countryman to you, even if I left my Verona when I was too young. I remember the language always—always!—but I speak it like an imbecile now. Is that what you hear—an imbecile? Look, my friend, I know every corner and every story in Barcelona. We will start with the park. Tomorrow. Yes?'

His words were tumbling out as if there was a great shortage of time in which to speak, and indeed that was well enough true, for I had no intention of going anywhere with him, despite his knowledge and his propensity for talk. Added to that, he was no countryman of mine. Any man who abandons Italy and makes his life elsewhere loses all rights to call himself Italian. That is my law. I myself was six days away from my home and I was already chafing to return to Italian soil. This man had been gone thirty three years, at the very least, and so he was a Spaniard, and a malodorous Spanish pig at that. I had no intention of spending more than the next few minutes with him.

I kept watching for Chiara. There were a hundred faces but none were hers. I said, 'So that was where a corpse was found, in Gaudí's park?'

'Güell Park. Yes. He was a young man. Not unlike yourself. Are you curious to hear more?'

'Not really.'

'No?'

'That's right.'

'Is that what you tell me, no? After I've made myself so vulnerable to you? Do you think I'm always so straightforward with my friendship? Then, if that is what you want, you dear and wise young man of letters, I will stay quiet as a tomb. How will you like that? Nothing will make me open my mouth. You see what you have accomplished? Beg me if you want but nothing will work. It is as if I have no tongue. Understood?'

'Yes, all right. Quite fair.'

We stared into different directions, he toward the busy roundabout in the Plaza de Catalunya where his yellow taxi cab had driven circles too many years, and me toward all the lovers so perfectly entwined and so perfectly detached in every corner of the Bar Zurich—and I saw them in such a way as I had failed to see my own love for Chiara, back in those tantalisingly obscure days when there had still been a chance for us. But for the hope that she might yet arrive in that bar I would have quickly taken the metro back to my hotel, then a night-train in the direction of any Italian frontier—but for that one vain hope.

It was after eleven in the evening and the bar was full of

students and workers and broken-eyed tourists such as myself, and despite her promise, the promise I'd extracted like money from a miser, Chiara might never arrive. For I'd found her again, after a space of three and a half years, at the old university in this city of Barcelona. I had found her between the morning English classes she taught to first and second year students. It was like a poor joke; a daughter of Rome teaching the language of countries she had never been to, English, in yet another foreign country, where her hundreds of adolescent students understood nothing of her own native tongue.

Chiara apparently failed to see the futility of this, for I discovered she was working on her doctorate and actively seeking tenure. I heard such stories of her from the people I found and courted, and I even found out where she lived. Every night I went to that house in order to spy upon her. I should have walked straight to her doorstep but she lived with a family, a family whose looks displeased me; I did not wish to meet Chiara again under the contemptuous gaze of that repellent patriarch or that moustached surrogate mother of hers.

So I therefore had contrived the moment when we suddenly faced each other in some busy hallway in some busy university building, both of us frozen in our tracks, with students shouting and running and lecturers entreating for peace. I'd thought it would be better if Chiara believed I found her by accident. My face must have betrayed all my fear and joy at seeing her again; but Chiara had long-since cast me out from her life, so much did I learn by gazing into her astonished eyes. Three and a half years separated us and three and a half years had made her beautiful. Time had added flesh to a winsome frame and had lengthened her miraculous hair. That hair was full and long, a symphony of black ringlets that tumbled far past her shoulders. It was with a shock that I saw it; without me Chiara had grown from a girl who had always seemed so pretty, into a woman.

Chiara gathered her wits more quickly than I, even though I was the one who was prepared, and before I could speak, before

I could utter a word, she spoke with a quickening voice that I was a thing from another time and another country, that in the face of my best intentions and despite my journey to her new city, no fairy tale ending could be expected by me, no romantic coda could be appended to our story; all this she spoke in that crowded corridor. Her manner was stiff and her chin was up. It was as if I was nothing but an unpleasant memory. Chiara's intention was that I would remain in the place where Chiara had put me, always and forever, cast out from her once true heart. But then she saw there was something to be learned by gazing into my own eyes.

Chiara's voice faltered and then she fell silent.

It was as if a kind of fear came over her. The running and the shouting of the students in the corridors counted for nothing. I was certain neither of us felt part of the surrounding world. That world melted away. All that mattered was the unspoken bond between Chiara and me. Her face became pink. It was a deep and sensual blush that extended down her throat and disappeared into her white shirt. I saw there was lace stitched around her white collar. How I wanted to touch it, that lace, and the soft skin underneath! A great sexual charge made my legs weak. If we had been truly alone I might have taken her in that corridor, standing up, against a wall, in any way possible, my fists bunched in her hair as if I was tugging at a lioness's mane. Chiara understood then. She saw I was far from finished with her. She saw the extent of my passion, and so the girl returned, the believing and erotic young literature student of three years and a half before, who had known only one love, and that one love had been me, Marco, her poet.

Chiara's eyes became bright and her white teeth bit at the inside of her bottom lip. My heart grew full, but she said, very quietly, as if she was afraid to speak, 'No, Marcello, you misunderstand everything.'

Now the old man bumped my elbow.

'Well,' he said, 'he was found in the early morning. The very early morning.'

His voice was gruff but deep. It was that great chest of his, nearly lost because of his appalling posture, yet sound enough to produce a voice of such timbre. He was wrong in his assumption about the way he used his original language, for he did not sound like an imbecile at all. He did not sound like a taxi driver either, at least none that I knew of. Somewhere in his past, most probably in his Italian past, that Spanish pig did have some finer breeding. He was close again, his breath all beer and broken promises of silence.

'This dead man, that was when they found him, as the sun was rising. One of our drivers went up into the park to smoke a cigarette and drink whisky. He liked to do that. He liked to say it was the least he deserved for the terrible night shifts he worked. He liked to think that if he could smoke a cigarette and drink whisky as the sun came up over the city, then he was one step ahead of his sleeping countrymen. There he saw a beauty few in Barcelona take the trouble to open their eyes to. The sun rising from the sea, glowing gold, no-one but he ever saw such a thing. A simple habit, his dawn journeys to Park Güell, and one that we can reasonably be assured he has been cured of. Ha ha! He found the dead man in the crooked and colourful bench that runs over the esplanade of the park. You have at least seen photographs of it? No? I wonder what there is that you have bothered to see. Tourists photograph it and have fits over it. Let them have their fits now.'

The old man started to laugh then he pulled his chair so that his leg touched mine. He smelled of stale clothes and even more stale days and nights. He looked like the life that awaited me if Chiara would not love me. He laughed a little more and tiny bubbles of spit marked his dry lips.

'Our friend, this night-shift driver, thought the dead man was asleep. Until he saw his eyes.'

'His eyes?'

'Ah. Now you're interested. I can tell you're interested now, my young friend. You won't want me to keep my mouth buttoned now, will you? His eyes. Gouged out. There, I've said it. What do you think of that? Gouged out and gone, the dead man's eyes. Pressed out by thumbs. Or maybe plucked by the beak of a hungry bird. Imagine finding a thing like that in such an outlandish place. Yes, it would change a man's understanding of the shape of the world. It couldn't help but play tricks with a man's mind, don't you agree? Tell me. What hatred—or what courage!—must it take to gouge out the eyes of a fellow human being?'

'I can't imagine.'

'You care to hear more?'

'I do have other things on my mind.'

'Other things? A young man like you? What could you have on your Italian mind? Ah, a girl of course. That would be so, some dark-skinned Catalan chica who wants to rub her face against your stylish clothes and hear stories of how you will take her to la bella Italia and love her up and marry her and make her have many bambini. For another drink I'll tell you a story no chica ever heard, and certainly no authorities.'

He looked me in the eyes, carefully.

'All right?' he asked. 'For another drink?'

I don't know if I nodded assent. He was compelling, in his way. The old man raised his hand for that surly waiter. Everyone around me spoke their foreign language. But for the old man I would have felt isolated and strange in that place, yet with him I felt strange too. He spoke his Italian fluidly, without any of the halting phrases peculiar to long-term expatriates, and he used words and sentences in a way that a taxi driver should not have used those things, but, in the midst of that, the old man's eyes were troubled and his hand was shaking. There was something of a fire in him and he was trying to quench it with beer. He was also trying to quench it, I thought, by telling the story of it. He was the most unattractive human being in the Bar Zurich and now he was my friend—of sorts. I almost felt sorry for him, or at least I felt a sympathy, the same sort of sympathy a priest must feel in the confessional when a sad man shuffles in and tells his story of loss and disaffection. Yet there was much more than that to this broken old taxi driver. I was tantalised by the idea of a horror that could make watery the eyes and unsteady the hands of an old man who, plainly, had seen so many of the evils a swarming city of millions can offer.

I opened my wallet and put down a crumpled note, an abominably large denomination. The old man's eyes widened with relief.

We had made our contract.

'The story only starts that morning in Park Güell. It was fifteen days ago today, no more. The night-shift taxi driver I spoke of, let us call him by his name, Giovanni. He was tired and he was depressed. It was his usual state of being. A man can live alone only so long. His wife was dead at least sixteen years and his five children, every one of them, shunned him for reasons he could not say. If he was a man of greater insight he might have seen that he had been an impatient and even a cruel father, quick with the leather belt and the smack of a young ear. There was no woman in Giovanni's life except for an old relative here, a neighbour there, perhaps, to be kind, we should include the two or three women who were regular passengers, but they amounted to no emotional involvement whatsoever. They were faces as in a crowd to Giovanni, faces that came and went, faces that passed saying nothing and disappeared leaving even less. Why is this important? Well, let us see the turns in Giovanni's story. Let us say that our Giovanni was a man who was left behind by life. Let us also say that our Giovanni was tired of life. But every night, on he drove, picking up passengers and delivering passengers, driving the streets as if he knew them better than he knew the lines in his own face, yet it was all as if he had only the one destination, always—Park Güell, and the dawn that would rise up every day over Barcelona.

'During this particular night-shift Giovanni had made a lot of money, at least by his standards. His pockets bulged with pesetas. His wallet was fat. There were student parties in every quarter, great student parties that only started after midnight or one a.m., with boys and girls calling for taxis and travelling, always travelling, becoming drunker, more garrulous, more and more out of control. Maybe it was the end of their studies. Who knew? Giovanni didn't bother to ask, for of course Giovanni was used to such nights. In thirty-three years he knew how to exploit such nights. So he drove like a demon, his head down over the steering wheel, and he never missed a green light or any pedestrian's impatient signal from the street. Students would pile into his taxi and he would take them wherever they wanted to go, more quickly than they had ever arrived there before. In his rear vision mirror Giovanni would see the boys slide their hands in between the legs of the drunken girls, he would see how homosexual men kiss each other, he would see how homosexual women touch one another. He didn't mind; he didn't care. He'd seen it all and worse, much, much worse, before. His pockets were full of money and that was all that mattered.

'So he kept going all through the night and the morning, criss-crossing the city, and finally the parties started to wane and it seemed a taxi was the last thing anyone in the world wanted. The time came when couples and groups of drunken, drugged students wandered up and down the streets like shadows, homeless and aimless. That was when Giovanni had the time to envy them. He envied the way they could hug one another and slide their hands between one another's legs, and kiss and walk so aimlessly, yet always with the youthful promise that there would be another night and another party, another beautiful lover and another beautiful lover's warm bed, even, and this Giovanni envied most of all, the promise of another lover's freshly brewed morning coffee. Such a simple thing, yet how he would have begged for such a thing.

'Giovanni did his best to put those thoughts out of his mind.

He started thinking of the light that would soon rise over Barcelona. He started thinking of his bottle of whisky and of his cigarette. Those were the only bits of peace—of fulfilment, even—that the world and his own aching heart would allow him. So perhaps he was not a man completely lacking in insight, but instead a man whose greater wisdom had come too late in life to be helpful. At the very least, to be fair, he understood beauty. Giovanni wanted beauty. He could not possess it but at least he could gaze at it.

'Soon he would set off for his usual destination, but then greed, or maybe it was even pity, made him pick up one last lost soul. I say pity for she was a dark, frail girl, and she seemed bewildered, and she was alone, and her hair kept falling into her eyes.

'When she came into the taxi the cold morning of Barcelona came in with her. A chill wind, and it filled the car. It struck Giovanni as odd, for during the whole long night and early morning he hadn't felt the cold once, or even been conscious of it, until that moment. And then she asked to go to a street beside Park Güell, and she made sure that he promised he would pick up no more passengers, and when they got there, to that street beside Park Güell, she seemed more bewildered, and the hair was always in her eyes, and she told Giovanni she had no money in her purse, none in her stockings, none in her shoes, but then it occurred to her, for Giovanni was insistent, and then angry, that if he would follow her, if he would just follow her, if that would be all right, she would pay him better than he could ever be paid with pesetas.

'Giovanni thought this over. It was curious. It had happened before, of course, there were always the whores who would rather give a taxi driver a minute of pleasure than part with their precious money. There were always the women, older, often, who had drunk too much and who would ask for just a moment of tenderness in the back seat of a taxi, from any driver. These are all the stocks in trade of driving a taxi in Barcelona or any other great city. But, for Giovanni, there had never been a girl so young, or so frail, or so forthright, and therefore so paradoxical. There had never been a student. And there had never been one with such eyes. Eyes, that when he saw them watching him from behind her veil of brown hair, were as mysterious as the night-time sea past the Barcelona harbours, that beautiful sea he could gaze at for hours. But this girl—no other passenger had ever seemed so haunting.

'Strangest of all was the fact that his visit to Park Güell with the girl coincided exactly with that time he always took his trip there. So it was just pre-dawn, and for the first time Giovanni would watch the coming of the dawn with another human being—of all things, with a young and seductive female. But in a way Giovanni was frightened. Of course in another and a stronger way there was a thrill inside him, the same thrill that had made him tremble on his wedding night, the same thrill that had made him weep when his first child had been born. For a moment Giovanni was lost in a fantasy, a fantasy where that young girl knew him, a fantasy where she had picked her time and she had picked her place because she had been watching him and waiting for him, through weeks and months, all because she was in love with him. She longed for him. But such a fantasy was of course impossible. The girl had been standing on La Rambla calling to a passing taxi. Giovanni could have been anyone, any man, any driver. Still, lonely and foolish man that he was, Giovanni fantasised.'

'But why should she have wanted to go to that park anyway?' I interrupted him. 'Surely there was something suspicious. It was dawn. What kind of place is that for a girl to go alone?'

'No, there are streets and homes in that quarter, surrounding the park. It wasn't suspicious at all. What was so odd was that a certain sense of fright began to melt the fantasy and to overwhelm Giovanni. For the first time in all his visits to the park his heart beat faster and the sweat stood out on his forehead. He found he didn't want the whisky. He found he could live without his cigarette, and that great golden morning too. He found the thought of all Gaudí's weird sculptures and twisting and turning architectures made him dizzy and sick in the pit of his belly. He began to think about his own small bed in his own small apartment. So he struggled, and he reflected, and what he eventually found was that despite his misgivings and his mind's rebellion and his body's trepidation, he could put all that aside for the one thing that was important to him, and that was a hunger, a growing hunger, unlike anything Giovanni had ever felt. It was the starvation of a child in a refugee camp. It was the thirst of a man lost in a desert. This hunger gnawed at Giovanni's insides, and still it grew. Beyond sense, beyond even life itself, he truly craved one thing above all else, and that was the fare the strange young girl was prepared to pay. No whore could have satisfied him now. No amount of whisky could have dulled his pain, nor could any wife have satiated him. He was tormented by lust, and it was for that fringe of hair that so carelessly fell over the young girl's face. It was for her black and mysterious eyes.'

'He was driven.'

'Exactly. By years of loneliness. You've known someone you've wanted to possess completely? You've known a passion so strong you would turn the world upside down to fulfil it?'

I thought of Chiara but I would not answer.

'Of course you do,' the old man said. 'That's why you understand this story. That's the very reason you're here in this bar. Ah.' He slurped his beer and rested his shoulder against mine. He was trying to beg another cigarette from those young people crowded and pressed around him, but it was as if he had become invisible. 'Maybe that's why you have such a strange set in your eye. Anyway, that's good.'

'Why is that good?'

'We'll see why later. First let me go on. Now. Our Giovanni was apprehensive enough to first try and take that frail slip of a girl into the back seat of his taxi. He would have her there and the debt would be paid. Let me be perfectly clear: at this point Giovanni would have wept, or worse, if she had somehow tried to renege on her offer. So Giovanni told her that it would be warmer and safer in the back seat. He told her he would be gentle and he would be quick. She told him there would be no need to be gentle or quick at all, that, better, he should be rough and he should use her for as long as he wanted, and if he tired, well, she was young and strong enough to deal with him. She told him she liked the look of him, even, she said, the smell of him. Giovanni was truly enkindled by those words. He could not remember a time in his life when words like that had ever been spoken to him. The girl seemed less and less bewildered. If anything, there was now a sharp point to her voice. Giovanni found a quiet spot to park, away from the streetlamps, where it was dark and still, but then the girl refused. She said that she lived in that very street with her parents, and her father was an insomniac, and her mother too, the whole family most likely were insomniacs, and she wouldn't risk them being out walking—at five a.m. mind you—and finding their only daughter, their sweet student daughter, with a taxi driver. Giovanni had to follow her into the park, as she had first said, or the offer was null and void.

'She made her way out of the taxi and Giovanni was left alone with the chill air and the thudding of his heart. By the stars still in the sky Giovanni watched that girl go, her wispy skirt swishing high on her legs as if the cold, to her, was nothing. He could see the way her hair blew. Had he ever touched hair like hers, long, golden-brown, so wild? Light was coming into the sky. Giovanni fumbled for his bottle of whisky and he poured a great draught down his throat. Then another. It didn't help. His senses were acute. His lust had a diamond edge, and that described the morning, for it was hard and sharp as a diamond. Giovanni pushed himself out into the early morning and rushed toward Park Güell before the girl could disappear forever.'

'This is not a true story,' I said.

'No? What is it then?'

'Some imagining of yours. Something you made up to explain the presence of a dead man in that park. If there was such a dead man.'

'You want me to stop?'

'Not now. It's quite amusing. The girl is titillating, of course, which is the effect you seek. Personally I might have done without Giovanni's family history, or the description of his boorish life and work, but you tell your story with a nicely ironic flair. So go on. I'm interested in sad Giovanni's fate. I don't think it will turn out well and I am already a little sorry for him. Which is, if you don't mind me saying, the hub of storytelling. Your audience must suspect what might happen, yet they must dread that it will happen.'

'You've broken my concentration.'

'I'm sure this vat of beer you're swilling down will do wonders for your concentration.'

'May I have another?'

'Yes, go on. Here's another, right on time. Where were you?'

'If you won't interrupt.'

'I won't.'

'So—Giovanni rushed through the park's entrance. The shapes, the statues, the colours and strange faces, the inlaid decorative work in the main staircase and in the soffit-work, it was all hideous and it was all beautiful, as if Giovanni was seeing the place for the first time. As if he was seeing it the way the master architect had seen it. Park Güell was alive with the things that only live in the corners of the imagination, or in the corners of the eye. Do I need to embellish that? No. I refuse. Giovanni climbed the grand staircase of the park's entrance, breathing hard, and there were creatures snapping at his heels. He could have sworn there were, but when he turned, which he did often, there was always nothing. And then that staircase led him out to the flat plain above Park Güell. The observatory.

Here the ground was sandy and gritty underfoot, and Giovanni saw that familiar, crooked, colourful, crazy bench that runs all around the plain's wide perimeter. It was the plateau of the park, from which every morning he saw the compass of the world. The wind was in Giovanni's hair and the sun was rising up out of the horizon. There was a fire of gold over the sea. It was the greatest and most beautiful morning since the dawn of time.

'The girl was waiting, silhouetted against that dawn, her wispy dress flying and her hair blowing. Between her legs Giovanni could see the rising, fiery sun, and it was as if it burned through her. Giovanni crossed the expanse of ground. With his big belly and his grey hair and his dirty fingernails, he felt as if he was the romantic lead in a Hollywood movie. He no longer felt the cold. He was no longer conscious of the creatures that scurried back and forth in the shadows. He felt nothing but that hunger inside, that lust, and when he took the girl roughly up in his arms—picked her bodily up because she weighed less than nothing—his mouth bore down into her white face and her red lips, and she was ready, and it was as if she was eating him. She moaned in the way that the wind moaned, and the two of them kissed all the more passionately, the girl's body trembling, her hands gripping Giovanni's hair and his shoulders.

'As for Giovanni, well, strength was coming into him, an in-human strength, as well as a kind of caving-in of the soul. It was as if he wanted to eat the girl alive and die in her arms all at the same time. Giovanni lay the girl down onto a curve of that crazy-crooked bench and he pushed up her skirt, and he followed her down, kneeling between her legs and deeply kiss-ing her there, but when he stopped he saw a shape laying on the bench beside him. Giovanni drew back, and he saw clearly what it was beside his right shoulder, and he let out a scream, and the world swayed. For the dead man was with them on that bench, and it was as if the dead man was only asleep, but he was all bloody, and he had no throat, and he had no ears, and half his face was gone, and his eyes were empty in his head.

'Giovanni fell back, scrabbling in the sand. The girl stretched voluptuously, like a cat coming awake, and she cradled the head of the dead man, she cradled his head in her lap, caressing cheeks that were no longer there, her hair falling over the stricken dead face, and then she looked up through the veil of her hair and her black eyes stared at Giovanni.

'Everything had gone out of Giovanni—strength, lust, even fear. He was beyond fear. His bladder had emptied but he wasn't conscious of it. All that was left in him was awe. Disbelief. And a silence that rocked his skull.

'The girl said, "Maybe I'll give you a chance," and Giovanni nodded his head violently, like a fool, and he could not get any words out of his throat. She said, "Tell me your name."

'Giovanni managed to speak his name, fumbling and spluttering. He was too transfixed to lie. He knew he was on the precipice of death. In any moment the girl's monsters would emerge from the shadows to eat his throat and his face and to gouge out his eyes.

'The girl stood up in a swift motion—nothing more than a blur—and she was over him. Her thin body covered Giovanni's, and though he tried to struggle away, scrabbling in the sand, the girl's tongue lapped at his throat and at his ears, and her fragrant hair fell in his eyes. Her hands held down on his hands, splaying him like a starfish. She sniffed at him. Giovanni could feel the way she pressed down on him, the way she panted so heavily. She was hungry. She said, "Luckily for you, you're too old and too ugly for us. Your soul is empty. There's no juice left in your life. There's no joy left at all. You taste bitter and sour. Maybe if you promise to help us we'll let you live. Maybe. You're so dead already, but there's a chance we could use you. And your taxi. And your fear of eternity. Will you help us?"

'"Yes ... yes."

'"Whenever we call?"

'"Yes—yes."

'The girl's hands moved over Giovanni, and then she had his

wallet, fat with pesetas from his good night's work. In a blur the girl was on her feet again and she was standing by the dead man.

'"Take anything, everything, it's yours."

'"You'd like it to be so easy, wouldn't you? It won't be like that, Giovanni De Mauro. Your life will never be the same. You will always remember me—and my friends." She had his taxi driver's licence out of his wallet, and with disdain she threw that fat wallet down at him. "So this is where you live. Not a very nice area, Giovanni De Mauro. No wonder your heart is so barren."

'The girl played with the licence. She waved it before her eyes as if it was a fan, or some kind of mobile for the wind to catch, and then she put it down into the dead man's face and wiped his blood with it. "Ah," she said, "this one was beautiful. A young man who had not yet even begun to lose the juice of life. You better go now, but if you speak a word to anyone—" She waved the licence in the wind. "Anyway. We've made our pact."

'"Yes. Let me go. Now. Please. I won't say a word."

'The girl turned away and Giovanni managed to push himself up onto his knees, and then to his feet. The girl kept her back to him, as if she was deep in thought, the wind still whipping at her dress and at her long hair. She looked frail again, just a breath of a girl, frail, frail, frail, but with a black heart. Giovanni was so much bigger than her. He told himself this: I am so much bigger than her. And she had his licence, and so he took a wary step toward her, then another, and then another. He knew he could kill her with a single blow, he could strangle the life out of that soft throat, or he could break the girl over his knee.

'Giovanni reached out with both his hands to grab her thin shoulders, and she turned and cried out and her hand swept past his face as if it was a great axe that could have beheaded him, and Giovanni threw up his arms in defence, and then he was running across that plain, falling, running hard again, his old man's heart seizing with terror and exertion.

'Just the once he managed to look back, and there he saw silhouetted against the golden dawn not one figure but five, and then ten, and then twenty, more, and they were surrounded by scuttling, indistinct creatures. There was a great crying in the air. By the time he was in his taxi Giovanni was weeping with fear, and he drove blindly, like a madman, and because he ran through every red light in Barcelona and because he nearly knocked down every early morning pedestrian who happened in his path, the police pursued him and eventually even managed to stop him, but when he was in the presence of those officers, when he was in the middle of their circle, on his knees, Giovanni was weeping again, this time with joy, because he thought he was safe and he would be able to tell his story and the police would protect him from the evil of the world.'

'Oh, don't tell me our hero tried to make police officers believe that story?'

'I'm glad you see he could not have been able to do such a thing, not in a hundred years. A taxi driver develops a certain cunning, you know, if he is to survive. At first he prattled like a madman, but when he was in their offices and he had time to think, Giovanni recanted. It was the best thing he could have done. The police investigation commenced. To every detective assigned to the case Giovanni was only the poor fool who had discovered the dead man and who, given the state of the corpse, had been understandably frightened out of his mind. In fact there was a certain amount of relief when Giovanni changed his story. After the first few days, he was left alone. And that is that. So. What do you think of this story?'

'Oh, I think there has to be a lot more. The girl promised to come to Giovanni. We certainly don't want to miss that part.'

'Yes, but Giovanni has not returned to his rooms. I told you he was cunning. He is in hiding. He lives in places where he would not be so easily found, and on top of that he moves daily. He makes sure to keep his taxi well-hidden and he does not believe he will be discovered, at least not by her. When he does drive, for extra money, he does so sporadically, and only in daytime hours. He has become a very careful man.'

'No.'

'What do you mean, "no"?'

'The more you explain, the less satisfying it becomes. Your story's at a loose end, that's its problem. We're abandoned in the middle of act two. I'm interested in this story. I'm interested in its content, you've succeeded there, but I'm also interested in its structure. Now. You can't possibly try to leave the story where it is, with Giovanni in hiding and, presumably, jumping at shadows, and I don't think you intend to. What about that girl and her coven of—whatever they are. We're in limbo. It's just not good enough, what you've told. We, I mean your audience, are prepared to believe these evil creatures Giovanni has encountered may be vampires, we may even hope that they are something worse than vampires, but we just don't know. Lack of information makes us only suspect what they may be. If for example we are given more information, little by little, that suspicion will turn to dread, and that's the effect you want. Do you see what I mean?'

'But this is a true story. It can't fit a formula.'

'A story is a story. It's all in the telling. Join a few pieces together or make up new parts for those that don't fit. What could be easier? Now. The girl's promise to come after Giovanni has to be fulfilled because it has raised our expectations. If that promise isn't fulfilled then the girl looks like a dupe, not some incarnation of evil. You could just as easily turn her into a comic figure now.'

'I see you've thought about story-telling.' The old man looked at me and then he leaned his head into his hand. He said, 'I suppose I can see that what you say may be true. I think that may be because the full story has not played itself out.'

'Ah,' I said. 'Now that makes sense.'

'It does? To you?'

'Of course.' I looked at him and something about his dull-eyed melancholy made me smile with a little more warmth. 'Let's get to the point, because this is what you've been driving at, rather clumsily too, I might add. The point is you picked me out of the crowd here. Don't tell me it was an accident. You chose to sit with me and you chose to tell me this story. Why would you do that, to unburden your soul? But it's Giovanni who needs to be unburdened, not you. Unless, of course, you are Giovanni. That is you, isn't it?'

'Well, yes.'

'Of course. And you believe wholeheartedly in your story, don't you?'

'Yes.'

'That makes it interesting, though I expect you will end your days in the insane asylum. Let's look at this question of unburdening the soul. Let's look at the logic of your story. The Giovanni you've described—the self you've described—may be cunning but you say he lacks insight. He appreciates beauty of course, that humanises him, together with the fact that he carries such a weight of loneliness in his heart, but you've given me the impression that the terrain of his heart is a complete mystery to him. Correct? In that case, for such a person, confession for the sake of confession just does not seem plausible, not for that character.'

'I see.'

'I hope you do. So, Giovanni had—you had—an intent other that confession when he—you—approached me. Excuse me if I labour this point, for you have to see your story in the way your audience will see it, and that will help you to understand how it is that, for the most part, they're always a step ahead of you. They will want to know what your goal was in coming to the Bar Zurich, and picking me out, and so on. They will want to know this very quickly, or again they'll be frustrated. Well, within the logic of your story, your goal could only have been to find a way to finish your story. You, the author of this living tale, if I can call it that, know very well you're stuck in the middle of act two. You say you believe this story implicitly, so that means you also know you don't want to spend your life in hiding, or with the threat of that girl one night appearing in your bedroom and taking out your throat. So you need a way out. There's only one way, at least within the reality you've created.'

'You're losing me.'

'I'm telling you I'm on to your game. And if I am, so is your audience. You came to this bar, populated as it is mostly by young university students, because you were seeking out a sacrificial lamb. Where else could your story go? What other twist could there be? Your intent was to find someone you believed that strange girl and her companions would accept as a sacrifice, then they might leave you alone. So you sat with me. You discovered that I'm edgy and nervous about a woman, therefore all the more vulnerable, and you discovered that I am very conveniently a foreigner who may not be missed by the authorities. And I have a young man's looks. You thought I'd be the one to help you conclude your story.'

'You think yourself so clever?'

'Yes.'

'But what you say, then, it could be done.'

'Oh, of course. For some reason or other I would have to let you take me to this Park Güell. Let me see. You would have to trick me, or get me drunk, or take me by force. Is that what you'd planned? You offered to take me there tomorrow—you were probably hoping that by the end of the night, when I was full of enough beer, you could talk me into coming with you to see that beautiful dawn. That would have been the easiest and the most probable option. You might have succeeded too, with a blockhead.'

'Now I can't do any of those things.'

'True. Well, all that's left is the possibility that I would let you take me there anyway.'

'I like this reasoning. Yes, indeed I do. Why would you let me take you there?'

'I don't know. Pride. To prove to myself that I don't believe your fantastic story. To call your bluff. To make a fool of you.'

'Then you'll come?'

'Absolutely not. In the context of the story what I've described is hardly a credible motivation for my character. I would have to balance my desire to show you up as a fool with my very understandable fear that you yourself could try to hurt me there, and then in your mind convince yourself that it was those phantasms who did it. And in that balance, fear would always win.'

'Those things are real. I swear it on my children's souls.'

'Still, no audience would accept me going there with you at such an hour. No half-intelligent audience, anyway. Another thing. What makes you think those creatures will still be at the park? A public place like that. If it regularly produced a half-eaten human body, the police would have been swarming long ago. They would have ploughed the very ground up to understand what was happening. They're not very sentimental, police, not even, I'll bet, about your sacred Gaudí. And there's nothing in your suggestion that particularly profits the sacrificial lamb, if you don't mind me pointing that out too. I get to make a fool of you, but if I'm dreadfully wrong, which I suppose must be seen as a possibility, or else our audience would have gone home by now, I lose my throat and my ears and my eyes. A most unattractive option. I'm sorry to spoil things for you, Giovanni, but there's plenty of other candidates in the Bar Zurich if that's what you really want, and they're all getting drunker. Why don't you try your luck with one of them? Your audience will accept that your first choice of victim was too smart to budge, and that you needed an alternative. Sociologists and rock musicians like to tell us the youth of today believe they have no future; well, here they are, disenchanted youth currently fill the Bar Zurich, why don't you go see if you can sell them a most concrete idea of "no future"?'

I laughed and old Giovanni sloshed down more beer. I laughed because my boredom with him had grown strong enough to bring out a familiar cruel streak, a streak I'd been at pains to suppress in my life, yet rarely managed to do. Still, in a way that I couldn't quite explain, I'd come to find him more diverting than I could have anticipated. Oh, but he was just a poor raving lunatic. I had to laugh a little more. This Giovanni De Mauro actually believed in the events he spoke about. There was a part of me, and I will admit this, that would also have liked to believe such a fantastic story. For the world is so dull and human beings so predictable, I almost wished there could be a proper end to Giovanni's tale.

Well, Güell Park was the last place I would have gone, either alone or with him, that night or any other night. What was important was my original reason for being in the Bar Zurich, and indeed Barcelona, and that was for Chiara, who, I now increasingly believed, was not going to keep our appointment. Maybe I'd tried too hard; maybe I'd frightened her. The next day I would have to try some new tactic. But I was sick to my stomach of tactics and covert moves. They were ultimately all so transparent, just as Giovanni's were. No. Chiara had probably learned of the way I had ingratiated myself with her friends and her colleagues in order to track her down. No wonder she'd been frightened off; but I would make Chiara see me, it was as simple as that. If I had to go to her home and face her adopted family—that ugly patriarch and his hairy-faced wife!—then I would. If I had to drag Chiara screaming from her home, I would do that too.

Because I loved her.

Just as I decided that, the old man, Giovanni, turned to me once more, rubbing his shoulder against my shoulder as if we were conspirators.

'You know, the sacrificial lamb is not usually supposed to understand how stories like this one turn out. I have to hand it to you. That's how you've stymied me, by being so much smarter than me. The lamb has to be an innocent. Pure. Vulnerable enough to bring out all an audience's sympathies. Isn't that what you would say?' He sopped up more beer, and went on in a hoarse whisper, 'So why don't you tell me about this young chica of yours?'

I swivelled and took him by his shirt. I didn't care who saw.

'You shut your mouth,' I said. 'Shut your filthy mouth. You can imagine any disgusting fate for me you like, but don't you entertain one thought about her or I'll be the one to be afraid of. You understand me?'

Another round of beer arrived. Now I was thirsty. The smoky atmosphere had made my throat parched. I shoved Giovanni aside and swilled a beer down, then pushed myself from the table. To hell with him. But it was agony to try and make myself leave that bar. What if Chiara did come and I wasn't there? She was my only concern, and I just could not believe she would be so steadfast in her refusal to come to me—not after three and a half years, not after I'd travelled so far to find her.

I stood in a corner, surrounded by laughing and yapping university types, and Giovanni pushed his way through them and stood in front of me, shuffling around as if he had an itch.

'What's the matter with you?' I said. 'I've got no more time for your story.'

His fetid body repulsed me, his eyes that had turned from sadness to cunning, even his lack of height. In a second I would make the waiters throw that drunkard into the street.

'You were right.'

'About what exactly?'

'About what you said. About that girl and her promise to come to me.'

'Oh, yes.' I didn't stifle my yawn. I turned my back to him. I wanted to humiliate him so that he might crawl off without there having to be a scene. But then I thought about what he said. That girl. Very reluctantly, I half-turned toward him. In an off-hand voice I said, 'Well?'

'She did find me.'

'So you've thought up a little more? I wouldn't bother, your story is irretrievable, and quite dull.'

He reacted then, really reacted. It shocked me to see the true fire in old Giovanni, the true outrage. Lunatic or not, he was most defi-nitely a man in spiritual pain. It was as if he'd had enough of me and my contempt. I pulled back from the way his ugly face glared up at me, at the way his crooked and yellow teeth were so bared.

He said, 'How clever you think you are, my beautiful Italian friend, my beautiful countryman, with your sharp wits and your sweet air of detachment.'

'Get away from me.'

'How superior you find yourself with your handsome clothes. Is that a silk shirt? How lovely. And your smooth skin. Do you use a facial creme? You fool. How beautiful it will be to watch that smug indifference leave your face, Marcello. You see? You're not the only one who thinks he is so clever. Can you imagine how I know your name, Marcello?'

I was stunned. I was physically stunned. 'No—no, I can't at all.'

'And how authoritatively you declared my story could only unfold in one direction. Ha! Ha! Ha!'

Giovanni's spittle sprayed my cheek and people turned to stare. Others moved away. Giovanni smiled a smile I did not like, but at least he stopped the staccato braying that was his laughter. How could he know my name? I was in fear then, and it was a terrible, unreasoning fear for Chiara. The old man waved his brown hand for more beer and he waited until the bad-tempered waiter brought it to us. Then we stood in that corner, and very slowly, and very deliberately, and with great delight, Giovanni told me the rest of his story, and it was a fable I had to believe, to the very last detail.

'Giovanni moved yet again, as he did every day, but this time it was in the middle of the night. The one-star hotel he had been in for no more than another weary day, and by that I mean daylight, well, it began to grow claustrophobic and small. Giovanni had stretched himself out on the bed, but as his breathing grew steady and his thoughts went to the awfulness of his predicament, he felt the walls pressing in and the ceiling falling down. The hotel had been a poor choice, worse than all the other poor hotels he had stayed in. It hardly deserved its single star. There he found he could not close his eyes for fear that the room would shrink around him and that he would awaken in a trap. He could believe such a thing, that he would close his eyes and when he opened them he would be in a box, and not just any box, but a coffin. Neither could he lay awake, for the bare bulb above the bed shone in his eyes, transfixing him like a rabbit caught in a headlight, and when he stared into that light the world was washed of all colour, and out of that dazzling white might walk the strange girl.

'Perhaps he could lie in darkness. Desperation made him try even that manoeuvre, but when he did turn out the light all sound seemed to intensify. He heard mice moving behind the walls, scuttling busily, and on top of that they started to scuffle amongst themselves most loudly; and then the hum of the night traffic rose up from the street, and the room seemed to throb with sound, and there were heavy footsteps too, in the corridors outside Giovanni's room, on his very floor, the top floor, where he had asked to be put, and he feared those footsteps belonged to that girl, and to her friends, and they were crawling toward him.

'In a violent action Giovanni pushed himself out of his bed. He gathered up his courage and he checked outside his door, and was greeted with the sight of nothing. In his room he could no longer breathe. With trembling fingers Giovanni buttoned a soiled shirt over his soiled singlet, for now he lived in a type of squalor. He believed he was most vulnerable during those few minutes it took to shave, or to shower, or even during the time it took to clean his teeth. He could not bear the sound of the running of a tap or the flushing of a toilet, for they masked other sounds, and Giovanni knew—above all else—he had to be vigilant for all sounds. No-one must be given the opportunity to creep up behind him in silence, and lay a cold hand on his shoulder, or touch his throat, or his eyes.

'Such little time had passed since that night at Park Güell, days and weeks only, yet already Giovanni felt he was going out of his mind, and it was not only his mind that failed him. The always strained tendons in his neck caused him excruciating pain, and his shoulders were now hunched as if he was constantly trying to make himself smaller, less visible. His knees creaked when he walked and they stiffened when he did not. And there was an aching in his belly, a solid aching, as if he had swallowed a rock and it refused to pass. To these ailments were added a hundred other discomforts; a twitching of the cheek that would start for no apparent reason and stop just as inexplicably; a swelling of the feet, like those of a pregnant woman, that would make him throw off his shoes and leave him unable to walk for hours. The final insult was the gamey smell Giovanni's body carried. Anxiety. The putrefaction of fear. Yet he could hardly risk the act of washing.

'His mind suffered because of his sleeplessness; he was always weary, for if he did chance to sleep he would jerk awake every few minutes, at some perceived movement, or presence, or imagined change in the air around him. Giovanni tried to face reality. He knew there was no point in pretending he could go on this way. Sometimes he wished that the girl had taken his throat out, that she had done it quickly and cleanly, that he was already wrapped in the sweet oblivion of death. Then, at least, he would not have to live with such apprehension, with such maddening vigilance! Yet, Giovanni did want to live. That was his irony. Sad as his life had been, heavy as his heart had been, he found he most assuredly still longed for life.

'Vague plans to leave the city, the country, the continent if need be, developed inside his sizzling skull. He would not stay in Barcelona. Neither would he return to Verona, for he could be traced there by anyone with enough diligence. He did not want to stay in Europe. He thought often of India, with its teeming millions, or of China, with its billions, but the place Giovanni decided he could best disappear was the United States of America, and in particular Los Angeles, Hollywood. For that was the place the newspapers always said human souls most easily vanish. Oh, in his more lucid moments, how he knew his ideas had slipped into insanity!

'Yet his most pressing need, for the while at least, was to vanish from that awful hotel, and find another.

'A few belongings—and clothes everything he owned was still in his apartment, where he must never return—were stuffed into the plastic shopping bags he used as luggage, and he left the room. He went down the dark corridors and staircase and confronted the night manager, who was asleep at his desk, and whom he roused with a slap on the shoulder. Giovanni paid half the room charge and walked into the night without listening to the manager's shouted admonishments of how Giovanni was morally obliged to pay the other half as well. He threw those plastic bags into the passenger seat of his taxi cab and he drove off at speed. He had no idea where he was going, he simply felt all the better for being out of that room. He was low on money, and low on petrol, but it felt good to drive, to cruise around the city, for that was the thing he did best. Maybe, it struck him then, the task of finding another hotel room could wait. For where was he safer than in a fast-moving vehicle?

'The lights and gaiety of Barcelona were invigorating. The more Giovanni drove around the city, the better he felt. How could he have locked himself in a hotel day after day? The streets were full of people and cars. This was the world Giovanni knew, and with a bold stroke he switched on the taxi's For Hire sign, and his luck was good, for he found fat fares, and that enabled him to buy a full tank of fuel, and then a sandwich, and then a chocolate bar. It continued that way all through the night, his luck staying with him so that each fare seemed more profitable than the last. His tips were excellent. Giovanni felt touched by angel's wings, for passenger after passenger remarked how lucky they were to find his taxi available; after all, the sudden Metro strike had stranded people all over Barcelona.'

'But that's tonight,' I said. 'I nearly didn't make it here. The buses are over-crowded and the taxis are all—you are talking about tonight, aren't you?'

'I like it when you start to catch on. The earlier evening, yes.

Let me continue. After one particularly generous passenger, who may not have realised his own generosity, for he was an Irish sailor full of alcohol, and sandwiched by two whores from the worst part of the city, Giovanni drove along with the Mediterranean to his left. Can you believe this: for the first time in an eternity Giovanni's heart was almost light. The sea beyond the harbour was dark and inviting. One day soon Giovanni knew he would set out on that sea, to his own undiscovered country. He drove by the immense statue of Christopher Columbus, that monument with its hand pointing in the wrong direction—to the east instead of to the west, how could the city fathers have allowed such a faux pas?—and then Giovanni turned the car and followed the heavy night traffic up along La Rambla.

'The cars there moved slowly. Halfway along they stopped altogether. There was street dancing, with hundreds of people lining the kerbsides. These crowds had gathered into tight knots and had created a bottleneck, a traffic jam of wild proportions. Oh, it was a night! It was as if everyone was captured in the city heart and there was no way out. Giovanni could hear music and drums and singing; he hardly minded having to wait there for he had no home to go to, and he was comfortable in his taxi, and he liked the way life brimmed around him; but all those feelings vanished when he turned his head and gazed out the taxi's side window. For the girl was standing at a prominent corner of La Rambla, and she was facing his car, and she was watching Giovanni's unshaven face.

'They exchanged a look, and then the girl smiled. It was a pretty smile, for she was indeed a pretty girl, but it sent a chill through Giovanni's body that ended with the flesh of his loins crawling as if alive. The wind that came across the harbour and passed around the iron legs of Christopher Columbus blew the girl's hair away from her face. Her skin was white, her lips were red, and her eyes were as dark as he remembered. Giovanni sat still, dead in the traffic, the air around his head pounding. He watched the way the wind whipped at her hair, and how that flimsy dress rippled over her thin legs, and then he had to hide his face in his hands for his nerve was finally gone. When he could bring himself to look up the girl had disappeared into the crowds trapped along La Rambla, but there was something else, something in her place, something even stranger.'

'What, for God's sake?'

'Another woman. Another young woman. Standing exactly where that girl had stood.'

I thought I knew then, and I shuddered from deep down inside myself. I thought my heart was going to give out. I took Giovanni by the shoulders and shook him.

'A young woman?'

Giovanni's teeth clattered with my force. He managed to utter, but not very well, 'Stop it! Or you'll never know another thing! Take your hands off me!'

With a final shove that pushed him against a wall I forced my-self to stop. I wanted to wipe my hands after touching that piece of human detritus. Giovanni straightened his filthy shirt and ran a finger around his grimy collar. A man-mountain of a waiter hovered near us. I could read his indecision, so I smiled at him as benignly as I could, and then I put my arm around Giovanni's shoulders. I hugged my companion affectionately and chucked his bristly chin. The waiter decided there was no trouble, only high spirits. I took my arm away from Giovanni. He should in-deed have washed. He stank like garbage left in the rain.

'That young woman,' Giovanni started again, 'seemed to be frantic. She saw Giovanni's stranded taxi and she ran toward it, calling as if he was about to drive away.'

'But you were caught in a traffic jam.'

'She didn't care. In a half-second she had moved into the back seat, and he could hear her breathing heavily as if she'd been running all the way up La Rambla.'

'And then?'

'And then they spoke.'

'Quick!'

'She told Giovanni the Metro strike had caught everyone by surprise, including her, and that she had been trying for an hour to find a vacant taxi. She said she didn't mind if they were stuck there for another hour. She said she would pay any charge, but she had somewhere important to go, and it suited her to at least have transport. Giovanni told her he would turn off the meter until they started to move, and she liked that, Giovanni thought she really liked him for that. He watched her in the rear vision mirror—with a seed of suspicion, of course—but when she smiled that suspicion left him. She was just a young woman who had somewhere to go on a chaotic evening. And she had a good heart too, that was visible to him plain as day because he thought no smile like that could be fake. You know the smile he saw. You probably know that smile better than anyone on this earth, eh? Giovanni knew then what he had to do. He had to do it because she was his only hope of salvation, fate had delivered her to him, and he would not tempt fate one more time. It hurt him that she wanted to speak, but they had so much time to wait inside that traffic jam, and her cheeks were flushed with a certain air of excitement, or expectation, and she couldn't seem to bottle that in. How Giovanni would have preferred her anonymity! But she spoke, and the things she spoke about brought Giovanni to the Bar Zurich.' Giovanni sighed. 'Do you want me to go on?'

There were no words I could speak. My mind was spinning. Finally, I said, very quietly, 'Please stop referring to yourself in the third person.'

'It's the only way I can manage to tell the story.'

'You have to stop it.'

Giovanni sighed again. 'I'll try. Maybe you're right.' He looked for more beer but there was none forthcoming. He said, 'You're wondering if Giovanni—I'm sorry, I'll try again. You're wondering if I hurt her. Yes, I've hurt her. Let me tell you that now. I've hurt her indeed.'

I was leaning against the wall and the ground beneath my feet was moving.

'So. We sat and waited for the traffic to move and we spoke about Barcelona. You know how these conversations between strangers go. It was the element of time. We had to fill that flat space. Silence for so long just seemed impossible. When she started to tell me about her work at the university that sense of calm and peace came back to me. It was her voice. Of course you know her voice. How it soothes and how it lilts, and how her Italian accent makes her all the more delightful to listen to. She told me she was very good with languages, and that in her three and a half years here she had learned Catalan, Castilian, and even Basque, though she felt more confident at reading or listening to those languages than actually speaking them.

'I said, "Miss, but you've mastered our Catalan. Except for your accent I would hardly have thought you were a foreigner."

'She said, "You still have an accent. Where are you from?"

'And I told her and we laughed at being two Italians trapped in a traffic jam in Barcelona. I said, "What brought you here?"

'She thought about that for a while, and I was under the impression that she would not reply, and when I looked back in the mirror the colour in her cheeks was high. I think it was her excitement that made her tell me.

'"It was a young man, really, the great love of my life."

'"But you're too young to have a great love! How old are you? Twenty-two, twenty-three?"

'"Twenty-three, now. When I knew him in Italy I was just a girl. We were students. He was the smartest one. I think one day he'll be a great poet."

'"So this great poet broke your heart? I can't imagine what else a poet would be good for."

'"No. He didn't break my heart. Well, in a way he did."

'What is it that makes people need to confess? I ask you that now, Marcello, just as you asked me. Is it that by sharing some hurt we think we can lessen it? And why to a taxi driver—why taxi drivers most of all? As if we care about the petty ins-and-outs of people's lives. The who-did-whats, the he-said-this and

I-said-thats; people believe the things that happen to them should hold equal significance to those unfortunate enough to have to hear about it. But then, this girl was different. It was her voice. It was the tone of her voice. It wasn't until the end of our conversation that I really understood. I'm sorry, I don't mean to be vague to you now, but I was intrigued and I was confused. There was something I was missing, yet I don't think any passenger in that back seat ever spoke so plainly, or from such a heart.

'She said, "It's very much on my mind tonight. We have quite a history. He and I were so wild together at university, it's a wonder we passed a single subject. Often we would forget our classes and go to his flat and spend the day and night listening to music and watching films. Do you mind me telling you this while we're stuck here?"

'I told her that was quite all right.

'"Well, he would give me books to read from his own library—his parents are wealthy—and then we would discuss those books late into the night, on journeys that seemed to us to be of the greatest discovery. That was part of what I liked about him, the way we could learn together, and that strange kind of intensity of his that could transfix me for hours. And then, you know what? He would suddenly break off from what he was doing or saying, and he would compose a poem, complete and beautiful, in one concentrated action. He didn't need studies. When I was with him, neither did I. You see, I could match him.

'"The conflict that developed with our parents was almost unbearable, but with a love like ours parents come to mean nothing. His was an industrialist family and they fully expected that when his studies were over he would enter the family business. Industrialists. To this day I wonder if they have a heart between them. The thought of following in his family's footsteps filled him with revulsion, and I begged him not to give in. My family expected me to graduate at the top of my classes, as I'd done all my life, but with Marco—his name is Marcello, but that's what I liked to call him—but with him my grades seemed insignificant. We were rising above anything as mundane as university. I started to fail, and there was a kind of glory in that. Every now and then I would write, the beginning of some great novel of my own, but it was Marco who was writing the type of poetry that should be collected in books, and so slowly it happened, because I thought his was the greater talent, somehow I sublimated everything of myself into his needs. I became no more than a secretary."

"'Yes, that's what men like. A cook in the kitchen, a whore in the bedroom, and a secretary in the office."

'She laughed at that and I can tell you I was surprised. Maybe in a way I'd wanted to frighten her off. To give her a chance to run out of that taxi and never return. I really would have expected her to be offended, but she stayed and somehow I still had the impression she liked me.

"'It made him so much stronger and me so much weaker," she went on. "It was a foolish thing, but then I was young and stupid and I only see now how easily women fall into such a trap. You know what I mean. Well, of course, the sharing stopped. Marco started to seem so much wiser. I realise in hindsight that he was simply focused, and I was not, therefore there was nothing left to do but follow. But how can a man love a woman who becomes so submissive, and how can a woman love a man who is so obsessed with his own inner world?

"'Something changed in Marco and I think it was because of me. He discovered he enjoyed his dominance over me, and as he became rougher and ruder within our relationship, so too was he in his dealings with other people. Somehow that only made him more attractive—to a certain element only, mind you. He developed more of a circle than ever while I watched on with nothing but distaste. His friends seemed to live to be near his intensity. Acolytes, I called them, but Marco didn't love me anymore and he didn't care what I thought.

"'His friends helped him to change. They all took drugs,

those free-loaders, and they all slept with one another. The spoiled underbelly of Roman youth. Partners became interchangeable. I shudder to think what Marco did when I wasn't looking, but he barely bothered to lie to me. He discovered hard and harder drugs, and his focus changed, from writing poetry to writing the most soulless pornography, which he sold under a pseudonym so as not to inflame his family.

"'Marcello only wanted the most offensive books in his home now—from pure, cheap sex magazines to so called 'erotic literature', but all it did was debase him, and he tried to debase me, and his demands became disgusting. What I wouldn't do there were ten other women who willingly would. And Marcello made the most of his allure. I could barely believe that a person who had seemed so beautiful, a master of such beautiful words too, could be revealed as being so corrupt inside. He tried to play games with me. They were meant to humiliate me, or maybe to make me see how pathetic I'd become. But when Marco's first poems were published, in his own name, all pretence of good intentions, university study, and love, went out the window. That was when I ran away from him, and in a way, I've been running ever since."

"'I think this traffic is about to start moving again," I told her. "Can you see that group of people dancing toward the fountain? Hopefully everyone will follow. Then we'll be on our way. And then I'll get the meter going."

"'You should have it going now, seeing that you've become my father confessor."

"'It's a taxi driver's lot. Believe me, I'm used to it. But this is a most unusual story."

"'I'm going to see him tonight, you know."

"'Really?"

"'He's found me—after more than three years. Marco wants me back and he's come all the way to Barcelona to collect me."

"'And of course, a young girl with a good heart, you've completely forgiven him."

'The traffic started to move then and I flicked the meter on. The girl smiled at that. I watched her in the rear vision mirror whenever I had the chance. I'd decided exactly what I would do, and I wanted her to feel all the more comfortable, all the more relaxed, because I could see I might only have one chance. If I botched that chance she would go shouting murder into the night and I would be ruined anyway. But what she said next surprised me.

'She thought for a while, and as we drove beside La Rambla I watched her profile. She was looking at the flower sellers and the painted actors begging for coins.

'She said, "You ask me if I've forgiven him? You want to know whether I'll take him back? The answer to that is no. Marco— Marcello—is a monster. The good I originally saw in him was a teenage girl's fantasy. I can't feel anything but hatred for him. I've been living with that fact for three and a half years. I've been living with the fear that he would come and find me. I never told him what went on in my mind. I ran away, and so I never let him know how I loathed and how I pitied him. It was the coward's way out. Since then I've died a thousand deaths from the expectation that he would arrive on my doorstep. Now he finally has. Why should I feel such fear? I'll only know peace when I look into his face and tell him what's in my heart. He's begged to see me tonight. Well, his reward is on the way."

'That was when I understood what had been so strange about that beautiful girl. She had the face of an angel but her voice carried such a bitterness! Her heart was so full to overflowing with hatred that it shocked me, it actually shocked me. If I'd let myself I would have felt sorry for what would have to come next to her, but her worries were not my worries. They would never be. We are all islands, and so I saw that my need was all the greater than hers. She had to die, to help me, and it was a pity—but a pity only—that she would never have the chance to speak her heart to this Marco. To you.

'The traffic jam had loosened. I drove quickly away from La

Rambla and for a while I stayed on all the busy main roads, but then I turned toward streets I knew would be quiet. She must have thought I was taking short-cuts to save her a few hundred pesetas.

'I said to the girl, "And what was your name? After such a story, I feel I need to know."

'I saw her smile. She said, "Well, I may have exposed my life, but I'll only tell you my name is Chiara."

'"Such a beautiful name. It's like music. Chiara. And that miserable creature waiting for you at the Bar Zurich is Marco."

'"I only think of him as Marcello now."

'And with that I slowed and then stopped the taxi. The blind alley we had travelled toward was dark. This was where Barcelona was dead. All the parties in the world could go on, but here there would always be silence. I swivelled in my seat and the girl, Chiara, looked at me with a hint of surprise. It struck me again just how beautiful she was, with her flowing black hair and her dark eyes and her simmering anger giving her cheeks colour, but I did what I had to do. It didn't take long. The girl slumped down and she didn't move again. With a three-point turn I drove the taxi away as quietly as I could, nice and quietly, and made sure not to attract the slightest attention.'

They kicked the two of us into the street a few seconds after Giovanni said that.

At first I was insane with rage, but then I thought, No, Giovanni has to take me to her. He's a lunatic, but how will it help me if I beat him senseless? The most important thing is to find Chiara, nothing else matters.

Giovanni's nose was bleeding and his bottom lip had split. In the Bar Zurich the waiters had been expecting some kind of outburst all along, we'd been that strange a pair, so I didn't get far with venting my anger on that human piece of merda. No sooner had I struck Giovanni in his bristly face, and then again, than the waiters pounced. They quickly wrestled us out of the busy bar and into the street and threw us down onto the sidewalk like yesterday's rubbish. They yelled at us but I couldn't understand a word. Then they left us with passersby giving us the widest berth.

Yet it was the best thing that could have happened. For the moment at least I could think clearly again, despite the way my heart shook inside my chest. It was a real quivering, and it cried out Oh, my Chiara! but I had to do more than weep impotent tears.

Giovanni sat on the ground nursing his face. It was all I could do not to attack him again.

'Come on,' I said. 'We can't stay here. They might be calling the police. Where's your taxi?'

'I am staying here.' Giovanni's shirt was flecked with blood. He kept a hand over his nose and his mouth. 'I'm not moving. You weren't supposed to hit me.'

'Can you blame me? Can't you see what you've done, Giovanni? You've completely imagined this nightmare vision about that ghoulish girl. There is no girl! At the exact moment you thought you saw her again on La Rambla she was replaced with somebody real—my Chiara. And now you've really hurt someone. Now you really do have trouble, all because of a sick fantasy. I pray that you haven't killed Chiara. Can't you see how innocent she is? Can't you see how ill you are? Just take me to her. Please. Take me to her. I swear that if we find her there won't be any police involved. You can take that trip to your own undiscovered country. You'll be free to run away. That would make you happy, wouldn't it? Now, tell me quickly. You did take her to this park, didn't you? That's where you've left Chiara? Tell me she was alive and safe when you left her, please.'

'Oh, she was alive all right. But I'm not moving from here. You can go to hell, for all I care. You weren't supposed to hit me.'

Giovanni looked as if he might cry. It was all I could do not to put my boot into him and kick him to death right there and then. Oh, how I would have liked to succumb to the rage that was eating me up from the inside. That Spanish pig had hurt my Chiara, God help him.

I walked circles, thinking, thinking, finally I said, 'But you've got your wish, Giovanni, don't you see?'

'See what?'

'You've fulfilled your original intent. In the story. You've found your true ending. Your audience is now poised for the final act. You can't deny it to them. Look at the beautiful irony of it! Your sacrificial lamb is now begging you to take him to your—what can I call it?—your killing floor.'

'You're only one of two.'

'Yes, but you came to me for a specific purpose.'

'That's right.'

'And it wasn't to hurt me with stories of how the woman I love has hated me all these years.'

'As if I care about that. I wanted to make you come to Park Güell with me, and if you knew your Chiara was there, I was sure you would. I thought two would be better than one. Can you understand that reasoning?'

'Of course. And you were right. Two sacrificial lambs, that doubles your chances with those ghouls, doesn't it?'

'How could they stay angry with me after that?'

'Come on, Giovanni. You've done well. I'm asking you now. Take me there.' I checked my watch but Giovanni still wasn't moving. 'It's after three in the morning. Let's go. That's where we have to go, isn't it, you did take Chiara to Park Güell?' I was thinking I would give Giovanni five more seconds. If he still didn't move, I would run for the nearest police station. 'You took her to that plateau you spoke about? That crazy bench? Is that where you left her, where the dead man was found?'

'No,' Giovanni mumbled. He took his hand away from his mouth and he wiped it on his dirty shirt. Then he shook his head in a distracted manner. 'No. People there. It was too early. Lovers. Kissing, whatever, admiring the view of the city. Looking at the moon, drinking the night breeze. Park Güell is enchanted. Couldn't take your Chiara there. You'll never find her. I can see how clever you're trying to be. I took her into the forest behind the park. You can look all you like there, but only I know where she is. Me, and those things.'

'Then take me to them. I'm not afraid.'

'You don't believe in them.'

'I do, Giovanni. Now I see you've been telling the truth all along. I want to go to them.' I squatted down by Giovanni and I took his shoulders in my two hands. He shuddered, waiting for me to hurt him, but I could see he wanted sympathy. He was shuddering because he feared being struck, but also because he feared he would cry his grief out to the sky.

I moved closer, and I put my smooth cheek against his rough cheek, and I said very softly into his hair-sprouting ear, 'How you've suffered, Giovanni. How you've suffered. A man should never be left to suffer alone, not the way you have. We don't always have to be islands; we don't always need to be so alone. I understand how it's been for you.' I held him all the more tightly, his stench swarming up into my nostrils, and I spoke most softly then, in no more than a whisper. 'Drive me there now, Giovanni. I'm completely in your hands.'

I closed my eyes and pressed my face to his, for long seconds, and his breathing started to follow mine. What a pair of lovers we must have looked to the passersby in that avenue. When I felt that enough time had passed I relaxed and kissed those hard, dry lips of Giovanni's. Then I looked into his face. Giovanni's eyes had rolled back into his head and only their whites showed.

I gently prodded him. I helped him to his feet. Tears fell down his face.

'Thank you, my friend,' Giovanni said. 'Thank you.' He looked with his hurt eyes just the once toward the Bar Zurich. 'I hear one day soon they'll be tearing that corner down. Good.' He snuffled into the cuff of his shirt, leaving more fat drops of blood. 'My car is down here.'

And so we walked to Giovanni's taxi, and climbed in, and I was on my way to Park Güell.

I barely took in those so-called magical surroundings. The park could have been the most beautiful or the most strange place in this world, but there was only one thing on my mind and that was to find Chiara. I'd made Giovanni leave his taxi parked crookedly in the street by Park Güell's entrance, and then to lead on ahead of me. I was full of suspicions and I would not give him the slightest chance to trick me. The park seemed to stretch away to my left but Giovanni was going down a set of rough and wet steps cut straight into the side of a hill. Down we went, and those steps ended in an expanse of thickets. Bushes and brambles there grew no higher than my waist but even in the darkness of that early morning I could discern the forest ahead.

'What are we doing down here?'

'I told you. I couldn't carry her into the park. It was too early in the evening. Lovers and sightseers.' Giovanni pointed in the direction of the trees. 'She's in there.' He was out of breath and his knees seemed to give him trouble. It must have been almost impossible for him when he'd come that way earlier, carrying Chiara in his arms. One of his legs seemed stiller than the other, and it made him shuffle, but I would not help him.

'Hurry,' I said. Giovanni seemed to falter. He was like a donkey hesitating on a trail and I couldn't bear the sight or the smell of him any longer. 'Go on. Where did you take her?'

Giovanni looked from the left to the right. I stood behind him and then I grabbed a fistful of his hair, pulling his head back.

'Do you think I'll put up with any more of your lies? Do you think I won't kill you if we don't find Chiara? Start walking!' And with that I pushed him forward. Giovanni fell heavily to his knees and hands.

'It's just that, in the dark, I'm not sure where. Please don't hurt me. Not again.'

Under the stars and sky Giovanni was just a shape in the dark. On his knees and hands, shaking his head from side to side, he could indeed have been a donkey that had fallen for the last time. Again I was consumed with a desire to kick him to death right there. His hand favoured that stiff leg of his. I made myself look away. My arms were trembling.

A wind had risen. All the bushes shook. In the sky there were a million stars, yet only the slightest sliver of a moon. It was cold too and it crossed my mind to wonder how it was I had arrived in that place, how it was that such a bizarre story as Giovanni's had come to involve me, and how strange that my true reunion with Chiara would occur here, in a forest, and not in the Bar Zurich. It must have been nearly four in the morning. In my mind's eye I could see Chiara lying as if asleep at the base of some great tree. She would be covered with fallen leaves, and she would be cold, but she would not have been exposed to the elements so long that it would have harmed her. When I took her in my arms and rubbed her shoulders and her cheeks she would come back to life and back to me. There would be no hate in her heart. I was the one Chiara would never hate, despite all Giovanni's black lies.

Up ahead, that forest moaned low. It was as if it was a great and dark world of its own, and it had mournful voice, but that was just the wind.

I helped Giovanni to his feet.

'Go on.' I pushed him, but carefully so that he wouldn't fall. 'We don't have time to waste. Do you understand?'

'I think it's this way.'

On we went, and as we walked through the first phalanx of great trees, and then amongst the wide and solid trunks of those deeper inside, the air was much colder and the perspiration on my face started to dry. I was trembling, but with more than that chill. It was anticipation and fear too. What if Giovanni had killed Chiara? There was a wind and a whistling, a soft song that if I concentrated, I could just hear. There was a sort of melody. There was woodwind, and choral voices, and the swirling and swelling of strings, but to try and grasp that melody was to try and grasp the last tendrils of a morning's mist. There was something though. Something quietly sacred about that place, some memory of the human race's first holy ground. Nature's own cathedral, I told myself, and when Giovanni spoke his voice was low and hoarse in that deep chest of his, and I knew he felt it too.

'Yes, I was right. This is the place.' Giovanni took a long breath and he looked upward, toward that canopy shutting out almost all light. His hands were clasped in front of him and I could not see his face. 'By that tree—the gnarled one that looks like the face of a witch. That was my marker. She's there.'

It was so dark and my heart was beating so fast. I had to make my way carefully or risk falling into some ravine. I called out, 'Chiara? Can you hear me? Chiara?' and the reply was that wind playing amongst the branches and leaves.

I stopped then.

But if this was a cathedral, then it was of some ancient religion of evil. I did not believe in God or scriptures or even in an afterlife, yet I knew there was no earthly good in this place. I could sense it. I listened carefully, for that whispery melody amongst the trees and for the sound of approaching footsteps. When I listened it was as if I could hear the forest's beating heart, and it spelled out a slow rhythm of death, death, death is coming to you. Yes, something was approaching with stealth and sentience, and it was coming down from the hills because it was angry and it was hungry, and there was good human life to be had, flesh and ears and eyes, but that most beautiful of all things too, the soul of a man who has not yet begun to lose the juice of life.

Me.

A blow sent me sprawling into the undergrowth and the world twisted and turned, spinning wildly on its axis. My head rocked with stars. I felt my face hit the wet and exposed root of a tree, but the shock of that roused me. In almost pure darkness Giovanni came at me again. He was swinging something above his head. I saw the looming silhouette, and then, just before he brought his arm down, the great trees allowed a sliver of light to shine through, and I saw Giovanni poised with his face all twisted with pain and hatred, and in his upheld hand there was the glinting of something silver and heavy. A wrench. That was why his leg had been stiff and he'd been such a shuffling old man—how could I have been such a fool? He'd secreted that weapon upon himself during the drive to Park Güell. The bastard. Yet in the instant I thought all these things he brought that weight down with every bit of his mad strength. If not for the darkness my skull would have been crushed to pulp.

Giovanni's aim was poor. The wrench thudded into the earth beside my ear. Finally I reacted. I pulled Giovanni down by his brawny arm, and then his stinking body was close to mine and we wrestled in the damp and brush. Giovanni was already screaming like the coward he was. At one point he was on top of me, and he stopped screaming long enough to try and crush me with the combination of his weight and barrel chest, but he was an old man and I was young. Soon I had the wrench in my own hand and it appalled me how fine that inert lump of metal felt to the touch, to the grasp. It was warm. I brought it down against Giovanni's skull, and as he twitched I brought it down again, then pushed him away.

He lay on the ground, moaning. But softly. It was more like a sighing.

I made myself get to my knees and then onto my feet. A great weariness had come over me. The back of my neck, near the right shoulder, burned as if I had been branded with a red-hot iron. I searched everywhere nearby for Chiara. I circled the tree that bore the face of a witch. There was nothing. I searched further. Nothing—only ethereal music and the steady beating of the forest's heart. Together those things told me I was indeed in an enchanted place, and far from alone.

Giovanni had been crawling. He slithered along the forest floor, a pathetic creature that has lost its legs. I took step after step beside him. Slowly he would stretch out one arm, pull himself over the ground, rest with his face buried in the leaves, and then put out his other arm and do the same again. His legs moved, or they quivered, his feet trying to find some purchase to push against, but they didn't seem to be much help. I let him go a little further. Then he was against a vast network of tree roots and he could not negotiate them at all. Giovanni came to a stop and only his fingers worked, gripping and squeezing amongst the rotten leaves of the forest floor.

I rolled him onto his back and the whole sum of his foul stench was released into the air. I fell to my knees beside him.

'Where is she, Giovanni?'

Giovanni's throat was choked with either saliva or blood. He coughed, and said in a weak voice, 'Home. She's in her bed, I hope.'

'What happened?' I propped Giovanni up and his throat seemed to clear. His head lolled and I shook him. 'Well?'

'She was … an angel. I couldn't bring myself to hurt someone like her. But you, if someone needs to die, it should be you.'

'She was coming to see me. How did you stop her?'

The wind rose up and blew in my face. I was conscious of the way that wind made Giovanni's eyelids flutter. There was enough light to see that he was blind to everything, for only the whites of his eyes showed. I shook him harder and his head was loose as a marionette's. He coughed up more of his blood.

'I convinced her that such hatred … it was wrong to show it … to anyone, even a monster of a young man. We talked about love and loneliness. We talked … a long, long time. She said she'd never had … a real friend, not in Barcelona.'

I kept shaking him. It was as if I was shaking the very words, and then the very life, out of that dull, old body.

Giovanni whispered, 'I made her see that if she loved you once, that was enough. It's wrong to hurt … those you've loved.'

'What did she say? What did Chiara say to that?'

Giovanni's whole body shook. 'The girl said "Yes".'

And then he stopped moving. There was no final sigh, no final appeal, no sign that death had taken him. Giovanni simply stopped moving. I was crying then, I think, crying not for him but for the humanity in Chiara. I lay Giovanni's head against the ground.

It was as I was kneeling there that the unexpected happened.

An eternity might have passed for all the conflicted emotions that had the time to run through me, but it was really only moments after Giovanni stopped moving.

For I felt Giovanni, some part of him—with my anti-theological stance I hesitate to call it his soul or his spirit, yet what else could it have been?—come into me. It was just like that, and there was a bitter taste, like eating onions or drinking ouzo. It was so strange it was almost amusing. I felt Giovanni's essence rise out of his body and then move inside me. No sensation could have been clearer.

Where I knelt was upon holy ground, or evil ground, but already then I was hesitating to use those emotive words. Maybe it was ground that was close to some other part of our universe, to that place where our eyes rarely see but which in our dreams and in our imaginings we understand all too well. I was overcome with wonder for I could not have thought Giovanni's story would end with his fetid little mortality entering my heart, but there he was, trapped, and he might never be released—perhaps not until I myself breathed my last. And if he tasted as dull as onions or ouzo, what might the life of someone vital be like?

I could hear, or perhaps I could feel, Giovanni's voice crying out. Something had happened to me that changed forever my views of heaven and hell and the limit of the human soul, and I was renewed.

There was life all around in that forest. Things were coming down from the hills toward me. No, I would not think the word evil. I would not fear anything that arrived. I would not call out to God for help. No. If there was a frail girl coming, I would take her into my arms. If there was a beast with a gnawing hunger, or some motley collection of strange little creatures that could do no more than scamper and scavenge for scraps, I would find a way to tame them.

Giovanni cried out inside me. Perhaps it was the wind blowing harder and I had lost my sanity. I thought I could smell the sea, the Mediterranean, all black and mysterious past the harbours of Barcelona. It crossed my mind that I would never return to an Italian frontier, that I'd passed beyond the simple notion that we are of countries. We are of worlds, and in that forest, in the diamond morning, I was poised at a new one. The stars and the sliver of moon, they understood everything. The trees shook themselves into life and a beautiful contentment filled my soul.

How, I wondered, would Chiara hate a man so full of the joy and the juice of life? Again, I knew it: I was renewed. She would see this in me, very clearly, when I arrived at her doorstep.

At first I sat on the ground, but it was damp and uncomfortable, so then I sat up on Giovanni's barrel chest, and waited.

Paris, 1995

THE CURRENTS

The Man

I.

Catherine's told him that this is the only way to do it. He has to fill his chest with air and hold it in as long as he can, which isn't as easy as it sounds—for a man of his age it's by no means a simple matter of taking a deep breath. Instead, he needs to concentrate hard, concentrate on filling every part of his lungs from top to bottom. He has to fill them as if they are a pair of great bellows, because only then will he have the chance to succeed. His lungs will have to inflate until they hurt; in the pursuit of this he has cried out in pain; not only that, but he has cried with pain too, tears running down his lined cheeks as if he were a newborn baby transplanted into the frame of an octogenarian. And when his lungs are full he knows he must keep his chest lifted high so that he will be able to hold onto his breath as long as he can.

Hold it a full two minutes, leaning forward until—well, Catherine says, he'll see.

When he was younger and more vital, no problem, of course. Not for someone who's enjoyed swimming, long-distance bicycling, and who was once good at almost all physical activities, though he'd never liked team-based sports. Too much of a loner, averse to the company of too many people, predestined to finally live alone. This is exactly what he does.

These days the hurt in his lungs is lessening. He's training himself to do this thing. He has just about trained himself to do it.

Today the memory of the worst of the pain is still very clear, but it doesn't scare him. How long can he hold his breath now?

Yesterday, one minute forty-three to maybe one-fifty-five. At this upper limit his mind swims, he feels faint, but it's better to persist, to keep trying and training, to trust the information Catherine has given him. She reminds him to go through it all slowly and methodically, day after day, week after week. There appears to be no rush. Discipline is the answer. So his old back arches and his spine cracks as the air comes in, as the air goes down, as he holds firm. He feels the way his body expands, and, despite the discomfort and threatening nausea, in a way he's come to like the sensation.

This morning there's definite progress. It's one-fifty-two on the first attempt and a personal best of one-sixty-six on the last. This after only five weeks of self-training. He tells himself, See, old man? pronouncing 'old man' as he always does, at least in his thoughts, with contempt. This useless old dog you've become can learn new tricks.

He breathes evenly and takes in the misty morning before heading back up to the great house, the three dogs at his heels. He thinks, I'm doing it, Catherine. About a quarter of the way to the house, despite expecting their good-morning feed, he watches the dogs tear away in hunt of the hare that must be tantalising their twitching nostrils. They might find it before it can disappear down a burrow; many days he comes across the torn-apart remains of some poor small animal. A hare, a possum, a chicken, sometimes a harmless green snake, other times the variety that evokes little sympathy: a brown or black, its head still whipping and eyes still sharp, despite its broken back.

Two of his three dogs are very good dogs, excellent for a country property. One is useless, but you have to take them the way they come.

The winter mist is rising from the green hills around him. It will be a good sharp day. The tennis is on, second week of another grand slam. He'll watch a match or two, if they don't go on too long, but he'll also make certain to sit under the shading branches of some trees with one of the latest books he'd ordered from the mobile library.

And, after all that, tonight it'll be a minute-seventy-five for sure.

2.

After a light dinner of baby spinach leaves, steamed endives, and tomato slices dressed with olive oil and oregano, and another two chapters of his book, no nightcap, no good match-up on the tennis to glide him past the midnight hours, twice he times himself while standing beside his bed. The Omega stopwatch reveals scores on the cusp of one-seventy-five, though not quite. Now we're close, maybe even close enough to try? He's not tired. It's been an easy and relaxing day—and he needs no more than five hours' sleep a night to wake perfectly refreshed. So why not try a small experiment, even with the frosty cold outside? He's only twenty-five seconds off the mark, isn't he?

He slowly and carefully dresses into warmer clothes, walks along the corridor and holds the banisters as he takes the staircase. When he's downstairs he calls his dogs from their dark, snug beds to follow him. Together their shadows move across the acre of moonlit front lawn. At the long gate at the top of the drive which leads down the hillside to the small country laneway below, he waits till his heart has found its regular beat. Refreshed and alive in this ice-cold breeze he tries his breath-technique a third time, the stopwatch glinting in his palm. The sweet cold air is like a potent force in his lungs; the Omega will tell no friendly lie; the count goes on. Seventy-two, seventy-three. Eighty-two, eighty-three.

Catherine, I'm nearly there.

He lets what is left of his breath whistle out and there's no great pain. That time it didn't hurt too much at all. What an achievement. One-minute-eighty-three seconds and no real discomfort. Seventeen seconds off; surely it can't make so much difference?

One day a long time ago, to impress Catherine when she'd only just become his wife, his second, and last of course, he'd swum powerfully underwater over three full minutes. She'd timed it. When he'd raised his head above the glistening surface of the Olympic-sized pool they'd gone to, she'd been on her feet, desperate and worried for him. Three-seventeen. He'd grinned at her concern, then so had she, bringing him a thick towel and wrapping his young muscular body up in her embrace. And that night, hadn't they made love for so long?...

Useless to think of physical abilities decades out of date, especially in the early a.m. of a new winter's day. And most especially when there's such a miracle to make.

So maybe the time has arrived. He doesn't want to wait anymore. If he can hold a great breath this long, is there really good reason to wait?

Catherine, is there?

No answer.

'We won't put it off,' he speaks in his gruff voice to the indistinct shapes of his dogs, who, keeping close by his legs, don't like the damp and dark. Their nostrils flare. Each dog is uneasy enough to want to stay within the safety of this small pack. Even if they catch the enticing scents of interesting, warm-blooded creatures somewhere away on this vast rural property, somewhere down this dark misty hillside.

He wonders at the way their haunches twitch and tremble. It must be something greater than hare out here; maybe they smell deer. A group of these elegant creatures is probably down the bottom of the hill, away in the mist. They've lived in this countryside for years, having escaped from Sam Hogan's property in 1973 and breeding happily ever since. Now protected by a council ordinance as well, woe betide any local or intruder who decides to interfere with them.

The moon shines above without the slightest trace of cloud to filter the light, but here, closer to ground, it's almost impossible to see a metre ahead.

But he doesn't want to put it off, not now, not after setting his mind to the task. He wonders how far he'll go, how far he'll travel—if anywhere at all. A grim smile comes to his lips. What fools old men are. Still, there are only three dogs and perhaps those deer to witness his imprudence. He also wonders if the trick to this magic will really be in the breathing, or if it will prove to require something else entirely, something Catherine has neglected to tell him about. It could be so. Holding one's breath, surely that's only how you start. At least he possesses the imperative she's told him so many times he'll need: belief.

Without it, don't even pretend to try.

3.

Despite the cold, anticipation dampens his palms. Little other excitement has entered his life these recent years. As age increases, the opportunity to feel one's own blood-rush decreases. The sense of the outside world becomes leaden. Sight dwindles, sounds lose their sharpness, light strikes with little intensity. Yet the inner world is where nothing changes. If anything, the inner life burns all the more deeply. As it does this minute.

He uses the quiet voice his dogs understand signifies his commands: Come with me now.

Despite their unease, the three obey as soon as he speaks, staying close. He wants to walk the distance, get a feel for his course the way professional sportspeople will walk the field or the court or the track upon which they will attempt to demonstrate skills they've honed over decades.

So he leads the dogs downward, sinking more deeply into the fog. If he never came back there'd be no one up at the house to raise the alarm. His mansion hasn't seen more than the cook, and tradesmen and cleaners, and the occasional paid consort, for a very long time. Since Catherine breathed her last. How much has he come to like aloneness? Perhaps too much, but it's always been in his nature and so that's that. He's got his dogs and often they seem more than enough company. Until his seventy-eighth birthday he'd walked them around all the near and distant country roads almost every day. Even after that, once or twice a week was not out of the question, though the distances grew shorter and the crucifying slant of this hill on the return journey finally became a major impediment.

Give or take some unevenness in the surface, he knows it remains eight hundred and fifty-three metres to the bottom, where the long driveway meets the narrow road the council decided to name 'Old Farm Lane'. When he and Catherine had first arrived here the lane had no name at all, and he'd preferred the anonymity of living in a place that could barely be found. For years Catherine's party and dinner invitations had included her exquisite hand-drawn maps.

Now, the further down he goes, the thicker the gruel. The dogs stay at his heel. Blanco, the youngest and most timid, the useless one, lets out a whimper. Blanco has been a disappointment though the cross-breed shepherd and akita has a terribly sweet nature; he would prefer his canine companions to be confident and sharp. Still, Blanco doesn't run off, even if he is trembling tail to nose.

After the long, careful downward trek the ground levels out. It's so much colder at the base of the hill. For decades he's walked off from this point, tramping into the surrounding fields so that he can hardly imagine any part of the local terrain that he hasn't covered. Often his powerful binoculars have accompanied him. He's seen rare birds hidden in treetops and packs of deer running and leaping from one pasture to the next; he's witnessed doe being born and he's seen platypuses in the creeks.

But they're close now, aren't they, the deer?

He remains quiet, keeps his dogs still as he listens. There's a pack for sure, impossible to tell how many creatures are gathered. He doesn't have a flashlight; his dogs press against his calves. Through the material of his trousers he can feel their warm trembling bodies, their breath. No doubt the deer already sense their presence, but they haven't decided to run.

How far away are they? He lifts his right hand and raises it up through the mist until his arm stretches straight. With his fingertips he searches in the dark. Maybe they're not quite as close as he thought, but he hears the wet breath in their nostrils, the soft clomp of their hooves moving slowly over moist dirt and wet grass. His dogs shiver. The mist is actually closing in, thickening. He can't make out his hand—then there's something like a swirling in the grey. The tips of a set of antlers pass close by, like catching a glimpse of a great ship's smokestacks out in the bleak ocean of a misty night.

Then there's another pair right next to him. The backs of his fingers touch the hard bristle of fur as the creature moves past.

Blanco cries. It's not quite a whine, more a moan of fear. That's enough to make the deer break and run. There's the heavy thudding of many, many hooves.

Ah! Blanco!

Still, nature has touched him. Nature, whom he is about to provoke.

4.

It's a tough climb back up the hill, enough to make his thin thighs burn and his heart beat heavily. In his life there has been time for music, making love, eating, drinking and the pursuit of pleasure—now there's walking and more walking, which grows harder from year to year, from month to month. This fails to fill him with too much regret because, if not for the walking, when his mind is at its most liberated, then this idea of how to catch the currents might never have come about.

An afternoon five weeks back, after a half-day's excursion with two of the dogs—young Blanco was still too troublesome and had to be left at home—he'd unpacked his lunch of cheese, olives and sourdough bread, and had sat in a clearing. He'd vaguely watched the treetops sway.

Some species of hawk soared nearby. In the slants of sunlight filtered by the branches, motes danced in the breeze. In a sort of meditation he watched nature undertake its day in its own uninterrupted way. He chewed olive seeds, drank water from his bottle, and tried to will himself into the landscape. I'm not watching this, I'm a part of this.

It had felt good and wasn't very hard to do; then a momentary unease had passed through him. Without the time to even try to understand what was happening, he next felt a sense of the world wavering in his vision, as if the fabric of reality itself had started to shimmer.

Oh my, this is it.

It wasn't going to be a bad place to die. He felt no great fear or desperation. No urge to try to get to his feet and find help. To die in this spreading meadow—it was even better than a peaceful slipping-away in his own bed, wasn't it?

Someone can find me here in nature, that'll be okay. Probably John Muller when he comes riding through with his slasher.

He lost strength and slumped, the side of his face pressing to the picnic rug, but instead of drawing his last breath he dreamed. Yet it hardly seemed a dream. Instead this vision of things seemed all too real.

He saw old acquaintances and his first wife Elizabeth, always-helpful little Beth, and his mother and father and two sisters too. Then there was the very tragic Virginia, his very first girlfriend, only a teenager when she'd drowned at a beach while holidaying with her family; Virginia's father had come to see him and tell him the news. Seventeen years of age himself, he'd wept for the better part of a year. Never even contemplated another girl until Elizabeth with her blonde curls and green eyes had caught his attention at Sunday mass, and they'd found a way to talk in a secluded cloister as the heat of a brutal summer's day baked the departing congregation outside. Married, no children, Beth felt ill and passed away—her funeral service marked the last time he entered a church, cathedral, any chapel of any kind. More solitude; eight years of total aloneness before Catherine lifted his life out of the familiar dirt of despair.

Each of these folk now passed him by, glancing his way with only mild interest, and no one beckoned him rise up and follow.

If it really was a dream it was a good one, because Catherine stood over him.

'Isn't it time to lift yourself up again?'

Then the sun was in his eyes and he had a blurred vision, a glimpse, of someone who could have been Catherine catching the currents above. Blinking more fully awake, trying to sit up there in the rug's shaded position, he thought that perhaps what he'd seen was the elongated shadow of some local bird, a soaring sparrow-hawk maybe. He wiped fresh, coursing sweat from his brow and tried to see past the branches of this lovely great elm, but she was gone.

That night, however, Catherine very kindly appeared once again. He slept and dreamed: Isn't it time to lift yourself up again?

On later nights Catherine revealed the simple sequence of required actions. He had notes jotted in a pad at his bedside, but it was the same thing repeated: Don't worry if it hurts, train yourself to hold your breath a full two minutes, then it won't be so much of a risk. All these weeks this has been his path and his objective. He's been training his old lungs to take in the air and make his chest lift.

Very straightforward indeed, Catherine. But to what end?

If she ever answered that question, upon waking he couldn't remember it.

5.

Back at the top of his hill he surveyed the sky. There was only the moon, no stars reaching out through the black.

He tells himself not to falter, not to doubt himself. Not to doubt his wife, whether she's real, an apparition or something else entirely. On the face of it of course he knows this procedure is foolish. If someone else described what he was about to attempt, well. At least he's not fool enough to try it off the peak of some bridge or over the side of a building.

Still—maybe he's mad? Those moments of disorientation, the world wavering in his vision, then that waking-sort-of-sleep in the forest. Recurrent dreams of a dead woman's visitations. He knew these could all be the effects of a series of mild strokes, or even the simple delusions of an old man whose mind has finally crumbled.

Yet he hasn't sought out his doctor because he feels fine. As for real doubts, well, he simply can't use them. Catherine would have said something like, Do what you well believe in and what you believe in do well.

So he steadies himself and ensures the rhythm of his heart has returned to its resting rate. Ready. He sets his feet and draws his breath, slowly at first, nice and shallow. Then he starts. He swallows the crisp morning air into his lungs, deep, deeper, more and more. His chest fills, rising. He forces himself to keep it slow. A certain amount of pain has returned but he persists until he reaches the critical point where he can't possibly take in any more air. The blood beats at his temples. Do it now. The dogs lean into his calves as he leans forward into the mist.

A minute. Must be a minute and a half now. More.

The test, his experiment.

A wave passes over him and it blots out the night and the cold.

6.

How much time has passed? His breath has completely left him and his old knees bump against the ground. They take his weight, then his outstretched hands strike the surface and they take his weight too. His wrists twist at the sudden catch of weight; his lungs ache, vision slow to return.

When he comes out of his swoon he's settled in the wet grass on all fours, at an angle, facing downward, but breathing again. The dogs are licking his face. He looks back over his shoulder. He seems to be some way down the hillside, but the thick mist makes it hard to discern just how far it is. The moments of getting to this point from up there, of exactly how he's arrived here, simply will not form in his mind.

He falls to his side and lies there, breathing deeply, lacking the strength to fend off his dogs, who worriedly lick his face.

Catherine, did I do it?

She isn't with him. The dogs are. At least the good two. Blanco is standing back a little, staring, dumb eyes filled with apprehension. Of everything the octogenarian might think about this experience, what most clearly crosses his old mind is this: I'll bring the dogs inside and let Blanco lie close, it must be awful to be scared all the time.

He breathes some more and finally gets to his knees, pushing the wet snouts of his two dogs aside.

Did I lift myself up, Catherine?

He finds his feet and gradually surveys the encircling mist. Catherine isn't with him. He senses that she's gone and that he's alone again, both inside and out. He'll try again soon, and many times, but a new thought has already come into his mind.

But who can I tell?

The Woman

I.

This was the better part of the job, she thought, the anticipation of arrival, and of who and what might greet her. Far better than the release of leaving the situation—when she might be exhausted and perhaps even a little darker in her soul, if the client proved to be quite different to what Selena had told her.

She liked the way this man Grant drove his Ford up the long driveway, not going too fast, giving her time to look around. After they'd left the suburbs behind they'd come through some very pretty countryside, and now this area seemed even more relaxed and beautiful.

The GPS on the dashboard confirmed the car was in the right

place. It was quite dark out, dark in that way it always is outside of cities, but the moon and stars were out, casting a silvery sort of glow to the scene. She liked what she saw and felt only minor trepidation—that, plus a soft sort of thrill tingling beneath her skin. She recognised why she had it: here was another journey into the transgressive. Added to which, the job wasn't going to be quick. No matter of a hello and an easy but firm ejaculation in whatever manner the client desired. Instead, she was going to be a companion until ten a.m. the next day. The bad thing was the potential for tedium; the good was that she could use an array of her skills, though she didn't consider these skills particularly sexual. She knew that, compared to other girls, she'd been well and truly promiscuous since the age of about sixteen, but in her mind, when it came to paid sex, she always used the word performance. Her job was acting in its purest form—an in-situ acting masterclass and stage performance combined, where she had the best role and there was absolutely no room for stumbles.

There was a bonus to this one too: the gentleman who'd made the booking, Selena had told her, had used the company's services a half dozen times in the past two years. He was of a very advanced age and would be no trouble at all. At each of his bookings the girl in question had come away as if from an overnight holiday, and with a sizeable tip. The client was too old to want more than conversation and to watch his consort moving, whether clothed or unclothed; in each case the tip had doubled the night's payment. One thousand, eight hundred dollars on top of the eighteen-hundred overnighter fee? Clients like this you dreamed about.

Less Selena's forty percent, she should pocket $2,160 for a single night's work. Combined with a few hundred dollars of her savings, this would pay her enrolment in the two NIDA classes she was still desperate for—an intensive course on advanced screen acting techniques (she'd passed the two prerequisite starter courses more than a year back), and a three-day workshop called Screen Test Essentials. She'd be able to pay her flights and get herself some decent accommodation. No lousy two-star motel like the last time, when she'd been trying to survive on a shop assistant's wage. Now that she'd discovered the benefits of Selena's type of life, she'd already been pricing out multi-night accommodation costs at Sydney's Intercontinental, the Observatory, the Wentworth ... not very bread-and-pub-grub actorly, not very Shakespeare-in-the-park, but God she was sick of dives. God she was sick of debt. And God she was sick of just about everything in her life.

No—everything that used to be in her life. She'd started over. She needed to keep reminding herself of that. And because the old man waiting out here in the middle of nowhere was one small stepping stone in the process of re-modelling her life, well, she would give him everything he wanted. Talk, companionship, stripping, and of course sex if he miraculously was up for it—anything but murder, as they say. She knew it ought to be strange to feel this way, but she already felt grateful for his call.

2.

'So you've never driven anyone else to this place?' she asked Grant when they first settled into his immaculately clean vehicle.

Grant, muscular, but not in a beefy way, shook his half-way-handsome head. 'Would have been one of the guys before me. Max or Jimmy maybe. I've only been working for Selena a couple of months.'

'Me too ... she says he's eighty-six.'

'You've either got your work cut out for you or you'll put him to bed with his pills and medicine. Why would he want an overnight?'

'The usual?' she mused. 'Ten percent sex, ninety percent lonely?'

'Guys are really like that?'

'Some ... maybe the older ones,' she said, though because of her newness she was no expert. She was also only a part-timer; Selena's trust and favours were things you needed to earn.

She knew she only had this job because a girl named Natasha, who'd first been allocated the octogenarian, had slipped in her bathroom and twisted an ankle. She was a late replacement and in reality had experienced no more than a dozen clients so far. Six, she remembered, had been in one of the city apartments Selena kept. Most of the others had been out-calls to hotels. Two had been overnight stays.

Despite her enthusiasm, the first of these had been monumentally boring. A man in his fifties, lonely and tired of life, who'd hardly even looked for a spark of inspiration from a young attractive woman like her. He'd been content to get drunk, come, and sleep. She'd left the next morning knowing about as much about him as he knew about her, and she hadn't needed to use any acting skills—all in all, a total disappointment.

The second overnighter had been much more taxing: he'd stayed awake with her until past five a.m., definitely on a mission to get his money's worth. A man made even duller than the drunk by bitterness, he'd still been angry at a divorce that had happened, she calculated, seven years back. But this client had tested her. She'd created the character she would play— half playful vixen, half dominatrix—and had performed her role until he'd finally, finally got his fill of her and started softly snoring. Washing his semen off her hands and chest for the third time in their encounter, with his brutal and hating words and sneers still in her ears, she'd looked out the bathroom mirror at the rising dawn. Then, naked and a little bruised, she'd gone to stand at the tall plate-glass windows where she silently considered the new day. Who can I be now? she'd asked herself. The question echoed in her mind as exhaustion made her go to his bed on slightly trembling legs and slip between the sheets. She'd fallen asleep without hearing her own answer.

Now she told Grant, 'It's sort of like, sometimes ... even if they're lonely and you're there, they don't know how to be un-lonely.'

'Un-lonely,' Grant spoke. Thirty-five at a pinch, he made a face, as if he hoped no such feelings waited anywhere in his future.

Then they were over the hump at the top of this incredibly long driveway and going through an open long rectangular gate. Grant slowed even more and let the headlights of his car play over the scene before them. To their mutual surprise, an ancient mansion was lit from inside, but only from two or three windows. The place sat in the middle of acres of cleared, green land. Plenty of trees.

'Wow—a ghost house.' He glanced toward her. 'One thing I know is you don't have to stay. Don't like the look of any place you're sent, just call it. There's a courtyard up ahead, see? I can turn the car around and we'll go back. Just say.'

She liked Grant, even though she'd only met him this evening. In another circumstance he might have been someone to be interested in. Pretty strong, okay to look at, but not so good-looking he'd be too much trouble with other girls. Half-way smart too. He'd said something about being an electrician and a fall, going on workers' compensation for back trouble. He couldn't do strenuous work for a year or two, but driving, easy. Cabs? Not for him. This? Perfect. There was a certain care-worn look to his face that she couldn't place. Thin skin. Lines where you wouldn't quite expect them in someone his age. Was it the weight of too many troubles; was he a drinker; did he simply play too hard in his private life?

'Selena says it's fine. He's used us before and just wants company.'

'Dunno the point of that, if he's so old ...'

'Other girls reported the same thing. No sex, just some touching. A little T and A, then a good night's sleep in his bed. Apparently the old man smell's the main thing that might bother me.'

'Ugh.'

'And if I can stand to be touched by dried-up hands.'

'Can you?'

'I hope so.'

Grant had slowed the car even more. It crawled as if hesitant about the big dark place. He peered through the windscreen.

'I dunno …'

'Selena's not going to send someone like me along to anything risky.'

'What's someone like you?'

She half-laughed. 'He said to make sure not to send a tough nut, some old hooker seen it all and made of leather. "Fresh and soft", that's what he asked for. So Selena was going to send Natasha.'

'Yeah, Natasha's really nice.' He glanced at her again. 'You fit the bill better.'

'Do I?'

'Far as I see.'

She almost blushed.

'But don't forget the rules, all right? Just after eight now. First call is from me and it's at nine on the dot. After that we text unless something's going wrong. Keep your phone close. If you don't answer or reply I'm coming up. I won't be far, and that goes all the way until I come collect you. If anything's happening you don't like, you feel nervous, scared, whatever, you know the key words?'

She knew them all right. Selena had drummed them into her head from the first day: 'Everything's hunky-dory, thanks'; 'It's a wonderful evening', or any gushy words to that effect; if there was actual danger she had to say or text anything with the words 'cool' or 'cold' or 'chilly' in it. She hadn't had to use them yet. Selena told her very few girls ever did.

'And if there's anything I don't like—' he produced an iron pipe from down the side of the driver's seat—'this connects with the old codger's head, no questions asked.'

'You're not going to need that. And anyway, Selena would get rid of both of us.'

'There's plenty of Selenas in the world. There's one you.'

She wondered if he was the protective type, or simply protective of her. She tried not to glance too long at his profile. Grant was really what you called rugged.

'We're not going to be making a good impression, like this,' she said. 'Let's get up to the house.'

'I'll check the place out. See if anyone else is inside.'

'Not in the rules, Grant. How would that make him feel?'

'Like the old dickhead he is,' Grant grumbled, but she saw he'd already given in. Selena's way of doing things was written in stone. Scouring a home-visit's house for potential trouble wasn't in the way they were supposed to nurture their clients' sensibilities. 'Just remember I'm not far. I call, you text, exactly when we're supposed to. Okay?'

A figure had appeared at the front door, which had opened. The silhouette was flanked by two dogs. Grant peered at those shapes, eyes narrowing as they pulled up.

'Strange business we're in.'

The car pulled up and she opened her own door. 'See you in the morning.'

3.

She knew the role she would play. She'd decided to be something like herself: an aspiring actor who'd never bothered with too much schooling, and who'd been able to get through most of her life on good looks and charm. The difference was going to be an almost total absence of failed love affairs; in her real life she had plenty of them, most of which she'd ended herself. The thing about her was, she simply started to feel the dead weight of others' expectations too quickly and too keenly. So-called 'love' and its daily demands simply ended up smothering her. Her mother, whom she'd nevertheless adored, had smothered her, had been on her almost every day of her life until she'd finally moved out. After that things between them had improved. Men, she found, had their own smothering ways. They wanted her as a sex-cat, which was fine, because she adored every aspect and variation of the sex act, but after torrid days and nights in some bedroom, soon enough the men she was with started to want more traditional things. For her to get the groceries; to serve up dinner; to clean and wash and to be waiting when they came home from work. She could manage a fair amount of all this, it was true, but when it moved into the norm, well, that was her cue to find the door, use the key and lose the key.

Fresh and soft?

Well, maybe she was and maybe she wasn't—but she knew she liked the part and could look the part.

Tonight's embodiment of herself would be a little gentler than the reality, modelled mostly on her mother. Her mother had been someone who'd had her own firm ways, but she'd also radiated goodness without any special effort at all. It pleased her to emulate that memory. The world could use a little more of this type of thing, she thought. I could even try to be little more like her in my everyday life. That might have been asking too much, but at least for this night she'd try. The client's request for someone 'fresh and soft' was something she interpreted as a request for tenderness and understanding. Well, she'd be a combination of the best parts of her mother, and of the almost insufferably sweet Melanie Hamilton from Gone With the Wind, and the tougher but just as good-hearted Rose Tyler from Doctor Who. Formidable combination: the role created its own energy in her.

She was stepping out of Grant's Ford and the two dogs sat like a set of curious gargoyles beside their still-indistinct master. She noticed there was a third dog, a white one, almost hiding further back inside the house. It was moving to and fro in agitation, clearly upset by the arrival of a car and a stranger. The other two, however, saw nothing to be afraid of: their tongues were out and their tails swept the dark wood of the polished floorboards behind them. She was certain that they remained where they were because the man hadn't given them the command to move; she liked that—he knew control.

As she emerged she gave a slight smile for her reception committee, but not a hugely fake one; she had no time for people who cheapened their smile by beaming at nothing. She closed the passenger door behind her and sensed rather than saw the grudging manner with which Grant eased the vehicle away. The client made no move to come forward. The Ford made a turn in the courtyard and its red tail-lights soon followed the driveway over the rise past the long front gate, disappearing. She wondered where Grant would spend his night waiting for her. Not at his home, wherever that might be—he'd said he would be close.

Now she moved forward with a confidence she hoped wouldn't be taken as either aggressive or presumptuous. She came up the front steps to the front door, and the client moved a little into the light. She had a better look at him: yes, he was very old indeed, but not in a particularly worn-down manner. She saw he was tall and had a slight stoop, but he carried himself with some bearing. There was pride in the way he stood there. Well, why shouldn't there be? He'd lived eighty-six years, according to Selena, and he was the master of this entire hillside paradise.

He took her hand and kissed it. She noted that his own hand was firm and dry and had no trace of an old man's palsy, of that giveaway trembling of age. She felt the way his eyes absorbed her.

'Hello,' she said.

He nodded. 'Please come in,' and he showed her the way.

She knew immediately that he found her pretty. It was some instinct, but she was sure he wasn't disappointed with Selena's choice. Gaining confidence, in the hallway she stopped and went down to her haunches and rubbed the two dogs' necks, actually cooing over them.

'Hello, beautiful dogs. You live in this wonderful house ... and you over there,' she gently beckoned the third, 'why not come closer?'

'That's Blanco. He's very shy.'

'He doesn't need to be scared.' She put out her hand. Very carefully the white dog approached, then nuzzled her palm. 'See, I'm not so bad.'

The three dogs lapped up her attention, adoring her. The client stood watching.

'This is a good start. They like your scent and your manner.

Even your aura.'

As he spoke she rubbed each dog gently. They actually groaned with pleasure.

'Come through—sadly for the dogs they'll need to go to their beds.'

The old man was clearly not of a mind to share her. He locked the three disappointed dogs out of the house via a back door that seemed to lead into a sort of closed atrium. She guessed they were safe there and couldn't get out, couldn't go off wandering the property at night causing trouble. He showed her a small downstairs bathroom where she could wash her hands. Alone a moment she did just that, and checked her face and straightened her dress. When she emerged, she found that he was sitting in a very nicely-lit living room and had poured her a cold glass of white wine.

'It's a Sauvignon Blanc, if that's what you like?'

'Thank you. And this house is extraordinary,' she said, moving into a deep armchair and liking the way it immediately made her feel comfortable. He made her feel comfortable too. The night was cool and there was a crackling fire in the fireplace. Very nice. So nice, in fact, that later if she needed to be naked in this room, it wouldn't be in the least bit uncomfortable.

'People usually want to know, so, yes, things are as they appear—I live in this house alone. It's the way I prefer things now, but if I had my choice my wife would be with me. She passed away seventeen years ago. Please don't try to offer kind words about this. I always keep dogs and there are a variety of people who come to the house. A cook and cleaner, men to tend the gardens and grass, the trees and so on. A property like this thrives on maintenance,' he smiled. 'Even though none of these good folk is any type of conversationalist, I never feel all that alone.'

It wasn't the way she would have chosen to start a conversation, but he seemed perfectly at ease talking about his circumstances.

'What if you get sick?...'

'Well, when my time comes it comes, even if it means I have to expire alone on the kitchen floor. But to cover most circumstances I've invested in an assistance alarm. If I were to need help, if I felt a heart attack coming on, for example, or some other medical emergency, I only need to hit the button. There's one in the kitchen, the main bathroom, and my bedroom. Also a portable device for when I'm moving about outside. It all works on a two-way system as well; if I'm buzzed and don't reply a carer is despatched immediately. In this way older folk like myself who are otherwise well can stay in their homes. Personally, I couldn't countenance some kind of retirement village. And a nursing home, heavens.'

'I can understand that.'

'Can you?' he asked with a sort of knowing twitch of an eyebrow, for what could she know about the lives the elderly led, the things they needed to face? She felt she'd made a slip, though he gave no indication of feeling this himself. If anything, he seemed very happy to have her with him.

'You're right. I probably can't really. I'm not even twenty-five. But I guess I can try.'

He shook his head slightly, as if to say she wouldn't need to.

'So there's not much more about me to tell. I'm long-retired. I made money in property investments and am quite well off. My interests are sports, literature, a little poetry, movies—though I don't go to them anymore—this house, my property, and my dogs ... it's not much of a story. And I don't ask for many young women to be sent to my home. Of course I never visit any. In general I'm no libertine or sexual adventurer but with beautiful young women like you in the world, if I had my time again I probably would be.'

As he'd said that, he'd smiled toward her. It wasn't a salacious comment, only a small compliment.

'Sometimes, but not often, I do feel slightly alone. Mostly when I need conversation, or if I've got something I want to demonstrate.'

'Demonstrate?'

He seemed to catch himself.

'Probably a poor choice of word, but yes, something like that. And despite your profession, it's nothing sexual. Nothing I need you to do. And by the way, I want to assure you that there's nothing here you have to worry about. I know better than anyone else what this house looks like to the outside world. I know how isolated it is. And I even know how I must seem. So thank you for coming. Thank you for not driving away.'

It was as if he'd seen into Grant's car and had heard the conversation between them. He was looking now straight into her eyes, and she liked that gaze, how sharp it seemed, how it seemed to connect them. This was certainly no infirm old man on his way out.

'It's very Gothic, this house, that's for sure.'

'The man who built it must have had a penchant for Victorian architecture. That's what drew me to it in the first place. I've always loved that sensibility. The old spooky house.'

'The best stories ever.'

'You like movies and books?'

'Movies. Books—' she scrunched up her nose.

'That's all right. I read a lot but there isn't an old horror film or ghost story I haven't seen. Would you like to know something funny? I even saw the original Dracula motion picture in the cinema, before I was ten. Not quite the first run, but close enough. People screamed and women fainted! I remember that. And Frankenstein with Karloff, not to mention The Invisible Man with Claude Rains. Classics, all. And very beautiful in their way.'

'I've seen those films.'

'Do you like them?'

'Absolutely. Movies are my thing.'

'Really? What does that mean?'

'My mother ... she was an actress. She used to take me to the movies with her all the time. From when I was a baby. And I'd go see her on stage too. Sometimes in the audience, sometimes from the wings. It was a great way to grow up.'

'She had some success?'

'A little. Mostly in theatre. A couple of soaps on TV but those didn't make her happy. She spent a lot of time teaching.'

'And you, learning?'

She felt the same blush coming into her face that she'd felt with Grant in the Ford.

'Yes.'

'One day?...'

'Yes.'

'Then I hope I'm around to enjoy one or two of your performances.'

She found his words very touching. She'd expected to be sympathetic towards him; she hadn't at all expected the reverse. Then she caught herself: but she wasn't acting the way she'd meant to. She wasn't playing the part she'd planned, This old man had simply brought out the real her. And without any effort at all.

'It's really beautiful here,' she said to cover her own thoughts. 'And I'm enjoying the night very much. But I want to make sure you are. That's the most important thing. So should we talk about what you'd like for the evening?'

'This, as it is.'

'Would you like me to do anything?'

'I believe you're well in the process of it.'

She smiled. 'How am I?'

'First—I'm so glad for the way you've dressed. No ridiculous red evening number with a plunging neckline, for one thing. Neither are you wearing too much jewellery, and if you don't mind me saying, with such beautiful skin, you're quite correct in not relying on too much makeup. The first thing I noticed about you? That simple lemon-yellow dress, perfect for a first meeting with a young man's parents, over dinner in their home, say. Flat-heeled pair of stylish sandals, so pretty the way they tie around your slim ankles and end in a bow. You have one silver ring on the smallest toe of your right foot. No idea what that symbolises, you must tell me. No disfiguring tattoos that I can see.

'Now, your hair. I see young women with hair styles better suited to Martians and cockatoos, but yours is honey-brown and demure. That nice sideways fringe and a neatly plaited ponytail. Perfectly judged. Your skin is darker than what I expected, so I think you must have some southern European or possibly even Middle-Eastern blood—though that seems at odds with your mother being an actress. All in all, you're a warm, sweet-looking girl. A young woman I could pass as a granddaughter or granddaughter-in-law, and who can't be faulted for looking so naturally and unselfconsciously sensual. So do I need someone like you to do anything for me? Let me tell you. Being in your presence is a gift for an old man. Selena's got a prize on her hands. You should remember that. Remember your worth.'

The clarity of his speech had almost taken her aback. Who was this man? What did he once do? And she knew those last words of his could have two meanings, both of which he'd meant. Her worth: in dollar terms to Selena and herself, in what they could earn together—and her worth to herself, the unmistakable admonition that she oughtn't sell herself.

But haven't you paid for me, old man?

A hot blush of unexpected anger was moving up her throat; she knew he saw it. Where was her acting ability now? But she also noticed the way he eased off, as if he was gently moving the two of them from a precipice.

'Actually, there is one thing,' he said. 'Do you like to eat? Let's move into the next room and see what I've prepared us.'

4.

Grant's first call came at the dot of nine. 'It's very warm with the log-fire,' she'd said, making sure not to make any reference to anything cool or cold. Grant grunted but she didn't think it was with any satisfaction—she thought he'd probably wanted an excuse to come collect her straight away. Then there was a text message, and another, all timed as they'd agreed it. Then silence. From here on in, as per the plan Selena always set down for home visits, she was only to contact her driver if there was trouble. There wasn't and wouldn't be, she was certain of that. The brief jagged edge to their conversation was forgotten and she was having a good time. The dinner, wow, that had been something. A roasted beetroot, carrot and walnut salad to start, followed by grilled swordfish drizzled with a blend of whisked olive oil, lemon juice, oregano, garlic and parsley. The same white wine with the courses but a Muscat to go with the dessert of poached pear with white chocolate sauce.

'You made all of this?'

'Some. I had my cook help me with the preparations.'

'You don't need a cook.'

'I do—without a companion I have no motivation.'

She'd made him go back into the living room while she'd cleared things away and neatly stacked the dishwasher. Her belly felt pleasantly warm, but wasn't in any way over-stuffed so that she needed to lie down and go to sleep. She liked this old man's company and she liked the things he'd done for her—so now what? She didn't have any familiar pattern to fall into; this would have been the perfect juncture to undress, to undress the client, to perform various acts upon him or herself or both, to let him lead her upstairs to the bedroom or to allow herself to be ravaged on the couch or on the floor in front of the fire.

She even felt a mild disappointment. Yes, he was old; yes, his skin was mottled and covered in liver-spots; yes, his hair was thin and yes, there was a slight old man smell to him, but if he wanted to touch her she knew she wouldn't recoil. If he wanted sexual satisfaction, she would be very pleased to give it. She felt that she wanted to do something to repay him for her wage and for this lovely night. It was as simple as that.

When she went into the living room he wasn't seated but was instead standing by the fire. In another light he could have been a strong, vital suitor waiting for his girl.

'I'm having a brandy. Would you like one?

'Let me pour it.'

She was a little light-headed but hardly drunk—Grant didn't have to worry. She'd been drinking water as well as the wine and Muscat, and she liked the idea of brandy before the embrace of sleep. She hoped his room and bed were clean—no, she was certain they would be. He might even want to shower before snuggling beside her; if so, she would take one too. It had grown very late. She sensed the silence in the vast countryside outside. It was safe in here; she felt good to be near him, in these rooms.

'Could you come closer?'

It was the first time he'd said anything like that. She put down the drink she'd poured herself, and did as he asked. She felt the heat of the crackling logs through her thin dress.

He turned and looked at her. He was taller. She looked up into his eyes. Eighty-six years, she reflected, what must it feel like?

Something had come over him. Some kind of slight change. She wasn't quite sure what it was.

'I've done something ... a little extraordinary. Unexpected and, I must say, confusing. It's had something of a surprising effect that, I think, I'm only feeling now. Isn't that odd?'

She had no idea what he was talking about, but some instinct told her to extend her arms over his shoulders, as if he was a much younger man and she was drawn to him. With a crooked grin that she hadn't quite expected, she kissed his lips. It was neither pleasant nor unpleasant. No other part of her body touched his: only her elbows so lightly on his shoulders.

'You make even the most pitiful man feel like a king.'

Now she did let her body touch his. She kissed him again.

'Have you ever felt the need to raise yourself up, change your circumstances, do something different in your life?'

'Yes,' she said, and without having expected it, tears sprang into her eyes. She felt the way his old fingers gently touched those tears, then he lightly caressed her face.

'Why?'

She struggled for the right words. Again, the acting was gone, completely out the window.

'I ... I just can't find my way ...'

'You want things.'

'... Sometimes I think I know what ... then I don't know at all ...'

'You're young. You should want everything. Make sure you go get it. Don't be scared of anything, any obstacles, any person. Push yourself out of the ordinary and the everyday. The whole world will try to make your feet like lead, but when you fly they'll be cheering.'

She smiled up at him. Her eyes were still wet but now she felt a thrumming over her skin. An electricity. It was almost as if these were the exact words she needed to hear. How had he known? She tried to kiss him again but his hand reached behind her dress and ran the zip down. Gently, but with assurance. He undressed her there, as she'd imagined a younger man would have done. She raised her hands and slowly undid one button of his shirt.

There was a new sort of hesitancy to his voice, but he said, as if surprised, 'Yes, I think so,' and with old skin on young skin the warmth of the fire was over them.

The Man, the Woman and the Driver

I.

He looked at her and thought he'd seen children asleep with less sense of innocence and tranquillity. She was lying on her belly with her head cradled in her arms. The dying embers of the fire made her look young and golden. Which she was. The girl had helped him to his knees, then to lie down and make love to her. Now she was naked and the side of her face revealed a young woman perfectly at peace. She probably had little idea how much it had hurt to get from a standing position to the floor; his knees, his hips, the small of his back—creaking, unbending, all as if they had broken shards inside them. Yet the small miracle had happened. He hadn't expected it; he hadn't wanted to do more than get to know some sympathetic young woman and do his best to show her what he could do. He had to share the gift with someone, didn't he? And in that person's eyes he would see the truth or lie of what he believed.

Catherine, he thought, why make me do it, then leave me so completely alone?

Nothing in the great house answered him; the only reply was the crackling of embers.

And now that she was asleep, what should he do? A young woman actually deep in repose because of him. Him. Selena, whom he'd never met, but with whom he'd had several interesting and amusing conversations by telephone, would probably laugh in disbelief. Even with some delight.

He thought of his lungs filling with air and his body wanting to rise with the currents. He thought of this young woman running her hands over his old parched skin. Somehow these two things blended into the same sensation. He thought of her small encouraging sighs—and as he remembered holding her face in his hands he recalled the way he'd wanted to tell her everything. She would have welcomed his story, he knew that, even if she disbelieved every word—for each of her kisses had been more loving than the next. How had she been able to do that without being repulsed? She almost reminded him of Catherine, when she'd been young and they'd spent so many golden days and nights enjoying one another. For years they'd experienced a sea of pleasure, until advancing years and the inevitable decline, the dwindling powers.

Well, it had been all right, every part of it. He'd loved Catherine, young, middle-aged, old—and when she'd died he'd felt a light leaving him. A light that drifted away.

On some current.

He was glad her eyes opened. Glad they opened and that she immediately had an unforced smile for him. He'd been buttoning his shirt, trying to not make a sound but still hoping she would come out of her slumber. He couldn't help smiling back at her. He was standing a few steps away and could tell she didn't mind the way he took her in. She seemed to enjoy it, as if this was a part of her job she liked and so was glad it was happening. Something she could readily understand within the conundrum he must seem to her: a man's eyes feasting on her body, wanting her.

Slowly she stretched and turned, sitting up but not rising to her feet. Making herself cross-legged like a red Indian, she stayed by the fire. The last of the flames created shadows in the hollow of her neck and across her breasts. Her hair was out now, the ponytail gone. He loved the way it fell to her shoulders. She looked untroubled; it was hard to believe this young woman gave such a beautiful body to men for money. Her body, and such a beautiful mind too.

Well, he had paid for her, and would again. He had no idea what Catherine's instructions had been leading towards, but this night had led him to this young woman. He wouldn't be greedy; he wouldn't pretend to be younger than his years; but he would call Selena a little more regularly now, and the only person he wanted sent to his house was the one with him now.

'What were you thinking just now?' she asked. Her voice was soft, as if she didn't want to break the mood.

'Why do you ask?'

'I don't know ... I'd say you were about a million miles away, but you're not, are you? You're just sort of ... thinking things over?'

'I didn't expect anything that happened tonight.'

'Are you glad?'

'Yes, but not if it was ... too unpleasant for you.'

'Not a bit. I'm happy.'

'Would you visit me again if I asked Selena?'

'Without a second thought.'

'You might need a second thought.'

'Why is that?'

He felt his own hesitancy for the absurdity of what he would say next. He wasn't at all sure that what he had to offer in the cold night outside was in any way real. Each time he'd attempted the magic his head had swum and though he'd ended up far down the hillside, usually on his hands and knees in wet grass and dirt, he had no recollection of how he got there. The startled eyes of his dogs could have meant anything.

And each attempt had taken its toll too—he found he needed to sleep and rest for longer and longer periods of time.

On his last try there'd been no mist at all. Clouds had obscured the moon and any deer had been far off in the forests. He'd told the dogs to sit, then had filled his chest to the full. The familiar sensation that approached elation had swept over him. No pain. He'd started to count, staring at the glistening clouds above. Fifty-two, fifty-three. Rain coming soon, always welcome. Seventy-three, seventy-four, seventy-five. Catherine in my arms used to always make me happy. One hundred and twenty-one, one hundred and twenty-two. Where are you now, why don't you come to me anymore? One seventy-nine. I wanted to be a poet, a painter, a writer, an artist, but all I was ever good for was making money and using my body, you always encouraged me, Catherine, you always believed in me, but I could never find the way to raise myself up—then he'd felt his connection to the world melt and blackness had dripped into his eyes.

There'd been a rising wind, he'd heard it traversing the countryside, making long grass sway, beating against his face, maybe even lifting him ...

He'd come back to himself with his arms wrapped around the wooden post-box at the bottom of the hill, far, far below in Old Farm Lane. Hanging on, he'd been gasping for breath as the dogs caught up with him and yapped and turned all around his thin trembling legs.

'A million miles away again?'

'What?'

There she remained, still cross-legged by the fire, naked, elegant and utterly heartbreaking. The sight of her brought a thought even more acute than his mystery of catching the currents: if there's no physical pleasure in the next life, no skin, copulations, breasts, thighs, no secret warm places and no sensual desire at all, how is it called Heaven?

'You said I might need to have second thoughts? Why would that be?'

He was past obfuscation; it was time to let her know. And whatever she decided from here, well, the matter would be out of his hands.

'Because I'd like you to come outside with me ... we'll take a short walk. I know it's cold and it's misty, but it won't be too unpleasant. It's past two a.m., as you can see,' he indicated the clock on the mantelpiece. 'I'm not inclined toward sleeping just yet—but perhaps I'd be taking advantage of your good nature?'

'The cold doesn't bother me. What would bother me is to go back to sleep when I could be spending more time with you.'

Those words from any other paid woman would been learned and delivered by rote. From her, though, they felt genuine.

'Then you'll need more than your dress. I'll find you some warmer things.'

'If you think I need it.'

He nodded and was about to leave, then he looked back at her.

'Do you understand you're a light in this world?'

She sat in the warmth returning his gaze.

Finally she said, 'What we're going out for, this is what you've wanted to show me all along, isn't it?'

He hesitated a final time.

'At the top of that long driveway you came through, at the gate, the hill descends from there. This time of year it can be quite full of mist. There are deer around as well. If we're lucky to see them up close, it can be a fascinating experience.'

'That's what you want me to see?'

'Not really ... there at the top, it's a matter of taking a very long deep breath and holding it, and leaning forward ... then ... almost ... losing yourself in belief.'

He saw the way she tried to deal with this information, to make sense of it. He liked the slight furrowing of her brow.

'Belief of what?'

He didn't reply because the words simply wouldn't come.

2.

Once she left this house and days and weeks passed, what she'd remember best, she thought, would be the thing that had surprised her most. Not how gentle he'd been, how courtly, or that wonderful dinner. Not even the curious things he half-spoke about, half-intimated. It also wouldn't be the fact that for one night he'd rediscovered his powers—well, it was almost that. More precisely, she would remember the vulnerability that had come into his face as his semen had poured into her. His features had cleared of age, expectations, disappointments and life's reversals. Even histories, artifice, everything. The true nakedness of a man had been in his face—and she was sure she'd never quite seen anything like it before.

Was that nakedness something that could happen in women as well? She thought it had to be. She tried to picture her face in moments of ecstasy—but no, she was wrong to think in those terms. Ecstasy, pleasure, physical release, all of that was incorrect. She had to think about vulnerability, of being carried toward the complete collapse of defences. One's own utterly helpless moment. Where was the role that would allow her to use such a thing? She'd have to find one because she was almost certain she would never be so defenceless in her real life.

He was only gone a few moments now, she'd listened as he'd slowly climbed the staircase and floorboards had creaked above her head. She stretched before the fireplace, then pulled some of her scattered clothes into her lap. She didn't dress, but instead found her mobile phone. A quick text to Grant? She decided she probably had time enough to call him.

There was a long pause, longer than she expected, then his voice was on the line. He sounded somewhat abrupt, or a little confused, as if he'd surprised himself by falling asleep or she'd disturbed him in the middle of some activity.

'Hey, are you okay?' she heard him ask.

'It's all fine, and wait till I tell you about him—he's really something. Were you asleep?'

'Sorta ... but there are things down here, it's strange, nearly made me jump. Took me a while to figure out, it's so dark—antlers in the mist. There's this big white stag and then smaller animals. Never seen anything like it.'

'Deer, you mean?'

'Right around the car, not even scared ...'

'Where are you?'

'Just down the bottom of the drive. Parked near his letter box. What a mist ...'

'Well, I wanted you to know it's been a good night and we're even going for a walk.'

'Now?' he sounded incredulous. 'Where?'

'Well, probably not far, he is old. Maybe just to the top of the hill, the way we came through. Dunno what's on his mind. Wants me to see the mist, maybe those deer ...'

'He's not weird is he?'

'Only in a nice way.'

'And where's he gone, how come you can ring?'

'He's getting me some clothes.'

'Then what are you wearing now?'

'I mean he's getting me warmer clothes.'

'Okay.'

'Good,' she said, because she couldn't think of anything else. Then she remembered what the old man had told her. 'He said something about the top of the hill, holding your breath. And believing.'

'In what?'

'That's the question.' There was a pause.

'Why is there a question?'

'I don't really know.'

'Bring your phone.'

'Okay.'

'I'll come get you if—'

'I keep telling you that you won't have to.' She stopped and looked upward. The creaking had stopped. Maybe he was coming down now. The living room was a little cooler, those last embers in the fireplace definitely dying. Wait—was the old man actually taking a little too long? She wondered about that. 'Better go, he'll be back in a sec.'

'Call me again, or just text "OK", something like that. Either way, ten a.m. I'm in front of the door.'

He'd spoken about all those old movies he'd seen when young, almost in their first runs. Dracula, Frankenstein, The Invisible Man. The way he'd spoken with such warmth and affection for those films, and even with regret, made her take a guess: maybe he'd wanted to be an actor or something, a writer or director. She could see him on a film set, giving a great performance or drawing out the best from young actors like her. If she'd guessed right, then it was such a pity he hadn't achieved what he'd wanted.

Push yourself out of the ordinary and the everyday. The whole world will try to make your feet like lead, but when you fly they'll be cheering.

She thought them the most beautiful words ever spoken to her. Maybe she wouldn't just fly down to Sydney and take those two courses; maybe she'd pack up and move and get into that world properly, make it happen for herself. She felt such affection for the old man right now, and that affection made her want to go find him, make sure he was all right. She knew that if she was a heroine in one of the types of films he'd mentioned, for all her good intentions audiences would be screaming, Don't go up the stairs! Get out! Are you crazy?

But that's what she was doing.

She felt no fear doing this, no hesitancy about this great old home. She simply wasn't the type for those kind of nerves. She'd been living alone in her own apartment for the better part of five years now, and though her mother always told her to find a flatmate, to live among other people, she couldn't recall very many occasions where she'd had to sleep with the light or the television on, or had come awake in the dark spooked by some or other imaginary thing. This place had good vibes, simple as that, and she believed vibrations, auras, whatever you wanted to call them, were things she was both receptive to and gave off. No wonder the dogs had liked her straight away. We're all connected. She'd felt good in this house the moment she'd stepped inside; she'd felt comfortable with the old man as soon as he'd welcomed her.

She was in her clothes again, of course, those sandals on her feet and the laces looped around her ankles. She went up the stairs and called for him. There was no reply. The staircase was carpeted and though it creaked these small sounds were hardly sinister. There were deep shadows all around, true, but for the most part things were well-lighted; she didn't expect some monster to jump out of the dark.

On the second floor it was easy to see where he must have gone. A corridor was nicely illuminated by very subtle ceiling lights. What she assumed to be several smaller bedrooms had their doors shut, but at the end there was one room open, a light on inside. She was certain that the sound of the creaking floorboards she'd heard above her had been from that part of the house.

'Are you there?'

3.

He washed his hands and doused his face, then took a long look at himself in the mirror. His appearance was no different to that of any other day or night; one small miracle of being able to make love certainly hadn't created some extra miracle of youth. He rubbed his face and his eyes and had to admit that he was tired. A more sensible course of action would be to send the girl home and go to bed, or, at the very least, to tell her a walk at this hour might not be such a good idea. They could call it a night and slip between the sheets. He would hold her close for some minutes, feel the warmth and scent of her young body, then the release of sleep would come.

But the hillside was calling. He needed to show someone. He needed to reveal this thing or have it proved for a lie. How would she react? What would she think?

Catherine, have I lost my wits now, is that it?

There was no answer in the mirror, no voice rising up from behind him, no sense of some message just waiting there in the empty air. He used a clean towel to dry his hands and the back of his neck, then he stepped out of the small bedroom en-suite into the bedroom. Did it have the old-man smell the very thought of which he detested? He tried to ignore the question and collected a warm coat for the girl, something fleecy that she could button up close under her chin. She would look sweet in this coat of his, he reflected. When they were outside in the cold night air he would like to embrace her close, if she would let him.

The light in the bedroom seemed to waver—there must have been a problem with the electricity lines. This semi-rural region was notorious for bad power service. Then it was back and for a moment he stood quite still as he took in the room. It was as if the image of everything, especially at the edges, had sharpened. Were fine-tuned. He didn't want to leave the girl alone too long, yet he studied this bedroom, those french doors, the windows and curtains, the split-cycle air conditioner in the wall that whispered so quietly when it was on. It was as if he had new eyes. Beside the bed was a pitcher of water, a tumbler and a bowl of fruit. He could actually taste the juicy flesh of the waiting peach and of the two apricots. Here were all the framed photographs of Catherine, some with him beside her, some of her alone. There was the official wedding photograph in its half-a-century-old frame. What of all the long years this room had been theirs and then become only his? Even the years themselves seemed sharper. He and Catherine had slept and made love in that bed—he saw it again, a marvellous yet immensely sad sight too—as if a thousand years ago. Yet here he still was.

He needed to take a deep breath. Maybe something inside was telling him he should make better preparations for this new attempt at the top of the hill.

So he tried to draw in the air, long and slow, as he'd trained himself, but it seemed too hard to do. The problem with the electricity came and went one more time: the room dimmed then returned to its normal state. His sense of that sharpness faded. Wait, wasn't all this a bit like the wavering that had happened out in that field, under the tree? His legs were trembling. Better sit down a moment, and so he eased himself into the very comfortable white upholstered lounge chair where some mornings he had coffee and read the newspaper.

I'm sitting down, there's not the breath of an air current, but I almost feel like I'm ready to float away.

He dimly perceived the shadow that passed into the room. It took him a little by surprise.

Oh my, it's you, Catherine.

4.

She found him sitting in a white armchair that was faced toward a set of French doors, as if to allow the moon and starlight to fall over him. No, she thought, it would be for the morning sun. He'd sit there with a gorgeous view of every new day, and the sunlight would fall over him.

She moved closer and though he was warm to her touch she knew what must have happened. His eyes were shut, his head was down and his mouth was only slightly open. Across his lap was a fleecy coat and his hands were over that; she thought he must have collected the coat for her, and she found this incredibly touching, that his final act of kindness had been meant for her. So she put her hand on his face. It's all right, it was lovely to be here, I'm glad I met you. Then she kneeled beside him and laid her cheek on his forearm. There was no pulse, no breath, the man was gone and the body was empty. Where, she wondered, where did you go? She noticed all the photographs, the woman who must have been his wife. Many stages in life: young, middle-aged, old. He hadn't mentioned her name.

Maybe you went to her. Wouldn't that be something?

In a minute she'd call Grant. He could come up to the house and together they'd ring an ambulance. At the fact of a death no doubt the police would have to come too. She felt no anxiety about this. She wouldn't try to run away from the scene, pretend she'd never been there, or, if caught, claim he'd been fine when she'd left. No—she'd tell everything exactly the way it had been. The conversation, the dinner, the fire in the fireplace. She'd even let them know he'd been able to make love to her. Let them think about that. And she'd be proud to say that she'd known a man like this, even if it had only been for one short night.

Who have you left behind? What will I do with your poor dogs?

She'd have to set them free soon, let them roam the property, maybe even come see their master.

The mobile phone was downstairs. It hurt her to have to leave him alone; she really wanted to sit with him until the official matters of death commenced.

He paid for me to be with him. But I want to.

All right, she'd go call Grant then come back. That would be okay.

With a final squeeze of both his hands with hers she left the bedroom and hurried downstairs. The home seemed colder. She knew that the embers in the fireplace had died, yet it was something more than that. No, she told herself even as she shivered and the gooseflesh raised on her arms and legs, the house is cold because it's a cold night, nothing else.

The living room felt empty. The air had more than a chill to it; it was frosty. He's gone, the room seemed to say; yes, he's gone.

She almost fumbled the phone but had the redial and now Grant's number was being called. She waited, shivering, and so much time passed she almost stopped to try again, then she heard his voice:

'Hey this is Grant, can't talk right now so leave a message.'

She couldn't believe it. All through the night he'd been so close, as if to seem no further away than the next room, now this. She tried again. The same answer message came. She stood where she was, breathing deeply. What should she do— just call the ambulance herself? Yes, that was probably the right thing. Then she shivered again and had to even out her breath. It was like a panic attack or something, what it must be like for people who suffer from acute anxiety. It was something that afflicted her mother, especially now she was older, but never herself. Still, she knew that if she regulated her breathing she would calm down.

What had the old man said?

... there at the top, it's a matter of taking a very long deep breath and holding it, and leaning forward ... then ... almost ... losing yourself in belief.

Now she would never know what he'd been referring to, but the part about the very long breath, that was helpful. So she tried it, feeling her quickened pulse starting to ease. She held the breath, half-closed her eyes, and soon felt a welcoming lightness coming to her head, her body, as if her feet could gently lift off the ground.

There, that's better.

She tried Grant one more time, and the message was all she heard.

Wait—he'd said he was down the bottom of the hill, just near the mail box. Maybe his phone had gone flat, or he'd accidently turned it off. She was certain he hadn't decided to leave her and drive off somewhere.

It wouldn't take long. She'd go get him, then they'd make the necessary calls.

It was cold, that was true, yet somehow this bitter post-two a.m. didn't feel quite as cold as it had in the house. Was she simply setting loose her movie-buff, actor's imagination, or had he been the warmth in that house, just as he'd told her she was 'a light'?

If only she could have known him more. What had his background been, really? His dreams. Who had he been?

The giant trees cast longer shadows but the moon was very bright and the stars were all out; there was an almost supernatural clarity to the property, a glow. Gorgeous. She resented the fact that he was gone, she would have liked to take that walk with him, but now she was going to the place he'd mentioned— the gate, then the driveway that ran down the hillside. What he'd said had been true: there was mist, a lot of it. It whispered in tendrils around her ankles, then when she was at the gate and looked down the direction the driveway took, all sense of the ground disappeared into the foggy gloom.

Wow, she thought. Dracula, Frankenstein, The Invisible Man.

5.

Grant was back up on the scaffolding. It was as if every drink he'd had, every bad bet he'd made, every argument with Sally about her boy Thomas, who was her boy indeed, the father long taken off for God-knew-where, well it was like all of that had combined to put him up here on this shitty day on this shitty job feeling well and truly shitty himself.

Hung-over, parched, burned out.

The drinking had become a stinker. Which made his gambling worse. Sally had done the tally and it was thirty-six thousand dollars. Thirty-six, four hundred and eighty-three, to be exact. Well, she was right: in the end every cent did count. So he'd opened a new bottle of something cold, absorbed her anger for about another ninety seconds, then let fly. He was smart enough to keep off the subject of money: he got into her for the kid, thirteen years of age and so mollycoddled that if some other kid at school raised a finger or a teacher cocked an eyebrow he came home crying about bullying and unfairness and all sorts of what-for. Instead of standing up for himself. Fuck, that made him mad; and fuck, that made him want another drink; and fuck, all of that together said, Grant, go put another grand on the numbers, this time they're yours. Nearly stupefied with booze and almost completely soul-eroded, that's exactly what he did.

My numbers. My win.

Except it never went like that.

Then the shitty day came and one of the stupid Greek builders he was working with on this site told him to leave the switchboard he was wiring, to come up here on this scaffold and help him with something the Greek ought to have done on his own.

Well, he went up. And while he was up there, two and a half good storeys off the ground, the Greek was swearing at the government about some new tax who would give a fuck about except some immigrant construction worker, and this strange thing came into his head, and for a second he thought he was home in his room and the bed was right there for him to drop into and catch some winks, and the world sort of shimmered and he let go.

Falling. Except it didn't even feel like that. It felt like he was soaring.

Then he didn't remember anything.

Later the doctors all had the same song: You are so lucky to be alive. Not to be a quadriplegic. We've got no idea why you're not worse off. It's like you came down limp as a dishrag.

Well, he didn't tell them, I did.

So now he was a driver.

Then thump and thunk and he was awake.

Jesus—what? Something's hitting the Ford?

For a couple of seconds he was disoriented. He'd wanted a little shut-eye, the mobile phone held in his hand on his thigh so that he'd be ready for anything the girl wanted, but he hadn't expected to sink so deep. It was like he'd fallen into a well. And what the fuck was this around him? The car was just about swallowed in fog and animals were out there. He shook his head in disbelief, tried to see into the deep dark past the windscreen, the side windows, the rear window.

Beasts.

Now he saw the antlers of a stag, a great white fucking stag. The animal passed in front of the Ford, came around the side, passed the driver's window and even seemed to glance in at him. There was mist at its nostrils, a pallid glisten to its soulless eyes. Primal as all fuck, ancient as antiquity. Except those eyes did seem to have a soul; did seem to have just one step more than simple life; did really see him.

There were more of the things. No other white stags like that one, but big brown deer with heavy, thick antlers, and does too, their young. Bloody hell. He almost laughed in amazement, now that the initial shock was passing.

The phone went off, ringtone plus vibration. He almost jumped again.

'… there's this big white stag and then smaller animals. Never seen anything like it.'

She was all right, just checking in. What was it, two-seventeen? God, she and the old man were still up. Had they been at it, him eighty-six-odd years of age? And now a walk in the freezing morning. Well, it was her job and his money. Whatever made the two of them happy. She wanted to let him know the old man would be taking her across the property once he got her something warm to wear.

'Call me again, or just text "OK", something like that. Either way, ten a.m. I'm in front of the door.'

God, he liked her, he had to admit that. Even liked the sound of her voice. He thought he loved Sally, and the boy too, even if the kid wasn't his, but things with Sally were getting old and this girl he'd driven out here tonight, she was sort of young. In a way that didn't mean anything about years. Fresh—the way even the prettiest and youngest of Serena's girls just weren't.

At least things were going okay. He was glad for that. Come ten, when he collected her, he'd drive her home nice and slow. Maybe she'd invite him in for a coffee or something. Or, if she didn't seem too tired, he'd suggest they stopped along the way. He'd get her some breakfast, something decent, and just sort of look at her. He knew he didn't stand a chance with someone like her. He knew he wouldn't pay for her either. That was something for the losers of the world, and maybe the eighty-sixers.

The deer had moved on but he could tell they weren't too far away. So when would he have a chance to do something like this again? Imagine telling Thomas: Hey, guess what, buddy, last night I walked with a pack of deer.

Grant reached up and set the courtesy light to 'off' so that it wouldn't illuminate, then eased open the driver's door. He slid out slow, felt his way along the side of the Ford to the rear lights, tasted the razor-sharp cut of the cold, and stayed where he was, peering into the grey fog. Some breath of a breeze made that fog stir. It stirred to the movement of the beasts, too. He'd never heard of anyone being attacked by deer—at least, he couldn't remember ever hearing about it—so he look some steps away from the car and followed carefully in the direction he thought they'd gone. He was even more careful not to go wrong, to get lost somehow: as long as he could feel the hard bitumen of the lane underfoot, he knew he was all right. As soon as it turned to grass or mud or dirt then he'd stop and go back to the car.

He'd gone upwards a little way, not having noticed that past the entrance to the old man's driveway, Old Farm Lane became an incline.

A little way more, then I'll go back.

The mist cleared—parted, really, as if by some godlike hand—and there the pack was, further away than he'd thought. They were at the crest of a nearby hill, all standing together with their undisputed leader at the front, the white stag. Breathtaking to see. They even seemed to be surveying this place, their land, their country. And him. Where was a camera when you needed one? Best he had was the one in the mobile phone back in the car, but that wouldn't have a hope of capturing a shred of this.

Something startled them, because the entire pack, except for the white stag, suddenly bolted out of view. Now alone, the stag seemed to raise its head. He could actually see moonlight shining off those tremendous antlers. Maybe it was sniffing the air, making sense of whatever the intrusion was. Did it turn its head towards the old man's great mansion on the opposite hillside? It waited a moment then bolted as well, graceful and powerful, gone.

All this cold and Grant had actually sweated into his shirt. He felt the perspiration on his forehead. That was, that was big.

Feeling a curious elation, the road surface safely beneath his sneakers, Grant trotted lightly through the mist back the way he'd come until he saw the outline of his car. Its panels were covered in cold condensation. He ran his hands over the roof then washed his face with his wet palms. The hour was getting to him. Next time, no matter which of Selena's girls he was driving, he would do no more than what was expected: a drop off, get home and put his feet up, and check in from time to time to make sure things were all right. A leisurely drive the next morning to go get the girl, easy money. That's all he ought to have done tonight, but something about taking this particular girl into this lonely countryside—well, this half-urban, half-rural in-between of a countryside—had made him nervous. The old house made him nervous. Added to which, of course, a night away was a welcome break from Sally. She was still mad at him and gave little indication of changing that attitude, maybe for weeks if not months to come. So one night of killing time and dozing in his car seemed a lot preferable to lying in bed with Sally's simmering rage all pent up next to him.

He slid into the driver's seat and automatically reached for his phone, clicking the backlight on. And bang, just look at that: You have three missed calls.

Three! And Jesus, they were all from her. Fuck it, she hadn't left messages.

A sort of nausea passed over him. Just when she needed help, where was he and what was he doing? Oohing and aahing over a bunch of deer like David fucking Attenborough.

Sick in his gut, Grant was about to call her back—three times? maybe the old man dragged her out of the house onto the property for something bad, she'd managed to run off, was hiding somewhere shaking and terrified; or maybe she was still inside, him stalking her; it could have been anything but he was such a fuck-up he better do something right, and right now.

The key was in the ignition and Grant gunned the cold engine, kicked the headlights up on high beam, reversed fast from the quaint little wooden mailbox that was just about all that said there was a home somewhere nearby, then screeched the tyres as he turned into the driveway and started uphill, accelerator flat to the floor.

Five seconds I'll be there, don't be scared, don't be hurt. There was that lead pipe by his seat. His hand reached down and his fingers scrabbled for it. Old man I am going to fucking kill you.

But he'd gone barely a hundred metres when in the pea-soup mist he caught a flash of something, just out of the corner of his eye, past the side window, an indistinct, moving blur that appeared as if out of nowhere and that he lost sight of as the car hurtled past, like it was something falling.

He slammed the brakes and the car slewed sideways across

the wet driveway. He lost control of the wheel but there was
nothing for the car to hit. It spun to a stop. He gunned the engine again and turned the vehicle in the direction of whatever
the fuck that thing was, and tried to get the headlights trained
roughly around what he thought was the right spot. The mist
was too thick even for these lights. They seemed to reflect back
at him. Nothing. Godfuckit. Should he get up to the house or
see if something was really there? What if it was just another
dumb deer, this one running down the hill and now already a
kilometre or two away? What if it was her, escaping? But it had
come out of the sky, hadn't it?

No, no. Just a trick of the night. He was about to jerk the wheel,
hit the accelerator and get up to the house, when he caught a
glimpse of movement. Somewhere in there. He climbed out of
the car fast, taking the heavy lump of pipe with him.

The mist was her heavy cloak and she was on all fours, hair over
her face, disoriented and shaking. He fell down onto his knees.

'Are you all right?'

'I don't ...'

What happened?'

'I don't ...'

He looked to the left, the right, glad for his grip on that pipe.

'Can you straighten up?'

She slowly did, with his help, but they remained kneeling in
the wet grass, enclosed as if the last people on earth. There was
no sense of anything around them. He couldn't see if someone
was coming, and he couldn't hear a thing either.

'Is someone after you?'

She shook her head. Her eyes would close and then half
open. She seemed sort of—sleepy. Not quite here. He watched
the way she slowly lifted a hand to her face and pushed hair
away from her forehead.

'Did he hurt you?'

'No ... I was trying to call you ... so I went to the top of the hill
... something happened ... I must have fallen ...'

He tried to see up that way. Fallen? Impossible. If she'd tripped or something, could she really have rolled all the way down to here? What was it, half a kilometre or something? She'd be dead, wouldn't she, and covered in grass stains and mud. Funny, when he'd seen the blur in the corner of his eye, it was as if something—well, her—had fallen out of the sky. No, not right. All just tricks of this maddening mist.

'Let's get you into the car. Let's get you home.'

She let him help her to her feet. The glare of the headlights, even on high beam, was muted by the wet soup they walked through.

'We have to ... go back up ...'

Like fuck he would. They were getting out of there and Selena could just manage things later.

He moved her on and there was so little sense of the world around them, even of the ground itself, that with every step he actually had the weird feeling that they were stepping into air, into space. It was even a little like the way he'd felt when he'd let go of the scaffolding that shitty day on the construction site, the opposite of what he expected, not a plummet at all but the sense that his nerveless body was lifted on some current.

'What are you doing?' he asked sharply, when he sensed her strangeness. His arms were around her shoulders, guiding her as if from a car accident or a plane crash.

'... just sort of holding my breath ... sort of believing ... I really do now ...'

6.

Dracula, Frankenstein, The Invisible Man.

It was as if she had a part in one of these old black-and-white classics, she could even feel the weight of the story and its expectations on her shoulders. An old Gothic mansion, a lonely old man, a young courtesan purchased for the night who ends up spending the last hours of his life with him. Then the way she finds his empty body, and our heroine's dash through the bleak mist to find her hero ...

If only there was a script for this, she thought. Some way to know how to play it out.

An ambulance, a body bag being zipped up, dull questions from sleepy police officers in the wee hours of the morning: was that any way to run the denouement of eighty-six years of living?

Then she thought again of the old man's own words, which now seemed like something of a clue.

... there at the top, it's a matter of taking a very long deep breath and holding it, and leaning forward ... then ... almost ... losing yourself in belief.

She was at the fence. Tall trees swayed to the chill breeze. The deep mist below seemed to be rising. The tendrils that had gathered around her ankles were now to her knees, the hemline of her yellow dress. Grant was down there somewhere. Why hadn't he answered his phone? Yet another mystery in this mystery.

Well, I'll believe in you, old man. It's the last thing I can offer you.

She followed the steps, even closed her eyes, and the night's icy air prickled and quivered like a sort of divine radiance in her lungs.

2014

ACKNOWLEDGMENTS

'Romeo Becomes Moonlight' appeared originally in *Moonlight Becomes You: A Crimes For Summer Anthology*, Jean Bedford, Ed; Allen & Unwin, 1995 and *Bareknuckle Poet Annual Anthology* Vol. 1 2015

'The Sleeping Stranger' appeared in *One Book Many Brisbanes* (2007) and *The Barcelona Review (2009)*.

'Sugarbaby' and 'The Currents' appeared in *Review of Australian Fiction* (2012 & 2014 respectively).

A different version of 'Cotton Year and Clock' was published as 'Sliding Across a Blue Highway' in *Influence: Australian Voices*, Peter Skrzynecki, Ed; Anchor Books, 1997.

'Where Bread is Sweet' appeared originally in *Meanjin* and *Paradise to Paranoia: New Queensland Writing*, Nigel Krauth & Robyn Sheahan, Eds; UQP, 1995.

'I Asked the Angels For Inspiration' was published in the anthology *Men, Love, Sex*, Alan Close, Ed; Vintage, 1995 and *Bareknuckle Poet Annual Anthology* Vol. 2 2016

'Park Güell' appeared originally in the novel *My Beautiful Friend* as 'The Story of the Dead Man', Random House, 1995.

www.ingramcontent.com/pod-product-compliance
Lightning Source LLC
Chambersburg PA
CBHW050958210726
48287CB00004B/1272